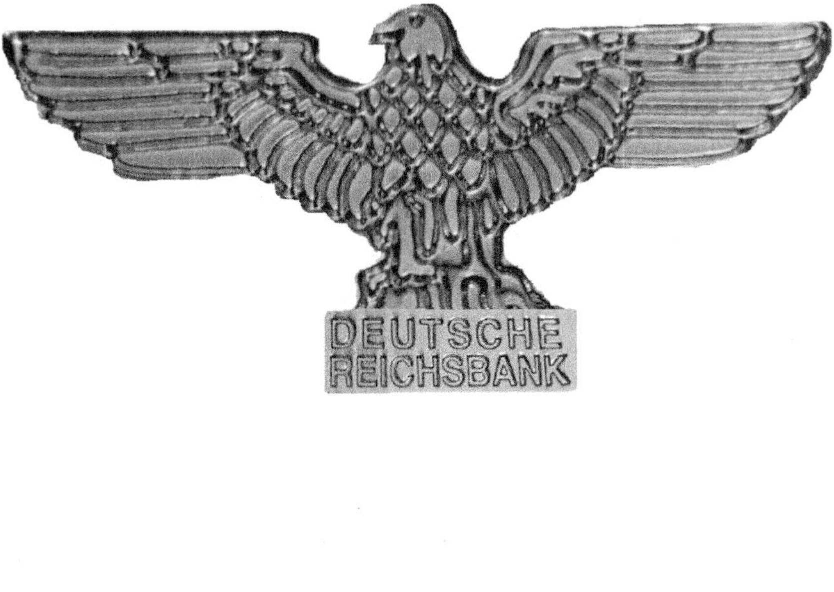
DEUTSCHE
REICHSBANK

BULLION

CHRISTOPHER KERR

First published in Great Britain in 2024 by
Kindle Direct Publishing

Copyright © 2024 Christopher Kerr
The right of Christopher Kerr to be identified as the author of this
work has been asserted by them in accordance with the
Copyright, Design and Patents Act 1988.

All rights reserved. No part of this publication may be
reproduced, transmitted, or stored in a retrieval system, in any form or by any means,
without permission in writing from the author, nor be otherwise circulated in any form
of binding or cover other than that in which it is published and without a similar
condition being imposed on the subsequent purchaser.

This book is a work of fiction. All references to characters, businesses, places, events,
and incidents depicted in this book are the product of the author's imagination and are
used in a fictitious manner. Where actual public speeches have been used, these will be
in the public domain and have not been altered.

Where the book refers to actual persons, living or dead, their words or actions unless
in the public domain are entirely fictitious and any references to these do not in any
way reflect or imply the opinions or behaviour of persons so mentioned. Whilst actual
historical events may have been used to place the story in context,
the author does not accept any responsibility or liability whatsoever for historical
inaccuracies in this work of fiction.

Printed on FSC accredited paper
Printed and bound in Great Britain
ISBN 9798333217783

British Library Cataloguing in Publication Data.
A catalogue record for this book is available from the British Library.

This book is dedicated to all those who have given the ultimate sacrifice

in the cause of freedom and justice during times of war,

and to those who have suffered and continue to suffer from abuses of power

or armed conflict as a result of

man's inhumanity to man.

'Each life is one precious individual.'

"Those who can win a war well can rarely make a good peace, and those who could make a good peace would never have won the war."

Sir Winston Churchill

Preface

In all of my books, I have tried to explore areas of history or contemporary affairs wherein there are aspects which warrant further exploration. I carry out exhaustive research in order to give my work both credibility and an accurate historical perspective. This often results in extraordinary revelations emerging about questions which have never been properly answered or explained.

As I approached the subject matter of 'Bullion', set against the disappearance of Nazi gold, I was ill-prepared for the astonishing, shocking, and profoundly disturbing evidence of the complicity of governments, powerful figures, and major institutions in what is probably the greatest financial crime in history. I could not believe the depths to which many sank in pursuit of personal wealth, or the involvement of reputable bodies in exploiting financial gain, cloaking themselves in descriptions of their 'probity', 'integrity', 'trust', and 'ethics'. The human cost of this public plundering was beyond belief in terms of the misery inflicted in the crime of, not only 'the Holocaust', but the looting by the Nazis of the countries they occupied. However, when the victors participate in, and perpetuate the crimes of the vanquished, does that make them any better, or are they equally, or more guilty than those they judge? The guilt of the victors exposed in my book is palpable and includes that of many commercial organisations which have flourished to become the multinational names we all recognise today, with foundations of shame.

The enormity of the subject matter was daunting as I uncovered so much material, much of it extremely painful to read. I was also angered by the cloak of secrecy that allowed so many institutions to participate in the financial atrocity of laundering gold and stolen assets in an orgy of hypocrisy and duplicity.

There never has been real justice after any war as competing factions seek the moral high-ground, usually at the expense of the truth. The Nazi German era was rightly vilified for the areas of evil it represented, but when it is discovered that those opposing Hitler's regime were also profiting from it, then history becomes a woeful reflection of humanity. The truth is that banks, financial institutions, investors, big business, and governments were all complicit in reaping the rewards of war, and in benefitting from the plundered assets of Nazi Germany.

I found the writing of 'Bullion' exhausting, and the length of the book increased beyond anything I had planned, but I wanted, if not needed, to expose so much. Even now, as I reflect, there is so much more that I could have included, but the book would have reached prohibitive proportions. To those whose awful stories may have been missed, I am truly sorry, but reward my hope is that I have illuminated a very dark period from which humanity should have learned. My wish is that readers will find 'Bullion' absorbing, moving, disturbing, and entertaining, but share in my outrage at what is revealed. Perhaps, we might ask ourselves the question: Could this happen today, or is it still happening?

Christopher Kerr

Maesmor, North Wales – June 2024

Prologue
The Diamond Wheezers

Saturday 4th April 2015 11:45pm
88-90, Hatton Garden, Camden, London

They were now gathered around the narrow gap which had been created in the early hours of the preceding morning, after they had cut through two heavy sliding iron gates. There had been six of them involved on that Thursday night. They had used a *Hilti DD350* industrial power diamond-tipped drill, boring through two-metre-thick walls, leaving three neat intersecting bore holes, of a width of half a metre, through the concrete wall into the vault. On the other side had been a heavy-duty safe deposit cabinet, secured to floor and ceiling, which they had attempted to push out by using a hydraulic ram. The equipment had failed and they had exited, without being noticed, at 7:50am, having been on the premises for twelve hours. They planned to return on Saturday night with a new ram, leaving twenty-four hours to ensure the break-in had not been discovered. One of the planners at the scene of the robbery, Brian Reader, aged 76, had exclaimed, "I'm too old for all this bleedin' malarkey. If at first you don't succeed, you scarper or else end up servin' porridge. I ain't coming back; I need some kip at my age, but I'll sort the launderin' after." Another of the gang, Carl Wood, decided on the Saturday, as they had arrived back at Hatton Garden, that their attempt was not going to succeed and backed out.

Now, just before midnight on Saturday 4th April 2015, having successfully forced the cabinet away with the new ram, three men faced the opening they had successfully created. The fourth gang member, John Collins, was positioned in an office at 25, Hatton Garden, keeping a look-out. As they peered through the conjoined circular drill holes into the vault, their excitement was palpable, viewing row after row of safety deposit boxes. "Looks like the Easter bunny's been; I fink we gonna have a nice bank holiday weekend, boys," remarked Terry Perkins, removing his yellow hard hat. He was dressed in a high viz jacket with 'Gas' written on the back which another of the raiders, Daniel 'Danny' Jones, said suited him because he never stopped "gassin'."

"Terry, you eaten too many pies to get through that gap", joked Michael 'Basil' Seed, beckoning to Daniel Jones, "C'mon Danny me old fruit, we'll half inch the loot and cut them lot aht."

"You better remember who the brains are 'ere," quipped Perkins. "Our old *China plate*, Brian Reader, may have ducked aht but he and I are the main reason you geezers are 'ere. We go back a long way and we done this before boys. Deposit boxes are favourites of ours; plus, there's no one better than Brian at laundering it. Don't forget Brinks-Mat and the Security Express raids back in '83. Two in one year and between us, me and Brian netted 55 mill. The *Old Bill* still fink most of it's buried, daft sods. Anyways, he gets his slice, yeah!"

The thin wiry figure of Basil smiled, "It was only an *egg yoke* (joke), you daft sod. How old are you, my son?" He looked Terry Perkins up and down, "67 bleedin' years old. You should know better at your age.

Villains like you should be settin' an example instead of leadin' poor young bleeders like me astray at only 55."

Perkins watched as Basil Seed and Daniel Jones squeezed through the hole, then passed them crow bars and angle grinders. Within minutes, two box doors, set in the wall, were opened and there was a cheer as Jones held up some diamonds in a mounting tray. This was followed by bundles of cash and, before long, some 500g gold bars were being passed through. Perkins cast his eyes over them, "Reader said not to touch the gold; can't see why. These are brilliant; marked *'Fein gold'* – nice and pure, sadly they're 'ramped' (hallmarked) but wiv a little smelting, we'd get more than *ten to fifteen bags of sand* (grand) for each of these. Best do what Reader said; he planned this lot, even though he's scarpered. Give some of them big boxes a good smacking; let's see what kind of dough these greedy bastards 'as been stashin'."

As the larger boxes were smashed open, more and more jewellery. precious stones, pearls, and cash were passed through which they began stuffing into bags. Suddenly Seed uttered an exclamation, "Jeeesus Christ almighty!"

"What's up, Basil, you *Charring Crosser* (tosser)?" responded Jones.

"Look at this *muvver!*" Seed grunted as he hauled out a much larger gold ingot than those initially found. "Looks like it belongs to Uncle Adolf; got a bleedin' swastika on it. 'Ang on, there's more of em."

"They're 12.5 kilos!" exclaimed Perkins. "Worth more v'an half a mill' each."

Seed had pulled out three more. "Well, I got 1.5 million *squid* 'ere and it's all bleedin' Nazi. They ain't got no need for it nah. Fank you Mr 'Itler. Don't mind if I do." They smashed into more boxes, and Seed triumphantly announced, as he retrieved and piled up the 12.5 kilo bars of gold, counting, "There's five, ten, fifteen, no sixteen more of the bleeders 'ere." He wrenched open some adjoining boxes and held up smaller bars. "Same wiv these; see, more swastikas – and there's quite a few of 'em,"

"Yeah, they 1 kilo, worth abaht fifty grand, but listen, my son, let's think about this," cut in Perkins, "I fink that's why Reader warned us off touchin' the stuff. I've 'eard about this Nazi gold. These geezers nicked it from a bank at the end of the war; their organisation is still around and they don't take no prisoners. The Jerries still do dodgy deals with it, buying favours over here. I've 'eard they use it for paying off the Old Bill. If we half inch it, they'll come for us. The Old Bill's one fing, but don't want no bleedin' Nazis chasing us".

"I'll take one as a souvenir," Seed stated. "My family was in the Blitz. My old lady and her *finger and thumb* (Mum) lived through the bombin'. They lost bleedin' everything in 1941 in a raid, so the Jerries owe me one."

Seed peered into one of the boxes, he retrieved a thick file. "Bleedin' 'ell, we got more stuff with swastikas on 'ere. He opened the file from which he extracted a smaller booklet in a black leather wallet. "I fink all this might have belonged to this gent. This looks like some kind of wartime military identity card." He whistled in surprise as he removed it from the wallet, examining it before holding it up. There was the bold symbol of the SS on the front under which was written, '*Soldbuch*' and beneath that, '*Personalausweis*'.

"Give us a '*butcher's*,' (butcher's hook – look) Perkins extended his hand through the opening and took the document. Inside on the left was a photograph of a serious looking man in uniform beneath which was his signature. Handwritten details were entered next to printed headings. His eyes were drawn to the rank shown on the left side of the document, *SS-Standartenführer* (colonel), and his name printed, Josef Spacil. Perkins closed it, "Aint no good to us, leave it wiv the bars; maybe, if they make it public, it'll be less likely that anyone will claim ownership of the gold; keep the bastards off our backs." He handed the ID back and Seed placed it on the file which he left next to the remaining gold bars.

As the first bullion bar was manoeuvred through the gap, Perkins looked down at the gleaming gold upon which was an eagle clutching a wreath surrounding a swastika. Underneath was written, *'Deutsche Reishsbank'*, then: *'12.5 kilo Feingold'*, with a number, *'DR076999'*.

"Yeah. Maybe I'll join you and *half inch* this. A little momento of our visit; I'll get emotional every time I look at the bastard. I'll straighten it out wiv Reader. Blimey, this ain't a bad job is it? Government's fault see; if they gave us more in our pensions, geezers like us wouldn't need to graft like this. Knock five hundred grand off my share, boys, I think wiv what we've got, it don't matter to me." The others laughed and Seed responded, "Give it a rest Terry, you'll have me in bleedin' tears, me old fruit." As more safety deposit box trays crashed to the floor, spilling their treasures to the waiting gang, they could hardly believe, or even estimate, the value of their heist.

1

The Poison Chalice

Saturday 25th November 2023 11:30am

Das Kauntinhaus, Pienzenauerstrasse, Bogenhausen, Munich

Heinz Friedrich Spacil had been a lawyer, and ruthlessly dedicated to his role, never accepting any incapacity, yet now, despite himself, he had to admit he felt tired after a prolonged illness; an illness during which he had reluctant to accept the diagnosis, or, indeed, the prognosis, but he had finally summoned his son to his home. His son, Karl Josef Biesecker, had refused to continue using father's surname, because of its Nazi association, having had it changed to that of his grandmother, Gretl Biesecker, in 1990, at the age of 20. The process had been complex but, as a young law student, he found a route by convincing the bureaucrat dealing with his case that using the name Spacil was causing him psychological trauma, which had to be attested by a clinical psychologist. As a young idealist, Karl had not seen eye to eye with his father, who, unlike many of his generation, refused to condemn Nazi ideology. Heinz kept a photograph of Karl's grandfather, Josef, in a black dress Nazi SS uniform on the wall in the living room, whilst in a glass case in the hallway, was a dagger bearing the eagle and swastika on the hilt, together with two medals; a *Deutsches Kreuz in Silber,* (Cross in Silver) and the *Kriegsverdienstkreuz 1 klasse mit Schwertern* (War Merit Cross 1st class with swords) on a blue velvet cushion.

Heinz had said to his son that his grandfather had been a great man in the former glorious days and that he had been proud when he was christened Spacil, albeit this was kept secret at the time, as he had been born out of wedlock to his father's mistress. His diagnosis of pancreatic cancer had come as a shock, but he had been feeling unwell for some time suffering with digestive problems and pain from his abdomen through to his back. He detested admitting to any illness or medical issues and had initially refused to consult a doctor despite his wife's remonstrations; however, he had finally been persuaded to undergo tests after an attack of severe pain. This had resulted in him obtaining illicit supplies of morphine one weekend, courtesy of *Die Spinne,* a secret organisation upon which he relied from time to time. His father, Josef, had introduced him to *Die Spinne* in his teens when he had been advised it was a mutual assistance network, a little like the Freemasons, except without the 'nonsense' of ceremony. His father had arranged for Josef to be given a job, following university, as an administrator in the financing section of the organisation, originally set up to assist former Nazis to escape after the war, under the leadership of the legendary SS special forces commander, Otto Skorzeny.

During Heinz's early adult life, he had been assisted periodically by *Die Spinne* in obtaining loans, ensuring he gained admission to the university of his choice, helping with financing issues, or in smoothing over minor indiscretions. However, he had become a brilliant defence lawyer and had soon generated his own substantive income. Although his father had been extremely wealthy, ensuring that he was well provided for as a child, he had believed in an iron code of discipline, and that meant that he expected Heinz to be self-sufficient and not depend on the wealth of his family.

Six months earlier, his wife, Marta, finding him doubled up with pain, had insisted he called for help. He had phoned the network number and within 30 minutes, a doctor had arrived, and morphine administered. *'Die Spinne'* had him admitted to the University Hospital of Ludwig Maximillian in Munich and within two days his diagnosis was given; they had also ensured he had regular visits by a care team and that morphine was available on demand. He had summoned Karl, having been informed by a leading cancer specialist the previous week that his care was now palliative. He had further been told that unless there was an unlikely remission, his survival might be measured in months at best. No one amongst his friends or in the family, apart from Marta, knew of his illness. Heinz was not a man ever given to admitting to, or showing, any sign of weakness.

Heinz had decided that the time was right to speak to Karl about matters he had never been able to share with him. He had tried to instil in his son from a young age not only the values that he had inherited of discipline and duty but much more. He had become dedicated to the movement that his father had spoken of with such pride, recognising the order that it represented. Germany had, in Heinz's view, become awash with, so called, liberal views, leading to a decline; a lack of leadership or direction, lawlessness, indiscipline, and political stagnation had infected the country, which had lost its sense of national pride and identity. His father had held an unswerving belief in a value system of which he had been a huge supporter and which he had served with distinction. After the end of the war in 1945, Josef Spacil had continued serving the *Führer* in a more secret role and, as

Heinz got older, he had taken him into his confidence. As a young teenager, Heinz had been enthralled by the stories of the Reich and he had felt pride that his father had trusted him to share the past. In most houses, allegiance to the Nazis was rarely spoken of openly after the war, but his father had ensured that Heinz knew and respected, what he termed as, his 'cultural heritage'.

Although Heinz had been conceived with his father's mistress, it had been accepted that he should live with his father and his wife. She had treated him well, acting as a second mother to him. He saw his real mother regularly but as her finances were limited, she was happy for his father to give him the life she could not. He had been brought up with values which his father proudly spoke of, exemplified by the vision of the greatest man he had ever known, the *Führer*, Adolf Hitler. He never spoke of him being in the past, or from the past, but always in the present tense. He would refer to him as "our beloved *Führer*" elevating him almost to the status of a deity. Dinners were held at his father's enormous house in the 1950's and 1960's at which military uniforms were sometimes worn and the Nazi salute given freely. Heinz recalled his father sometimes calling him in to meet with those present. It was at one of these that he had first been introduced to Martin Bormann which was something of a surprise as he had been told at school that this man had died in 1945. He felt a sense of honour in that his father had placed his trust in him, making him party to secrets he was sworn to keep. He was brought up to believe in National Socialism which was placed as more important than Christianity in his house, although his parents were Catholic.

During the 1960's, he had witnessed covert Nazi meetings and events where notorious guests would appear, about whom his father would tell him stories. Apart from Bormann, he met Hans Kammler, the former head of the secret advanced Nazi Weapons programme, Karl

Dönitz, who had become supreme commander of the German Navy after masterminding the U-Boat campaign, Heinrich Müller, the former Chief of Gestapo, and, amongst many others, Otto Skorzeny, a special forces commander in the war, who was a regular visitor to his father. They were all well-guarded, and many events were shrouded in secrecy. In his early twenties, he began attending the secret meetings and he was introduced to the highly secret world of a covert financing network masterminded by his father, and assisted by other leading former Nazis. In 1962, Heinz was taken by Josef Spacil to meet the board of Directors at the Bank for International Settlements in Basel, Switzerland. There he was introduced to the bank's management team by Thomas McKittrick, a former president of the bank. He was an ebullient American who had also been a regular visitor to Josef Spacil's home for as far back as Heinz could remember. He learned of the bank's pivotal role in providing international banking facilities to the Nazi regime and the critical part it still played in assisting with the movement of funds globally.

In those years, before his father's death in 1967, Heinz had been entrusted with more and more information. He began to organise financial 'clearance' matters under the watchful eye of his father. Heinz understood the need for secrecy to protect those who had been true patriots of the Fatherland. He was a pragmatist, recognising that covert money transactions were essential in the interests of the movement or *das Geheime Vierte Reich* or GVR. (the Secret Fourth Reich) This was an all-embracing movement, represented by many others, authorised by Hitler in early 1945 after the failure of the Ardennes Offensive, which would only take in the most loyal and dedicated supporters. Their responsibility was to safeguard and uphold the principles of the NSDAP (*Nationalsozialistische Deutsche Arbeiterpartei*), the National Socialist German Workers Party, or

Nazis, in a post-war Germany, should the war be lost. This was the highly covert umbrella of the NSDAP after 1945, which was supported by the central financial body of the GVR, controlled by Josef Spacil. The philosophy was that strength lay in there being a number of bodies, secretly unified, which would be harder for the post-war revisionist authorities (or post-Nazi traitors) to attack in both East and West Germany. Heinz was in his early twenties, and, despite having obtained his law degree from the *Ludwig-Maximilians-Universität München* or LMU, he was also very adept in financial matters on which he had been coached from a young age by his father.

Today, Heinz had decided was the right time to talk seriously to his son, Karl, although he knew he could not pass on the mantle for the management of the *Versteckte Vermögensfonds* (hidden assets funds) or 'VVF', as it was referred to by the inner circle. He could feel his life was ebbing away and it was time that he, at least, gave his son something of his legacy, and a chance for much more. He was proud of Karl who, in many ways, was something of a contradiction. He had eschewed all his father and grandfather stood for, yet he had always admired the military. As a boy, he had a fascination for uniforms, playing for hours with toy soldiers and setting up mock battles in his room. Even as young as nine, he was studying how commanders had drawn up battle plans and would replicate these, setting out lines of troops in formations with cannons, horses, or vehicles. However, he would concentrate on battles from Roman times, the Napoleonic era, or the First World War, and avoid anything from the Second World War. Once he had attended school and learned of the Nazi era, he had refused to acknowledge or talk about his grandfather's role or consider his father's views other than to condemn them. Heinz had learned that, once Karl had entered his teens, it was pointless attempting to discuss the past with him, and, for the sake of unity in the family, he had not pursued the matter with him. His younger daughter, Gretchen, was far more amenable and had an inquisitive nature about the past. She was five years younger than Karl and had pursued a career in accounting. She was ambivalent about the Nazi era, neither showing any support nor condemning it. "History must never be hidden," she had said to him. "there were ideals on both sides that people fought for, and many that were betrayed by the leaders. Was Stalin any worse than Hitler, or any better? There were many that profited from the war, making a fortune from investments in arms, vehicles, and from commodities." The irony of her career, which had developed into international fraud investigation, was not lost on Heinz and he was proud of her. There had been one major family row when Karl had announced, as a left-wing student radical, that he was adopting the surname, Biesecker. However, Heinz had decided after this, that he would avoid areas of contention and, for the most part, the family had been a harmonious unit. His wife, Marta, was four years older than Heinz, but retained the fitness and agility of a much younger person. The daughter of a former Waffen SS Colonel, she had never forgotten the smiling face of her father as he held her for the last time, before leaving in 1942 for the Russian front. After being taken prisoner by the Russians during the battle for Stalingrad in January 1943, he had died, or been killed, in captivity. He had served in a unit attached to the 6th Army which had surrendered with some 91,000 being taken into captivity. Of those, less than 6,000 returned after the war and Marta had never forgiven the 'Eastern Savages' as she described them. Neither would she ever countenance any criticism of Nazi Germany, and Karl had learned never to debate the issue with her from a young age.

When Karl had opted to join the army, Heinz and Marta genuinely felt enormous pride, and they both attended his passing out parade in

1995 at the *Offizierschule des Heeres* in Dresden, meeting his seventy-five- year-old grandmother, Gretl, there. She had always been very close to Heinz and would regale him with stories of "the glorious days of the Reich", as she referred to them, but had become wary of talking on the subject in front of Karl, despite not understanding his rejection of that period. Now, she was still alive, and at 103 years of age, she lived independently, although within a monitored sheltered complex on the outskirts of Munich.

Karl had settled well into army life and had seen combat service in Bosnia, Kosovo, Iraq, and Afghanistan. In 2005, he had been accepted to join the elite special forces unit, *Kommando Spezialkräfte* (KSK) and had been awarded Germany's highest medal for valour, the *Ehrenkreuz der Bundeswehr für Tapferkeit*, (Cross of Honour for Valour). Heinz had remarked to Marta and other close friends, but never in front of Karl, that he would have made a wonderful officer in the SS. Karl's medal award ceremony received no publicity because of the covert nature of his mission, although his parents were permitted to attend. The only information he shared with them was that it involved operations against *Al-Qaeda* and the self-proclaimed *Islamic State*. He had achieved the rank of *Oberst* (Colonel) and rarely spoke to his parents about his work. Although he had never married, he did have a partner, Inge, but they did not live together and neither wanted children. As Inge said one day to his parents, "Karl is married to his job, but says that when he retires, perhaps he will go down on one knee. I would never pressure him because it is his life."

Heinz had invited Karl and Inge to join them for a long lunch, as he had important matters he wished to discuss. It had been agreed that Inge and Marta would go shopping in Munich in the afternoon so that they could talk. They arrived punctually at the precise time agreed of 11:30am, a characteristic which Heinz admired, as his father had insisted upon, before him. As soon as the signal from the electric gates was triggered, Heinz arose from the armchair in which he increasingly spent long periods, often sleeping. He smartened his tie in front of the large gold framed baroque mirror in the drawing room, and straightened his vintage check tweed blazer. He was determined not to stoop, despite the gnawing pressure he felt inside which sometimes forced him to double up in pain, but he had taken a liberal dose of morphine on the advice of the visiting doctor who now attended the house on a regular basis.

His son arrived dressed smartly in a mid-grey *Trachten* jacket with buttons to the neck, complemented by a velvet collar, a blue top handkerchief, pressed black trousers, and polished laced shoes. Karl was fifty-three years of age but appeared much younger with an athletic build gained from a dedicated regime of fitness. His blond wavy hair was unfashionably parted and, Heinz reflected, he looked every inch an army officer despite being out of uniform. Inge was more informal in a pair of jeans, over which she wore a cream sweater with a neckerchief and light brown jacket. She had auburn hair to her shoulders, worn with a headband, appearing very chic. As a former fashion model, she maintained a pride in her appearance, despite preferring to dress down. Ten years younger than Karl, she was highly independent, and successful. After four years modelling, she had taken the unusual step of serving eight years in the *Bundespolizei* (Federal Police), where she had excelled, achieving the rank of *Polizeioberkommissar (Senior Inspector),* which had given her some commonality with his military background when they met. Now, she ran a small chain of boutiques, unusually selling fine fashion clothing, combined with up-market household items giving them a unique and sought after status.

Despite his disagreements with his father, Karl respected him, admiring his disciplined way of life, and his achievement in the wealth he had created for himself. He was unaware of Heinz's role in the GVR or the control held by him of the funds of the *VVF,* but believed his father's success came from his law practice which, to a degree, was true. As he entered, he hugged his mother and turned to shake hands with his father, before they, too, briefly placed their hands on each other's shoulders in a perfunctory embrace.

Although Karl was shocked at his father's appearance, which exhibited substantial weight loss, he did not show this. "*Mein Vater,* it is good to see you; it has been too long. Have you learned to retire yet?"

"*Niemals,"* (never) came the reply, with a laugh, "I have too much to do in my work to keep your mother in the manner which she demands. Come join me for a *Frühschoppen;* (morning beer) I have some excellent *Hefeweizen* (wheat beer). I also have some fine Riesling for the ladies."

"Just one glass," Marta stated emphatically, "I need to be focussed when Inge chooses the latest, most chic and expensive fashions to suit the lifestyle which my frugal husband has always begrudged me."

The atmosphere continued to be light-hearted over lunch, although, perhaps, a little forced, which was served by the housekeeper and cook, Greta, who had been retained by Heinz for over forty years. It was obvious to both Karl and Inge that Heinz was seriously ill. The text message Karl had received from his father the week before hinted at what he guessed, with a heavy heart, was to be a defining meeting. It had simply stated, *'My son, I need to see you most urgently. I regret that I have not been in good health of late and, as the great Roman poet, Virgil, wrote, 'Tempus fugit'*". Karl had not seen his father for nearly a year but both the rarity of a communication from him, and the wording were sufficient. His father never admitted to being ill, or complained, even when he had been unwell; it was not his way. Karl was at the Augustdorf military base supervising the training of a covert unit due to be sent to Afghanistan. He had immediately contacted his commander at HQ in Calw requesting compassionate leave which was instantly authorised. He was anxious to spend time alone with his father and was relieved when Marta stated that she and Inge needed to leave for their shopping trip.

Heinz invited Karl to join him in his study which was a large room, with a huge arched window split into multiple panes, with stained glass panels in the apex, overlooking the large garden and small lake beyond. There were floor-to-ceiling bookshelves lining two of the other walls and an ornate frame at one end in which was a portrait of Bismarck. Comfortable leather armchairs were set around the room and by the window was a large mahogany double pedestal desk on which were two quill pens at either end of a brass inkstand. Heinz settled himself slowly into an armchair motioning Karl to another. There was a knock on the panelled door, and Greta entered with two crystal glasses containing *Asbach Uralt* brandy and a bottle.

"The Doctor says I should not drink." Heinz grunted with a laugh, "Ach, what difference does it make?" Karl already sensed what was coming before the next words but he still felt the shock as his father spoke them.

"I am dying, Karl. For once, I am unable to control what is happening, nor give orders to change things. My illness is terminal. I have a tumour on which they cannot operate. Even now, with all the money I have accumulated, it is worthless in the face of illness." He lifted his glass reaching over to touch it against Karl's. "I have weeks, maybe months, who knows? *Prost!*" He laughed again at the irony of his toast, "*Prost*...I wish huh?" Karl felt unaccustomed emotion building inside him; he rarely showed his feelings but he felt a wave of deep sadness, wanting to do what they had rarely done, and hug his father.

He managed, "I'm sorry, Papa, so very sorry to hear this." His voice was choked.

Heinz stood, a little wearily, and walked over to a small filing cabinet by his desk on top of which was a stout wooden box with black iron reinforced corners, with a metal handle on either side, and a lock on the front, which he picked up with some difficulty, waiving Karl away, who moved to assist him. Then he carried the box over to where he had been sitting, lowering it onto a side table next to his armchair. "I have so much to unburden, and this…" he tapped the box, "will unlock many secrets, and answer questions you have after I am gone." He glanced briefly at the portrait dominating the wall opposite, and had a moment of inspiration in order to lead in to what he knew would be difficult. He pointed to it. "You see this picture? Do you know where it came from?"

Karl glanced upwards at the imposing figure, "I only know it is our redoubtable 19th century first Chancellor of the German Empire, Bismarck."

"An original;" his father replied, "it is painted by Franz von Lenbach but there is much more." He sat back down with a deep sigh. "This painting once hung in the Reich Chancellery." He saw Karl wince and quickly added, "Please; you must allow me to speak openly at this time whatever thoughts you have. This is important to me and time is not on my side."

Karl felt a pang of guilt at the reaction of anger which had welled up from old scars of sparring with his father as a young man. He held both hands up in a placatory motion.

His father swirled the brandy in his glass for a moment knowing this was the time, before continuing. "Your grandfather, Josef, left me this painting. He was proud of it as it had once had pride of place in Hitler's study. In fact, Hitler gifted it to him during the last days of the Reich in April 1945." He watched his son suppress yet another reaction. "I know your feelings about the Nazi era, and I have always respected them, but equally, I think, we must recognise the loyalties and actions of others, no matter how misplaced, from our past. You have inherited much from his character including a love of the military, discipline, tidiness and order. You were always frustrated, as a child, if we were late for anything and, in that area, you were uncompromising, just as you are now. You began tidying your room from an early age, and were never happy how others left it. These traits are inherent in your character and I recognise much of myself in you, as well as your grandfather. My father was an honourable man and took pride in his efficiency, expecting much of those who worked for him, and he was uncompromising in his standards. I want you to know about him because you never knew him. In his day, he achieved much, and was successful in all he tackled; he would accept nothing but the highest standards, which he exemplified himself.

"Like you, I was presented with much about our history after the war. I was too young to remember it having been born in 1942. However, I do recall the deprivations suffered by Germany in the late 1940's and through the 1950's. There was this incredible burden of guilt which was thrust upon us constantly in school, in university, and in the media. Your grandfather gave me an alternative view of our history which, as a boy growing up with a negative view of my country, was a welcome alternative. He would recall the great days when Germany was united, powerful, proud, and respected under the guidance of the *Führer*. He was an economist and spoke about the miracle turn-around in the economy and the incredible patriotism which engulfed the country after the crippling reparations resulting from the 'Treaty of Versailles', in 1919, after the First World War.

"As a boy in the 1950's, I wanted to believe in my country and feel proud of it instead of the constant shame which was forced upon us. My father gave me a different vision, and one I was drawn to. He confided in me that there were many like him, who were not wishing to take up arms, but to achieve the aims of the movement through more modern means."

Karl interrupted, "The movement, what movement? Surely, the Nazi Party was banned after the war. All displays of the emblem, or association with Nazism or the promotion of Nazi ideology were criminalised, I thought, in 1945."

His father paused before replying, as he recognised that to continue would break the code of secrecy that had surrounded his adult lifetime, and also create a security risk. He knew he needed to tread carefully, yet he was also deeply aware of his mortality. "Karl, please understand that more than 10% of our population were members of the Nazi Party at the end of the war. The vast majority of all who worked in financial, administrative, and legal bodies were members. They could not all be dispensed with. The country had to be reconstructed and managed. Most of those who had been part of the Nazi regime were reinstated in the administrations which followed. Even when you were born, the majority of those in authority were former Nazis. Many of Hitler's generals ended up as senior, and highly respected NATO officers. You stated over lunch you had travelled home from the army barracks at Augustdorf. This is named the *'Generalfeldmarschall-Rommel-Kaserne'* (Field Marshal Rommel Barracks) is it not?"

"Yes, but Rommel opposed Hitler," countered Karl.

"*Mein Sohn*, he may not have been a Nazi, but he remained loyal to Hitler and did not join or approve of the July bomb plot to assassinate him in 1944."

"He was killed by them or forced to commit suicide," said Karl forcefully.

Heinz looked at his son, knowing that he had so much he needed to tell him, yet inside, a part of him was unsure. His voice softened, "Yes, he was a good man, but fell victim to some of the fanatics who were engaged in hysterical mass revenge killings after the assassination attempt on Hitler.

"Karl, I have much I need to tell you today and the knowledge I give may be 'a poisoned chalice', but I need to unburden myself, and, in so doing, give to you an inheritance with which you may do what you will. That is your choice, but it is because I love you as my son, that I must pass to you a secret which may alter the rest of your life."

2

"Suffocated by Gold"

Monday 21st January 1939 9:30am
Das Kabinett Zimmer, Reichskanzlei (Reich Chancellery),
Vosstrasse 2-6, Berlin

The Cabinet Room was enormous by any standards, imposing, and grandiose; the impression to all was that they were part of a great, powerful, and unstoppable purpose, driven by 'him', and his inspiration filled them with pride. The monumental nature of the destiny of which they felt a part seemed to be epitomised by the incredible building which many had entered that day for the first time. They were seated either side of a twelve-metre-long table on which was a ruby edged covering, embroidered intricately in an exquisite blush pattern. At either end of the cloth as it overhung the table were two matching squares from which hung four gold tassels, with three woven *Hakenkreuz* (swastika) symbols separating them. Ornate brass table lamps adorned the centre of the table in which shades were set giving a curiously homely warmth to a highly formal setting. There were twelve polished dark wood-framed plush chairs either side, covered in a classical red and gold patterned fabric; black eagles were on the seat backs with gold wings clutching a swastika in a wreath with their claws. At the top of the table stood an empty, more grandiose chair which awaited 'him'. The grandeur was added to by floors carpeted with sumptuous rugs in a diamond shaped blue and red pattern. Walls in polished mid brown marble, with hints of red in the pattern, were separated by timber panelling at intervals in which were neo-classical oil paintings. As they gathered, they were dwarfed and awed by the six-metre height of the ceiling with its neat symmetrical panelling. Two double five-metre-high framed doorway entrances dominated one end of the room, in the centre of which was a magnificent tapestry depicting a wild horse being restrained by Roman figures. At the other end was another double doorway of equal height, through which they knew 'he' would enter.

The air of anticipation was palpable and conversation was in hushed voices. There was a hierarchy with the guests at one side facing the chosen few on the other, on whose shoulders 'he' had bequeathed epic responsibility. *Reichsführer* Heinrich Himmler was dressed in his black dress SS uniform, with silver collar flashes, his eyes darting down the table, from behind his wire-framed rounded glasses, taking in the demeanour of those attending, his air of derision noted by others who would not publicly speak of it. His reputation as the ruthless leader of the SS meant he could enjoy the fear he engendered in others. Next to him in a brown lounge suit with a red armband in which was the black swastika in a white circle, was Joachim Von Ribbentrop, his hands clenched in front of him, his swept back thin blonde hair over a smooth featured face set in contemplation at what may follow. He had been summoned with a brief call at 10:00pm the previous night, and all engagements, as *Reichsminister* of Foreign Affairs, were immediately cancelled. To his left was the portly figure of Hermann Göring in the light blue uniform of his beloved Luftwaffe, which he had built up over the preceding six years, his 'Blue Max' medal for gallantry at his neck. In contrast, the diminutive but lively Josef Goebbels was dressed in a somewhat overstated pin-striped double-breasted suit, with the enamel maroon Nazi Party badge on his lapel. His hushed words resulted in a guffaw from Göring, as he recited an experience from the night before, drawing a grimace from Himmler, who had no time for this propaganda spouting fool. The thickset figure of Martin Bormann, increasingly important in Nazi Party administration, was in a brown uniform, talking in hushed tones to the deputy *Führer* Rudolf Hess, whose black uniform was similar to that worn by Himmler. Hess's thick eyebrows were furrowed in concentration as he took in minute details communicated to him by Bormann, with a legendary ability to absorb information without taking notes. Albert Speer sat in a dark business suit, quietly proud of the reaction he had received from colleagues regarding his design and building of the Reich Chancellery in which they now sat. The magnificent edifice had been completed two days ahead of the desired impossible deadline set for him just one year before. It was just two weeks since the New Reich Chancellery had been opened, much to the delight of the *Führer,* who had lavished praise upon him. Speer had opened a red folder, crested with a gold eagle and swastika, in front of him, and was sketching ideas for statues and pillars which he still wished to add to the building complex.

The two most senior German Army (*Wehrmacht*) officers, *Oberst Generale* (Colonel Generals) Wilhelm Keitel, and Walther von Brauchitsch, attired in military field grey uniforms, sat nearest to the top of the table in earnest conversation over the forthcoming campaign to subdue and absorb the remaining parts of Czechoslovakia into the Reich. On the other side of the table were six men who, in contrast to the many uniforms present, were all dressed in formal suits with ties, many with winged collars. They wielded less influence or power within the Nazi hierarchy, although they were not averse, if not relishing being selected for service to the Fatherland, to which three were financial contributors. Some felt nervous at being summoned to 'his' presence, wary of being so near to the pinnacle of absolute power; others displayed a pompous arrogant air, or had an element of competing self-interest. All would claim to be proud of what had been, and what was being, achieved in the Reich in the six years since 'he' had assumed power.

Hermann Göring, unable to resist a little mischievous satire on an occasion of formality, uttered words to ease the tension, drawing some restrained laughter, "I suppose the *Reisemarschal* ("Travel Marshal") will perform his usual tiresome role as Master of Ceremonies." His disparaging remark about the adjutant to the *Führer* drew a furious look from Himmler, who had nothing but disdain for this man whom he regarded as decadent with his irreverent, cynical, humour. As if on cue, the two enormous panelled doors behind the head of the table were opened wide by a man most recognised as *Standartenführer* Julius Schaub. He was in his early thirties with swept back black hair, attired in a brown uniform, and polished black boots. He straightened, pausing for a moment as he clicked his heels, announcing, *"Meine Herren*, our *Führer, Deutschlands Führer, und Reichskanzler, Heil Hitler!"* His right arm shot outwards in the Nazi salute, as all arose around the table echoing the words, their arms also raised.

The sound of purposeful steps was heard, and then the unmistakeable figure of Adolf Hitler marched into the centre of the entrance, as Schaub stepped to one side. He paused in the doorway, his eyes surveying those present, and his jaw set with a purposeful look giving no hint of warmth or emotion. Then, he slowly extended his right arm, holding it out stiffly, exerting a commanding, powerful, and total air of authority over the room. His neatly brushed dark hair was cut short at the sides and parted to the right, with the front longer and combed in a diagonal curve over his forehead, and his unmistakeable, signature, squared moustache was meticulously trimmed. He was in a double-breasted brown tunic, with three gold buttons either side, worn over black trousers with no belt or webbing, and unlike many there, was not wearing boots but highly polished shoes. His shirt was white, worn with a tie matching his uniform jacket, in which was a gold eagle tie-pin, whilst, on his left arm was the red and white Nazi armband with a black swastika. He wore his customary wound badge or *Verwundetenabzeichen* from the Great War below his chest on the left side, over which was the Iron Cross, and positioned above, the small golden edged round senior party badge of the NSDAP with the swastika in the centre. They remained standing as he walked forwards, dropping his arm, but at the table, he bent his arm upwards from the elbow with the palm of his hand facing backwards, uttering one word in a guttural voice, "*Heil!*".

He then gestured to them to sit, but he remained standing, folding his arms. There was absolute silence as the doors were slowly closed by Schaub behind him. The *Führer* looked distantly, as if reaching beyond the room, then placed his hands on his hips, before raising his right hand, his index finger outstretched. He began quietly, "My destiny is now being realised which was to inspire the German *Volk*, give them purpose and reverse the betrayal of Versailles, imposed upon us by the International Jewish dominated economies of those who sought to suppress us. Now, no one can impose any more on *Deutschland*...no one! *Niemand!*"

The repeat of the last word echoed around the room as he sharpened his tone, then more quietly, "First, I had to create the foundation for our great destiny, with the unswerving will which Providence bestowed upon me; I held a vision and strength of resolve that would refuse to be thwarted. In less than twelve years, I had taken the *Nationalsozialistische Deutsche Arbeiterpartei* from obscurity to become the greatest movement in German history. I have led the Party to become admired, recognised, and feared throughout the world;" His voice rose, "One vision, one will, *ein Deutschland, ein Reich, ein Führer!"*

Rudolf Hess stood up, driven by awed admiration, his arm stiffly outstretched, as he shouted the words, "S*ieg Heil!"* As if on cue, all those on Hitler's left followed suit, repeating his words, whilst those sitting opposite in suits, responded more slowly, not having been used to such drama, but nevertheless feeling inspired by the words of this extraordinary man, the like of which no one had seen before. It was as if his words spoke to each person individually, yet stirred up a sense of belonging to 'him', to 'his' will, and to Germany.

Hitler, once again, raised his arm from the elbow, in the more relaxed style of Nazi salute he had introduced, then he folded his arms, holding the rapt attention of the room. "It was in 1921 that I assumed the role of Führer, which I laid down as the '*Führer Prinzip'* (leader principle), and in my political testament which I wrote within '*Mein Kampf'* in 1925, I clearly defined my purpose of establishing one leader. More and more German *Volk* welcomed the clarity I gave in my vision of a strong *Deutschland* led by an iron will. Have I not already delivered much of what I promised? Since we were swept into power, and then seized control of all institutions in 1933, we have shown to our people and to the world the miracle of National Socialism. First, I committed our intention to rip up the Treaty of Versailles, and then, under my direction, our army has been built up to become the finest, disciplined, and most well equipped in the world. Is that not true, *Meine*

Generäle?" He swung round to face Kietel and von Brauchitsch, fixing them both with his steely blue eyes.

The two men stood and snapped to attention, von Brauchitsch responding, *"Jawohl, mein Führer.* We could not have asked for more. We now have 98 divisions and 1.5 million well-trained men with more in training. We also have 9 Panzer divisions, each with 328 tanks."

Hitler held up his hands, acknowledging the numbers with a brief smile. As the officers resumed their seats, he turned to face Göring. *"Herr Generalfeldmarschall,* I believe that you also have benefitted from my decision to challenge and oppose those who tried to weaken the inevitable rise of German strength with your Luftwaffe."

Göring rose more slowly, with a broad smile, giving the same more relaxed right arm salute that Hitler had used previously. He pushed his chest out, enjoying the moment, drawing a visible grimace from Himmler, who hated what he considered was an odious display of self-importance. *"Mein Führer,* I can announce we have 370,000 men, but this number is rapidly growing. Production of new aircraft is increasing but we already have 1000 new fighter aircraft and nearly as many bombers. I regret that I must announce that we may have broken the provisions of the Versailles Treaty by some margin which permitted us to have no aircraft and no Luftwaffe. Please accept my apology." There was laughter around the table as Hitler smiled, and Göring finished with, "The betrayal we suffered at the end of the Great War has been reversed because of your boldness and leadership, for which, Germany owes you gratitude." He nodded as he spoke the final words, before retaking his seat.

The Führer appeared to look into the distance as he began again, "I recognised that we needed to seize the moment when I observed the increasing weakness of the democracies with their endless arguing, lacking the decisiveness of true leadership. In France, the growing force of socialism threatens their old regime, whilst the communists are rising in strength; their seats in the Chamber of Deputies have grown seven-fold. The threat may not only be to their state but could spread to face Germany against which, in time, we may be forced to act. In Britain, their democracy has been rocked to the foundations by the abdication of their King, setting faction against faction. Many in their highest social society are debating whether they should act, looking at our stability with envy, admiring the order we have achieved and the unity of our people for the new Germany. The Great Depression has weakened America, and shown up the failures of their system reliant on individual greed; now, respect for their law is breaking down accompanied by a huge increase in crime. They failed to protect their identity by allowing massive contamination with unfettered immigration, importing Jews, and Slavic filth from Europe. "Here in Germany, we recognised just in time the threat we faced to our Aryan race and the purity of our Germanic heritage. We too have suffered at the hands of the Jews, but now we are taking steps to eradicate them from our society, to cut out the poison of the Zionist serpent, to achieve what I term, "*Judenrein*" (cleansed of Jews). We must be wary of the international Jew, which will attempt again to infiltrate, against which I will make a stand, committing myself totally to the future of a greater Reich, fortified by the purity of our blood and our natural superiority. When the time came, I answered the calling and under my leadership, we have virtually eradicated crime, made our streets safe, and allowed our businesses to prosper." His voice sharpened in tone, increasing to a crescendo as he waved his right fist emphasising each point, as every person in the room was transfixed. "We have restored our national pride, retaken our power, re-established our culture and regained our Fatherland, our *Deutschland*."

This time it was Goebbels who exclaimed, *"Sieg Heil!"* echoed by others in the room.

Hitler stopped, pushing back his forelock, which had dropped across his face with his dramatic delivery.

"Providence called me to our great task which is to build our strength, and become the bastion against the scourge of communism, and the vile Bolshevik threat from the East. First, I had to secure the German state and begin retaking what had been stolen from us by plundering Jew dominated countries, and free our people who were trapped by borders within which they did not belong." He waved his index finger at each person in the room as he spoke, never pausing, nor needing notes. "All of you have played a critical part in our great and historic mission. *Ja,* you, *ja,* you, and you, and you, and you...and especially you, *mein Reichsminister* Goebbels...you manage to exaggerate even my words to the masses and, I'm told, they believe you!" As the *Führer* raised his eyebrows with a rare jovial look, it was obvious to those who knew Hitler well, that he was in an ebullient frame of mind, but they equally knew that his mood could rapidly change at the slightest perception of opposition or weakness. This was a moment for laughter, but each knew that he would constantly evaluate their reaction and they could rarely relax in his presence. Hitler strode to the window looking out over the Chancellery garden at the neatly laid pathways intersecting the newly grassed over areas. He rubbed his hands together and turned,

"*Meine Herren,* I have taken on the burden of leading the Reich because I knew that my will was tied to the hopes of the German *Volk;* my life only then assumed the role that destiny had chosen for me. I am now surrounded by the symbols of the Party with which I became great, and which has become great through me; but we have a new and greater task ahead. We must create a financial foundation for our future, which will reinforce our power, securing the Third Reich beyond our lifetimes for the next thousand years.

"In only six years from 1933, when I became the undisputed *Führer*, I was massively endorsed by the people of Germany because they believed in my vision and purpose. We immediately began the process of *Gleichschaltung* (Nazification), ensuring that National Socialism was at the centre of every aspect of our culture. In 1933, we strengthened our grip on the Reich by banning all opposition elements that cause the weakness suffered by democracies; by doing so, we made National Socialism the Party of the Reich for the Reich. I had the will to challenge all obstacles, and ensure that Germany could free itself from the shackles imposed upon us in the great betrayal of 1918, and the criminal plundering of Germany under the provisions of the Versailles Treaty. I knew that decisive leadership was the primary factor. For that reason, I made the Reichstag irrelevant in 1933 by ensuring that any decision I made could not be challenged by either the president or any opposition. In 1924, I described the Versailles Treaty as a sham and a disgrace, and that this dictated peace represented an unprecedented pillaging of our people. I now believe it was not only driven by desire for revenge by our enemies, but that it was the work of Jewish financiers against whom we will exact our own revenge. In 1935, I ripped up the Treaty by introducing conscription, committing our Reich to an army of unprecedented size and power. In the same year, we took back the Saarland because the German population there voted to be part of the new Reich. Of course, we influenced some to vote the right way because only through seizing power can you exercise power. I recognised the feeble democracies would not act to oppose us when we marched into the Rhineland in 1936, as Deutsche *volk* lined the streets, cheering our troops. Then in 1938, we welcomed Austria into the Reich in the *Anschluss*. We had to persuade the chancellor to resign and, for some reason, he agreed after we had explained the alternatives." He threw both his hands in the air emphasising astonishment causing Hermann Göring to guffaw loudly, as others joined in the laughter.

Göring then added, "Yes, he did not wish to die resisting the will of the people!"

Hitler nodded before continuing, "I knew this was the time for Germany to re-assert its identity, and unite all *Volksdeutsche* living outside our borders under the protection of *Heim ins Reich* (Home in the Reich). Hence, I did not hesitate to march into the Sudetenland region of Czechoslovakia last year, despite the pathetic protestations of British Prime Minister, Neville Chamberlain, and a little posturing from the French. They actually agreed to give us the territory without even involving the Czechs. This is my kind of diplomacy. Strength dictates any solution imposed on the weak. Now our people in the Sudetenland are in the Reich. We will not stop there; we are exposed and threatened by the vile tyrannical curse of communist Russia and for that reason, we must secure our borders, and expand the living space for Aryan people in the East with our policy of *lebensraum* (room through expansion). Czechoslovakia will cease to exist and if the Polish do not see sense, and give us access to Danzig, we will smash them into submission." His fist had slammed onto the table as his last words were delivered in a shout. All those in the room rose, their arms extended, as Hitler stood, his arms folded, with a triumphant gleam in his eyes. His tone lowered as he spoke earnestly.

"Now, it is time to take action to secure our economy. On 30th January, I will give a speech to members of the Reichstag in the *Krolloper*" (Opera House) to celebrate the six years since I came to power. I will make it clear that Germany will no longer tolerate the Jewish financiers who contributed to our demise whilst they profited.

I will say that if the Jewish financiers start a war, this will bring the annihilation of the Jewish race in Europe. *Meine Herren*, they have already started that war, and my words will be propitious for what will follow. Now, we will plunder their coffers, as they did to us. *Herr Reichsführer ...*" He turned to Himmler, "Your SS will execute my will; this will be achieved under your direction with your gift for ruthless, meticulous planning." Himmler, sprung up, clicking his heels, "*Jawohl, mein Führer.*" His face showed no emotion, only a cold expressionless look, his eyes unblinking as he responded.

"We must take back from the Jews our own reparations for what they have done to us. I am today authorising the setting up of what I am calling, "*Versteckte Vermögensfonds"* (hidden assets fund), which will be maintained separately from our main exchequer, and only those within this room will know this. We need the co-operation of an international bank wherein we can place and exchange the "*Versteckte Vermögensfonds."* A few days ago, I discussed this plan with the president of the Reichsbank, Hjalmar Schacht, but he did not share my vision. For this reason, I have replaced him with a more loyal member of our Party, *Reichsminister* Walther Funk." He gestured to a middle-aged, thick-set balding man with a heavy build in a sombre three-piece suit, a dark grey tie, and an NSDAP badge on his lapel. "*Herr* Funk, please inform those present of the ideas we have discussed."

Funk stood up, removing his glasses, holding a file which he referred to as he spoke. His voice was deep, "*Mein Führer, meine Herren,* when I was appointed General Plenipotentiary for Economics last year, the Führer made me aware that we needed more weight on the international markets to match our growing military strength. We are now partially controlling a Swiss bank that operates outside any political control or interference." He paused, adding, "or so they think." He smirked as there was a polite ripple of amusement around the room. "In fact, we have three members of the board of that bank here today. I am one of those." He gestured to two men sitting to his left. "I think most of you will know Emil Puhl, the vice president of the Reichsbank, who is another director." The man stood briefly, bowing towards Hitler, and then to the rest of the room. He had cropped hair, a small moustache, and was smartly dressed in a black suit and spotted tie. "My other colleague is Paul Hechler who, I can inform you, is Assistant Manager at this bank which is called, the Bank for International Settlements, based in Basel in Switzerland." The smaller, dapper figure of Hechler in a pin-striped suit and thick hair with grey at the sides stood briefly, nodding towards Hitler, who acknowledged him with a brief wave of the hand.

Funk continued, "We all sit on the board as directors of this bank and, I can tell you, we share the board with a fellow Italian, who works closely with *Il Duce,* and is an admirer of both Mussolini and our Führer. The bank was ironically set up to facilitate the process of transacting our reparations in 1931 and deals are done outside of regulations on a daily basis, with very few questions asked. There is a name being put forward for the next president who is an American, with substantial investment interests here in Germany, by the name of Thomas McKittrick. He has also worked with our banks here in Germany and has a vested interest in our prosperity. We are now controlling many parts of this institution." He looked up with wry smile, "Not even you, Herr Goebbels, my former boss in propaganda, could make this up as no one would believe you!" This time, it was Hitler who laughed loudly and the rest of those present followed. Funk added, "I can inform you that the bank has now become one of the most powerful in the world, attracting some the most influential bankers. This will provide us with the vehicle to meet the policy needs of the Reich and the wishes of the Führer." He bowed again, then raised his arm in salute before sitting down.

Hitler now stood, pausing as he looked around the room with his piercing blue eyes; then, placing his hands on the edge of the table, he leaned forwards, speaking his words in a precise manner. "I have asked three outstanding businessmen to attend this meeting here today who will also play a part in my economic plan. These are first, Günther Quandt, who is involved in manufacturing automobiles and is a supplier of arms and equipment to our forces. Next to him is Hugo Boss, who supplies uniforms to our armed forces and who has, I think, benefited very directly from my decisions. Finally, the manufacturer of fine National Socialist porcelain, and designer, Karl Diebitsch, has joined us. The *Reichsführer's* SS have greatly benefitted from his outstanding capabilities as he designed their uniforms and much of the insignia. These three men are shining examples of the National Socialist principle of working together to benefit the state. All of them use low-cost, efficient labour from our concentration camps which has assisted them to prosper, and contribute more to the Reich. My mission will be to both reward business and enable Germany to prosper as we expand, using our hidden labour assets.

"Let me now turn to gold and currency. I have no time for gold nor any wish to base Germany's wealth or currency on this and, had I done so, we would not have recovered because we had none. We have made it possible, without gold and without foreign exchange, to maintain the value of the German mark. Behind the German mark stands the German capacity for work, while some foreign countries, suffocated by gold, have been compelled to devalue their currencies. When the time comes, I will use currency as a weapon of war. Despite my determination never to rely on gold, all of us representing the awesome power of the Reich, must increase our power by any means, and if that requires exploiting the weaknesses of other nations, then we must seize the initiative. For that reason, we shall seek gold, procure gold, store gold, and secrete vast quantities in the *Versteckte Vermögensfonds*. "One day, when we have triumphed in our great endeavour, and realised our destiny in the east, we will recognise there is no longer any need for individual nation states with their own currencies and identity. Europe will be united with Germany the rightful and dominant force, and our reserves will give us the foundation from which the dawn of a new united Europe will arise. *Heil*"

The room echoed with the response, as those around the table stood, their right arms extended, before breaking into applause as Hitler sat down and reached for the telephone in front of him, ordering tea and biscuits for his guests.

3

A Bent Clodhopper

Tuesday 7th April 2015 8:10am
HQ – Metropolitan Police, New Scotland Yard, Victoria Embankment,
City of Westminster, London

The alert, when it came from the EOC (Emergency Operations Centre), via a 999 call from a security guard, was, at first, treated no differently than any other. The operations map for Holborn District of the London Borough of Camden was activated, and checked in by the allocating Sergeant as a jewellery theft at number 88-90, Hatton Garden. First response officers were alerted and within four minutes, the sound of a police siren preceded the first car pulling up at the front of the building, its blue lights flashing, containing two uniformed officers, followed by two more in a second vehicle a minute later. The call was also logged for the attention of 'The Flying Squad', and five minutes later, an unmarked car was despatched with armed officers, Detective Inspector Keith Anderson, and his partner, Detective Constable Rodger Bentham.

The first officers on the scene, Sergeant Derek Knowsley and Constable Mark Pearson, were met by two men; one in a dark business suit with smart grey parted hair, introduced himself as Abdul Kareem. He explained he was the Sudanese under-manager; the other, a somewhat overwrought security officer dressed in a black military style sweater over uniform trousers and boots, gave his name as Keefa Kamara, and volunteered he was aged 54. He confirmed to the officers he had worked there for 14 years and excitedly babbled he had never experienced anything like this before, and that, in his view, it was "a mission impossible". The officers calmed him down and told him to take deep breaths before continuing. He then explained he had arrived for work at around 7:45am, as usual, after the bank holiday weekend. The front door was secure, showing no sign of forced entry. There had been an alarm activated the previous Friday morning just after midnight, which was on the log, but after checking the entrances to the building, no further action had been taken other than the incident being recorded as a false alarm, which had happened a number of times previously. Sergeant Knowsley had stopped him to direct the second two officers on the scene to the entrance in order to prevent anyone from entering or leaving the building. At that moment, DI Keith Anderson and DC Rodger Bentham arrived, briefly introducing themselves and flashing their warrant cards. Anderson was slim, aged fifty, with wavy blonde hair, greying at the sides and was wearing a mid-grey suit with a tie loosely fastened under an open collar. Bentham was broader, in his thirties, with swept back dark hair in a black leather jacket with a t-shirt underneath. After Sergeant Knowsley had briefly summarised the position, DI Anderson told Kamara to continue.

The security man felt a sense of importance which masked his nervousness as he spoke. "Yes, it was me who called you. So, just after I arrived, I proceeded towards the vault when I noticed a door with its lock askew, and observed absolute chaos beyond. There were wires all over the place and signs of a break-in. When I reached the vault, I could see through the viewing window a complete mess; there were safety deposit boxes all over the floor with their lids forced, and valuables strewn everywhere. I also found the basement fire exit door unlocked which gives access to Hatton Garden Courtyard. I then called the police, but I haven't investigated further or touched anything."

DI Anderson turned to Kareem, "What is the value of the goods you have here?"

Kareem looked confused for a moment before replying, "I do not know; it could be hundreds of millions of pounds, but it is impossible to tell because it is not catalogued; all the deposits are confidential."

"Jesus," Anderson responded, "What kind of goods do you store, sir?"

Kareem was trembling as he blurted out, "We never know, but right now there is gold, jewellery, and precious stones all over the floor with cash strewn everywhere. We have hundreds of deposit boxes here, but I can see many are still intact."

"How many boxes do have, exactly, sir"

"There are 999, but only 500 in use."

"Can you identify the owners?"

Kareem lifted his shoulders in an uncertain gesture "Yes, by name but, once the boxes are opened, we cannot identify what may belong to who. This is confidential to protect our customers."

"You haven't done that too well, have you, my old son," muttered DC Bentham.

"So, let me get this right," DI Anderson said directly, "You've been robbed, or more pointedly, these poor bastards who have trusted your security have been robbed. You have no idea what belongs to who, nor what has been nicked, nor even what it is worth; am I right, er, sir? "

"Yes, that will be correct unfortunately." Kareem gestured with upturned hands.

"Who owns this place?" Anderson replied. "I need to get our legal boys to check this. I can't get my head round it."

"That will be Mr Manish Bavish, sir, but he is not here."

DC Bentham cut in, "Very convenient. Where is he? Do you keep a record of that?"

Kareem smiled weakly, "I am afraid he is in Sudan with his father, Mr Mahendra, who is also an owner, but we have not seen him either for some time."

"Gawd save us," Anderson replied. "Right, hang on one second. He turned to Sergeant Knowsley. Sarge, get uniformed to send in 10 officers to secure the building and start asking questions of neighbours etc. I'll leave you and Constable Pearson to organise. You know the drill. Anything noticed unusual, that sort of thing. We'll go down the vault."

"What about BWV, Gov? (Body worn video) Shouldn't we wait for forensics?"

"Give it a bleedin' rest, Sergeant, I been doing this job since you were in short pants. I might declare a Major Incident here; but before I get my arse kicked for wasting police resources, I'm checking the crime scene if you don't bleeding mind. If you want to file a report to IOPC (Independent Office for Police Conduct), I'm equally sure your stripes will be removed for wasting police time." He spoke the words laughingly but disparagingly, turning to Kareem. "Right then, let's try to find out what you don't know about what is missing, and how you going to give back what you can't identify." He glanced across at Bentham, winking, "How we going to record this if we don't even know what's been nicked. They might have been really nice *tea leaves* (thieves), and decided to put it all back." He looked directly at Kamara, "Has anyone else entered the vault since the robbery; anyone at all?"

"No sir," came the reply. "I know that crime scenes should not be interfered with."

"Good boy." Anderson replied, then he glanced back to Kareem. "Come on, Abdul, let's see what you broke into, and then you can show me where you stashed the loot."

Kareem looked horrified for a moment until he saw the wink and the smile which Anderson gave him. He led the way through a corridor past a lift which Kareem explained had been disabled by the thieves. On reaching the entrance to the vault, there appeared to be no damage until they were shown to a basement room, in the wall of which were bored three joined semi-circular holes through a two-metre thick wall. "Jesus H Christ" exclaimed Anderson, as he peered through, seeing piled up battered safety deposit boxes on the other side. There were also gems scattered on the floor and some bank notes. He pulled some gloves in a packet from his jacket pocket, as Bentham did likewise, then turned to Kareem, "We'll have a quick *shufti* round. You stand outside in the corridor, me old fruit. We don't want any evidence compromising, do we? Right, Rodger, you going to need to breathe in a little. You need to get *'er indoors* to stop stuffing you with chips."

"Piss off!" came the reply. Bentham had, long ago, dropped adopting any deference to his superior, except in front of certain other superior officers. Both men had worked on many operations together, building up a healthy respect for each other's abilities and, outside of work, they enjoyed a close friendship. Anderson chuckled, before turning to wriggle through the gap. Bentham spoke cheerfully to Kareem, "If we not back in 15 minutes, call the cops." Then he followed Anderson into the vault.

As they entered, Anderson noticed a small black document, next to a file on top of a cabinet, and his eyes were drawn to it as it had an eagle and swastika motif on it. He picked it up and studied the inside. When he saw the name, his heartbeat quickened, thinking back, and then with almost unsuppressed excitement, he exclaimed to Bentham. "Christ, I know this geezer. You know I'm well into World War II stuff; well, this bloke on this Nazi ID looted the Reichsbank in Berlin just before the end of the war in 1945. At that time, our lot let it be known that most of the money had been found in some German mines to cover up incompetence and stop the Ruskies getting involved. However, a huge chunk of it was never recovered and there was a lot of naughty stuff going on under wraps. A fortune in Nazi gold had disappeared, whilst looted art treasures and stolen currency were being traded on the black market; even the Mafia were involved. No one knows the value of what the Nazis nicked but some believe it was worth billions in today's money."

DC Bentham, who was looking through the debris of smashed and twisted safety deposit boxes suddenly uttered an expletive, then again, "Christ almighty, Gov, look at these bleedin' gelt bars which might link to what you talking about. Blimey, this is heavy." He lifted up a 12.5 kilo gold bullion bar. "It's got a swastika on it, for God's sake. There's a load more of them here. I could roll them over to you on these bloody pearls littering the floor." He started lifting some of the boxes then gasped, "Oh my Gawd almighty, there's a whole heap of gold bars here, some big, some small...must be more than a couple of dozen of the smaller ones."

Anderson walked over to him, and they stared, wide-eyed, at a sight neither had experienced seeing before. They spoke quietly and earnestly for a few moments before Anderson went back to the drilled vault entrance, wriggling through the hole, making his way back to the manager who was standing in the corridor looking anxious. "Right, Abdul, I'm declaring a Major Incident here. No one goes near this vault. I want you to show me how these villains gained entrance or how they exited your, er, high security building. Where's this fire escape door?" He turned back to Bentham, "We'll block all access down here until forensics arrives. I'll check out how the building was compromised and I'll be back here shortly."

At 9:45am, DI Anderson called in and spoke to the duty Sergeant at Flying Squad HQ. "This is DI Anderson, senior FOA (First Officer Attending) at the premises of the Safety Deposit Company Ltd, at 88, Hatton Garden: I'm declaring this a Major Incident. This is a serious crime with a suspected large theft of cash, gold, and jewellery from a major breach of a secure vault. PIP 3 recommended plus we may need involvement of NATIS (National Investigation Service), because of the sensitive nature of items discovered bearing the Nazi emblem." Within a minute, the phone bleeped in the office of DSU (Detective Superintendent) Craig Turner, the head of the Flying Squad. He decided, in turn, to notify the Met Police Commissioner, Sir Bernard Hogan-Howe, as he was concerned that this may run as a major press story. The Commissioner ordered that they should withhold any immediate press statement although he authorised that Turner should visit the crime scene personally, requesting that he report back directly to him by midday.

On arrival at the scene, the head of the Flying Squad was greeted by Anderson who took him straight to the vault. More uniformed officers had now arrived and a police-taped cordoned-off area had been erected around the front of the building. Forensics investigators were on the scene dressed in white overalls, and a scene of crimes officer (SOCO) was directing those photographing, recording, and gathering evidence. Abdul Kareem, together with a small team of officers, had been instructed to contact all safety deposit box owners who had been affected by the robbery.

After the initial survey of the scene, forensics reported that there were around seventy of the smaller sized safety deposit boxes smashed open and twelve of the larger boxes out of the five hundred in use. On viewing the scene, there was something familiar to Turner about the manner of the bore-hole access to the vault which he recalled he had seen before in a robbery reported by Interpol. By 11:00am, after talking to another officer who gathered intelligence on international crime at NATIS (National Investigation Service), he had been sent an image by text of a very similar robbery which had taken place in Germany in 2013 at the *Volksbank* in Berlin. The method of entry to the vault had marked similarities and he made a mental note that they needed to liaise with police in Germany to look at potential links between the two crimes, not least because of the swastika marking on the gold bars. That morning, the police and the manager had only been able to make contact with five owners, but the feedback was already alarming. The value of the contents of the twelve boxes that these owners declared stood at around 15 million pounds. None of those contacted were owners of the larger boxes which had been forced open, which made the prospects of the size of the haul daunting. The last thing Turner wanted was to be added to the statistics of largest robberies on his watch. In the entire history of British crime, the biggest heists had been the Knightsbridge Security Job in 1987 and the City Bonds robbery of 1990. The latter had fallen apart rapidly with most of the bonds recovered, but the Knightsbridge job netted the thieves over £40 million which was equivalent to over £124 million in today's currency values. Now, it could be that this heist might be well in excess of this amount. Clearly, the figure would need to be underplayed to the press but he knew, from experience, that this was a political decision and not one which fell under police responsibility. However, Turner had another headache to deal with, which was the matter of the ten 12.5 kilo gold bars recovered with a swastika on them. For years, there had been an alert to keep a close eye out for anything which might link back to the biggest robbery in history at the end of the Second World War. Senior police officers were briefed that a fortune in Nazi gold which disappeared in the closing stages of WWII had never been recovered. This included a vast quantity that had been looted from the Reichsbank on the orders of Hitler. The briefing stated that if any links to this were ever discovered, that such should be treated as 'Classified'. Any information was not to be shared except at the highest level, and then only as authorised by the home secretary or the prime minister. Turner called Anderson into the office used by Abdul Kareem, asking all those there to give them some privacy. "I understand you entered the vault this morning. You should have waited for forensics; serious questions are going to be asked about this at the highest level."

"Yes, apologies about that, sir, but I did not want to declare a 'Major Incident' without good reason. Especially knowing the pressures we are under for budget cuts right now. You're damned if you do, and damned if you don't. I wouldn't like to be in your position right now."

"I'm not looking to hang you for it, Keith," replied Turner, sighing, "you're too long in the tooth for that, but trust me, this is going to be scrutinised from above and the press will be all over it. Was anyone else with you?"

"Only my oppo, sir, DC Rodger Bentham, but he was never out of my sight."

"Where is he now?"

"End of his shift, sir. I sent him home 'cos there was nothing else for him to do here once we'd closed the place down and got forensics here. In hindsight, not a good move on my part, I'll omit that bit from my report."

Turner lent forwards, fixing his eyes on Anderson, "Keith, I need a faultless and meticulously worded report. The last thing we want are a load of conspiracy nutters saying we might have a bent *clodhopper* in the *Sweeney*. I have a feeling this is going to be very big, and our political masters will want answers. First stop for me is the Met Commissioner."

"Good luck with that one, sir, I don't envy you."

12:30pm – Office of the Metropolitan Police Commissioner
New Scotland Yard, Victoria Embankment, London

The large panelled door opened, and the Commissioner, Sir Bernard Hogan–Howe, entered the conference room with a bulky file under his arm accompanied by the Director of Communications, Martin Fewell. Sir Bernard was a slim man, in his late fifties, with neatly trimmed greying fair hair wearing a white police shirt, and black tie, with silver epaulette badges. Fewell was a little younger, wore a grey business suit and, thought DSU Turner, a somewhat overstated tie.

"Good afternoon, Craig," the Commissioner began as he sat at the head of the polished cherry-wood table, "it seems we might have a storm brewing with this one. I think you know Martin." He gestured towards Fewell, "Clearly, this needs delicate handling and Martin needs to craft something for the press. What have we got so far?"

Turner was sat to the Commissioner's right opposite Fewell, who opened a tablet, and began typing as they spoke. "As you are aware, sir, we have a break in at number 88-90 Hatton Garden which is a major secure safety deposit and storage facility. Looks like they gained entry over the bank holiday weekend, and, as there is no sign of forced entry, we may have a suspected insider. They dropped to the basement via a lift shaft, bored three holes into the outer wall of the vault, forced a secure fitting the other side, giving them access to the vault. Sir, most of the security cameras and street CCTV appears to have been disabled but we do have some footage. They wore masks and balaclavas and cameras captured a white van which was used in the robbery."

"How much was nicked?" Sir Bernard asked, his eyebrows raised.

"I'm afraid we don't yet know, sir, but it appears it could be one of the biggest we have faced. They don't keep records there of the value stored but the villains knocked off seventy-three of the smaller boxes out of the 500 in use so it could have been worse. However, there were also 12 larger boxes forced which contained heavier stuff such as bullion. Typically, the facility store jewellery, precious stones, gold and currency and, from our investigations so far, we think that we could be looking at the upper end of tens of millions, possibly in excess of 100 million.

"Oh Christ!" Sir Bernard exclaimed, "that means our political masters are going to be sticking their noses in. Ok, what about the Nazi link?"

"Two things there, sir; with regard to the Nazi connection, we have recovered ten 12.5 kilo gold bars and four 1 kilo bars of gold, bearing the swastika which, surprisingly, the thieves left behind. We have established that some of the boxes containing the gold are registered to a German investment company, based in Switzerland, by the name of *VVF AG*. We have quite a file on them stretching way back. The company was set up in late 1945 with the suspected involvement of former Nazis; we do know they have substantial assets held by Swiss banks. There were rumours that *VVF* were involved in questionable trading after the war using assets seized from the Jews."

"This is getting worse and worse," Sir Bernard muttered, "I think I need to brief the PM on this today." He turned to Fewell, "Needless to say, Martin, not a whiff of this to anyone, not even with one of your so called, 'Off the record' briefings. I do not want any reports being released by our friends in the media saying, 'undisclosed sources are saying'. Clear?" His voice had assumed a tone of uncompromising authority." Fewell had substantial experience in media relations having held senior roles for iconic BBC News programmes such as *The World at One, Newsnight,* and the *One O'clock News.* He had also been responsible for developing *Channel 4 News* before becoming Director of Media and Communications at the Met in 2012. He immediately recognised the sensitivity of the crime and understood the position which the Commissioner needed to adopt.

"Sir, I think a very simple statement concentrating on the crime and nothing else will suffice. We can deflect the press's attention by talking of the imperative of catching those responsible in any interviews. Clearly, the fewer knowing either the size of the haul, or the Nazi connection, the better."

Turner added, "Another line we are pursuing, Sir, is that there was a raid on the *Volksbank* in Berlin in January 2013 which has striking similarities to this one, so we may need to begin opening up lines of enquiry in Germany."

Sir Bernard sighed deeply, "I'm afraid I think we are onto something much bigger than any of us might imagine here. Press briefings should omit any sensitivities or details regarding the content of the larger boxes. You know the sort of thing; give them accurate figures on the number of boxes compromised, and then we will later issue a modest estimate of the value of stolen items. Seventy-three boxes out of 500 doesn't sound too bad. I think, in order to uphold our reputation, which, God knows, has taken a battering of late, we need to demonstrate the seriousness with which we are treating this, and use the incident as a confidence building exercise. I'm afraid, Craig, I think I need to appoint someone with more senior credentials to oversee this, but working alongside you. You can act as SOI (Senior Officer Investigating), but I suggest joint press conferences etc., you know the drill. I'll smooth things over with the PM and the home secretary. I'm going to bring in MI6 to pursue the German connection because of all the sensitivities. I'll deal with you directly, but have you any idea who you might appoint as SPOC?" (Single point of contact)

"I'll nominate the Flying Squad officer who was first there, DI Anderson. He's a good man; due to retire in the next couple of years with a long, unblemished record. His superior, of course, is DCS Paul Johnson of the Flying Squad; he can be our immediate front man to the press."

The Commissioner made a note, then opened the thick file he had brought in as he entered. "The file on the missing Nazi gold or *'Raubgold',* as it is called here, goes way back when and much of it has never been uploaded anywhere. I've never studied it in detail. The first entry is in 1945, but it links to another from 1940 recording something called 'Operation Andreas'; all very hush-hush as they used to say."

At 3:51pm on 7th April 2015, a press statement was released by the Met, *"Flying Squad officers are investigating a burglary at a safety deposit business in Hatton Garden EC1. Enquiries continue."*

Sir Bernard appointed Police Commander Peter Spindler (uniformed special commander) to oversee the investigation, and contacted his opposite number, the director of MI6, Sir Alex Younger, requesting assistance with a probe into *VVF AG* and links to Nazi activities.

3:30pm 10, Downing Street, London

The plain black unmarked Range Rover was equipped with blue lights to front and rear which were flashing, having carried the Commissioner from HQ, and which now swept through the gates allowing entrance to Downing Street; armed police saluted as the vehicle passed through. He was alone but the PM's secretary, Sir Jeremy Heywood, had made it clear that the PM wanted a joint meeting with Sir Bernaard Hogan-Howe and Sir Alex Younger from MI6. As the car drove up to the kerb outside No 10, the shiny black door to the Prime Minister's office and residence swung open. Sir Bernard, dressed in his full police uniform, pulled his hat, with silver embellishment 'scrambled egg' on the visor, to his head as he emerged. Some press cameras flashed from opposite and he paused to give a brief, but business-like wave, before entering the building. He was ushered to the reception room outside the PM's office where the suited Sir Alex Younger was already sat, studying a tablet screen perched on his legs. He looked up with a smile of acknowledgement.

"Jesus, Bernard, what have you lot dug up this time? I have enough on my plate dealing with the Islamic State issue right now. Belgium, Australia, Canada, the US, and France in the last year, quite apart from the carnage they caused in Iraq; mark my words, we will be targeted next. Now, we appear to be facing a foe from the past?"

At that moment, there were footsteps, and the home secretary, Theresa May appeared, dressed in a red jacket and black skirt, carrying a briefcase, her face beneath her bobbed greying hair was set in a determined look. She stopped, to shake their hands with a brief smile, before entering the PM's office. Seconds later, the double black doors, with their gold trim, swung open and Sir Jeremy Heywood invited them to go in. As they entered, David Cameron rose from his polished desk in one corner, in a blue suit and matching tie, although his shirt collar was loosened. He appeared, as always, very smartly dressed, added to by his neatly parted thick hair and he greeted them with a friendly smile of acknowledgment.

"Thank you, Sir Jeremy." The PM spoke the words with a finality which, his secretary recognised, was an invitation to withdraw. As the doors closed, the PM rapidly took command of the meeting. "First, let me say nothing of what we discuss here today will be communicated outside this room, unless I directly authorise this, except, of course, for operational purposes. Ok, as I understand it, we have had a major robbery at Hatton Garden which could be the largest we have ever faced. In addition, this has unearthed some Nazi gold which may be linked to that which disappeared in 1945. Looking at your initial briefing, Sir Bernard, I concur that we are going to have to downplay the size of the robbery for reasons of public confidence and, for once, the press have no idea, as yet, that anything particularly unusual has occurred. Now we need to look at something more concerning, which is that the German company owning some of the boxes, *VVF AG,* appears, from your initial summary, Sir Alex, to have been founded by former Nazis at the end of the War. The company has been accused of laundering monies and gold looted during the War, including that confiscated from the Jews. We then have something of an issue because the source of this gold may be linked to the wartime activities of the Swiss based Bank for International Settlements. As I understand it, during the War this wretched bank was under the presidency of an American, with a board including the vice president of the Reichsbank, and other Nazis. Incredibly, the board also included the governor of the Bank of England, Sir Montagu Norman, and a director of the Bank of England, Sir Otto Niemeyer. I see from your report, Sir Alex, that

Niemeyer was chairman of this bank when war broke out, and vice chairman until after the War ended in 1946. They sat on the board alongside known Nazis, not only before, but during the war." He paused, scratching his head as he looked at the briefing askance, rhetorically posing the question, "They did this, whilst Montagu Norman remained governor of the Bank of England? How the hell Churchill permitted that, heaven knows. Have I summarised this dog's breakfast correctly, so to speak?"

Sir Alex Younger responded, "Spot on Prime Minister, I regret to say; and I do not think we should go public on any of the gold connection as it would undermine the confidence in the financial sector, not least by our friends in the Jewish community, who are already kicking off about antisemitism in the political establishment. My concern is to find out why there should have been any bullion deposited here, and whether it may lead us to the fortune that has never been recovered."

"You did the right thing by coming to see me, gentlemen. Right, we need to keep the lid on this. No press briefings beyond a normal robbery investigation. I suggest we peg the value involved to around 15 million and, as we have no way of knowing the real amount, that should survive any post-event revelations causing us difficulties or embarrassment."

The home secretary interrupted, "Prime Minister, we cannot expect investigating officers to keep quiet or, indeed, misrepresent the truth. It would not sit well with me to be party to any attempt at disinformation or, to coin a phrase used by a former cabinet secretary, being 'economical with the truth.'"

The Prime Minister looked exasperated, "Theresa, whilst admiring your reputation as a person of the highest integrity, we must remind ourselves that we are dealing with a matter here of national interest which may well also be labelled one of national security. First, we have the natural sensitivities to the fact that this country may have been a safe haven for Nazi gold, quite apart from the hornets' nest which could be stirred by a press investigation. Imagine if it came out that we had been helping to run the Bank for International Settlements, during wartime, sitting on a board with Nazi Party members and that this might be linked to the laundering of looted Nazi gold. That to one side, we would then be embroiled in a further row because in 1945, it was stated by the Americans and ourselves that most of the Nazi stolen gold had been recovered. Clearly, we are then in a position whereby our Jewish friends will want to know what our part was in covering up monies which were stolen from them in the Holocaust.

"We also know that there has been post-war infiltration by Nazis into the political and financial establishment of Germany, the United States, and, I regret, the United Kingdom. We do not want to instigate a situation whereby all these factors combine in a tsunami of scandal that could affect our standing as the financial capital of the world. Notwithstanding all of that, and the passions this might inflame, we have the political reality which is that anti-EU sentiment is running at an all-time high in this country, not least in our own party. If any of this gets out, Nigel Farage and his bunch in UKIP will have a field day and, my God, I can imagine a scenario whereby the Euro-Sceptics get their way and we end up exiting the EU."

"Forgive me," Sir Bernard Hogan–Howe interjected, "but I regret that such political issues are not those which must concern my role, except, of course, where they may affect public order. However, I can emphasise that my officers do sign the Official Secrets Act and we can cite this case as falling under the national security banner, only sharing any intelligence or findings from the investigation on a 'need to know' basis. I can ensure that only the most trusted officers are deployed and that all reports come via my desk for clearance. Might I suggest, Prime Minister, that your government operates on the same principle."

"Good point, Sir Bernard," the PM replied, "the last thing we need, and I trust you agree with me Theresa, is a COBRA meeting on this, or, even worse, sharing the situation with our Lib Dem Deputy PM, Nick Clegg. Once that 'politically correct' mob in the Lib-Dems get hold of this, there would be no stopping the trouble they'd cause, notwithstanding which, we need to keep Clegg onside until we can increase our majority in the House. The sooner we can dump them and get on with our agenda unimpeded, the better.

"Our priority now is to get this cleaned up and dealt with. Sir Bernard, put every resource you can into cracking this. I can authorise an additional budget if you need it. Sir Alex, I think your people need to look at the German links, especially, the robbery in 2013 and the involvement of this *VVF AG*. When Churchill said, "We are fighting to save the whole world from the pestilence of Nazi tyranny", I cannot imagine that he would envisage we would still be doing so over seventy years later."

4

Das Geheime Vierte Reich

Saturday 25th November 2023 3:00pm

Das Kauntinhaus, Pienzenauerstrasse, Bogenhausen, Munich

Heinz had decided to be totally open with his son as there seemed little point in hiding anything anymore. "The strange thing is, Karl, that as I approach the end, all I have worked for has little or no value, yet I place more value on things I have seldom paid enough attention to. You know, I have walked here in the beautiful gardens surrounding this house this last year observing things I have never seen before. I was enchanted by our wonderful cherry blossoms bursting into flower in early spring, surrounding the path to the lake, followed by the colourful pansies and violas. I watched the beautiful rhododendrons making a wonderful display of pink, white and red all around us; I noticed all this, and the song of the birds, as if for the first time and, I regret, probably the last." He stopped for a moment and Karl leant across, placing his hand on his father's arm, giving a comforting grip. The old man's blue eyes were focussed distantly, and he patted his son's hand for a moment. "The edelweiss was lovely, and, of course, the cornflowers looked incredible, bringing a vibrant blue-violet colour to the landscape. I have sat out on so many days reflecting on my life and wondering how I may be judged. Wood avens are still giving us a display, even this late in the year, and you know what they say about these flowers? They ward off evil; perhaps they might protect me or, perhaps, repel me for what I have done." He sighed.

Karl spoke softly, "*Mein Vater,* do not think this way. I have been guided by you all my life and I respect you for who you are. I know we have disagreed about the past, but that is what it is, the past!" He emphasised the last words.

His father was shaking his head. "I worry how I may be judged by the Almighty. Did I do the right thing in following my beliefs or was I motivated by avarice, or status? I think my conscience should be clear, but there are days when it is not. He reached for the bottle of *Asbach Uralt*, and topped up their glasses, raising his to touch Karl's, "*Prost!*"

"My son, there is much I need to tell you and, perhaps, it is as much to unburden my conscience as it is to impart information. I hope you will not be the one who judges me most harshly because..." He paused, then, "I used the word, 'believe' before and that has underpinned my life despite how others may view this. As I approach the final curtain, I have doubts about myself, yet my beliefs remain. How strange that my conviction is tested by my conscience."

"Papa, you will always by my father, and I look up to you for the strength you have always displayed." Karl gripped his father's arm for the second time reassuringly.

Heinz's eyes assumed a more focussed look, "Ah yes, the values represented by the mantra passed on to me by my father, 'Strength through discipline.' He used to tell me that this was his second most important guiding life principle; his first was, *'Meine Ehre Heisst Treue'* (My honour is loyalty). This, as you may know, was the motto of the SS in which he served, with distinction during the war, reaching the rank of SS-*Standartenführer* (Colonel). I have wanted to tell you more about him before, but your principles, which I do admire, prevented this. *Ach* so, now is the time. You may do as you please with what I am about to reveal, but please remember that I have taken a great risk to make available to you what I will now reveal; an inheritance, perhaps, which your own conscience must dictate whether you accept." He opened the box which he had placed on a table by his chair when they had first entered the room, pulling out a photograph of his father dressed in his SS uniform, which he passed to Karl who tried to suppress an expression of distaste he felt for what his appearance represented. He looked at the surprisingly boyish face of his grandfather under a cap clearly displaying the death's head emblem of the SS.

His father continued, "He was a good soldier, like you, and his record of service was exemplary. Papa had started life working as an accountant, but saw career opportunity with the rise of the Nazis. He joined the SS in 1931 and rose rapidly through the ranks being promoted to SS-*Sturmbannführer* (Major) by 1934. In 1940, he became commander of the security police and SD in the Netherlands; however, despite showing outstanding ability as an administrator, Himmler did not consider him ruthless enough, and he was replaced in 1941."

"Thank God for small mercies," Karl interrupted, surprising himself that he was genuinely interested. This was an area his father had never attempted to discuss with him before. "Please do carry on, Papa, I am finding this really fascinating."

His reaction removed the trepidation his father had been feeling about what he was revealing, giving him confidence to carry on. "Despite this career setback, Papa excelled as an economist and organiser, and had also worked in locations which were under fire, showing a cool resolve to get things done for which he was decorated. He was posted to serve in Russia, organising and heading up the policing of the occupied areas. His efficiency in carrying out his role combined with the highly effective removal of gold and currency from Russia to the Reich was noticed. His success in this resulted in his recall to take over the administration of the *Reichssicherheitshauptamt* (Reich Security Main Office) or RHSA and secured his promotion to SS-*Standartenführer*. During his time in office, he had impressed many, including Walther Funk, the Reichsbank president, who suggested to Hitler that he should be entrusted with certain key tasks in protecting gold reserves, and concealing assets. He was noted for his creative accounting skills which enabled large amounts of gold to be siphoned off and transferred into a secret fund which I shall come back to.

"His reputation as an economist grew; so much so that he was selected by SS-*Obergruppenführer* Ernst Kaltenbrunner, the overall commander of the RHSA, for a vital mission. The RHSA was the Reich Security Main Office and Kaltenbrunner also ran the SD which was the intelligence agency of the SS and the Nazi Party. Kaltenbrunner was a brutal fanatic and had a reputation for cruelty including the execution of prisoners; your grandfather despised him but, of course, could not show it. Hitler approved Papa's selection and he was eventually entrusted with an historic task in April 1945. This was to remove a massive amount of money, valuables, and gold bullion from the Reichsbank in Berlin, and take it to a place of safety. The bank had been extensively damaged in a huge American bombing raid in February 1945 and a highly secret operation began at that time to gradually transport currency and gold bullion out of Berlin. However, events overtook the removal process as the Soviet forces had reached the outskirts of Berlin far more rapidly than expected on 20th April 1945. Urgent action was needed and your grandfather led a military operation to remove what they could from the Reichsbank, in what was, in effect, the largest bank robbery in history on 22nd April 1945. He marched in with a detachment of the SS and ordered the staff to open the vault at gunpoint. Vast quantities of currency, valuables, gold rings and gold coins were removed with an 'official' value estimated at $130 million. In today's money, your grandfather managed to steal over $2 billion."

"*Du Lieber Gott!*" Karl exclaimed. "*Das ist ja nicht zu fassen!* (that's unbelievable) What happened to it all? Did it get found by the Allies?"

"Most of this was never recovered but it was claimed at the time that virtually all Hitler's hidden gold and valuables was discovered stashed away in the Merkers potassium mine three hundred and twenty kilometres south west of Berlin. So much was covered up at this time by the Allies, partly for consumption back home, and partly because the monies involved could have had a destabilising effect on the post-war economy. But there is much more that has been hidden which is that of the gold, valuables and currency removed from the Reichsbank after February 1945, excluding what Papa removed subsequently, over $6.5 billion has never been recovered at today's value."

Karl whistled in astonishment, then raised the finger of one hand, "I think I have heard of this, Papa; is this what has been called the '*Raubgold*', rumours of which, if I recall, are dismissed as conspiracy theories when they arise."

His father slowly shook his head, giving a knowing smile, "Of course it is ridiculed, with the connivance of our intelligence services. It is an embarrassment to the state; too many powerful people have been involved…still are, and not, I stress, only here in Germany. I regret that I have been complicit in that. He leant forwards, grasping his son's arm; "Karl, this is still being covered up because of the enormity of what occurred in 1945, and the collusion of the financial sector and other institutions in what followed. You see, the value of what was removed at this time was far, far, greater than has ever been admitted. The figures I gave you do not include the hidden assets fund which Hitler set up in 1939 known as *Versteckte Vermögensfonds* often shortened to *VVF*. This was specifically set aside from state assets in order that it could provide additional funds for other purposes where no trace would help the cause of National Socialism. Towards the end of the war, Hitler saw it as being the economic foundation of a network, providing the basis of the 4th Reich.

"Returning to the bank heist in April 1945, you may have noted that I used the word "*official*" when I described the value of what had been taken. This merely covered what your grandfather and his accomplices could arrange to safely transport by air which was, at the time, the safest method of transport out of Berlin. The Russians were closing in fast and attempting to encircle the city. However, there were still substantial quantities of gold bullion remaining in the Reichsbank, some of which formed part of the *Versteckte Vermögensfonds*. This was too heavy to be transported ay air and Hitler was adamant that this should not fall into Soviet hands. There was still a relatively safe road out of Berlin to the south west, and Papa volunteered to lead a well-armed and heavily escorted convoy and attempt to reach Obersalzberg via that route. Despite a fire-fight with an *Ivan* force, they got through and proceeded south to the Bavarian Alps where further adventure awaited, not least with the Americans, who were far more, shall we say, laid back and entrepreneurial. Many GI's went home as rich men, I think." He laughed, recalling the many stories his father had told him about his desperate efforts to secrete the vast fortune for which he was responsible, when all around him was in a state of collapse. He touched his glass to his son's again as he chuckled.

"At that point, huge quantities of gold were buried in ditches, in rivers, under houses, and with loyal friends who lived close by Hitler's house around Berchtesgaden; our people displayed extraordinary ingenuity; everything was accounted for meticulously and later recovered. We were also arranging regular shipments to other safe locations, including banks in Switzerland on whose confidentiality we could rely. Your grandfather had an incredible strength of mind. He surrendered to the Americans in early May 1945 and led them to decoy sites where small amounts of gold were recovered, distracting them from where vast caches were hidden, and never discovered. I think I have inherited some of Papa's skills for concealing gold, but more of that later. It was after the War that your grandfather's role was to be pivotal in managing the assets.

"The value of the *Versteckte Vermögensfonds* had built up over the war years and was kept secret from all in the Nazi hierarchy but a chosen few at the very top. However, because of his trusted position and financial reputation, this information was eventually shared with your grandfather by Ernst Kaltenbrunner. Ironically, because your grandfather was appalled by Kaltenbrunner's cruelty, excesses and corruption, as Chief of the RHSA, he testified against him at the Nuremberg war crimes trials. Kaltenbrunner was executed by hanging in 1946. Karl, you will not believe this, but by 1945, the *Versteckte Vermögensfonds* were worth $970 million which in today's value would represent over $15.5 billion with most of it held as gold bullion. This does not include a staggering quantity of gold and valuables which had not been officially added to the *Versteckte Vermögensfonds*, but which was looted or appropriated into the Reich. These were stored in various secure locations during the War, but removed and hidden by units of the SS in 1945."

Karl was shaking his head in utter astonishment, his eyes glazing over as he wrestled with the staggering value of the missing bullion. He looked up at his father, his face expressing utter astonishment, as he quickly thought back over the figures for official, and hidden records. "So you are saying that, if we include the *Versteckte Vermögensfonds*, over $24 billion has never been recovered, plus that which was hidden by the SS, and more which Grandfather took out of Berlin by road in a convoy. *Mein Gott*, that is more than some countries raise a year in tax revenue. How do you know all this?" In his mind, he was already dreading what he might hear next.

As his father was about to speak, his face contorted, as a searing pain spread across his abdomen and into his back. He bent over double, gasping, motioning to the electric bell push indicating that Karl should summon Greta. Moments later, she entered and, noting how Heinz looked, immediately left the room, returning with a syringe which, she explained to a startled Karl, contained morphine. She grasped his father's arm and swiftly injected him, asking if he needed the warming cushion. Within seconds, he raised up, white-faced, then sat back in his seat taking deep breaths, then reached for Karl's arm, "I'm sorry..." he whispered, "Please...I must continue. One minute..." He put his head back and closed his eyes.

Karl looked on feeling helpless, "Papa, I am here for you. Can I do anything?"

His father did not reply but shook his head as Greta re-entered with a heated cushion which she placed on Heinz's stomach. He opened his eyes, and slowly straightened up, muttering his thanks to Greta as she left the room. "I do not think I have much more time left on this earth, Karl, and so much to tell you. There are papers in this box that I will give to you and which will give more detail on what I am telling you; there are documents and letters which my father gave to me plus others that I have added. One thing that may help you is that the Nazis kept meticulous records."

"Help me in what, Papa? This is all incredible and shocking, but I still do not understand why this may affect me nor what part you may have played."

Heinz attempted to rise, but struggled with the effort, saying in a weakened voice as Karl helped him up, "Please, I like to see the last of the day over the trees and the lake. I value this more than gold which Hitler once stated he felt suffocated by. I think that is how I now feel." Karl walked him slowly to the tall, arched window. His father's eyes had a glazed faraway look as he stared out across the large lawns in the fading light of day with long shadows thrown across the expansive garden as the watery sunlight filtered through the trees on a cold still wintry late afternoon.

He patted his son on the back, "You know Karl, I planned how I was going to tell you all this but now I hardly know where to start." He looked at his son with tired eyes, his face drawn, and Karl felt a deep pang of sympathy for his father, noticing, with a shock, how frail, vulnerable and changed he looked from the father he had known all his life. "Come, time to finish what I have started," Heinz muttered in a more determined voice, motioning back to the seats and Karl led him slowly away from the window.

"So, my son," he said, as he refilled his glass with brandy, "I should begin at the beginning, *nein*? By the mid 1960's, I was, of course aware of my father's key role in looking after substantial investment groups, which were part of a highly secret organisation, with its roots in the Nazi era. Papa did not hide his involvement in the Nazi network, known as *Die Spinne,* which assisted fugitives to escape or in assuming new identities. Many former Nazis, at that time, were being rounded up, once again, for war crimes trials which had resumed in Germany.

I was, by then, a defence lawyer and had become involved in representing or assisting teams in defending many notable or notorious figures from Hitler's regime. I did not judge them for what they had done although many were clearly guilty of heinous crimes or "excesses" as your grandfather called them. I was at the *Auschwitz-Prozess* trials of 1963 where most of the accused got away with light sentences. We managed to secure legal definitions based upon whether a defendant had been 'following orders' or had carried out killings when not following orders. In the former cases, they were judged as being accomplices to murder and received light sentences. Only the latter cases received a heavy sentence but there were only six of those. Then, I was instructed in the Treblinka Trials which started in 1964, and the Sobibor Trials in 1965. I regret that many guilty of "excesses" were never brought to justice and, of those who were, most escaped with a mild sentence. I was not proud of the part I played in this, which still torments my conscience. However, by now, I had come to believe in the principles of National Socialism, but not the manner of enforcing them in the era of Adolf Hitler.

"Your grandfather remained an unapologetic committed Nazi, and I admired him for his loyalty and dedication to his beliefs. By 1966, he began giving me more and more responsibility for the control of the assets which, by now, had become much larger. I was proud of my father's trust and gladly accepted when he invited me to become involved in his investment group. We were financing what was called a new Reich which was being administered from Argentina, under the direction of the former head of the Nazi Party under Hitler, Martin Bormann. *Die Spinne* had assumed a much wider role assisting many former Nazis in obtaining senior posts in institutions including the security services, the armed forces, the police and even the judiciary. We were successful in infiltrating business organisations, the civil service, and the government, not only here in Germany, but also in Britain, and the United States. We had former senior military personnel who had once sworn an oath of allegiance to Adolf Hitler, working in NATO high command.

"When Papa died in 1967, I was formally approved by the governing body of the new Reich in Argentina to continue administering the asset base through a front company. This had been established in 1945 and eventually became a public investment company by the name of *VVF AG*. Your grandfather ensured I was well provided for before he died and sold his holding in a major supermarket chain which he had ran after the war, transacting this through *VVF AG* in 1965. He then allocated me a sizeable shareholding within this investment group which had huge assets."

"*Ich glaub mich knutscht ein Elch!*" (I can't believe it) Karl exclaimed, "It sounds like the Reich flourished after the war. You are telling me you financed this? How could you do this?" His voice registered his shock and anger.

"Please do not condemn me for what I believed in." Heinz said imploringly, "You have no idea what it was like in those days. Shame for everything German; no national pride; just guilt and more guilt constantly thrust at us. You know what Papa did? He restored my belief. In the 1970's, the country was slipping into anarchy and there were killings on the streets, and bombs detonated by extremists. Social unrest began to explode with militants emerging such as the Red Army Faction and the Baader-Meinhof gang. People openly expressed that if Hitler was still in charge, this could not happen. We craved order and so I believed in what I was doing in a drive to attempt infiltration of those who had embraced National Socialism into every walk of life. We represented order, discipline, and national pride...We believed!" His last words were spoken with fervour before he sat back exhausted, breathing heavily, and closing his eyes.

Karl was torn between the anger he felt at what he was hearing and compassion for the old man; his father, who was struggling to hold on to life; then he regretted his previous outburst. He spoke his words in a quiet, more measured tone, "I am sorry, Papa, but all my life, I have not even wanted to think about all this. This is the past. We are a new Germany now which does not belong to that period or those beliefs."

His father held up both hands in a placatory manner, "There is more, much more, which I have had typed up by Greta into a testament which is for your eyes only. It is in this box which I would ask you not to open until my death. My son, have you heard of *das Geheime Vierte Reich* or the GVR?" Karl felt almost numbed by the enormity of what he had already heard, and shook his head in a resigned manner, shuddering at the thought of a secret Reich existing.

"This is the organisation formed immediately after the war, which is split up into many bodies reporting back to the leader who is now based here in Germany. Former prominent and trusted members of the Nazi party were invited to be part of this new organisation in 1945 which soon flourished, financed by the *VVF* which was, in effect, a new exchequer. Prominent businessmen became donors such as Hermann Schmitz, the CEO of IG Farben, the former giant chemical company, now incorporated into organisations with which you may be more familiar; names you will recognise such as AGFA, Bayer, and BASF. Schmitz was a prominent supporter of Hitler and part of his business was moved to Auschwitz to exploit slave labour, a move organised by Heinrich Himmler. His company produced huge quantities of material needed by the German war machine and, incidentally, they manufactured *Zyclon B* gas which was used in the gas chambers. Another major donor was Günther Quandt who supplied the German armed forces with, amongst other things, arms, uniforms and vehicles during the war, with interests in Daimler-Benz, BMW and VARTA. His businesses also used slave labourers and there was even an execution area set up in his Hannover factory. He had been appointed by Hitler as *Wehrwirtschaftsführer* or as a leader of the military economy."

Karl interjected, expressing shock in his question, "Surely these people were prosecuted after the war?"

His father put stress into the words of his response. "This is why I am telling you all this. You have no idea how powerful the influence of the GVR was after the war. The case against Günther Quandt was dropped, and Hermann Schmitz, who had received a token four-year sentence, only ended up serving three. You know where both men ended up afterwards? On the board of the Deutsche Bank."

"Oh *mein Gott!*" Karl exclaimed, holding his head in his hands, as his father continued, "Enormous power and influence is exerted through the GVR in government, and they hold vast financial assets. Hitler had a vision, which he announced in 1940, of a post-war Europe united in one union, dominated, of course, by Germany, with power ceded by independent states to a central governing body. Does this sound familiar? Does this resonate with today's European situation?

"Now, perhaps, with what I have told you, you will understand why I said to you that I am tormented by my life's work." He let out a long sigh, pulling a face which reflected disturbing memories of the many compromises he had made between what he often justified as being pragmatic, using a mantra he had developed of actions being "in the interests of the many."

He continued, "You will recall, as a young man, that Germany was split into east and west, but we had people on both sides. By the mid 1960's, we had successfully infiltrated the East German regime, the so-called German Democratic Republic with 10% of their administration being former members of the Nazi Party. The communist regime operated with secret police, the Stasi, who were incredibly vigilant, obsessed with keeping our people out. In West Germany, it was easier and we had more success with 67% of former Nazis in the administration. At this time, we all shared the desire for a unified Germany, and, in 1989, we judged the moment was right to encourage and participate in the mass protests, leading to the fall of the Berlin Wall, which you will remember."

"Ah yes," Karl responded, "my days as a left-wing radical were overtaken by the euphoria of reunification. I went to the demonstrations and climbed on the Berlin Wall. I broke off a piece, which I still have in a mounting, at home."

His father replied, "We too, felt that euphoria, but then the cracks began appearing in our unity. Militants in our ranks stated that this was the time for action, advocating the use of violence, whilst others adopted a less radical approach. Our agenda became blurred with self-interest creeping in, resulting in corruption, and, to a degree, I became disillusioned with the movement which was losing direction and purpose. I remained loyal to the traditional values of National Socialism, especially national pride, and respect for authority in an organised society not afraid of embracing its cultural heritage. However, I was opposed to violent extremism in order to achieve our goals. As a kind of insurance against the unknown, I began hiding gold in much the same way as my father had done before, using creative accounting in order that there was no trace of certain hidden reserves I started building.

"All was going well until 2013; there was a robbery at the *Volksbank* in Berlin when thieves successfully bored into the vault. Substantive quantities of gold belonging to us were taken. We could not claim for our losses or report them, as the gold did not officially exist, nor had it been declared. Then, in 2015, another robbery, almost a carbon copy, in London at a vault in Hatton Garden, where a fortune in currency, jewellery and precious stones was taken but this time some of the gold was left behind by the thieves. The discovered gold was hushed up by the authorities because it was marked with swastikas and considered politically sensitive. A secret investigation was launched but dropped in 2020 after the villains responsible for the London robbery were all apprehended. We have contacts within the British police who informed us how many bullion bars were discovered on the floor of the vault. The amount of gold recovered is less than what was officially recorded as deposited by the GVR and, Karl…" he paused in order to add a finality of emphasis on his words, "even less than that which I had secreted there that the GVR have no records of. I had decided to leave this unaccounted gold to you and your sister, Gretchen. It is, and was, untraceable, although I have recorded the unique numbers of the bullion bars which are listed in this box. Of course, we know the thieves must have taken this and, as they were all apprehended, we know who they are. However, there is a further problem. My former assistant manager tells me that the GVR are dispatching a special unit to visit the crooks involved in the robbery. I had held off on this until they were released from prison but, apparently, all are now free apart from one who will soon be out. None of those involved have confessed to the authorities how much they took in the robbery, and, for the most part, where it is hidden, although they have surrendered some of the loot to avoid longer sentences."

Karl was incredulous, "*Mein Vater,* I am speechless and cannot imagine why you should even think I would want this, but that is another matter. My question is how all this gold was hidden for all these years and never discovered."

Heinz turned and looked him straight in the eyes, "Karl, you would not believe the hypocrisy of financial interests. You know where most of the *Raubgold* is? With the most trusted institutions in the world; much of it is deep under the Alps in the Gotthard region of Switzerland known as the Gotthard-Vaults. In addition, deposits of gold have been placed in banks all over the world; we even sought permission to place some in the Vatican Bank." He put his head back, exhausted, and closed his eyes.

5

Trust and Integrity

Tuesday 9th January 1940 10:00am
The Bank for International Settlements, Gegenüber Schweizer
Bahnhof, Basel, Switzerland

They were seated in the rear of the chauffeur driven limousine, and had travelled the short distance from the Grand Hôtel Les Trois Rois to the bank which was situated next to Basel Railway station. Thomas McKittrick had arrived to take up his new post as president of the Bank for International Settlements, known as the BIS, two days previously, which he was familiar with, having carried out work there previously. He felt some trepidation, as he peered out through the sleet streaking across the car windows, at the unimposing entrance to the bank situated in what had been the Savoy Univers Hotel between buildings forming part of the station. His mind was evaluating the enormity of the task facing him in a world rocked by the outbreak of war. The dinner he had shared the previous evening with his fellow passenger, Marcus Wallenberg Jnr., had brought the contradictions and compromises he knew he faced into sharp focus. The *Mercedes Benz Pullman* limousine had arrived at the impressive frontage of the Grand Hôtel Les Trois Rois, also known as the Hotel Drei Könige am

Rhein, on Blumenrain, Basel, at exactly 9:30am. Thomas McKittrick, dressed in an immaculate pinstripe suit, mused that the timing was typically precise; a trait he had come to admire in his old friend and mentor.

McKittrick, at fifty, was ten years older than Wallenberg, but over the preceding nine years since meeting him through his father, the Swedish banker, Marcus Wallenberg snr,, he had come to respect Wallenberg's advice and guidance. McKittrick had served with Marcus Wallenberg Snr on the German Credits Arbitration Committee, based at the Bank for International Settlements. This had been established to oversee German reparations after The Great War, and to assist German businesses to deal with debt and investment issues. Wallenberg Snr. had tutored McKittrick on many aspects of international finance, guiding him on the intricacies of making sound financial judgements based not only on fiscal, but political considerations.

McKittrick was born in Missouri, and after graduating in law at Harvard, he had worked for the National City Bank, and had been assigned to assist with the establishment of a branch in Geneva, Switzerland. He joined the US army during World War I, before being seconded to British military intelligence. Subsequently, he had taken a position with Lee Higginson, a Boston based investment bank, and, after joining his firm's London office, he built up a wealth of international connections in the financial sector. He had a reputation for being meticulous in his work, whilst possessing a warmth in nature which helped in developing relationships and gaining trust; skills which had earned him a position in the firm as a partner.

Marcus Wallenberg Jnr. had become a close friend, but also had proved to be of considerable help to him because of his position, substantial wealth, and connections. He was deputy CEO of Enskilda

Bank based in Stockholm, but with offices in Basel, and held board positions with a host of other major European companies. As they had dined together the night before, they had discussed the potential for the war in Europe expanding to become a global conflict...

McKittrick had voiced his deep concerns. "I figure things are going to get pretty tough for the British if this war escalates. I worry because the world has relied on the City of London for hundreds of years as the global financial centre. I think the British Empire could collapse under a concerted German offensive. Look at what has happened in Poland and Czechoslovakia; Hitler has taken the Rhineland, absorbed Austria into his Reich, and seems unstoppable. Right now, things are pretty quiet, but there are rumours that Germany may attack France. We are facing uncertain times, my old friend, and we could be in for a whole heap of financial turbulence."

Wallenberg had surprised him with his reaction, as he gestured to a waiter to refill their glasses with Champagne. He began to laugh as he sat back, "We are bankers, Thomas... bankers. You know when banks make the most money? When there is uncertainty or war, and now we have both." Marcus was a tall man, slim and athletic in appearance, maintaining his fitness, despite the demands of a growing business empire; he had represented Sweden at international level at tennis in his youth. On the court, he exhibited the same single-minded commitment to the game as he did with his focus on financial affairs. He was dressed in a maroon double-breasted dinner jacket, a black bow tie, with a white carnation, and his appearance was debonair with neatly parted blonde hair, slicked back, reflecting a self-assured manner. He leant forwards, "Thomas, my father has taught me that in finance and banking, we must learn that neutrality is the key to good business. Taking sides or exercising moral judgement is not in our sphere of responsibility. Our duty is to provide a safe haven for our clients' assets and give them best advice on how they can build upon their wealth. If we become the judge, or, indeed, the arbiter, then we are guilty of losing the impartiality which provides our strength. We can seek the higher moral ground at this momentous time, yet gain from the misfortunes caused by the proclivities of others; not taking sides in our sector is, assuredly, the more noble path to take." He pulled out a cigar case, offering one to Thomas, "This is why we want you here; to smooth over troubled waters as the new president of our bank."

They moved to the smoking lounge, with a view overlooking the Rhine, and took seats in one corner on regency style chairs surrounding a small mahogany table. A gold standard lamp added opulence to the room which had large windows with floor to ceiling maroon velvet curtains. McKittrick spoke earnestly, "The world is teetering on the edge of what may become a global war, and we have directors of the bank, and members, from virtually all the combatants or potential belligerents. I am a lawyer by training but I think a diplomat is what is required here."

"Thomas, my dear Thomas," Wallenberg smiled ingratiatingly, "You have the skills needed here, because the world can see you are not a banker, but a man who has served to arbitrate on banking issues. You are the honest broker and you are American. Your president does not wish to become involved in the war and most in your country favour a policy of isolationist neutrality. My brother, Jacob, and I have powerful friends on all sides and we intend to prosper at this time through the needs of all for international banking from our own neutral position. We own businesses that can assist the war effort on all sides with vital supplies such as ball bearings, steel, aluminium, and trucks, whilst also affording banking facilities. Last year, Germany wished to access gold held in an account with the Bank for

International Settlements belonging to Czechoslovakia which Germany had invaded and occupied, but they could not legally access the account which belonged to another country. So, we assisted them, or should I say the Bank for International Settlements did. The money was simply transferred from one BIS account to another, which the German Reichsbank also had access to. You may ask, under whose authority? I can tell you this was orchestrated by none other than Montagu Norman, the governor of The Bank of England; yet Britain was on the verge of war with Germany at the time. You see, what unites us is our integrity and neutrality, and that is our strength because we are bankers, proudly independent, raising ourselves above the politics of war."

McKittrick was incredulous as he tried to absorb what he was being told. "Marcus, are you telling me that the governor of the Bank of England helped Nazi Germany effectively steal or plunder from a country it occupied? Jesus H Christ. What the hell am I getting into here? How in holy hell did he manage that?"

"Not steal, Thomas, that would be crude," came the reply swiftly, "but merely smoothing over transactional banking issues in a policy of what I term, 'fiscal enablement', based upon account authority. Montagu Norman, you must remember, is one of the architects of the BIS from its inception in 1930. He believes passionately in retaining banking independence, hence he wanted to form a bank run by bankers for central banks without external interference or political control. We are truly international, serving the interests of our members without favour but, of course...with reward. Put simply, Morgan enabled the transfer of Czech gold from one BIS account to another BIS account. Of course, our neutrality was observed; it was not us that subsequently removed the gold from an account accessible to the Reichsbank; whilst we understood that Czechoslovakia may have been occupied by

Germany, it is not up to us, as bankers, to form any judgement about the issues of national sovereignty."

"Hell, I need a drink," McKittrick declared. "You wanna join me in a cocktail, say a large Kirsch?"

Wallenberg smilingly replied, "Ah, the diplomat is in you, ordering a Swiss drink. I think I will opt for a Kirsch Royale, to add a little more length to the drink with fine Champagne. You see, all this on the tab of the bank too; commerce buys a little cultural pleasure does it not?"

Now, as the chauffeur held open the door, and they alighted from the Mercedes outside the entrance to the Bank for International Settlements, McKittrick could not help but feel a tinge of excitement in his new role. He loved a challenge and having thought over the conversation with Marcus the night before, he was relishing the prospect of mixing a little Machiavellian ingenuity into his financial strategy for the bank.

As they entered the tiled floor reception area, a secretary sitting at a desk beneath a crystal chandelier announced that all the other attendees of the meeting scheduled that morning had arrived. The building retained many features of its former role including, curiously, the keys still hanging behind the reception desk for bedrooms which now served as offices. On the wall was a brass plaque in which were engraved the words, *"Integrity governs our trust"*. After she had made a brief call, a young bespectacled man in a black suit with a winged collar and tie appeared, announcing himself as Per Anders, a junior investment assistant. He shook their hands and bowed before asking McKittrick and Wallenberg to accompany him. They proceeded down a carpeted corridor to a large set of double polished panelled doors which gave access to what had once served as a dining room, but was now the boardroom. Anders knocked on the door, then entered, announcing, "I have the honour of presenting Herr Wallenberg, the deputy chief executive of Enskilda Bank, and Herr McKittrick, our new president." There was applause from the men present who stood up around the long cloth covered table as they entered the large room. Anders took the two men to one end of the table where two empty chairs were positioned. A short dapper man with receding hair walked forwards, his hand extended to McKittrick, speaking with a pronounced French accent. "*Bonjour,* I am Roger Auboin, the General Manager of the bank; this is a great honour. Permit me to introduce my colleagues and our guests; I think some of whom you may already know."

There were twelve men sat around the table, and McKittrick did recognise some faces, but others were unknown to him. They were all dressed in dark suits, and some, McKittrick noted, wore the maroon and white enamel Nazi Party badges on their lapels. As he glanced around, the whole situation appeared surreal to him as he was sharing a room with people who were opposing combatants in the war; this sense increased as they were introduced to him. "*Monsieur,*" Auboin spoke with the ingratiating demeanour of a head waiter, "permit me, *s'il vous plait,* to present the management present. I have the honour to introduce the chairman of the bank, Sir Otto Niemeyer, who, despite his name, is English and is also a director of the Bank of England." Niemeyer, a well-built man, wearing a winged collar and tie, bowed briefly, shaking McKittrick's hand, saying, "Delighted to meet you, old boy. We have many challenges to face together, but here, we run our own affairs, free from political interference. Damned fine thing too, I say."

Auboin continued, "May I present the assistant manager of BIS, Paul Hechler." The man in front of McKittrick with slicked back black hair, clicked his heels, raising his right arm in a Nazi salute, before stiffly shaking his hand.

"I hope that we can build economic connections at this time which will not compromise the *Führer's* vision." He was wearing a round Nazi party enamel brooch, and a tiepin of an eagle clutching a swastika. He did not wait for Auboin, but brusquely continued, ignoring the Frenchman, "I am accompanied today by the President of the *Reichsbank*, Walther Funk, and the former President, Hjalmar Schacht, who is also a Minister – without – portfolio in the government of the Reich." Walther Funk also clicked his heels, raising his right arm, but the more genial bespectacled Schacht bowed, placing both hands around McKittrick's as he looked directly at him,

"I think a steady hand is very much needed here. I was a founder of the BIS and sometimes I see this incredible institution as my bank."

Hechler ushered another man forward, "We are also fortunate that the *Führer* sees this meeting today as so important he has directed that the deputy president of the *Reichsbank*, and director of BIS, Emil Puhl, should attend." Puhl, with shaven hair, also wearing a swastika badge, raised his arm and clicked his heels, speaking in an abrupt manner.

"The *Führer* has decreed that we will need to preserve the security of our reserves which have grown as a result of the new territories of the Reich," adding ominously, "and will continue to do so as the Reich expands. As a neutral president, we welcome you and trust that the war will not impeach upon the integrity of the bank."

Auboin now pushed himself forwards, "Please, *Messieurs*, we must follow protocol, and now I am delighted to present the Secretary of BIS, Signor Rafaele Pilotti." A short man, dressed immaculately, with a neat moustache, walked forwards bowing deeply and dramatically. "Your Excellency, it is a great honour to welcome you. My government and, in particularly, *Il Duce* himself, extend a warm hand of friendship to you, offering you our full support in your new role."

McKittrick interrupted the proceedings by saying, "Gentlemen, I would propose we dispense with further formalities and that you each announce yourselves, as you speak. I suggest we cut to the chase and get this meeting started." He turned to Pilotti, "Can we fix to get a cup of coffee?" Pilotti bowed again before going to a telephone on one of the smaller tables surrounding the room, and muttering in a low voice, then raising his head, he announced, "*Gentiluomini*, not only coffee, but fine tea is on order."

McKittrick took his seat at the top of the long table, undoing his briefcase from which he extracted his notes. "Forgive me gentlemen, but I don't care much for protocol, and I have condensed today's proceedings in order that we can discuss real issues without skirting around them. I shall circulate *ditto machine* copies of a shortened agenda I have prepared.". They studied the papers as they were passed down the table.

Inaugural Presidential Agenda for BIS Meeting
Chaired by the President – Thomas H. McKittrick
09.01.1940
HIGHLY CONFIDENTIAL

Independence and Integrity
Occupied Territory Assets
Jewish Property
Gold Reserves and Loan Repayments
Disposal of Reichsvermögensfonds
Asset Source Analysis
Dividends and Payments to Members
Post-War Bank Policy

McKittrick examined his notes for a minute, before a knock on the doors preceded a trolley being wheeled in bearing two large urns containing coffee and tea, together with plates bearing an array of small cakes and biscuits. He then began addressing them, "Gentlemen, we are facing war on what may become an unprecedented scale, and I am grateful that representatives from the nations involved can sit together in a civilised manner that becomes us as bankers and businessmen. Our decisions today will affect not only the security of this bank, but the recovery of our economies when this war is over. This is not a time for despair, but a time to realise opportunity; we also need to invest in a better future which will bring stability and prosperity to us all. We must put in place firm foundations for ensuring that whatever the outcome of hostilities, our businesses are protected in a post-war world, and our investments secured. I will now turn to the first item on the Agenda."

Marcus Wallenberg raised his hand, "Please!" He stood as McKittrick nodded, "Marcus Wallenberg, Deputy CEO of Enskilda Bank. My brother, Jacob, is CEO, and my father, Marcus Wallenberg Snr., is Chairman. Both the Allied and Axis powers in this war are benefitting from factories which we own, producing ball bearings, explosive materials, armaments and vehicles. We will prosper assuredly as a result of the conflict. We do not judge the combatants, but merely supply the demand. As such, we are neutral, just as we see the BIS must be viewed. My brother, Jacob, is a regular visitor to Germany and is known personally by Adolf Hitler. For my part, I liaise with both the United States and Great Britain and we can, therefore, be seen not to favour either side. Our view is that the bank's integrity depends on its independence and neutrality." He sat down as McKittrick continued. "This is a fine example of how we can remain above the conflict and assure that we provide the fiscal stability that the world needs at this time. We are uniquely privileged in that we have a stake in our own bank, independent of all external political controls. Careful banking diplomacy at this time will ensure our survival. We have the privileged status of diplomats; we can cross borders unchallenged, without having our bags searched, and, to safeguard our status, we must be seen at all times to be above reproach, guarding our position as the bastions of the integrity which we uphold. The neutrality of the bank must apply to all transactions, and I now refer to objections which I understand have been registered over our acceptance of what is shown in the agenda as *Reichsvermögensfonds*. I understand, this refers to those assets seized by the occupying forces of Germany?" He turned to the assistant manager, Paul Hechler, raising his eyebrows.

Hechler rose sharply to his feet, clicking his heels, "*Herr* President, these are split into two areas, the *Fonds des Reichkommissariats* which are monies raised by the Reich in what you term 'occupied territories', and the second are the *Fonds der Judenfrage,* (Funds of the Jewish question) which relates to money which we have confiscated from the Jews as part of our programme of *Arisierung"* (Aryanisation)

McKittrick, noting that a smartly dressed man in an accentuated pin-stripe suit was rising to his feet to object, raised his hand signalling that he was moving on. "Gentlemen please, I know these are challenging times, but we have much to cover. Let us turn to the next item; occupied territory assets."

A dapper man with a beard, sporting a bow tie and pince-nez glasses stood up, "Mr President, Montagu Norman, governor of the Bank of England and a member of BIS. I have some experience on this issue. We had to facilitate access to Czechoslovakian assets by Germany, after the occupation. We took the view that the right to access national assets held in the bank must pass to the executive authority which exercises sovereign control over a nation. This had clearly occurred in the case of Czechoslovakia. It was not up to us to judge the right or wrongs of Germany's claim on the territory, merely to ascertain which government was in control."

Opposite him, the man who had attempted to interrupt previously, stood abruptly, "Leland Harrison, US Ambassador to Switzerland, may I speak frankly?" McKittrick nodded as Montagu Norman sat down. Harrison spoke in a measured tone, "I find this distasteful in that if the sovereign rights of a nation were violated by Germany, then we cannot claim we are neutral if we assist the Nazis to plunder the assets of any state suffering arbitrary aggression. Whilst the United States has maintained neutrality, thus far, the action by this bank breaches the code of banking integrity which you claim to uphold."

Walther Funk leapt to his feet, "We took action to protect Germans isolated by the ruinous impositions of the Treaty of Versailles. You dare to question the actions of the *Führer*...You Americans think you are perfect. Look what you did to your own native people, stealing and plundering. Do not criticise us, Mr Ambassador, for protecting our own *Volk!*" His voice had risen as McKittrick held his hands up in a placatory gesture.

"Gentlemen please", another sitting next to Harrison stood, "Per Jacobsson, economic advisor to the BIS. I was one of the architects of this bank. We must work together, whatever our views, in the interests of all banks who have a holding in this institution, not least for the nation states who rely on us. We must leave political considerations to one side, no matter how well or ill-founded. In that, I agree with our president. Politicians decide policies, but in our rising above such matters, we assume the higher ground here."

An imposing man with neatly parted hair, and a commanding demeanour then stood, "John Foster Dulles, lawyer, specialising in international affairs, holding many connections in the US Government. Gentlemen, I assisted in reducing the over burdensome reparations imposed on Germany after the Great War. For that reason, Herr Funk, I hope my credentials are impeccable." The German nodded his head brusquely as Dulles continued, "These are times when great moral questions may arise, and who amongst us can be the arbiter on these issues? It seems to me that many of the items on the agenda might benefit from as little in writing as possible because, as a lawyer, I can vouch for the fact that indictments or otherwise depend on what is written down. I have much in common with my colleague here, Leland Harrison, and I know his motives to be honourable but we live in a world of *Real Politic*, and, for that reason, I am of the opinion that, following the suspension of Board Meetings of the BIS last year, we should grant to our new president the power to make the right decisions, unfettered by our natural concerns or loyalties. He has been chosen because he has earned enormous respect from some of the greatest bankers in the world, not least from you, Mr Wallenberg, and your father, and your brother who, as we know, is highly thought of by Adolf Hitler. I believe we should carefully consider the guidance we might be able to offer the president of this bank, but without being prescriptive."

The genial, bespectacled figure of Hjalmar Schacht now rose, his words delivered carefully, "You may know that I have opposed many policies of the government I serve, not least the handling of the Jewish question. For these reasons, I resigned, but the *Führer* still felt I had much to offer as an economic advisor, and to my surprise, I was retained in government. I have even been awarded honorary membership of the NSDAP, being presented with the gold party badge."

"Where is it?" Paul Hechler interrupted in an arrogant, aggressive tone.

Schacht ignored him, not even acknowledging the intervention, "I am a great friend of the governor of the Bank of England," he nodded towards Montagu Norman, who raised his hand with a smile, "and we are proof that what may divide us should not break down that which unites us. My belief is that we must take difficult decisions to preserve international banking and the stability of our currencies and reserves. The sensitivities that I and others hold about the Jewish question must not jeopardise our financial institution. Therefore, I endorse the words of my esteemed colleague, John Foster Dulles. I propose that no full minutes of our considerations today are recorded and that we trust the integrity of our president."

The delegates did not leave the Bank for International Settlements that day until darkness had descended over the city of Basel, and it was a very tired Thomas McKittrick who returned to his suite in the Grand Hôtel Les Trois Rois. There were no records of the meeting other than a brief summary of 'discussions with colleagues', handwritten by him. *"After in-depth considerations, on my first official day as president, broad agreement was reached that we must preserve the independence, neutrality, and integrity of the bank whilst ensuring that there are post-war structures in place which guarantee the survival of key industries whatever the outcome. It is not the place of the BIS to judge, but our strength lies in our independence. All agreed that the gold standard might be the best preserved medium for assuring interest payments are honored by any borrowing member of the bank. Agreement was reached that BIS may access gold reserves held by any member to secure repayment. The issue of the disposal of the Reichsvermögensfonds and the Jewish Question remains unresolved, but all agreed that preserving the status of BIS above such matters was the ultimate priority. The bank cannot and will not prevent the deposit by any country of assets with BIS and it would be contrary to our strict code of independence to become involved in judging how any member procures their assets. My colleagues placed their trust in my rectitude and judgement to resolve any issues in the absence of Board Meetings for which I am grateful."*

6

'The Last Testament'

Friday 5th January 2024 10:30am
Church of St Georg, Bogenhausen, Munich

The funeral had been well attended, with many notable guests there from government, the financial sector, and industry. Karl was surprised to see senior offices from the armed services. He had worn his dress uniform with the distinctive red beret, as a Colonel, which his mother had insisted upon, stating that his father had been a lifelong admirer of the military and that it had been one of the proudest days of his life when Karl had passed out as an officer. The service had taken place at the Church of St Georg, in the Bogenhausen district, according to his father's final instructions, despite pressure from outside the family to hold it at the cathedral of Frauenkirche, the largest church in Munich. Karl was informed by his mother that all of the arrangements had been organised and paid for by an organisation that his father had been involved with, but of which she knew Karl would disapprove. He surmised, from the revelations which his father had shared with him, that this was *Die Spinne*, which had been alluded to, even within the funeral service. No expense had been spared, and they had been driven slowly over the 1.5 kilometre journey to the church, in a long procession of black limousines in which every family member had been allocated a place. His father's coffin had been draped with the traditional red, black and white flag of the German Empire with the Maltese Cross emblem. Karl had remonstrated with his mother that this had links back to a dark past but she was not to be swayed and he knew, from his life experience, that once she had made a decision, nothing would move her from it. He was only thankful that a flag bearing a swastika had not been used. His mind was in turmoil as he sat beside his mother in the church, hardly able to take in the fact that he would never again hear the calm reassuring guidance of his father, nor share in the intense discussions they had held in his final days. In those last weeks, he had developed a closer relationship with his father than he had ever had before. He had found real empathy, despite having kept an emotional distance from his father throughout his adult life stemming from his teenage years when he had discovered his roots. He could not reconcile the role his grandfather had played in the Third Reich and the overt Nazi sympathies held by his father, with his own distaste of the past. All that had become less important as he had watched his father's life coming to an end, despite his fierce determination to combat or ignore the symptoms of his illness. In those days, Karl had seen another side to the man whose beliefs he had despised in his formative years; instead, seeing a sensitivity and a nagging remorse which represented a contradiction to all he had stood for in his life. He felt for his father in his final days as he had unburdened those aspects of his life about which he held regrets.

Now, he was going through the motion of a ceremony but feeling very distant from those present and increasingly unnerved by what he was witnessing. He had watched with a resigned detachment when they had arrived at the church, as a group of men had formed up, dressed in black uniforms he did not recognise. They had saluted as the hearse drew up beside the entrance, then, as the coffin was removed, one had marched forwards, laying a medal on top, shaped like a Maltese cross, with a red, white and black ribbon which was neatly placed in a 'v' shape. The uniformed men had then performed the role of pallbearers, carrying his father's coffin slowly inside. As they had entered, the organ had played the national anthem, *'Deutschlandlied'* and he noted that some amongst the congregation began singing the words, with others joining in, and a chorus of voices could be heard voicing the final words in the stanza, *"Deutschland, Deutschland über alles, Über alles in der Welt!"*

What was he to do with what his father had shared with him? He knew he could not ignore it and, he thought, if he did, he would be betraying the final trust his father had given to him. Yet, already, what he knew filled him with concern about not only his country to which he felt fiercely loyal, but the institutions upon which democracy relied globally. How could the world have allowed so much, ignored so much, and hidden so much.

His interest was sparked as the priest announced that a eulogy would be delivered by a distinguished former colleague of Heinz Spacil, and he watched as a man with thick silver hair, wearing shaded glasses, and a dark grey suit with large lapels stood up in the congregation. He had not met him before nor did he recognise who he was, although he had seen his name in the order of service over which he had exercised no input. He noted, as he walked forward from his seat a few rows behind them, that he nodded to some on either side as he passed, stopping to bow to Karl's mother. He then proceeded to the lectern and Karl watched incredulously as he lifted his right arm, bent at the elbow in a gesturing wave to the congregation, yet positioned the palm of his hand back. Was this just a gesture, or a perverse coincidence? The move appeared to be executed in a manner not dissimilar to that he had seen Hitler do in old newsreel footage. He announced himself as Franz Niemeyer and that he worked for the Deutsche Bank. His voice was strong and authoritative as he spoke, clearly at ease addressing large gatherings.

"*Meine Damen und Herren,* today I deputise for *Der Leiter* (leader) of the organisation for which Heinz Spacil worked so tirelessly, Heinrich Hackmann. "*Der Leiter* is not here for security reasons, but has personally vetted and approved what I will say. I have known the man who we have gathered to honour today for over forty years. He was a family friend as was his father before him. Both men dedicated themselves to Germany, and despite how others may judge our past, we should remember those who served their country not with shame, but with pride." There were murmurings of approval from around the congregation. "My address can scarcely do justice to the dedication of Heinz Spacil to a burden he inherited from his father, Josef, who, in turn, was the genius who ensured that Germany rose from the ashes of the destruction inflicted upon us at the end of Second World War. Our industries recovered quickly, backed by careful investment which, first, Josef oversaw, but which Heinz continued when he took over in 1967, ensuring that we achieved domination economically in post-war Europe, culminating in our playing a leading and unassailable role in the European Union. This great project was a legacy left to us from a past we are no longer allowed to speak of. But it was here in Germany that our leaders had the vision that national barriers between European nations should dissolve in an economic union; a union which Germany would inevitably grow to lead. The supreme irony in all of this is that our greatest supporter in the achievement of our aim was France!" He threw his hands up in a mock gesture of astonishment, drawing some laughter from the congregation. "Heinz recognised that in the new era, we should embrace, support and promote that economic vision. We have prospered as our great country reunited, liberated from the Soviets, who remain, under a different guise, just as much of a threat now, as our forefathers recognised a hundred years ago. We prospered, after reunification, defying the pundits of gloom, and much of that prosperity, and that of Germany, was down to the genius and foresight of Heinz Spacil. He took over the great responsibility of managing *Vermögensfonds* which had grown in the post-war era under the direction of his father, Josef Spacil, a man who had the temerity to walk calmly into the Reichsbank in April 1945 and relieve them of their assets at gunpoint. As a banker, I can say this man was unashamedly the greatest bank robber in history." There was more laughter. Niemeyer raised his finger, "Josef had the vision and foresight to organise the post-war management, and distribution of investments which helped us to secure our position in the world today. We needed men of his stature after the war as we gradually re-integrated those of talent back into business, government and our armed forces.

"Josef protected the security of assets used to re-invest in the recovery of our businesses by using some of the safest financial institutions, even securing an offer of help from the Holy Church; yes, even the Vatican bank assisted us. With God and bankers on our side, nothing could stop us." There were murmurs of amusement, as he paused, and even a ripple of applause.

Karl listened with incredulity to the brazen words of Franz Niemeyer, hinting at what was, in effect, the collusion of major institutions in the disposal of Nazi assets. He witnessed the approval in the expressions of some very senior officers from the military who were attending, together with others he recognised from the world of politics. Niemeyer was speaking again, "After the war, our former military commanders were recruited into NATO, our Luftwaffe aces retrained to fly jets, our armed forces re-formed, whilst former civil servants returned to their positions. So, in banking and commerce also, we recognised that we needed the brilliance of businessmen who had lost their positions or been accused of being accomplices in the excesses of the previous regime. These people were invaluable in the reconstruction of Germany and the resurgence of our industries. Heinz recognised this, defending many in court, as a brilliant lawyer, allowing those of talent who had merely cooperated with the former regime, to assist our country in the drive to prosper and recover. He continued the great work of his father, investing prudently, exerting influence with those in power, not only here, but on the international stage, building a new Germany which was no longer defined or shamed by its past. In the modern world, his vision gave us back pride, and prosperity that many said was impossible as Germany reunified. Many of us here today have benefited from what Heinz achieved, and there is the hope now of a new future; a future in which he was quietly working to bring much needed political change. The hope is grounded in the realisation of the need for strength in leadership that has been lacking, which we and other countries are recognising across Europe; a recognition that we have suffered from years of weakness in government." Niemeyer concluded by stating that a testament to who Heinz Spacil was, and what he had achieved, lay in the number of distinguished people in prestigious positions who were in attendance. His words filled Karl with horror in the realisation of how pervasive the influences of the past were in the modern world.

Afterwards, as he walked slowly behind the coffin as it was carried to its final resting place in the crisp, cold of the late January morning, Karl spoke quietly to his sister, Gretchen, "These bastards are still around, still believing in that vile creed that ruined our country, and which was responsible for countless millions of deaths."

Her reply shocked him, "Karl, we cannot condemn an entire generation for what excesses the leadership of the time may have promoted. There were many patriotic Germans who believed that sacrifices were necessary to bring order and give the country back some pride. It is time to stop living in the shame of the past. Did we stop buying Volkswagens because Hitler helped design them? We have to embrace pragmatism and recognise that Papa lived in the economic reality of a bleak post-war divided country and he did what he felt was right."

He did not argue as he watched the ornate coffin being lowered, and tried to recall the remorse and the contradictions that his father shared with him in his final days, recognising that, perhaps, he had judged him as a person too harshly in life. He had to reflect that he too, had faced many difficult choices on active service in the military.

After throwing a white rose into the grave, he turned to walk down the long path back to the waiting limousines. As he did so, a tall, well-built, middle-aged man, with short, cropped blonde hair dressed in a long leather coat, wearing shaded glasses, stepped towards him, flicking open a wallet containing his photo ID from the *Bundesnachrichtendienst*. *"Bitte, Herr Oberst Biesacker,* I am *Major* Dieter Metz from the BND. May we speak for a brief moment?" He looked round furtively, ensuring no one was in earshot before continuing, "I have documents for you, prepared under the direct orders of your father." He took a slim brown package, sealed with tape from his inside pocket, looking around again before handing it to Karl. "Please, Herr Biesecker, watch your back as you are in great danger. Trust no one in authority no matter how high their office. We will do our best to protect you, but our great movement has been compromised by extreme elements. Also, in the pack there is a card with a number you can call for assistance, for anything, including armed response, at any time, day or night. You nominate your own six-digit code; they will not ask for your name, unless you wish to give it. The card may be used anywhere in the world. I must go. My condolences, your father was a great man." Before Karl had the opportunity to respond, Metz had pulled the collar of his coat up, and walked briskly away, exiting via a gate which led to some trees beside the church. Karl thrust the package into his inside coat pocket and hurried down the path to join his mother and sister in the leading limousine. He knew in his mind that the decision he had hesitated over for the preceding two weeks was now made. As the procession of vehicles began moving away, a man in a flat cap and donkey jacket, spoke into the microphone clipped to his collar, then glanced down at the screen of his mobile phone to check the quality of the pictures he had just taken.

Two weeks previously:

Saturday 23rd December 2023

Das Kauntinhaus, Pienzenauerstrasse, Bogenhausen, Munich

Despite it having been only four weeks since his previous visit, the deterioration in his father's health was all too obvious. A couch had been organised for him in his study although the visiting doctor and nursing staff had advised that a bed be set up downstairs. Heinz was a proud man and refused to permit such a disruption to his home. He had stated that if he was to die, he wanted to still see the lake and his beloved gardens until his last moment through the long windows of his room which he would not permit to be spoilt by a bed.

Karl had been contacted by his mother in the preceding days, urging him to join the family for what she knew would be his father's final Christmas adding that she thought he may not last out the week. Karl had sought compassionate leave from his commanding officer which was immediately granted. Surprisingly, General Hoffmann had stated that he should take as much leave as he needed and not to be bound by the customary two-week limit. "Your father has many friends in high places who exert considerable influence and you need not return to duty until you are ready to do so. All pay and allowances will be unaffected." The General had finished the interview with the words, *"Viel Glück!* (Good luck) which Karl had thought, at the time, a little curious. He had spent Friday night with Inge at her apartment situated at Bachmair Weissach Lake, a fifty-minute drive from Munich, and they had driven to his parents' house in the morning, arriving at midday. Karl was shocked at his father's appearance as he was shown into the study by Greta. She had said to him, as they had left his mother with Inge in the large lounge at the opposite end of the house, "He will not be with us for much longer, but has demanded to spend some time alone with you. I see his life ebbing away each day." She wiped a tear from her eye with a handkerchief, choking over her words, "Forgive me, but I spent a lifetime with him." She was seventy years old with grey hair, tied back, dressed in a suit over which she wore an apron. Karl gave her a reassuring squeeze on her shoulder before she knocked on the study door. The voice was as commanding as ever, *"Kommen!"* Heinz Spacil was lying, half propped up on pillows, on a couch under blankets, his cheeks hollow, with sunken eyes reddened, surrounded by dark circles, whilst his white hair seemed thinner. Despite this, he half waved, raising a weak smile as he saw Karl, nodding as though to communicate that he knew what Karl was seeing. Greta began bustling around him, moving tissues, a plate with untouched toast, and filling a glass with water from a jug. "Stop fussing me woman," he ordered, "and give me some peace with my son. Out, out, out!" Greta looked up at Karl, with a mock smile of surrender, and left the room.

His father stretched out his hand which Karl shook, then placed both his hands around his father's saying, "*Mein Vater,* it is good to see you. *Frohe Weihnachten* (merry Christmas)."

The old man laughed weakly, "I do not think I will be doing much partying this year but we can celebrate you being here. Will you join me in having some *Asbach Uralt*. The doctor says I should not mix this with morphine, but what do I care." He pressed an intercom by his side, ordering the drink, then turned his head to look out of the window, as Karl sat in a chair next to the couch. "My life has been too busy, Karl, much of it covering up the indiscretions of others in which I have been complicit. Like you, I had ideals once, ideals which I know you despise but they had a place and some of them still do. Here, looking through this window, I see the beautiful hand of nature, and seek refuge in the peace this brings. I listen to music, and let my mind drift to better times, but then, I ask myself whether they were better." He stopped for a moment, listening, gesturing Karl to do the same who up to that point had not noticed soft orchestral music playing in the background. "You hear this? It is Wagner; he only wrote one symphony but it is a masterpiece, yet undervalued and ignored by many; it is '*the Symphony in C major*'. "He closed his eyes, moving his hand as though he was conducting the music, with a serene expression. Then, he turned to Karl, "I am proud of you, my son, for pursuing your military career." His voice altered, and then he coughed, his face contorting with pain.

At that moment, Greta entered, carrying a bottle and two glasses on a tray, placing them on a side table as she went over to Heinz who waived her away. However, she had also brought in a dose of morphine which she injected, ignoring his protestations. As she left the room, Heinz closed his eyes for a minute, then, with a sigh he looked out over the garden once again. "You see the *Erica Carnea*, already spreading a pink carpet near the lake. I wish I could walk again along the bank of the River Isar." He had a sadness in his eyes which were distant, then in a wavering tone, "Alas, I will not see the daffodils this year."

"Papa you cannot know this..." Karl's words sounded almost pleading, yet he could see the life in his father fading away.

"Please, I need to tell you." Heinz's voice became suddenly more insistent; he pointed to the tray and Karl poured out the brandy. He attempted to pass the glass to his father who grasped his hand guiding him to hold it steady as he took a drink. Then he fixed Karl with a deep look, focussing on what he wished to say. "Karl, I want you to seek what I have left you; whatever you do with it is a matter for you. You recall I told you that we had deposits of gold at the Hatton Garden Safe Deposit facility in London. After it was robbed, the police reports show that they recovered ten 12.5 kilo bars of gold bullion; which means that ten were unaccounted for with a street value of over 8 million Euros; there were also twenty-six 1 kilo bars missing with a value of a further 1.7 million Euros. Six of the 12.5 kilo bars were for you and Gretchen which no one knows about, and which I hid, using accounting methods passed on to me by my father. They cannot be traced although the serial numbers are recorded which you will find in this box which I have left for you.

"We have people connected to all those who deal in stolen gold, or 'fences' as they are called. If any of this *Raubgold* had turned up, we would have known about it. The police were not looking for it because they did not know of its existence. Even if I had ordered a secret investigation by our own people, they would not have known about the six bullion bars that I kept for you and Gretchen. Until last year, nothing was heard of the gold; then one of the fences operating in the Hatton Garden district alerted us that two 1 kilo bars carrying the eagle and swastika motif had been brought in. We told him to accept the deal and attempt to establish the identity of the person involved; nothing too heavy as we didn't want to scare him off. Turns out he was just a mule and had been instructed by others whose identity he did not know. We left him alone as he said whoever had instructed and paid him would use him again within a year. Our people checked out his identity and curiously, he was known as a police informer."

Karl sighed in amazement, shaking his head, as he absorbed what his father was telling him. He leant across to help his father have another sip of his brandy, after which Heinz continued, his voice now stronger strengthened by his determination to impart what he wished to say to Karl.

"Regrettably for the thieves at Hatton Garden, they were quickly apprehended, but the only link we have to our missing gold is with them. We were going to move on them, but it was too difficult because they were in prison, and not kept together. One of the ringleaders is still there, and another recently released. That is why I have obtained security clearance for you to act unofficially as part of German Intelligence in what can be passed off as a sensitive enquiry into the gold recovered, because of its Nazi origins. You speak English, and if you travel to England, you may recover what is yours."

Karl took a large drink of his brandy, before placing it back firmly on the table by the couch. "And if I don't want anything to do with this *Raubgold*?"

The old man raised both hands to stress his words, "If you do not act, then what is yours and Gretchen's will be returned to the GVR. Karl, although I gave my life loyalty to this organisation, the unease I now feel dictates that you do not let them take this. There is much more which I have referred to in a letter I have left for you. There are dangerous extremist elements Karl and what they could do to this country fills me with dread. I can still remember terrorism on our streets when the Baader-Meinhof and the Red-Army Faction were running riot in the 1970's and 1980's; there was lawlessness and senseless killings. It might interest you to know that some of those crazy left-wing militant terrorists are now on the ultra-right" He sighed deeply, motioning Karl to help him with another drink. "My duty to Germany is done; my conscience is wracked by guilt, but…it is now too late for me." He breathed a long shallow rasping breath, as his head dropped back on the pillows, and, for a second, Karl feared it was the end, but his father reached out his hand. "We cannot rectify what is in the past, but we can build a better future. I do not regret my beliefs, just the corruption that pervades everywhere money is involved. Money, I am afraid, buys power, influence, and nurtures greed in many that consumes them, so that they must have more. Perhaps, my son, if you are successful in recovering the secret bequest that I have left for you, you can use what is in my testament to help bring them down."

Karl looked slightly surprised, "Testament – you mean your will?"

"*Nein, nein,*" came the response in a weakening and tired voice, "It is in the box I showed to you, which is now in my safe. In there you will find an envelope sealed with wax addressed to you containing a letter which explains everything. There are many more items in the box which I placed in there these last months to give you some background and evidence, should you wish to use this but, Karl…" he moved to the side grasping his son's arm, "I do not wish you to use what I give you to attack or undermine the GVR. The core principles behind it underpinned the foundations of my life and although the values may have been perverted by some, I will not die, as too many have done, being ashamed of my past. Yes, I am guilty of helping those I should not have, but that does not compromise my loyalty to the Fatherland."

His grip loosened, as he lay back again muttering, "I love you and admire you. I thank God I have you as my son."

His eyes closed, and Karl felt a confliction within, yet the power of his father's last words overcame all of this as he leant forwards kissing his father on both cheeks before embracing him with the words, "I love you too, Papa, and I am proud to have you as my father." This was the last in-depth conversation he would ever have with his father in his final days and was not referred to again by Heinz until the night he died when he whispered to his son, "Do not forget my testament and never forget my love for you which will remain after I have gone." He had then drifted into sleep from which he never awoke.

7
Operation Andreas

Saturday, 10th February 1940 11:00am
The Berghof, Obersalzberg, Bavaria

His voice rang out as he stood at the middle of the long table in the dining-room surrounded by fifteen others seated on gold chairs, some in uniform, and others in smart suits, whilst he wore a simple double-breasted grey military tunic displaying no rank insignia, with his Iron Cross decoration beneath a gold Nazi Party badge. Light flooded the room from the large windows positioned between the ornate polished panelling giving a view across from the Obersalzberg to the dramatic Alpine mountains of the Untersberg beyond. As always, all eyes were on him, with rapt attention to his every word. The *Führer* spoke, "The British are calling this 'the phoney war'," he said in a high-pitched tone with an element of mockery, "but we will surprise the weak fool, Mr Chamberlain, who, just over a year ago was proclaiming, 'peace for our time', but I think he forgot to ask us our intentions!" He gestured with his hands turned upwards and outwards, which was followed by laughter from around the table. "I pledged to the German *Volk* that we would overturn the outrageous impositions and plunder of the Versailles Treaty, ensuring the security of all *Volksdeutsche* living outside the Reich. History will be on our side, judging our irrevocable right to seize back the territory dividing Germany and preventing our access to Eastern Prussia. I recognised the weakness of those who opposed us and now we have smashed our way through Poland, shocking those who thought we would not dare. Germany has triumphed over the *Untermenschen* (subhumans) in a first step of our glorious mission of *Lebensraum* to liberate territory creating space for the expansion of our superior Aryan race. No one will stop us, no one can prevent what Providence has destined for the Reich, *Niemand!"* His voice had risen to a crescendo and he slammed his fist down on the table to emphasise the last word as *Reichsführer* Heinrich Himmler stood, raising his arm, exclaiming "*Heil,"* swiftly followed by others in the room.

Adolf Hitler nodded, acknowledging their salute which he returned with the familiar half stretched arm, bent back at the elbow. "*Meine Kameraden,"* he continued, "before we strike to secure our frontiers in Europe, we must plan our economic warfare strategy, and how we propose dealing with the Europe of the future. As my Generals formulated military plans, I tasked our economists to prepare a vision for a future Europe united by a creed loyal to the will of the Reich. My view has long been that in unity of purpose lies strength and, for that, we need to work with those in occupied countries, to tear down borders in a new united Europe; a union of states which will provide a bastion to the threat from the east. Today, we have the most senior representatives present from our great *Nationalsozialistische Deutsche Arbeiterpartei* in the form of Deputy *Führer* Rudolf Hess, *Generalfeldmarschall* Hermann Göring, *Reichsführer* Heinrich Himmler, Reich Minister of Enlightenment and Propaganda, Joseph Goebbels, and my private secretary, *Reichsleiter* Martin Bormann." As he mentioned each person's name, they stood, all wearing military uniforms, clicking their heels, giving the Nazi salute. "My most trusted comrades will ensure the success of our epic purpose. All economic elements of our strategy will be co-ordinated under the office of the *Parteikanzlei* (Party Chancellery) under the direction of our Deputy *Führer*, Rudolf Hess, but..." he raised his finger in the air, "for our great purpose to succeed, as I announced to many of you in January last year, we need to involve our great businesses, our economists, and, of course, those from the banking sector. My monumental plan will be grounded, not only on our invincible military might, nor on the strength of our unopposed political will, but also with the mobilisation of economic weaponry which will confound our enemies. For this to succeed, we will utilise the skills of others within this room united behind four great strategies, geopolitical European integration, business investment, exploitation of our resources and international banking initiatives to secure our financial reserves in the *Reichsvermögensfonds*."

The Führer was in an exuberant mood as he leant forwards on the table. "Each of you in this room will play a critical role in expanding the Reich, built on the financial and military resources of an unimaginable scale as we throw our enemies into an historic state of economic chaos and collapse. I think many will know Walther Funk, our Reich Minister of Economics and President of the Reichsbank. As a former assistant of Herr Goebbels at the Ministry of Propaganda, we can, of course, trust that every word he utters is true." The *Führer's* humour contrasted with his customary austere, authoritative presence, instilling fear and admiration equally in those around him. Funk was sat opposite Hitler, a plump figure with receding hair dressed in a black suit with wide lapels. He stood and clicked his heels, nodding his head in deference towards the *Führer* who gave an acquiescent sign with his hands to address the meeting.

"*Mein Führer, meine Herren*, I have completed an analysis of our position in Europe and how we can secure our economic future, maximising our return on assets realised from our expansion, our future expansion, and our programme of *Arisierung*. As a result of the *Führer's* inspirational leadership, we are already increasing our national assets from the procurement of financial resources from the *Reichkommissariats,* or occupied territories, and the *Fonds der Judenfrage*. We have begun translating this into gold reserves through our membership and management role in the Bank for International Settlements in Switzerland. We have in place an agreement that as we draw monies from the bank in the form of loans, the bank may, in turn, secure the repayments based upon our guarantees which are backed by our gold assets. In this way, no one is directly involved in assisting the Reich other than securing their investment from gold reserves we allow them access to. A financial arrangement which compromises no one, not least the reputation of international bankers who are only too anxious to assist in this...er... procedure."

"Bravo!" Hitler cut in, wringing his hands together in delight.

Funk, his forehead shiny with sweat, could not suppress a hint of a smile as he then stated, "As we obtain more gold from those who have shamelessly exploited Germany, taking back our assets, I can confirm that over 100 million dollars (two billion in 2024) has already been realised from our programme of *Arisierung* which we anticipate will grow exponentially as we cleanse Europe of Jews in our policy of *Judenfrei*. The *Führer* has decreed that we must secure our borders which means there will be more *Reichkommissariats* and, *meine Herren,* in conclusion, I can give a positive report for the financial year ending December 1940, and yet, it is only January!" There was further laughter; then, from the corpulent figure of Hermann Göring, "I would like to propose a vote of thanks to the *Juden* and all the *Untermenschen* for their generosity to the Reich," causing yet more hilarity in the room.

Funk pulled on both lapels, taking on an air of superiority as he announced, "The *Führer* asked that I prepare the ground for the future of Europe and produce a paper on this. I can now confirm that this is completed and will be circulated to all present at this meeting together with my colleagues who sit with me on the Council of Ministers for Defence of the Reich. I can also confirm that Emil Puhl here, our vice-president of the Reichsbank and Director of the Bank for International Settlements, has agreed with the president of the bank, Thomas McKittrick, that we should prepare a financial plan for a post-war Europe, as the perceived strongest power after our inevitable victory." There were murmurs of approval as Funk reached for his notes in a somewhat flamboyant, effeminate manner which infuriated Himmler who grimaced at this man he considered to be an odious homosexual who should be disposed of. Funk opened his arms, in a gesture which reinforced Himmler's loathing, "*Meine Herren*, I give you a brief summary of our plan for Europe after our victory." He began reading: "The post-war European large-unit economy must be a unified German dominated structure which achieves organic growth, resulting from close economic collaboration between Germany and European countries. We might term this a European Economic Community. The most important currency of post-war Europe would, of course, be the Reichsmark which will assume a dominating position. The enormous strengthening of the power of the Greater German Reich, will, as a natural consequence, bring with it a strengthening of the Reichsmark. Eventually, the aim would be a single currency across Europe. But before that, conversion rates would have to be tightly controlled to avoid wild fluctuations and disruptions. Only then could currency union be achieved. I have termed this 'European Monetary Union.'" He continued to read extracts from his paper which, he stated, he intended to present as a blueprint for a post-war economic future to other leading economies through the Bank for International Settlements. He concluded his report with a summary.

"We would benefit as the leading economy in a new European union of states. The post-war continent would stand firm in its defence of Germany and German economic interests. This new united Europe will not accept the imposition of conditions of a political or economic nature from any European area because we will enforce the central economic policies freeing member states to trade more efficiently. *Danke.*" Funk finished reading from his paper with a look of triumph, wiping beads of perspiration from his brow with a handkerchief as Hitler began clapping, joined by all around the table.

The *Führer* stood again, leaning on the table with both hands as he addressed them, "So, this will achieve our objective of European integration and the banking arrangements to secure our financial reserves. My vision for the Reich requires exploitation of all resources available to us. This is coupled with the need to ensure the growth of our *Versteckte Vermögensfonds*. On the advice of *Reichsführer* Himmler, I appointed *SS Gruppenführer* Oswald Pohl to oversee internal economics and construction and ensure my will is executed. Herr *Gruppenführer,* bitte." Hitler sat down smoothing the front of his dark brown hair back, and folding his arms as he listened.

Pohl, a short man with greying hair, jumped to his feet, clicked his heels, and extended his arm stiffly. He was attired in a black dress SS uniform, with silver rank shoulder boards and oak leaves denoting his rank on his tunic collar. On his tie, he wore the maroon and white circular Nazi Party badge. "*Mein Führer,* with your permission." He nodded abruptly towards Hitler in a bow who motioned him to continue. "We are now using a great and growing resource to contribute to your monumental purpose of strengthening the Reich.

Under your leadership, we began dismantling the Jewish influence pervading Germany after 1933 by restricting their ability to operate businesses, forcing them to transfer their assets to Aryan control, for a fraction of their value. In this way, we turned the tables on the Jew who has so damaged the German people, plundering our money and property. We recognised that a strategy of honour was required in the transfer of Jewish businesses to German hands. It is the Party's duty of honour to support Party comrades who may have suffered economic disadvantages and help them achieve an independent livelihood. I am overseeing the transfer to our members of businesses we have made available, which achieves a noble objective. I am also executing an initiative harvesting the Jews and others in concentration camps as a highly efficient labour resource. I am fortunate to live in a wonderful area near Dachau, and visiting the camp has given me a unique insight into the hidden asset value of this resource. Our exploitation of this has enabled our great businesses to flourish and establish manufacturing centres close to the concentration camps we have established. I believe some of our business representatives here will attest to the efficiency savings this gives, lowering costs and increasing production.

"The other area to which I have been able to contribute significantly, has been in the accounting for the assets seized. Here we are assisted by the fact that there can be no accurate financial measure on the property of the Jew that we may discover or recover in executing our policy of *Arisierung*. This means that we can use shrewd accounting methodology to divert assets to the *Versteckte Vermögensfonds*. I have been assisted in this process by the extraordinary skills of an accounting genius who has earned my admiration and, *mein Führer*, already, he has found ingenious ways of making gold disappear from official accounting records. I think we can make great use of him in the future, especially as we expand the Reich. His name is *SS Sturmbannführer* Josef Spacil." Pohl stiffened to attention, clicking his heels, and sat down.

Himmler clapped his hands together as he looked around through his circular pince-nez glasses triumphantly, glorifying that this was an SS man, as Hermann Göring found it hard to hide his disgust; Himmler was a man he despised and whom he regarded with utter contempt. There were others in the room who shared his view but all recognised the enormous power he wielded in the Reich through the SS, and the fear he engendered with his reputation for the brutal disposal of anyone who stood in his way.

Hitler now stood again, "We must dedicate ourselves to increasing the financial might of Germany. For that, we must strive as our glorious *Volk* dedicate themselves to productive labour or military sacrifice for the Reich. We must never believe that our community exists on the fictitious value of money but on how we labour; that is what gives money its value. Our future lies in a race in which the people dedicate their lives to the Reich which will then richly reward them. We must destroy interest rates or charges with efficient use of resources including exploitation of those who have exploited us. Our fight is with the races that represent money. Money has been our enemy as the Jew's power is the power of the money, which multiplies in his hands effortlessly and endlessly through interest, and with which he imposes a yoke upon the nation. But now we are the masters and the Jew recognises that we have become the masters. When the weak democracies condemn our policies, I ask the question: 'If a thief takes your money and you take it back, does that make you also a thief?'

"The Reich needs money but this will reward the *Deutsche Volk* because they have earned the rewards which labour gives. Money is of no importance other than to ensure the means to reward that labour and dedication. Gold has no value to me, but Germany requires economic power for the people to thrive and expand. For this, we require the foundation of gold but we will use this new wealth to confound and annihilate our enemies. We will destroy those who oppose us, and their resistance will feed the will that drives us at this historic time. Now, as the enemy trembles, wondering what our next step will be, we will strike where they least expect it; strike without hesitation, and strike for Germany!" His tone had increased until he bellowed the last words out. The room was transfixed, as he held them in awe with the clarity of his vision and purpose. Then, in a quieter voice, "Whilst our invincible forces move forwards, we must demoralise the enemy from within by surprise, terror, sabotage, and assassination. This is the war of the future which we will fight from today." He paused, looking around, his face suddenly softening, "But, *meine Herren*, I think it is time for lunch, after which I will announce our new controlled inflation weapon which will stun our enemies and undermine their economies." He pressed a bell-push behind him and seconds later, there was a brief knock on the double doors, and a man entered, dressed in a white jacket. He clicked his heels, bowed, then briefly raised his arm in the Nazi salute. *"Mein Führer?"*

"Ah, *Herr Sturmbannführer* Linge, lunch for our guests." Hitler turned back to those around the table with a rare smile, "For those who do not know this man, he is no ordinary valet, but also a member of the *Führerbegleitkommando*, my escort protection unit. He is an elite, highly trained combat officer and a marksman. So, if he feels I am threatened by any of you, he will shoot you. Shall we take some air." This was followed by polite laughter as Hitler left the room with all standing, raising their arms in salute.

They took a stroll in the crisp midday sun on the upper patio of the *Berghof* as orderlies discreetly led some of the guests out of Hitler's sight to smoke cigarettes which was forbidden in his presence. They stared out at the spectacular Alpine scenery, with the rugged view of the towering peaks across the valley stretching as far as the eye could see. Hitler stood on the edge of the balcony fixing his eyes distantly, stamping his feet every now and then in the cold muttering odd words to Martin Bormann who remained by his side.

The guests stood in separate small groups, not wishing to return to the warmth of the interior until the *Führer* made the first move. There were some moments of levity as Fritz Tornow, Hitler's dog handler, appeared leading a German Shepherd, handing the lead to Hitler who immediately bent down, releasing the dog which ran around him, stopping to lick his hand before assuming a begging position as he stroked its neck, ruffling the fur. "You see," he said loudly, "she understands the meaning of obedience. The more time I spend with some people, the more I love dogs..." He looked up with the hint of a smile as laughter echoed across the terrace. "This is Blonda; she is nearly 11 years old and suffering with arthritis but, even now, if I ask her to climb a ladder, she will do so. She respects order and discipline, traits which the German *Volk* understand are needed to secure our great Reich." At that moment, Heinz Linge appeared, marched to Hitler, and raised his arm. "*Mein Führer, das Mittagessen wird serviert*" (lunch is served). Hitler patted Blonda, giving the command, "Go home!" and placed the lead in the dog's mouth, which exited the terrace, gingerly walking down the steps to where Fritz Tornow was waiting, although the dog often returned without further command, to her kennel.

The *Führer* walked back inside the chalet style building proceeding directly to the dining room which was laid for lunch with a fine white porcelain dinner service. The soup plates were inset with a golden eagle above a wreath surrounding a swastika to the left and right of which were the letters 'A' and 'H'. All the porcelain items were similarly gilded including the side plates and serving dishes which were on trolleys behind each line of seats. Four orderlies stood, with their white-gloved hands crossed in front of them, against the far wall. Crystal wine glasses etched with a similar crest were set amongst an array of silver cutlery on the table. As the guests filed in, they stood and waited in deference for the *Führer* who was speaking in a low voice to Linge who nodded as he received his instructions. Then he spoke, "*Meine Herren,* I have ordered an excellent vintage Mosel wine to accompany lunch which I trust meets with your approval. I do not suppose any of you would prefer to join me in apple juice and Indian tea?" There were titters, before Hermann Göring quipped, "*Mein Führer*, as your nominated successor, I must set an example to the people and endure the wine. In fact, the greater example I set, the better." Hitler acknowledged his humour with the wave of both his hands in mock exasperation, then looked upwards, as if seeking a divine connection. "At this moment, let us be guided by Providence in our sacred duty to the Reich. *Heil!*" He raised his hand with the final word, as all in the room responded, *"Heil,"* raising their arms in unison. Hitler then sat, gesturing to all to do the same.

The meal was then served with the orderlies bustling around the table, commencing with lentil soup, which was followed by marinated beef, mashed potato, and vegetables, whilst Hitler, a vegetarian, was served with egg dumplings. There were various conversations around the table although, if Hitler spoke loudly, all would cease talking to listen. At one point, the *Führer* broke away from small talk stating, "The fine porcelain which we eat off today is known as *Allach Porzellan* assisted by production measures with reduced costs, resulting from exploitation of assets from our camp at Dachau. I understand, *Herr Reichsführer,*" he looked up with his piercing blue eyes fixed upon

Himmler, "you have authorised the use of prisoner skills, but, so far, have shied away from using Jews. Why is this?"

Himmler looked uncomfortable. He did not like being questioned on any aspect of his administration or decision making and would not put up with this from anyone else. He attempted to look pleased to have been consulted, "*Mein Führer, die judensau* (jew-pig) may contaminate what they come into contact with."

Hitler responded, "I have decreed that we exploit every asset at our disposal and, in that, we must make sacrifices, even if it means utilising the Jew. They have exploited Germany and must be made to pay back what they have taken or serve the Reich to compensate. All available resources will be used in my policy dedicated to the sole purpose of German victory." Himmler snapped his head forwards in a bow. After lunch, they drank tea in the Great Room, which had a huge floor to ceiling window overlooking the Untersberg mountain. Linge informed those who had never been before that the window retracted into the floor giving a spectacular, open-air view of the snow-capped mountains and which was opened when the weather was warmer.

When they reconvened, the table had been completely cleared and, as they sat down, Hitler remained standing, and paused to build up the dramatic tension, his hands on his hips, as they had seen him do at rallies. All were transfixed, as he then addressed them, "I spoke before lunch about our new economic or controlled inflation weapon, but which Herr Funk has informed me breaks international law." The shaven headed Reich Minister for Economic Affairs and Reichsbank President, Walther Funk, looked very uncomfortable as Hitler spoke, recognising that to oppose the *F*ührer could result in instant removal from office at very least, incarceration in a concentration camp, or even death. However, Hitler looked at ease as he stressed the words he spoke. "My will is unflinching in the face of the monumental struggle that lies ahead. I cannot be bound by petty bureaucracy, regulation, or law. Such constraints are suffered by weak democracies limiting their power to take decisive action. When I became *Führer*, did I stop to concern myself about petty rules or archaic procedure? *Nein*! I swept aside such considerations in order to create and strengthen the Third Reich. Only I had the foresight, strength and will to lead Germany and regain our self-respect and dignity, unfettered by votes and argument. Let that be the territory inhabited by our enemies who lack the resolve of our nation as we eliminate all opposition to our purpose. Now we must seize control, not only of territories we may overcome in our policy of securing the borders of the Reich and expansion in the east, but... of our economic destiny. We will destroy the economies of those who dare to oppose us, starting with Great Britain, presided over by that pathetic weakling, Chamberlain, who will beg us for peace against the might of our resolve. My new plan which I have named *Unternehmen Andreas,* will unleash generations of instability in their currency, and levels of inflation never before experienced. We shall revisit upon them the economic misery which they imposed on us in the betrayal of the Treaty of Versailles. Most of you will know the *Chef der Reichsicherheitshaumptamt* (head of Reich Security), *Gruppenführer* Reinhard Heydrich. *Herr Gruppenführer?*"

He sat down, as a tall slim figure next to Himmler at one end of the table stood up in a grey SS uniform with swept back dark blond hair. He had youthful features, but his expression bore the look of ruthless determination, backed by a reputation for a fanatical dedication to duty, supported by deadly methods. His eyes were blue and his look unwavering, speaking his words in a clipped, precise manner.

"*Mein F*ührer, upon your command, I have organised a unit who are masterminding the production of forged British banknotes; only these are forgeries like none before. We are creating banknotes that are so perfect even experts will not be able to tell the difference from the real ones. These will be perfect copies, utilising materials that are identical to those used by the British. We will flood their markets with excess counterfeit notes, introducing inflation, purchasing gold, adding to your reserves, Herr Funk. What could be more perfect as our banks increase their assets whilst the British economy inexplicably collapses with hyperinflation?"

Joseph Goebbels interrupted, "*Ein grotesker Plan, aber wundervoll … einfach Genial!*" (A grotesque plan, but wonderful…simply genius) Heydrich continued, "We will also exchange the currency for Swiss Francs and US Dollars, strengthening our own economy, whilst the British will be plunged into financial chaos: eventually their currency will no longer be considered a world currency. Our own financial and military domination of a future Europe will be assured, and secured. *Heil Hitler!*" His right arm shot out, before he sat down.

Hitler rose again, nodding and beating his right fist into his left hand, "History will judge this time as the epic point in the resurgence of Germany, as Providence chooses this moment to sow the seeds for our future as the largest economy in Europe. *Heil!*" The echoes of their voices, joining in a chorus of admiring responses, rang out.

8

"If money go before, all ways do lie open."
(William Shakespeare: 'The Merry Wives of Windsor')

Saturday 6th January 2024 2:00pm

Das Kauntinhaus, Pienzenauerstrasse, Bogenhausen, Munich

'*My father, your grandfather, oft repeated to me the oath of loyalty he had taken in 1931 which, he told me, he retook each year on November 9th to commemorate the 1923 Munich Putsch. "I swear to you, Adolf Hitler, as Führer and Chancellor of the German Reich, that I will be loyal and brave. I pledge obedience unto death to you and those you appoint to lead. So help me God."*' Karl's blood ran cold as he read the chilling words in his father's letter, reminding him of all he had discovered and detested about the living memories of the past held by both his father and grandfather and the significant part that both had played serving the Nazi cause. He was sitting in his old bedroom at his parents' house on the floor above the study, taking in the view of the gardens that he had listened to his father speak so warmly of in his final days. Inge had left that morning, leaving Karl, at his own request, in order that he could begin examining his father's papers and, in particular, the contents of the box he had referred to as containing his testament.

He had just retrieved his father's large box from the safe set into the wall, behind the lower half of one of the bookcases in the study which was hinged to hide its location. After Inge had left, his mother had presented him with a large envelope containing the safe combination. This was sealed with red wax which he also found disturbing as, within the seal, was a round imprint in which was set the Nazi spread-eagle winged emblem. He had excused himself saying that he would need time alone to absorb what his father may have written.

The previous day, after the funeral service, and a luncheon in a local hotel, Karl had returned to his parents' house and spent the last hours of the day talking with his mother, sister and Inge reflecting over his mother and father's lives together. Greta had served them a light meal at 7:00pm, after which Karl had retired to his father's study with the package he had been given after the funeral. He had sat at his father's desk, slitting open the sealed flap, emptying the contents. He took a sharp intake of breath as he spied a plastic ID card for the overseas covert Intelligence branch of the *Bundesnachrichtendienst* containing his photograph, a standard issue wallet containing a further BND ID card, both of which bore the name Karl Geldmann. He smiled ruefully at his father's final humour referring to the word *'Geld'* (money). A further document was an authority to use lethal force and carry a weapon abroad on covert operations. In a plastic folder was £1,000 sterling in £20 and £50 denominations together with a British Barclays Bank debit card and a pin number attached with a paperclip. The name on the bank card was Timothy Warren. He whistled in surprise as, beneath this, was a passport carrying the same name, and a UK driver's licence. His heart beat quickened as he opened a further folded paper issued by the Federal Government authorising the purchase of a business class flight from Munich to London-Heathrow. A typed briefing stated that he would be met at Heathrow by a representative from the German Embassy whenever he chose to fly, arrangements for which would be automatically triggered when he used the flight voucher. Finally, there was a light-grey thin plastic card, which carried a curious logo, he did not recognise, depicting two diamond shapes one above the other, the top shape in red, and the bottom black, with a triangular pattern crossing at the centre. A telephone number was printed beneath with (24 hours) written in brackets. He raised his eyebrows, as something seemed to connect with the logo shape but he could not place it, slipping the card into his wallet.

He had retired to bed that night, feeling overcome by the strain of the day's events; despite denying it to himself, he already knew he would pursue the assignment his father wished him to undertake.

Now, sitting at the small red leather covered writing desk in the bay of the large windows overlooking the grounds and the sweeping lawns to the lake beyond, he was slowly absorbing what he was reading. He had gingerly opened the large stout brown envelope his mother had given him which was reinforced with card. He had retrieved some papers clipped together, on top of which was written, *'Kritische Information.'* Typical of his father's efficiency, he had smiled to himself, recalling the reputation Heinz held for tidiness in all things, signified by his meticulous filing, his insistence on his clothing being laid out folded in a highly ordered manner, and his preoccupation with punctuality, times and schedules. It was one thing that Karl had admired and, indeed, had inherited to a degree, which served him well in the military. Under various titles was the safe combination, the passwords to his father's laptop, and that of his mobile phone, together with a list of personal bank accounts, access information and details of investments. At that point, he had decided to retrieve the box from the safe and bring it to his room where he could examine the contents, and especially his father's testament, without being disturbed. He placed the box down by the desk and returned to the envelope.

He extracted some more sheets stapled together on the front of which was the heading, *Contacts (All are members of das Geheime Vierte Reich)*, beneath which was written, '*Security password – to be quoted on contact with senior personnel which should afford you co-operation – 'Adler-Geldbörse'* (Eagle Wallet)

There were some further subheadings and telephone numbers with brief annotations and others with more detail which he read with some astonishment. These included:

Der Spinne - im aubersten Notfall (In case of extreme emergency) He grimaced, recognising this as the organisation set up by the Nazis at the end of the war to assist their escape from the Allies and provide ongoing support in obtaining new identities. He read on:

Friedrich Völker – My former financial deputy

The Controller of the Versteckte Vermögensfonds, Dr Wilhelm Dexheimer

Oberst Konrad Kaufmann - The BND Deputy Political Director of Covert Operations

There was a further heading under which there were a number of names and he shook his head in disbelief at the senior ranks of some appearing on the list in the *Bundespolizei* (Federal Police*), Bundeskriminalamt (*Criminal Police*),* Bundestag Members, MEP's, and the *Bundeswehr (*Army*)*

Finally, in a small envelope was a key which he assumed, with a tinge of excitement, would be for the box. He reached down, inserting the key in the round iron lock, and was relieved to discover it fitted. His heart pounded as he turned it and found that he could lift the hinged lid, folding it back until it was held by restraining chains. He peered inside; there were neatly stacked files, and some papers, but it was the thick envelope on the top which caught his attention carrying his name on the front in his father's neat, precise, italicised handwriting. Once again, the flap was sealed with red wax imprinted with the Nazi eagle and swastika. Opening the envelope, he shuddered with a pang of emotion, as he thought the last person to see what he was about to view, was his father. He extracted a number of A4 typed sheets holding them between both hands as he read. The opening of the letter was surprisingly brief and to the point, which was, he reflected, more like the father he had known in life, than the more intimate connection that he had shared with him in his last days.

'Lieber Karl,

This letter contains my testament to you about my life which I know has always troubled you greatly. It is my final wish that you learn about the elements of my work that have caused me the most disquiet and with which I have failed to come to terms. What you do with this is a matter for your conscience as much as it will be if you are successful in your hunt for my final secret bequest to you. By the time you read this, you will hopefully have been contacted by the BND with whom I arranged your cover. Please proceed with caution because you will recall my warning that you will not be the only person seeking answers regarding the Raubgold. The value of our assets is almost inestimable but runs into billions of dollars and, as such, brings out the worst human characteristics, even in those we think we can trust. 'With money,' as Shakespeare says, 'all ways do lie open', but, equally, he says, that it is the cause of 'quarrels against the good and loyal, destroying them for wealth.'

I turn now to the loyalty which I have given all of my life to das Geheime Vierte Reich. I never questioned this as I grew up respecting and believing in all that Adolf Hitler stood for. Before you were born, a large portrait of the Führer used to hang here, openly displayed in the dining room of this house. I can remember my father standing in front of this, with others who visited, and them executing the Nazi salute. Loyalty was absolute and Hitler continued to have a hold on those who had witnessed his regime long after the war." Having read the chilling oath of loyalty to Adolf Hitler, the words, *"I pledge obedience unto death",* the phrase swirled in his head, and he placed the letter down, walking to a corner table where Greta had left a bottle of *Asbach Uralt*. After pouring himself a generous measure, he moved over to the window, standing by the desk, staring out and reflecting. 'Why such loyalty? What was it about Hitler that had gripped a nation and inspired so many to commit the most horrific crimes? Why? Why? Why?" he said out loud. "Surely my own grandfather could not have been involved in acts of such barbarity. *Mein Gott.*" He spoke the last words weakly as he sat back down and warily picked up the letter again. Almost uncannily, the next paragraph addressed his thoughts.

'In the box, there are documents which will show those areas which have disturbed me most. Many of these were referred to euphemistically after the war as "excesses" committed by a few who exceeded their orders. However, the more I looked into these 'excesses', and the source of much of the Versteckte Vermögensfonds, the more uncomfortable I became. Some of the gold came from occupied territories, or through clever banking arrangements with currency exchanges and loan repayments. Although, in today's world, this might be called money laundering, my father believed these were legitimate arrangements which were not called into

question by our main bankers at the Bank for International Settlements. In this, I continued to play a significant role both in protecting the funds, and increasing their value, from the time I took over on my father's death in 1967.

However, I will now turn to what was referred to as 'Fonds der Judenfrage'. This gold had been gained from the most depraved acts of mankind that I have ever come across in my life. When I understood how it had been obtained, I could not reconcile this with my creed of loyalty. Whilst I believe, and still believe, in the tenets of National Socialism, I was reviled by the savage, cruel, and utterly unjustifiable policies of confiscating Jewish property which, in itself, was reprehensible, but the policy of genocide was unforgiveable. When I discovered the depth of collusion of many leading figures in this vile practice, I became disorientated and full of a sense of self-loathing in that I could be part of anything resulting from such acts. On realising the depths of depravity to which many had sunk, I was filled with a sense of guilt that I was associated with this. Do you know that they even removed the gold teeth of those they were exterminating in the gas chambers. having this melted down at the Reichsbank and made into bullion bars. What kind of people could do this? I cannot believe that the Führer would have sanctioned such a policy. Yet, Karl, within the box you will discover evidence which is so damning, so shocking, that our business leaders were not only complicit in this, but profited from it. Many of these were the founding fathers of our current economic success, together with some of the present-day corporate giants that are household names.

The heritage of some of our leading businesses is tainted with their involvement in one of the greatest horrors of recent history. This was all hidden or not spoken of at the end of the war in the interests of rebuilding our economy, preparations for which had been put in *place by the Bank for International Settlements and agreed by the United States and Great Britain. What trials there were at Nuremberg were engineered to result in light sentences of those mired in guilt, which were shortened afterwards or even resulted in no indictment at all, as a defence was accepted of being a "Mitläufer" or follower without being directly responsible. This was often despite damning evidence of guilt. By this time, the war or war crimes trials were of no interest to the victors other than as a sop to the voters and former servicemen, whilst those directly implicated had the business skills necessary to maximise a return on investment by rebuilding Germany's industrial strength.*

I met many of these people and Papa would introduce them to me as leading players in the restoration of Germany. At that time, I accepted them and helped them, when I was in a position to do so, by lending them money and investing in their new ventures. However, in my later years, I began to discover their willing collusion in the so-called 'excesses', and my doubts about the GVR took root. There were many former officials, gestapo men, and members of the SS who remained fiercely loyal to every principle of their understanding of National Socialism and who openly defended the policy of extermination camps. Anyone who thought differently were labelled 'apologists' but we were many.

Despite my concerns, I was conflicted, because I believed in the idea of a strong leadership driven by an unswerving principle of service to the Fatherland. The anarchy of democracy is weakened every few years by pandering to the voters with foolish policies in the pursuit of power. I watch other European countries crippling their state economies with increased spending on welfare which, in turn, weakens the resolve of the working man to be a worker. Look at the breakdown in law and order across the world, and the price we pay for our weakness in the soaring crime figures, whilst unchecked immigration is leading to a dilution of our German race and culture. I know you will not agree with me and, my son, I am proud of your principled standing. That is the dichotomy in my views because, under Hitler, there were no views permitted other than those which were approved by the leadership. By the late 1960's and early 70's many of us in das Geheime Vierte Reich were appalled at what had been done to the Jews, and by the evidence of genocide committed against many others. We remained on the far right of politics but recognised the 'excesses' for what they were. However, a fanatical breakaway organisation from the GVR who call themselves the Reichslegion would not condemn any actions of Hitler's regime.

This extremist faction split from the GVR in 2010, declaring only they were the true followers of Adolf Hitler and demanded that they should be given a percentage of the Versteckte Vermögensfonds. They promoted violence as a legitimate method of achieving their aims, even establishing a paramilitary force like the former SS, known as the Deutsch Abteilung or DA. They know we control huge assets and they have in-depth knowledge of some of the places where we deposited elements of the Versteckte Vermögensfonds.

We held gold in the Volksbank in Berlin which, in January 2013, had a similar raid as that carried out at Hatton Garden. We had gold stored there with a value of over fifteen million euros, all of which was stolen. None of this was recovered but we think those responsible for the Berlin robbery were linked to the *Reichslegion. No one has ever been charged in relation to that and, believe me, that is because they have people loyal to them in high places and others who have infiltrated the police and security services. They also know that GVR gold is missing from what was officially recovered from Hatton Garden, and its value. Yet, despite similarities in the robbery at the*

Volksbank and Hatton Garden, we are unaware if the Reichslegion had links with the crooks responsible, all of whom appeared to be retired or semi-retired local villains. We have informers in the Reichslegion, who tell us that they are interested in pursuing the Hatton Garden thieves. Remember, however, there is no record of that which I secreted for you and Gretchen.

Initially, the Reichslegion were considered by our leader to be extremists and that we should merely distance ourselves from them; that was until they began to be a threat. Our leader, incidentally, at that time was Manfred Göring, the grandson of Reichsmarschall Hermann Göring, the Führer's deputy and leader of the Luftwaffe,."

Karl gasped, his eyes widening at the name, Göring, which seemed to jump off the page as if mocking him. His head was reeling with the enormity of all he was being exposed to. How much more could he take in? Nevertheless, his eyes were drawn back, irrevocably needing to learn more.

'*He stepped back three years ago because of a major leak to the press right in the middle of the Covid pandemic* [1] *which was eventually gagged at enormous diplomatic and political cost. Although still very much involved, he appointed Heinrich Hackmann, as Lieter. Both condemned the Reichslegion as criminals, comparing them to the SA under Ernst Röhm, who attempted to oppose Hitler's views, and was eliminated in 1934.*'

Karl stopped reading as he recalled the significance of the name 'Hackmann.' That had been mentioned in the eulogy given the day before by the banker, Franz Niemeyer. He made a mental note that he would attempt to contact Hackmann or Niemeyer before he left for England in order to fill in some blank spaces about who he may be up against; a thought given more relevance as he read the final

(1) **Covered in previous book, 'The Barbarossa Secret'**

paragraphs of his father's letter.

'My son, these people in the Reichslegion are dangerous fanatics who will stop at nothing to achieve their aims and you need to be very careful. They have records of our assets and want to recover or steal any of the Raubgold they can get their hands on.

Matters came to a real head in October 2022 when we were moving gold bullion, with a value of over 10 million euros, under our own armed escort, from the underground secure facility in Zurich to Stuttgart. Just after crossing the Swiss/German border, the armoured truck and escorting vehicles was stopped at what appeared to be a police roadblock just outside Gottmadingen. It was all so brazen but well executed. They halted traffic behind the armoured vehicle first, and then, half a kilometre further on, they stopped the truck, at which point twenty-five well-armed soldiers appeared in black uniforms, disarmed the escort, and ordered the vehicle down a side road before they blew the doors off with high explosive. Within fifteen minutes, they had unloaded the gold and disappeared. The only people who knew about the movement were within our organisation and, because of the sensitivities of what we were moving, we could not officially alert the authorities about the nature of what had been taken. Much of the bullion carried Reichsbank swastika markings.

Despite a huge police operation, only abandoned vehicles were discovered. No one has been arrested in connection with this, but we are pretty sure that the Reichslegion are responsible.

At this point, Hackmann ordered that our own security forces should attack leading figures in the Reichslegion and I'm afraid this has led to what might be called gang warfare. In the summer of 2023, with the gains made by the AfD Party, there were moves in Germany to *have the party banned as an extreme right-wing movement. For this reason, a fragile peace was negotiated with the Reichslegion to prevent a political backlash from the violence erupting, but they could move against us at any time. We know that within the GR we have informers, and, for this reason, you must trust no one. Our financial losses are in millions, and I fear for our future unless these people are rooted out but that is not a matter for you. There is only one who I can vouch for which is my former deputy, Friedrich Völker, who is on the list I have left for you. If you need more information, he is a good man whose father worked for me for many years, and they have strong links to our family from the past. He lives here in Munich and is an extremely talented financial expert with inside knowledge of the VVF.*

Much of what you will find in the box will evidence the laundering of our assets during and after the Second World War by those who knew the source and assisted us. Some of this is in the public domain but much has been swept under the carpet as 'inconvenient', or covered up, especially the activities of the Vatican Bank. What you do with all this is entirely up to you, but it eases my conscience to know that I have released evidence to you about the plunder of gold, much of it taken in the most barbaric manner from the Jews and others dismissed at the time as 'Untermenschen'.

My final wish is that neither you or Gretchen are ever exposed to the contradictions I have had to face, nor that you are ever tortured as I have been, by self-recrimination over a life's work protecting a belief in a creed as I have done, but part of which I now question. The world cries out for strength of leadership, but this should never be at the expense of the weak, or on exploitation based on racial origin. Throughout my life, I have tried to guide you, and be a good father and I hope, despite all, you will remember me with some fondness,

or, perhaps, even in a word that has never come easily to me, with love.
Take good care of your mother, who has always supported me and would never accept any criticism of either Hitler's Reich or the GVR, nor ever would she question my motives. Please be tolerant and understanding of her.
Dein Vater

Karl folded the letter with a deep sigh, and could not suppress a wave of emotional sadness which swept over him, not just for his father's passing, but also the realisation that he had never really known him as he should have, nor reconciled his own differences with those principles his father represented.

After Greta had served lunch, Karl decided he would leave with the box and study the contents more closely back in his apartment. Before leaving, he retrieved his sidearm from his suitcase, a *Heckler & Koch P30L* which was his preferred weapon of choice in the special forces. He already sensed that he may be facing danger, reinforced by his father's letter. He strapped on his shoulder holster, into which he slipped the compact handgun, after checking the magazine which he released out of the handle, pushing it back in again until it clicked into position. He spoke briefly to Gretchen, informing her about the sensitive nature of some of the information contained in the box, dating from their grandfather's activities during and after the war. He stated that he would share all that he discovered with her, but that there were some security issues he needed to clear up first. She trusted and respected her brother, accepting what he said without question other than giving a typically dry humoured response, *"Mein Bruder,* when you men finish playing soldiers, and you wish the more measured input from a woman, perhaps I will assist you," to which he replied, "I will inform one of my most senior officers; I am sure 'she' will be delighted."

After loading the box and case into his silver *Mercedes-AMG Gt,* Karl bade farewell to his mother, who, in typical stoic fashion when he enquired whether she would be okay, told him that she just had to "face life and get on with it." He swung the car round, heading back down the gravel drive onto a minor road, flanked by trees, which linked onto the Bundesstrasse 2R ring road heading back towards his riverside apartment at Harlaching. The traffic was light, and he gunned the 4 litre V8 engine, enjoying the response as the Mercedes leapt forwards sweeping onto the ring road, but failing to notice the motorcycle with two riders which was now following him 50 metres behind. He slowed down to take a left at the junction with Grünwalder Strasse, and it was then he became aware of the bike approaching fast down the centre of the road. His old instincts from years of active service with the *KSK* kicked in with a wave of adrenalin as he caught sight of a short automatic weapon being swung out from the pillion passenger as the bike roared closer. He swerved the Mercedes left to block their approach as his hand reached inside his jacket for the familiar grip of his weapon. The bike was now on the pavement and shot forwards swerving back into the road as it drew alongside; there was a flash from an *MP7* machine gun, and Karl ducked, hearing the burst of fire and accompanying bangs on the exterior of his car; his driver's window crazed as two shots penetrated, missed him by inches before the glass shattered. He jammed his foot on the break, then slammed the car into reverse, skidding the wheels as he wrenched the wheel to the right causing the Mercedes to lurch sideways blocking the road as an approaching vehicle shrieked to a halt to avoid a collision. Now, the motorcycle had turned and was nearly back upon him; he brought up his handgun, aiming through the open space left by the window, loosing off six rounds in quick succession and watched, as the bike slid to the floor, colliding with a parked car, throwing the riders into the road. He pushed his foot to the floor and the tyres squealed as he swung the car back to face forwards, speeding away, seeing one man lying motionless on the road in his rear-view mirror as he shot forwards. Sweat beaded on his forehead as he realised how near had come to being fatally injured.

By the time he had reached the underground carpark at his apartment 1.5 kilometres away, he had already decided on a course of action. He was grateful for the secure access through steel doors, having barely acknowledged it previously, which was activated by a coded lock system. In addition, there was a security concierge who controlled any entry to the apartments from non-residents.

In his lounge area, his heart still pounding, he reached inside the box he had brought in from the car, extracting the envelope containing the contact details his father had left him, then took out his mobile phone and tapped in a number. On hearing the brusque greeting of "Kaufmann", Karl spoke back with the voice of authority that his military background gave him. *"Herr Oberst,* this is *Oberst Karl Biesecker,* I believe my password is *'Adler-Geldbörse!'"*

There was a pause then, *"Einen Moment bitte"*...another pause before, *"Guten Tag, mein Kamerad...*your father was a national hero, and his father, *mein Gott,* he was a legend."

Karl responded, *"Danke, Herr Oberst,"* suddenly realising that he had uncharacteristically, not prepared himself for this moment, nor the part he now recognised he would have to play. He spoke calmly, slowly, as he was accustomed to doing when engaged on special forces operations, "I am proud of my father and the part my family have played in protecting the Fatherland." He was listening to his own words with incredulity and wincing as he spoke yet, strangely, the subterfuge came easily to him, and he began to almost enjoy what he was doing. *"Herr Oberst,* there has been an attempt on my life in the last hour and I think this is connected to a mission my father gave me, to look closely into the robbery of the *Versteckte Vermögensfonds* and the infiltration of the *Reichslegion*. It will not be long before the police arrive here, and I need freedom from awkward questions right now." He related the events that had taken place with the attack he had suffered in his car.

The voice at the other end was condescending, giving him a reassurance that police matters would be taken care of and that such trivialities were not worth consideration. "Karl, please, no more formalities; you may call me Konrad. I will resolve this situation within the hour. It is nothing. We will pass it off as extremists of some kind. I will arrange for your apartment to be placed under 24-hour guard. Please, give me 15 minutes."

Karl sat, with a drink of *Schnapps,* staring at the box his father had left for him, drawn to it, yet also full of trepidation about what he may discover within. Twenty minutes later, his phone buzzed, and Kaufmann informed him that police issues had been taken care of and security was being placed around the building. His voice then assumed a more genial note, "So, Karl, exactly what brief did your father give you, because he gave few details when requesting your BND identity, other than he wanted you to investigate the level of infiltration by the *Reichslegion* into our UK based financial clearance arrangements."

At that point Karl hesitated, wondering whether, perhaps, he had already given too much away; however, in this game of cat and mouse, he also recognised that to have done so had increased his credibility. In his military intelligence work, he had been taught that it was imperative, if under interrogation, to weave a narrative as near to the truth as possible, even giving away certain intel unknown to adversaries. This would then allow the feeding in of more misleading information from which an advantage might be secured. He decided to appear as if he were taking Kaufmann further into his confidence.

He spoke earnestly and quietly, "Konrad, my father stated that we, in turn, had successfully planted double agents within the *Reichslegion*, and that we had penetrated to a senior level within the organisation. He said that it was like going back to what he termed, "the good old days before unification", when we had people not only holding positions within the West German Government, but many in East Germany too." Karl now decided to appear more convincing by relating a genuine disclosure of a secret event his father had shared with him during discussions they had held in his final days. "I recall that in one remarkable conversation I had with my father, he told me that on 9th November 1989, the night the Berlin wall came down, the East German security forces were poised to open fire against those protesting and climbing on the wall, with automatic weapons. My father said we, in the GVR, had decided the time was right to move against the communist vermin and so we instructed one of our people, Günter Schabowski, a high-ranking communist party member and spokesman, to create confusion about the right of East Germans to cross into the west. He authorised large payments to Schabowski and other border guard officers. This has never been revealed and so, even you will not be aware of this. In effect, Nazi gold helped to reunify Germany and this, my father said, was one of his greatest achievements."

Kaufmann expressed his astonishment, and Karl knew that he had achieved his objective of being viewed as someone who could be trusted as part of the GVR. However, he recognised he was playing a perilous double game as he was not aware of who was involved in the *Reichslegion*, including Kaufmann.

Kaufmann returned to his previous question, "So, Karl, what was the brief your father gave you?"

"I had no specific instructions," he responded which, he reflected, was true, "but he asked me to undertake a covert mission to ensure the UK reserves of the VF were not being compromised or endangered by betrayal from within. I think this is why I have been targeted. Someone knew I had been selected for this purpose and they do not want me looking too closely into the UK robbery in 2015, or investigating the losses we suffered. Despite his stepping back, he knew our assets were being targeted, especially after the brazen attack on our armoured vehicle in 2022." Karl added for authenticity, "He said he trusted no one anymore in the GVR and, therefore, he turned to me. He was not prepared to see his life's work sabotaged."

"Ah, OK, please keep me informed about your progress, Karl, especially if you uncover anything. Is there anything else I can help with?" Kaufmann's voice had become irritably condescending again.

"Perhaps, a car…" Karl responded, "Oh and I'll need repairs organising for my Mercedes which has a number of bullet holes and a missing window."

An hour later, he received a call from the concierge informing him that a pick-up truck had arrived together with a driver who was leaving a car for his use. He went back to the list of contacts left by his father and keyed in a number.

"*Hallo, is das Friedrich Völker?*"

9

The Love of Money

Tuesday 20th August 1940 6:00pm
Cabinet War Rooms, New Public Offices (NPO),
King Charles Street, Whitehall, London.

The smell of cigar smoke hung heavily in the air, signifying the presence of the Prime Minister, as Brendan Bracken approached, having left his bedroom down the corridor which also served as his office in the underground complex. There had already been three air-raid warnings that day, preceded by the eerie wailing of the warning sirens raising and lowering before the droning of aircraft could be heard in the sky. He knew they were on the way to attack RAF bases and other defence targets such as *Chain Home* or CH stations, with their huge masts which could detect incoming aircraft. They had watched from the terrace of the House of Commons, overlooking the Thames, that lunch-time, cheering as they saw the trails of RAF aircraft intercepting the bombers. Bracken had remarked to a fellow MP, Major General Edward Spears, "We are damned lucky to have such fine chaps; I wish I could say I felt sorry for those poor Jerry blighters they shoot down, but I don't. Fearful business, but there's a war on thanks to the dreadful Mr Hitler." The reply from Spears was typically blunt, "Listen old boy, the only good German, is a dead German. Mark my words, the Hun will be bombing cities next. Thank God we have Winston Churchill as PM or we probably would have caved in to the Jerries like the damnable Frogs did under Pétain."

That afternoon, Churchill had addressed the House of Commons:

"The gratitude of every home in our Island, in our Empire, and indeed throughout the world, except in the abodes of the guilty, goes out to the British airmen who, undaunted by odds, unwearied in their constant challenge and mortal danger, are turning the tide of the World War by their prowess and by their devotion. Never in the field of human conflict was so much owed by so many to so few.

All hearts go out to the fighter pilots, whose brilliant actions we see with our own eyes day after day; but we must never forget that all the time, night after night, month after month, our bomber squadrons travel far into Germany, find their targets in the darkness by the highest navigational skill, aim their attacks, often under the heaviest fire, often with serious loss, with deliberate careful discrimination, and inflict shattering blows upon the whole of the technical and war-making structure of the Nazi power."

As a long-standing supporter of Churchill, Brendan Bracken had become his Parliamentary Private Secretary and now had a pre-briefing to give to Churchill which he had been told needed to be kept 'hush hush' at all costs. He was a dapper man, always well-dressed, with thick wavy hair, and was wearing a pin-striped suit with a white silk top-hanky; a brown document folder was held under his shoulder. He smiled at Churchill's personal secretary, Kathleen Hill, who was sitting outside his bedroom office at a small table desk on which was a typewriter. "Kate, you're looking fairer than ever, brightening up this cave we live in." He spoke with a soft Irish bur, and she blushed, but smiled demurely, bowing her head as he passed to knock on the door.

"Come!" came the loud, familiar growling voice.

Churchill was reclining on his bed, propped up by a number of pillows, in a silk dressing-gown, wearing half-moon glasses below the eyes, with a cigar in one hand, and a glass of whisky in the other, from which he took a drink, before placing it on a side table and picking up a sheaf of papers in his lap. "I think the tide is turning in this Battle of Britain which I deem to represent one of the greatest challenges to the might of our empire in its proud three-hundred-and-fifty-year history. This empire for which, I believe, it was not only my duty to serve, but a calling for which I have long prepared. In the words of Emperor Marcus Aurelius, "A man's true pleasure is to do the thing he was made to do," and, indeed, I have always known that one day, my destiny would be to lead, not overcome by adversity, nor daunted by it, but rising to the great task and privilege that leadership bestows."

"Fine words, Winston," cut in Bracken, "Would you be leading yourself, Sir, to be pouring me a glass of your fine Johnny Walker's Black Label?" delivering the words with a mischievous smile indicative of their close relationship. Churchill gestured to the bottle and then to a set of crystal tumblers on the long dresser lining the wall running parallel to his bed.

As Bracken moved to pour himself a glass, Churchill swung his legs off the bed, "So, after my speech today, and the increasingly good news in the air, one is tempted to say, "'Bring me no more reports, let them fly all, 'Till Burnam Wood shall come to Dunsinane,'"

Bracken, added two lumps of ice from a silver bucket, lifted his glass towards Churchill, who responded with a like gesture, then downed his in one brief motion, as Churchill did the same. As he moved forwards to take Churchill's glass, Bracken sighed, adding to the levity of their exchange, "I trust, using the analogy from the same play, 'Macbeth', I believe, you are not going to call me, a 'cream faced loon.'

May I?" He pointed to an armchair as Churchill nodded with a growled, "Pray continue."

"Very well, Prime Minister, but first, I must compliment you on a jolly fine speech in the House today, following many others that you have made, since assuming office in May, which I know has greatly contributed to the sense of unity and purpose by all the parties behind your leadership."

"Yes, yes, Brendan, but please, may I remind you, there is a war on and so I have neither the time nor the vanity to indulge myself in such platitudes, no matter well earned, or indeed deserving. What news?"

Bracken removed a five-pound note from his folder, handing it to Churchill. "Sir, the Home Guard picked up some poor chap off the beach near Hythe yesterday and retrieved £5,000 in cash" (equivalent to over £350,000 in 2024)

"Where on earth is he from?" The PM questioned with some surprise. "Doubtless, they apprehended either a miscreant, having stolen the money, or someone who must be well-connected, in which case, we can trace his people."

"Neither, I'm afraid, Sir, it appears he is from the Channel Islands, or, to be more accurate, from Jersey."

"By Jove!", Churchill responded loudly, "What in heaven's name is he doing here?" As he spoke, he was re-lighting his cigar, puffing large clouds of smoke which were drawn into the fans whirring above the room.

"Sir, he would not speak initially; however, Captain Richard Tomlin of the Home Guard is apparently a veteran from the 'last lot', when he served in military intelligence. He informed our investigating officer, despatched from SIS (Secret Intelligence Service), that he used a well-trusted method employed in the Great War for breaking prisoners."

He paused, taking a sip of his whisky, mischievously taunting the Prime Minister, who he knew did not tolerate lengthy briefings.

"Go on! Get on with it!" Churchill did not disappoint. "I have the Nazi hordes attempting to break down my resolve, traitors from within seeking to negotiate peace behind my back, fifth columnists infiltrating our society, the threat of invasion, and an incompetent private secretary who cannot be succinct."

"If I may be permitted to interrupt and get to the point", retorted Bracken with mock exasperation. "Apparently, he gave his name as Simon Lloyd but his identity card said he was called Reginald Lloyd and when he was challenged about that and where he had got the money from, he refused to speak further. Tomlin then stated to his hapless prisoner that he would be executed as a spy forthwith. The police arrived and the prisoner was told by them, after speaking with Tomlin, that they had no powers to halt the execution, irrespective of whether he answered police questions. Tomlin then, apparently, made a terrific play of lining his men up and pinning a piece of paper over the chest on this poor blighter's jacket. There was no blindfold, and the men raised their rifles as if to fire, at which point, another officer appeared and shouted, "Stop" and, after an altercation between Hamlin and the officer, he approached the terrified prisoner, stating that under an order given by His Majesty the King, he could grant clemency if the terrified prisoner would answer a few questions. He then sang like a canary, as they say."

"Damnably irregular and, I might add, breaches the terms of the Geneva Convention to which we are signatories and, doubtless by which we may well, one day, be held to account. Of little matter, at this juncture and at this momentous and precarious time in our history, please continue."

Bracken nodded towards Churchill's glass and taking note of the acquiescent nod, he began pouring two more measures, adding a squirt of soda. "Apparently, the poor devil is a Jew, and he stated that he had been dropped off with some others in a dinghy from a German. However, that is not the most interesting element of this business, Sir." He stopped to take a drink. "Damned fine whisky, if I may say so."
"If you do not come to the point, Brendan," boomed Churchill, "I shall, myself, summon a firing squad to end this tedious procrastination which is a proclivity, or, perhaps, affliction peculiar to those born in the Emerald Isle. Now get on with it man!"
Bracken's look suddenly became more serious, "Sir, the extraordinary thing is that this poor fellow was recruited by German Intelligence and given one simple task, which was to spend money. In return for his 'loyalty', his family would be spared deportation, because, of course, Sir, the family is Jewish. That is why he did not wish to speak."
"Confound it man, why do the Germans want to spend any damned money, least of all in Great Britain and why use a Jew?" Churchill now moved away from his bed to a small desk, extracting a pen from the inkwell, he began to take some notes, his eyes now totally focussed peering over his glasses at Bracken.
"I think it is because of their fluency in English, and the Jerries will not wish to use any of their own valuable *Abwehr* agents for such an innocuous mission. He was recruited with many more who were all given the same training and have been landed in various locations all over Britain. The treasury have conducted tests on the money the poor fellow was carrying and discovered that the notes are forgeries; incredibly good forgeries which damned near fooled our experts, but, nevertheless, Prime Minister, forgeries!"
Churchill's brow furrowed, "Are there no depths to which the despicable Hun will sink with their barbarism under that monstrous

tyrant. '*This tyrant, whose sole name blisters our tongues, was once thought honest.*'" He uttered the last words with his voice rising, expressing incredulity on the final word, then "but not by me. I warned about the storm clouds gathering over Europe in January 1935 and few heeded my propitious words."

Bracken raised his finger as he responded, "Ah, again, you quote from Shakespeare's 'Macbeth', which I believe Sir, to be one of his best. Returning to your warning, sir, I believe I was one of the few who agreed with you, and, moreover, I also recognised that your man, Hitler, was a damned cad." Bracken spoke emphatically but quietly.

Churchill raised his hand, asserting his authority, "We must call together those we can trust, which does not include all members of the War Cabinet, but merely those who can directly assist in facing this threat and finding a resolution. I want British Intelligence involved, so summon Colonel Stewart Menzies, the governor of the Bank of England, Sir Montagu Norman, oh and that economist chap, John Maynard Keynes."

"Prime Minister? Keynes?" Bracken was surprised that a mere advisor to the Treasury was being invited. He was used to summoning Menzies as the Head of SIS (Secret Intelligence Service), but the PM's instructions seemed highly unusual.

"Yes, yes, shall we say 11:00am on Monday," Churchill responded, "Keynes is, quite simply, the only man I have ever met who understands how to blend brilliant economics with sound political direction and expediency. Oh, and one last thing, Brendan, old chap, keep the reason for the meeting hush hush from Norman, and, give him as little notice as possible. The damn fool fraternises with the Hun far too much, and I have never found it in my nature to trust bankers, nor, I might admit, have they much time for me. Money, my dear Brendan, money assuredly is the source of many woes. As it says, I believe, in the First Book of Timothy. *'For the love of money is the root of all evil: which while some coveted after, they have erred from the faith, and pierced themselves through with many sorrows.'*

Friday 23rd August 1940 10:00am
The Grand Hotel, Chateau d'Oex, Switzerland

The dinner, the night before, had been sumptuous, all financed by the Bank for International Settlements, which had re-located its headquarters to the imposing hotel, in May of 1940, because of the threat of the growing war in Europe. The deputy director of the Reichsbank, and BIS director, Emil Puhl, had requested that the president of BIS, Thomas McKittrick, convene a secret economic conference, involving key financial players from the world of banking, specifically from the United States, Switzerland, Britain, and Italy. This would be presided over by the president of the BIS, the purpose of which was to enable Germany to put forward a plan to establish a more secure European economic financial framework for the future. Representatives were to be invited from the Swiss National Bank, the BIS, the Bank of England, Enskilda Bank, and the Reichsbank, together with influential figures from the USA who had both political and financial connections including the US Ambassador to Switzerland.

The delegates attending the dinner, which was held in the grand Baroque dining room of the hotel, had been carefully selected and vetted by Thomas McKittrick and Emil Puhl. The list had been compiled in consultation with US Ambassador Leland Harrison, together with John Foster Dulles, who had major political and financial connections, both in Britain and Germany. The guest speaker was to be Walther Funk, the president of the Reichsbank, which had drawn objections from BIS director, and governor of the Bank of

England, Montagu Norman. However, he had been reassured by McKittrick that Funk would avoid any contentious issues and concentrate on proposals for a post-war strategy offering Europe increased financial stability and unity.

The impeccably dressed Marcus Wallenberg, in a white dinner jacket, matching bow tie and maroon cummerbund, had been prominent at the top table emphasising the opportunities that needed to be seized upon during wartime. He spoke eloquently about banking institutions taking the higher ground, maintaining integrity by remaining above the political spectrum. This, he said, allied with the substantial commercial opportunities which existed if international businesses followed suit, recognising that their customer's geographic location or allegiance should not compromise their potential. The table quietened as he spoke, with an uncompromising authority, the guests listening with keen interest. "Here, in Switzerland, we gain from our neutral status and this encourages others to favour our financial institutions. US, German, and British businesses, and those from countries now incorporated into the German Reich, all need to look outwards, without restricting our markets because of the conflict. Demand during such times increases in certain sectors, and supply must adapt to this where this does not conflict with national political considerations. If there are sensitivities, business can invest through international banks, such as the BIS, into other enterprises operating within a territory which may be considered an enemy."

As he had finished speaking, a tall man, with receding hair, stood, in a black tuxedo, crying out, "Bravo. Where there is demand, there needs to be supply." Then, turning to other guests, he announced, "I am John McCloy and I am an American lawyer acting for a German business, I.G. Farben, with a subsidiary in the United States. Commerce and business must not suffer because of war, but prosper and provide whatever is needed, wherever it is needed. That is capitalism at its best, thriving despite adversity."

The German assistant manager of the BIS, Paul Hechler, his hair almost shaven, with a small moustache and wearing pince nez glasses spoke, with a thin voice in a measured unemotional tone, "These are difficult times but we, in Germany recognise that we must seek out ways of sensibly trading and maintaining financial stability within all the territories now incorporated into the greater German Reich. The gold reserves we are building should enable us to trade across all borders using the anonymity of our great banking institutions. Our debts can be settled using our reserves as security ensuring the highest standards of probity and trust are maintained. The differences that divide us must not prejudice our position as guardians of financial stability internationally. I agree with Herr Wallenberg; his Enskilda Bank is an exemplary example because they provide banking to Reich business and, indeed, help our government by securing materials we might need. Suppliers based outside the Reich benefit who would otherwise lose our market because of the war. Our great industries need supplies just as those of our adversaries do, and we hold German businesses interests invisibly through subsidiaries in countries which may oppose us. As we all know, all countries have a demand for certain key products and supplies are sourced from manufacturers irrespective of their nationality using the banking system. This is the reality of supply and demand. "

The former British chairman of the BIS now interjected. He had stepped down when board meetings were suspended, at which point they had agreed that McKittrick, as president, should take overall control during wartime. Sir Otto Niemeyer was an imposing figure dressed in a black dinner jacket and matching bow tie with a winged collar. He spoke in a cultured British accent. "Look here, old boy, whilst I accept and, moreover, endorse the need of the bank to maintain a policy of neutrality, I am a tad uncomfortable with the disposal of what you chaps term the *Vermögensfonds*. If my sources are correct, I believe you people are taking money and valuables from the Jews and popping this into this damned fund. I find the whole business raises a question about our integrity; frankly this is just not cricket, my good man."

"Hear, hear!" The words were spoken by US Ambassador, Leland Harrison, who added, "I have many Jewish connections including a member of the World Jewish congress here in Switzerland, Gerhardt Riegner. He informs me that Jewish people have not only had their possessions taken, but are being placed in so called labour camps, with credible reports emerging that some are being killed. We cannot turn a blind eye to such matters and the United States will not be complicit in what we believe may be a crime against humanity."

The thick set figure of Walther Funk responded in a surprisingly genial tone, despite his reputation for more passionate outbursts. "Gentlemen, may I reassure you that we will be inviting the Red Cross to visit our camps, where we are encouraging work with humane facilities for the residents. Our motto adopted within our camps is *"arbeit macht frei"* (work sets you free) which is not just a slogan. We had communists who were threatening the stability of our country, and Jews who infiltrated the heart of our financial system. We decided to act for the benefit of the German *Volk*. We are proud of the new Germany and all of you can bear witness to the miracle of our economic recovery. Yes, we take decisive action which some may find unpalatable, but this is for our people who have been exploited, robbed, and threatened for years. We have delegates on the ICRC (International Committee of the Red Cross) and have our own internal *Deutsches Rotes Kreuz* (German Red Cross or DRK) which is already ensuring that humane standards are achieved in our camps. This is rumour, *meine Herren*, malicious rumour, designed to discredit the Reich. We are setting up centres where these people can live in safety, enjoying better conditions than many others in our civilian population." He turned to Leland Harrison, "*Herr Ambassador*, I know we have had our differences, but is this not the reason that banking must rise above political or social considerations? Your own country and many others are benefitting from our sound economy. Business in both the United States and elsewhere have subsidiaries based in Germany from which there are huge commercial positives. Gold, gentlemen, gold is the answer, which has no identity or source other than a value upon which we can all agree, even with our adversaries. Gold is not a currency tied to country, or political doctrine, but guarantees security globally. Surely, we must embrace those areas which unite us, and leave the politicians to decide national direction."

The tall, commanding figure of John Foster Dulles spoke, "Ambassador Harrison, my friend Leland, raises a principle which I am sure many share. However, my brother and I have been involved at the centre of international politics for years engaged in the establishment of new institutions and international security measures after the turmoil following the Great War. We must maintain fiscal stability in the interests of international commerce. This war will assuredly end and our primary goal must be to ensure that businesses survive both within the country of the victor and in that of the vanquished. Let us place our differences to one side because, we are the guardians of the future of the world. Our task is critical, and one which must not depend on moral judgments, but on sound commercial principles which will avoid the chaos that would result if we failed to remain outside of the tragic conflict engulfing so many nations. I propose a toast, to global peace protected by financial security." They stood up, touching glasses to right and left, and, as they resumed their seats, the Master of Ceremonies announced that guests may now smoke. Within minutes, the air was filled with cigar smoke and an atmosphere of conviviality was enjoyed as they waited for Walther Funk to speak. He left the room to gather his papers and prepare for his speech.

Dulles signalled to Leland Harrison to join him, and moved to an alcove away from the table, with maroon velvet curtains gathered each side of the entrance. As Harrison joined him, they spoke in low voices. Dulles started, "For Christ's sake, Leland, don't rock the boat with these Nazi bastards. I have spoken to the president and it is more than likely we will join this war within a year, but we have to protect our commercial interests right now and, more importantly, after this Goddamn shindig is over. We got General Motors and Ford with plants in Germany right now, quite apart from our interests in oil which we are shipping to both sides, using ships of non-combatant nations. These guys got considerable influence on Capitol Hill, and we gotta be seen to be protecting their asses. The US is making money out of the Krauts, and we cannot afford to compromise that. We got investments in Sweden which are booming through iron-ore exports, but if that bunch of fanatics in Berlin get too hacked off with our attitude, they will cut ties, even the illicit ones. Hitler is one unprincipled son of a bitch, yet he is loyal to the core to one principle, and if he gets wind that we are posturing too much about the Jews, he will break off business links with the United States. Listen, we can make money out of this situation."

Harrison took a long draw on his cigar before exhaling in a sigh, "Darn it, Allen, we cannot ignore the persecution of these people. I have reports that they are systematically murdering them. Jews have had all their property seized, are prevented from working, and are being rounded up and put in camps that some are calling death camps. This is happening right now under our noses, and you are asking me to be complicit in a policy of appeasing these sons of bitches. Heck, we can't just do nothing."

Dulles put his hand on Harrison's shoulder, "Leland, I am not suggesting we do nothing; I am connected with the FBI, and we can work, covertly, to help the Jews. The president has plans to expand our foreign Intelligence service to prepare for entry into the war. We will not stand idly by but, Leland, remember the pain of the depression, mass unemployment, the Wall Street Crash, and the unprecedented poverty that overtook our nation in the Great Depression. We gotta be realistic and recognise the fiscal imperatives and that means doing business with those we may not like." He looked earnestly into the eyes of his old friend. "War is a tragedy, but this brings with it the greatest potential for economic growth in our history. The American people will have more opportunity to prosper than at any previous time whilst our businesses will expand massively. We have to recognise that sometimes realpolitik must over-ride our humanitarian ideals. This War will provide the biggest stimulus to our economy, and, from that, millions of Americans will benefit. I will ensure you receive help with the Jewish problem. However, we must publicly champion the need for our financial institutions to be free of political "concerns", whilst we can quietly assist with 'other issues' without speaking too openly about them."

The Master of Ceremonies announced that guests should return to their seats to listen to the speaker. A podium had been erected on a raised stage in the corner of the room, and then, the MC announced, "*Meine Herren,* please welcome the distinguished economist, international banker, former director of the Bank for International

Settlements, Reich minister for economic affairs and president of the Reichsbank, Herr Walther Funk." As one, all rose to applaud as Walther Funk appeared, from the side of the stage, bowing for a moment, before smiling and waving a hand in greeting. His large frame took up a position behind the podium, checking his bowtie set in a starched white shirtfront with an almost military gesture. As the guests sat, his shaven head was already covered with beads of perspiration, and although he did not cut an inspiring image, the interest from friend and foe alike was real. He uttered his opening words in a genial manner,

"Today the world is at war, but we meet in peace, as friends. As a gesture, the *Führer* has today ordered me to deliver you his personal assurance that he will protect the position, security, and standing of the Bank for International Settlements and, further, that the territory of Switzerland is inviolate. In stating this, he assures all that we may safely return to our headquarters in Basel."

He stopped speaking as there was a smattering of applause around the room accompanied by the odd cry of, "Hear, hear!"

"Well, gentlemen, what a pity the world is not run by bankers!" His remark drew some laughter. He raised his right hand, pointing a finger in the air to emphasise what followed. "Assuredly, as was said to me over dinner, this war will end and we must plan a post-war Europe which is united as never before, so that war is no longer an option. I have conceived a revolutionary plan for European unity which is led by financial considerations. If we become so completely unified not only through a political union, but a monetary union, it would be commercial suicide for any European nation to consider war, and that, *meine Herren,* is exactly what I propose." There were audible gasps of astonishment around the room. "Impossible, I hear your thoughts, but hear me out. Through our military and political consolidation, we have brought into the Reich, Austria, the Sudetenland, Czechoslovakia, France, the Netherlands, Belgium, Denmark, and Norway. Why should these countries not be absorbed into an economic and political union. My plan, which has the approval of our *Führer,* is to create the strongest monetary, fiscal, and political union in history." He slammed his fist down on the podium, and, at that moment, the room hung on his every word. He wiped sweat from his brow with a handkerchief. "We are burdened by petty bureaucracy, regulation, legal differences, and tariffs. These breed more bureaucracy, prevent growth, and stifle enterprise. That is the word which surely unites us in this room, enterprise! Enterprise which fuels our economies, and stimulates demand. Just imagine the abolition of all trade tariffs, de-regulation, free trade, a uniform legal framework, and monetary union. My vision is one where we achieve a single currency, and the creation of a true confederation of states in what I am calling, 'The European Union'." There was spontaneous applause and the deputy manager of the BIS, Emil Puhl, cried out an unrestrained, "*Heil Hitler!*". Funk held both hands up in a gesture of thanks, then continued, "We believe the Reichsmark will emerge from the war as the strongest currency. Initially, this may be adopted by the Greater German Reich as that of all the nations who are now *Reich Kommissariats* but we will commit ourselves to surrender this, in the interests of European Unity, in favour of a new European currency." Dulles leant across to McKittrick, whispering in his ear, "Dang it, these guys have gotten one hell of an idea, and despite my revulsion of the Nazis, I have to admire this one."

Funk now became more business-like, strident, and self-assured, "I can say that as result of countries being absorbed into the Grater German Reich, we can exert overwhelming influence over the policy of this bank. However, *meine Herren*, we wish to act in a spirit of cooperation and will not impose our will at this point. We wish all to agree that, until this war ends, gold will provide the security upon which financial exchanges may be made; gold, which carries no identity and frees our transactions from political or moral judgement. Financial integrity must be at the foundation of all our dealings. Today I place my plan here at the BIS demonstrating Germany's open commitment to peace and financial security for the future, guaranteeing incredible investment opportunities." There was more applause, but Montagu Norman turned to Otto Niemeyer, "Dash it all, old man, Winston is not going to like this; he is not going to like this one bit."

10

Arbeit Macht Frei

Monday 26th August 1940 11:00am
10, Downing Street, London

Sir Montagu Norman, clad in a long Victorian style light jacket, over a shirt with a winged collar and cravat, sporting a straw fedora worn at a jaunty angle, was certainly not in a light-hearted frame of mind. He had been abruptly summoned from the banking conference on a post-war economic strategy by Germany which appeared to give a commitment to the survival of the commercial interests from all combatant countries, some aspects of which, he grudgingly accepted, appeared to have merit. The conference had met on the Saturday morning, and broad agreement had been reached that confidential lists should be prepared of figures central to key businesses in each belligerent nation. These would then be shielded from any post-war action by the victors which may prejudice their position or their commercial interests. On both the German and British sides, secret guarantees were to be given, and the relevant business personnel informed, so that financial confidence could be maintained in the markets. At 12:30pm, he had been called to an urgent phone call from the British Embassy in Bern, and was connected with the Right

Honourable David Kelly, British minister to Switzerland (equivalent to Ambassador), who informed him that the Prime Minister required his attendance at Downing Street on Monday morning; he was advised that a vehicle had been despatched to collect him which would arrive within the hour. Norman found it damnably inconvenient, if not impertinent, that he should be summoned, at such short notice, and in such a manner, without even being given the courtesy of a reason why. "Dash it all, I am here in Switzerland; how the deuce does Winston expect me to be there? Does he not realise there is a war on?" His words were expressed in an exasperated voice to the minister who made it politely clear that this was not a mere request. Frankly, Norman was pretty tired after the banking dinner the night before and his involvement in the conference. Now he was being informed by the minister that he was to travel directly to London. Whilst Kelly's manner was urbane, Norman was left in no doubt that he had no choice in the matter and that he was to excuse himself from the conference immediately without giving the true reason. His cover-story was that he had to leave because his wife had taken ill. Arrangements had been made for him to travel to London that afternoon on an American Airlines *Douglas DC3*. This was assigned for US diplomatic travel which was immune to Swiss neutrality restrictions, and also safe from the possibility of German attack. His butler had scarcely time to pack, before a Cadillac limousine drew up outside the hotel bearing a stars and stripes pennant, which had whisked him off to the airport at Dübendorf, where he had boarded the aircraft, landing at Croydon airport at 8:00pm. He had then opted to stay two nights at the Savoy Hotel in central London where he knew he could relax in some comfort and receive good service.

He now paused, placing his briefcase on the ground, inserting a cigarette into a holder which was lit by his driver, as he faced the familiar panelled door of 10, Downing Street, before ascending the single step, passing between two policemen who saluted. He was met by Churchill's Principal Private Secretary, Eric Seal, dressed in a formal dark suit, with large lapels and a winged collar, who brusquely shook his hand. "He is not in the best frame of mind, Sir Montagu, I have to warn you; he has just been briefed that the Romanian monarchy is about to fall, and it looks like a new fascist dictatorship will be established." He led the way through the shiny black panelled door, with its ornate polished brass knocker and large number 10 set in the upper centre. As they proceeded, Norman felt a growing unease about what was to follow. He had already experienced a very uncomfortable meeting with Churchill, shortly after Churchill's appointment as Prime Minister in May of that year. He had smarted, after being quizzed about what the PM described as "collusion in Nazi plundering undertaken by the international financial sector", and that Norman himself might be described as "an architect in the construction of this unseemly Tower of Babel."

The Private Secretary led him through the entrance hall with its chequered floor, overshadowed by an ornate Victorian lantern, and antlers on the wall above a fireplace, down a long corridor into the ante-room outside the Cabinet Room. There, he was greeted by the familiar, tall, but slightly stooped figure of John Maynard Keynes. The two men knew each other well although Norman's outlook was more conservative on financial matters. He was concerned at the ambitious economic policies advocated by Keynes which he regarded as somewhat reckless; despite this, the two men had a healthy working respect for each other. Although Keynes had developed radical economic theories and had closely advised government on changes, Norman had a career based in the banking sector with traditional values. His natural leaning was towards the stabilising effect that gold reserves gave, whilst Keynes advocated a fiscal policy of borrowing, in order to stimulate growth, whilst retaining more political economic control.

"How are you, old boy?" Norman began, removing his fedora, and shaking Keyne's hand. "Tiresome business this; most inconvenient. Lord knows why Winston has summoned me to a meeting; have you any idea what the devil is going on?"

"Not a clue, I'm afraid old chap," came the reply from Keynes in his distinctive precise tone. He was dressed in a three-piece business suit with a tailored waistcoat, buttoned higher than the norm, just beneath his Old Etonian College tie. "My brief was merely to attend a meeting to consider wartime economic strategies and that I need not prepare for this. I confess, it does seem a little extraordinary. Only a decade ago, Churchill and I did not agree on much, but, I suspect, he enjoyed debating our differences."

At that moment, the door opened to the Cabinet room, and the familiar smiling figure of Brendan Bracken emerged. "Holy Mother, protect us," he spoke in an exaggerated Irish accent, "It's the men we trust with all the money, so all will be well." He shook their hands warmly, adding in a low voice. "Winston is in combative mood, so my advice is to do more listening than speaking."

He ushered them through the double doors, between two pillars to a long cloth covered table beyond. Churchill was standing, wearing a long dark jacket, a spotted bow-tie, and a matching lapelled waistcoat across which a gold watch-chain hung. He had a large cigar held in the side of his mouth. Also in the room was the head of SIS, also known as MI6, Stewart Menzies, the chancellor of the exchequer, Sir Kingsley Wood, and the home secretary, Sir John Anderson. The Prime Minister waived an acknowledgement to Norman and Keynes, grunting, "Pray, be seated." He removed the cigar from his mouth, and lent on the table, staring at each of them in turn, over half-moon glasses, then spoke authoritatively,

"Gentlemen, I have been briefed that Hitler, and his band of dastardly thugs, have concocted a monstrous plan to disrupt the heart of our economy." He banged his hand down on the table three times, adding gravity to the moment. "As Napoleon rightly concluded, *'the infectiousness of crime is like that of the plague'* and, like the plague, our nation has become infected or, one might say, invaded, not by Nazi jackboots, but by an economic blitzkrieg which has caught us napping. All over Britain, there are being relentlessly injected into our economy, counterfeit bank notes by fifth columnists, emanating from Hitler's Reich; notes of such quality, that even our experts are challenged in detecting them. The effects of this heinous attack on our financial foundations cannot be under-estimated and my instinct is that we must make an historic decision, upon which the constancy of the British Empire may rest, for, upon our stability, much of the civilised world relies. Indeed, the structures of our civilisation may be threatened, against which we must direct all our fiscal ingenuity or skulduggery which, doubtless, may be skills held by those in this room. We must not quake, nor shrink in the face of this assault, but counter this with a resolute and clear strategy which protects our nation, ensuring the future security of our economy which provides a foundation upon which we will re-build our future, when the tyranny of the Nazi regime is overthrown. We cannot afford the panic or a run on the banks which assuredly would follow if this became known, but neither must we hesitate in taking whatever steps are necessary in order that we can defend our island from this plague." He sat down, reaching for a table-lighter, before re-lighting his cigar and puffing thick clouds of smoke.

Maynard Keynes raised his hand, as if seeking permission, before speaking in high pitched tone, "If I may be permitted, gold, Prime Minister, in gold, Sir, may lie our salvation."

Churchill looked at him askance, "My belief, reinforced by the scars of your criticism of former policies which I espoused, was that you were opposed to the gold standard, Sir."

"Indeed, I am, Mr Churchill, as fiscal intervention by government linked to responsible borrowing, in order to invest in growth is the way forwards; this, Sir, provides the shield against inflationary pressures. However, if the stability of our currency is under threat, then gold is our salvation, if used as a weapon against the enemy."

The chancellor interjected, "In heaven's name man, how the deuce do you expect us to weaponise gold?"

"Elementary, my dear chap," responded Keynes with a touch of triumph in his voice, "the Germans use the international banking system for trading directly or indirectly with suppliers, many of whom are situated outside Germany. Much of their banking is carried out via Swiss banks, and, in particular, the Bank for International Settlements. Now, look here, as I understand it, they borrow from the bank, and use gold, much of which they have seized, as security, which the bank accesses and draws upon to repay the accumulating debt. Through the offices of our own Montagu Norman here, as governor of the Bank of England, and a director of the BIS, we can deposit British currency into the bank, which may be used to secure the Nazi loans, and then repay our exchequer, using their gold. This could easily be achieved with a little internal account wizardry. You know the sort of thing, robbing Peter to pay Paul and all that."

"Are you suggesting..." thundered Churchill, "that we finance the Nazi gangsters and their dastardly war machine? That is treason, Sir, I could not possibly even consider, nor condone, nor even be party to such an outrageous strategy wherein I might be judged a traitor to the empire."

"Indeed, Sir, and that is why I am suggesting that neither this meeting, nor those decisions that we reach, are minuted, and further, that all such activity is carried out covertly through the office of Stewart Menzies and the SIS. Clearly, it would be unseemly and dishonourable for a British Prime Minister and, moreover, a gentleman, to be involved in such matters."

Churchill's face changed from a determined scowl to a half smile and then, with a twinkle in his eye, as he rose from his seat, "By Jove," I am intrigued, if not utterly dismayed and appalled by such considerations; so much so, that my humour has improved, which will doubtless be assisted further by a glass of the finest Johnny Walker's Black Label whisky. Please do join me. I am minded to quote Thomas Jefferson, who, with some portent, penned the words, '*I believe that banking institutions are more dangerous to our liberties than standing armies.*'"

Tuesday 3rd September 1940 9:30am
SS-Schule Haus Wewelsburg, Schloss Wewelsburg, Büren, Westphalia

Some had arrived by air to the Luftwaffe base in Werl that morning, whilst others had opted to accept the *Reichsführer's* hospitality to stay the preceding night in the castle.

SS-Sturmbannführer Josef Spacil had been summoned the previous Friday by his commanding officer, *SS-Obergruppenführer* Oswald Pohl, who had informed him that they had been invited to a special conference by *Reichsführer* Heinrich Himmler to consider new economic and commercial initiatives based upon the Dachau model. Spacil had carried out a study of Germany's first labour camp at

Dachau earlier that year and had compiled a report on exploiting prisoner resources. He had put forward proposals to build a mutually beneficial partnership with business using the available low-cost labour provided by the prisoners.

Now, they were travelling in the rear of a large *Mercedes Pullman* limousine flanked by two motorcycles with armed outriders as escorts dressed in black SS uniforms which was unusual; the SS had more recently adopted to wear the field-grey uniforms matching the colour used by the *Wehrmacht*. Their driver informed them that black uniforms were issued to those assigned specifically to the *Reichsführer's* personal guards at Wewelsburg. Spacil and Pohl were both attached to the *SS-Wirtschafts-und Verwaltungshauptamtes* (SS Economic and Administration office) where Spacil's skills on finance matters had earned him rapid promotion plus the recognition and admiration of colleagues. He was an imposing man, well-built, with youthful features although he was in his early thirties. More recently, he had been posted to newly occupied Holland where he had been given command of the Security Police and the SD or Nazi Intelligence service. In this role, he was examining the optimum methods of maximising the financial return to the Reich from occupied territories. Liaising closely with Oswald Pohl, and at the request of Himmler, they filed confidential reports which were always labelled, *'Streng Geheim - Reichsführer Sache'* (Top Secret – Matter for the *Reichsführer*). These would be sent by special courier to Himmler and were not permitted to be read by anyone else. Pohl was a shorter, older man with receding greying hair, possessing a deceptive genial look, yet he had gained a fierce reputation for efficient organisational and administrative skills. He was utterly ruthless in his duties and never accepted failure, nor considered that anyone or anything should prevent the achievement of agreed objectives. Both men felt a sense of apprehension, and in Spacil's case, even nervousness, as Himmler was now perceived to be the most powerful man in the Reich, after Adolf Hitler. Most recognised that he held more authority than Rudolf Hess, the deputy *Führer*, and Hermann Göring, to whom Hitler had bestowed the title of *Reichsmarscall des Grossdeutschen Reiches* earlier in the year. The SS had become a massive military and security organisation with over 300,000 men and was expanding fast with the growing Reich combined with the demands of the war.

"I hope Uncle Heine is in a warm and jovial mood; perhaps, he will tell us a joke, *ja?*" Pohl remarked, and they both laughed, easing their apprehension. The *Reichsführer* was known for his uncompromising cold aloofness, rarely ever showing emotion, or even tolerating humour. On odd occasions, when he did smile, it was often more for show to suit the occasion than an expression of feeling.

"I think he should be dancing with joy at our outstanding record of *Arisiering, Alseidlung und Judenrein*" Spacil responded. (Aryanisation, re-settlement, and Jew cleansing)

"The problem is, Josef, what can we do with all these *Judensauen?* I am organising the building of camp after camp after camp."

"I think we may get some answers today, *Herr Obergruppenführer,* despite the *Reichsführer* never giving anything away before an important meeting, I have heard rumours that there are many leading industrialists and businessmen attending today. My headache at this point is to resolve how we extract the most revenue from the new countries being absorbed into the greater German Reich."

Himmler had made it clear that financial matters in the occupied territories needed to be overseen and guarded by the SS to avoid corruption. In addition, he had ordered that the systematic confiscation of all Jewish assets must be swiftly undertaken, and had emphasised that the seizure of any gold held in private possessions was the highest priority. Any gold realised from this process must be immediately transported back to the Reich. As the new territories were *Reichskommisariats,* all gold reserves were now designated assets of the Reich, although each occupied territory would govern its own economy.

As they approached the enormous Renaissance castle with its huge towers, flanking tall imposing walls in which were set lines of windows, Spacil, who had never been there previously exclaimed, "*Mein Gott,* it is utterly magnificent."

"*Jawohl,* Josef, and all financed and organised by my office," Pohl replied, with an expansive flourish of his arms. They stopped at a guardhouse by a barrier and the driver informed the guards of the identity of his passengers at which point they immediately raised their right arms stiffly. One checked his list, before announcing their arrival to the castle via a telephone. The guards were also in black SS uniforms, matching helmets, and red armbands with a swastika in a white circle. They were waived through towards an archway, where more guards stood either side, which they approached over a bridge spanning the moat beneath. As they entered a cobbled courtyard, a guard of honour stood outside the main entrance, and, after a command was shouted by an officer holding a sword, they snapped to attention, before presenting arms. At that moment, the car doors were held open by two further SS soldiers, and an officer stepped forwards, clicking his heels as his right arm shot out in the Nazi salute.

"*Heil Hitler, I am SS – Gruppenführer Karl Wolf. Willkommen auf Schloss Wewelsburg.* Please, follow me."

He led the way through two large timber doors, studded with iron, set in a stone archway flanked by two guards who jumped to attention as they passed; the noise of their boots stamping in unison reverberated around the courtyard. Wolf led the way down a long corridor with traditional iron lighting braces on the walls many of which were bare stonework, whilst some were rendered with white plaster. Heavy wooden doors were set in oak frames creating a traditional, historic appearance. There was much activity the with uniformed SS officers and men exiting and entering rooms as they were passing. The ceiling was low and vaulted and supported periodically by arches or thick stone columns. Spacil noted that the décor was simple and lacking in decorative elements that might be expected in such a large, magnificent building. As they walked, Wolf spoke, as if reading Spacil's thoughts, "The *Reichsführer's* orders were that this castle would represent the spartan spirit of the SS whilst capturing the Germanic traditions. The décor is sparse, symbolic of our single-minded dedication to the *Führer* and the Reich. The principles we adhere to are Teutonic in origin linking us to our great past and our cultural heritage. A research centre has been set up to examine historic links between National Socialism ideology and that of our ancestors. Here, we study genealogy, pre-history, ancient history and medieval history, examining how the purity of race ensured our Aryan superiority. Apart from a wonderful collection of paintings, you will see symbols around of Germanic culture and ancient runes, whilst our *Hakenkreuz* (swastika) is also integrated into the decoration." They descended some steps, then down a smaller walkway towards a large archway outside which two guards stood. Wolf stopped and turned to them, then glanced at his watch and spoke earnestly, "*Es ist Viertel vor zehn* (It is quarter to ten). As you will know, the *Reichsführer* is always precisely on time. As the hour strikes, he will enter. All other guests are assembled in the *Obergruppenführersaal* (General's Hall) of the North Tower where I will now take you. Please note that smoking is *verboten. Heil Hitler!*"

He opened the double arched doors and announced, "*Bitte, Mein Kameraden, Herr Obergruppenführer Oswald Pohl und, Herr Sturmbannführer Josef Spacil der SS-Wirtschafts-und Verwaltungshauptamtes"* Wolf stepped back, Spacil's eyes widened as he took in the scene. The circular hall had an air of spartan grandeur with twelve thick pillars supporting arches, beyond which were floor to ceiling windows with a vaulted roof above. These surrounded an open space where a long conference table was placed around which he noted the faces of some he knew. At one end of the hall two enormous banners were draped down the wall, one in black, bearing the SS symbol in the centre, the other in red, with a swastika set in a white circle. On the SS banner in gothic writing, the words, '*Meine Ehre heist Treue'* were displayed. Between them was a large portrait of Adolf Hitler, in a commanding pose, his hand on his hip, overlooking a rural backdrop. The walls and pillars were white reflecting the white and grey marble flooring, giving the room almost a sense of majesty. To the left of the conference table, inlaid in the floor was a darker marble with a circular array of symbols appearing to represent the sun.

The uniforms around the room were all SS, although there were also dark suited civilians present. The bulky familiar figure of Ernst Kaltenbrunner rose from the table, who raised his right arm stiffly in salute before walking to them, shaking each by the hand. He spoke in a jovial tone, "*Wilkommen, meine Freunde,* it is good to see you."

"Ernst, you old dog," responded Pohl, what is the *SS-Oberabschnitt Donau* (Austrian SS division) *Politzeiführer* doing here? Haven't you enough on your hands with *Gleichschaltung* (Nazification of people) in the Österreich after the *Anschluss*?"

Kaltenbrunner smiled broadly, the large scar which ran down his left cheek gave him a Machiavellian look, Spacil thought. He had met him before and found his detached bearing a little unsettling.

Kaltenbrunner cupped his hand to his mouth, as though sharing a confidence, "I have overseen construction of two concentration camps at Mauthausen and Gusen. You should take note of my ability in your economics office. I used the prisoners to make their own camps."

"*Arbeit Macht Frei!*" (work makes you free) interjected a voice, drawing laughter from around the table. The normally implacable face of Reinhard Heydrich broke into a broad grin as he added, "You know we have erected this sign above the gates of Dachau to give our guests a positive attitude when they arrive, ja?" Heydrich was well known to all present as the head of Gestapo and secret police in the *Reichssicherheitshauptamt* with a reputation for uncompromising efficiency and callousness. There was more laughter as another added, whom Spacil and Pohl both recognised as *SS-Oberführer* Rudolf Höss, the recently appointed commandant of Auschwitz, "*Jawohl*, I have had the same sign erected over my camp gates, made by the inmates at no cost; this is wonderful prisoner economics."

Kaltenbrunner guided Pohl and Spacil to seats he had reserved for them near the head of the table, gesturing to a man sitting to his right, "I am not sure if you know SS-*Obersturmbannführer* Adolf Eichman, the director of *Räumungsangelegenheiten,* our eviction department dealing with the Jewish question, helping us deport and cleanse the Reich of *Juden.*" Eichman stood up straight, clicked his heels, and bowed stiffly.

At that moment, the door opened and Karl Wolf entered; he stood to attention, as he raised his arm, "*Heil Hitler, meine Herren; der Reichsführer!*" He stepped back and all stood as Heinrich Himmler entered, pausing briefly to give the Nazi salute, saying in a cold, yet high pitched voice, "*Heil!*" Every right arm in the room was extended in response as Himmler purposefully strode to the head of the table, carrying a folder. He was dressed in a field-grey uniform with silver braided shoulder boards and collar badges of oak leaves surrounded by laurel set in black squares. His tie-pin displayed SS runes; above his top left pocket was a thin medal ribbon; a thick belt was fastened around his military tunic at the waist below which he was wearing jodhpurs and shining jackboots. His mid brown hair was shorn high on his head, and his face, with a barely perceptible thin moustache, was expressionless. His cold staring grey eyes, behind his signature round wire-framed spectacles, surveyed the room looking at each person in turn. There was utter silence as his presence exuded authority and inspired fear in equal measure. *"Bitte, hinsetzen."* (Please, sit) It was a command given by a man whose orders were never questioned. He passed his folder to Wolf, who extracted a sheaf of papers, selecting one, which he handed to the *Reichsführer* who glanced downwards before taking his seat.

His voice was almost a monotone, yet the words were pronounced with a preciseness on each syllable which held the rapt attention of everyone present. *"Meine Kameraden von der SS,* most of you will know each other and I shall not waste time with introductions. However, I will name our civilian guests, starting on my left, in turn, and as I do so, please raise your hand. You will know, of course, Walther Funk, our *Reichsminister* of Economics and president of the Reichsbank."

Funk's arm shot out as he curtly blurted, *"Heil Hitler"*.

Himmler's face showed a moment's annoyance at the interruption as he continued, "Vice President of the Reichsbank, Emil Puhl, Paul Hechler, the assistant manager of the Bank for International Settlements based in Switzerland, and Wilhelm Keppler, the secretary of state at the Foreign Office responsible for confiscated industries. Next to them are the following senior executives: Herman Schmitz of Bayer Pharmaceutica and IG Farben, Gunther Quandt from Varta and

AFA, Ferdinand Porche of Volkswagon, Hugo Boss of Hugo Boss AG, Carl Thalmann of Kodak, Friedrich Flick of the Flick corporation and Mercedes Benz, and Alfred Krupp of the Krupp organisation. Some of these men have also been appointed *Wehrwirtschaftsführer* (military economy leaders) but..." he paused, adding emphasis and drama to the words that followed, "three of these men are directors of the Bank for International Settlements in Basel, and Herr Funk is a former director. Your role, after today, is critical to the future of the Reich. We are all here with three matters to resolve; the first is the Jewish Question, the second is the exploitation of the economic benefits of our concentration camp system, and the third is the need to increase our gold reserves. I have been greatly assisted in finding a solution to all three areas from the valuable briefings given to me by *Obergruppenführer* Oswald Pohl *und Sturmbannführer* Josef Spacil. Please, stand!" He looked directly at Pohl and Spacil who sprang to their feet, their right arms stretched out in unison. Himmler flashed a brief smile, as he applauded them, immediately joined by the others around the table, ceasing as Himmler raised his hand in a gesture that he was continuing.

"We have acted with considerable humanitarian restraint and patience in dealing with the Jews. This will now cease!" He slammed his fist on the table to emphasise the point. The room was still and there was a sense of cold tension. "I am dedicated to the Reich and I have the strength to carry out whatever policy is necessary or execute any measures, with one sole purpose; to eradicate the Jewish contamination once and for all. Now is the time to act." He nodded to Wolf who handed him another set of papers which the *Reichsführer* briefly studied, then looking to right and left down the table, he stared at each of them in turn. Spacil felt real fear as Himmler's eyes fixed upon him for a moment, recognising that this man had absolute power to decide whether any of them lived or died.

"All three of the matters I have described are linked to the Jewish question. First, we asked that the Jews emigrate, but too few did so, and this policy failed. We confiscated their assets, but still they would not go. So, we assisted in their removal to Jewish areas but this operation, organised by *Obersturmbannführer* Adolf Eichman, has been slow and inefficient. The Jews have prospered at the expense of the German *Volk* so, now it is time for them to work for the benefit of the Reich. Why should the Jew not contribute if they remain here? This, *meine Kameraden* from the economics and banking areas, is my kind of economics. If we add the Jews to the available low-cost workforce available to business in the concentration camps, that would increase availability of a valuable resource, would it not *meine Geschäftskollegen?*" (my business colleagues) Himmler looked up at the dark suited men lining the table to his left, with a hint of a wry smile, and was met with a chorus of enthusiastic affirmations, with heads nodding and "*Jawohl, mein Reichsführer...das ist Genial!*" (this is genius) from Friedrich Flick.

Himmler nodded in response, then in a menacing, uncompromising tone, "All businesses loyal to the Reich will prosper through exploiting prisoner resources and, where appropriate, set up manufacturing or industrial facilities near camps where the labour will be readily available. In this way, your profits will grow and you may impose long hours in order to increase productivity. In my view, if these people are worked to death, you are doing the Reich a great service. Our policy has been weak, and, in that, we are failing in our duty to the *Führer*. We will now execute a new plan; we will round up all Jews and remove them to the camps or to ghettos which will be sealed off to outsiders. At present, we have only 50,000 prisoners in our camps. Within six months, we will increase this to 200,000, and then double this figure within the year. The capacity of Dachau and Auschwitz will be massively increased, with new camps added bearing the same name, whilst prisoners will be used in the construction of more camps across the Reich. However, I want more efficiency, and to that end, we will introduce accommodation economies which means increasing the number of inmates per square metre in their quarters. Jews will be available to your factories at a low cost, which I will reduce further for any payments made in gold. On that subject, any gold remaining in Jewish possession or held in any bank is to be seized and appropriated to the Reich and, a large proportion, as I direct, will be deposited with the Bank for International Settlements to accounts which only I shall designate."

He turned to Wolf, "*Bitte.*" Wolf extracted the next document from the pile, passing it to Himmler, who briefly scanned it before looking down the line of SS Officers to his right. "Our historic mission is to cleanse the Reich through *Arisierung*, and members of the SS must rise up to this noble challenge, evoking the historic deeds of the Teutonic Knights. Our sacred duty must be to enforce this bold and historic policy and my personal orders are to massively increase our efforts in this monumental purpose. The SS is tasked with arresting those who are Jews, Gypsies, sexual deviants, homosexuals, criminals, those with unacceptable religious beliefs, or anyone who opposes National Socialism, or might be viewed as a threat to the Reich. If anyone resists arrest, or does not cooperate, they are to be immediately executed. Future generations will thank us for creating our Germanic master-race free from the filth of contamination. You will all receive a summary briefing of this meeting from *SS – Gruppenführer Wolf,* with my detailed directives before you leave. My orders will be acted upon immediately, *Heil Hitler!*" He stood and all those in the room did likewise, their arms extended, as Himmler walked out, followed by Wolf.

The youthful faced commandant of Dachau, Alexander Piorkowski, whom Spacil knew well, remarked dryly, "There will be many thousands of Jews, I think, who will come to realise that *Arbeit Macht Frei.*" Ripples of laughter filled the room releasing the pent-up tension.

11

Pandora's Box

Monday 8th January 2024 9:30am
Rumfordschlössl, Englischer Garten, Munich

Karl had arrived early for their 10:00am meeting, and was walking slowly around the ornate colonnaded frontage of the 17th century building as though admiring it, but his trained eyes were darting all around, especially in the bordering shrubs. It was bitterly cold and he wore a *Bundeswehr* issue Ushanka style hat, underneath which he had a scarf pulled across his face, the purpose of which was more to conceal his identity than to shield against the wintry conditions. His military coat collar and lapels were also drawn up, his left hand clutching a thick square cornered briefcase, whist his right hand was buried in his pocket gripped around the handle of his *HK P30* handgun. After satisfying himself that there was no one watching the building, and that the few people walking nearby appeared to be tourists or those taking a leisurely morning stroll, he ascended the steps of the Rumfordschlössl and entered, feeling the welcome warmth within. He approached the reception, flashing his BND identity card for the first time, receiving a cursory nod in response. After asking the receptionist whether there was a private room available, he was shown into a small study used for student seminars, whereupon he sent a text message informing his visitor of his location. As he waited, he checked the sash window opening, then looked out over the trees and the large grassy areas beyond, evoking memories of the time he had spent with his father in recent weeks. He sighed, barely able to take in the enormity of the situation in which he now felt heavily involved, and the speed with which events had unfolded. His father's death was almost overshadowed by the extraordinary revelations he had been made aware of, all of which had been exacerbated the previous day with the discoveries he had made when he had examined the contents of his father's box.

He had awoken early and made himself a coffee, then, switching out the lights, he had peered through the curtains at the short drive leading to the front entrance to the apartments and the underground garage beneath. There was a police vehicle parked to the left of the garage entrance, and an unmarked car on the restricted roadway which bordered the river Isar beyond. He reached for his binoculars, and scanned the vehicle, clearly making out two figures sat inside whom he assumed were part of the security detail guarding the premises, parked there to enable a swift response, or pursuit, in the event of an incident. He had received training in exactly such tactics within the *Kommando Spezialkräfte* as part of military urban counter-terrorism measures. *'At least Colonel Kaufmann has been as good as his word,'* he thought, although he recognised he was in the unenviable position where he could trust no one, as his father had stressed in his final letter to him. He looked across at the mid-brown box with the reinforced black iron corners, reminiscent of some medieval money chest, with its large lock centred to the front securing a hinged hasp which, unusually, had a loop which was fastened by a lock housed inside the structure. He felt as though he was being drawn to it again, yet wanted to resist for fear of what more he may discover within. He looked more closely at the box noticing a faded label on the side. The writing was barely legible but, as he looked, his eyes widened as the words became clearer, written in German gothic script, *'Reichsbank – Goldbarren – VVF'*, underneath which was a barely legible Nazi stamp of an eagle and swastika. *'VVF...VVF; where have I heard this?'* He almost spoke the words as he clutched at his thoughts, which had absorbed so much in recent days, then he did speak, pronouncing each syllable in a gasp of realisation, "*Versteckte Vermögensfonds!*" He was in possession of a container that had been used to contain assets of the Third Reich. Then with a resigned, "*Ach*, so, it can only get worse...," he had reached over to pull the box to him, retrieving the key from his jacket pocket. He felt a sense of trepidation, tinged with undeniable excitement that he was on the edge of something extraordinary, yet foreboding. He let the lid fall back on its restraining chain, peering inside and examining sections which were marked with tabs containing headings. His eyes were drawn to one containing the words, *'Reichslager-Arbeitsressource'* (Camp work resource) extracting a beige file, the edges browning with age, which had typed across it the words, *Die Wehrwirtschaftsführer Umsetzung des Reichslager-Arbeitsressourcenprogramms* (Military Economy leaders implementation of the Reich Camp Labour Resource Programme), underneath which was the eagle stamp and bold letters displaying the date 04.FEB.1942; the words surrounding the circular stamp were: *SS-Wirtschafts-und Verwaltungshauptamtes*. Karl opened the file, almost warily, knowing that this contained information his father wanted to reveal to him.

Inside were a number of A4 sheets of yellowing paper, stapled together, fronted by a sheet which, once again, bore the Eagle and Swastika logo, underneath which in stark gothic lettering, was one word: *Zwangsvirtschaft* (Compulsion economy). On the page beneath, there was a neat tabulated table, typed in landscape, and his eyes widened as he took in the significance of what he was seeing, shaking his head, and sighing deeply. On the left were names of businesses, contact names, and their position. The next column had a single heading of *'Zwangsarbeiter'* (Slave labourers), divided into sub-categories which were headed: *Militärinternierte* (Military internees/POW's), *Zivilarbeiter* (Civilian workers), *Ostarbeiter* (Eastern workers) and the last category, *Juden*. However, it was the fifth column which made him take a sharp intake of breath. *'Hinrichtungen und Sondermassnahmen Autorisiert'*. (Executions and special measures authorised). The final heading was *Anwesenheit im Konzentrationslager* (Presence in Concentration Camp). Beneath the headings were ticks confirming the category of workers used by each business, but it was the well-known names that profoundly shocked him, together with the realisation that they had knowingly used slave labour. Co-operation was one thing, but this, this was collaboration in the exploitation of those incarcerated in concentration camps. He decided to compile a list on his tablet, condensing the names listed to businesses that he recognised. There seemed no reason to do this but he recalled his father's words in his last letter to him, '...*It is my final wish that you learn about the elements of my work that have caused me the most disquiet and with which I have failed to come to terms. What you do with this is a matter for your conscience.*' He had a sick feeling as he typed the names, pausing every now and then to check via Google, a present-day, better-known identity, annotating this against the original:

Altana – Originally part of AFA

Kodak AG

Siemans AG

IG Farben incorporating Bayer and BASF

Fordwerke (A subsidiary of Ford Motor Company)

Flick KG (Run by Friedrich Flick; became one of Germany's richest men after the war, and a major shareholder of Daimler-Benz)

Daimler

Friedrich Krupp AG, later ThyssenKrupp

Bosch

Adam Opel AG – A subsidiary of General Motors

Volkswagon

Messerschmitt AG (Now part of Airbus)

Hugo Boss

AEG

Accumulatoren-Fabrik Aktiengesellschaft (AFA) incorporating Varta

Auto-Union AG (Now Audi)

BMW – Originally part of AFA

Zeiss

DAPG – A subsidiary of Standard Oil

Dornier

MAGGI – (Part of Nestlé)

Mercedes

Porsche

Rheinmetall

Shell (Germany)

Telefunken

Wintershall now Wintershall DEA

Most of the listed businesses had a tick beneath the *'Hinrichtungen und Sondermassnahmen Autorisiert',* indicating that their factories could chillingly execute slave workers. He shook his head in disbelief at the barbarity that had become institutionalised under the Nazi regime, evoking further words from his father's letter, *'The heritage of some of our leading businesses is tainted with their involvement in the one of the greatest horrors of recent history.'*

He placed the file on the table next to him and reached back into the box, retrieving a greetings card, on which a note was clipped from his father, *'Liberated from BIS files; note sender and recipient! See file for sender.'* On the front were the words in decorative script, *'Ein deutsches Neujahr der Gemeinsamkeit mit der IG Farben"* (A German New Year of togetherness with IG Farben) The card was edged with blue corn flowers, white ribbon, and pine branches. Below this was a factory building from which a red fluttering Nazi swastika flag flew, under which were depicted smiling faces of workers, and the words. *'Beste Wünsche'*. He opened the card, his heart quickening as he read, *'To Herr McKittrick and my wonderful friends,*

For their friendly greetings for Christmas and the New Year, and for their good wishes for my 60th birthday, I am expressing my sincere thanks. In response, I am sending you my heartfelt wishes for a prosperous year for the Bank for International Settlements.

Viele Grüsse,

Hermann Schmitz – Geschäftsführer

Karl recognised the name of the company from the previous lists of those employing slave labour, and he glanced back at the original table seeing the ominous words, *Hinrichtungen und Sondermassnahmen Autorisiert* ticked. His mind was reeling as he thought, *'Mein Gott, the mindblowing hypocrisy of these people, putting workers with cheerful expressions on a card, when executions were permitted of slave labourers!'* He peered into the box which had a spring-loaded mount holding certain files together at one end in alphabetical order, typical of his father's thoroughness. He found a file on Hermann

Schmitz almost immediately, which he spread open on the table; inside was a summary sheet with the photograph of a well-presented man in a suit, swept back grey hair, with a neat, trimmed beard, and a self-assured expression. Karl scanned the summary:

Name: Hermann Schmitz

Date of birth: 1st January 1881

Place of Birth: Essen

Education: Nuremberg Commerce College

Studies: Engineering and Metallurgy

Career: Industrial production for Metallurgische Gesellschaft – advisor at Board level until 1914

1914: Enrolled for service in the Great War

1915: After sustaining wounds, appointed Reich Commissioner for Materials in War Dept

1919: Took part in Versailles Treaty negotiations on nitrates production matters

1919: Joined BASF, appointed to Board and then as CFO, on the creation of IG Farben, in 1925

1927: Joined Nazi Party

1933: Elected to Reichstag for NSDAP

1935: Became CEO of IG Farben

1938: Appointed Wehrwirtschaftsführer by Adolf Hitler

1939: Appointed director of the Bank for International Settlements

1941 IG Farben factory established at Auschwitz

1948: Convicted of war crimes and Crimes against Humanity and receives four-year sentence

1950: Released from prison and appointed to supervisory board of Deutsche Bank in Berlin and honorary chairman of Rheinische Stahlwerke AG

Date of Death: October 8th 1960 in Heidelberg

Karl was shaking his head with incredulity, gasping as he read that Schmitz had been appointed to the Deutsche Bank. On a separate sheet was the simple heading, *War Crimes and Collusion* committed by IG Farben. There were listed brief details under sub-headings which included:

Medical Experiments on Prisoners
Terrorisation, Torture and Murder
Prisoner Executions and Shootings
Inhumane Treatment and Beatings
Exploitation of Slave Labour
Involvement in Extermination through Labour Programme
Involvement in Mass Extermination through supply of Zyklon B for Gas Chambers

A buff folder had written on it, *Vernichtung durch Arbeit* (Extermination through Labour) With some trepidation, he opened it to reveal a briefing paper, browning with age, on top of which was the eagle and swastika logo. The heading was Natural Selection and Work within the Concentration Camps. The briefing was concise and addressed to all Camp Commandants. It began by confirming that it had been drafted in accordance with the orders given by *Reichsführer Himmler* on 3rd September 1940. The document specified that increasing numbers of prisoners or assets would be transferred to the camps as a result of Aryanisation of occupied territories and within the Greater Reich. This would lead to an influx of Jews who had failed to emigrate or re-settle, and who would, therefore, be required to contribute through work. Karl's eyes were drawn to one section, *"The Jews must not be given special treatment and Commandants must ensure maximum efficiency through work performance. There will be no minimum hours, with breaks permitted for eating purposes only. The arduous nature of the work will, by natural selection, lead to a reduction in those fit enough to continue working. The rest are of no value to the production requirements of the Reich, and may be dealt with appropriately. All those given the special status in the business economy of Wehrwirtschaftsführer will ensure that businesses maximise the release of this new asset.'*

The document was signed by *SS – Gruppenführer* Reinhard Heydrich, displaying the title; *Chef der Sicherheitspolizei und des SD*.

As he read, Karl felt physically sickened, despite a long military career in which he had been directly involved in combat missions and exposed to the brutality of warfare. He recognised the euphemism in the language which was still employed by the military of today, masking the graphic, and less socially acceptable nature of some assignments. He began to appreciate the disillusion his father had felt, and how deep-rooted the links were between those involved in war crimes and those within the commercial, banking, and financial sector. He replaced the file, reaching for that of Thomas McKittrick.

As he read the notes on McKittrick's appointment and role as president and effective controller of the BIS during the Second World War, he became both engrossed and shocked at the same time. Here was an American who was clearly involved in covering up the activities of the bank using the cloak that it was 'above politics', even after the entry of the United States into the war in December 1941. This political 'even handedness' seemed to be the justification for collaboration with the Nazi regime, and the disposal of its plundered assets. In his file were a number of notes recording decisions and meetings, but one particular paper caught his attention, and as he read the contents, he felt a deep anger at the level of complicity by what were meant to be trusted institutions. There were not only links to the Holocaust, but direct involvement in the laundering of Nazi Germany's assets, turning a blind eye to the source. The document was short and factual:

Minutes of BIS Meeting
Subject: German Shareholding in BIS and Voting Rights
24.04.1941

In attendance:

Thomas McKittrick (Chair)
Sir Otto Niemeyer
Paul Hechler
Emil Puhl
Sir Montagu Norman
Hermann Schmitz
Rafaeli Pilotti
Per Jacobsson
Ernst Weber

1. *The Chair convened the meeting summarising that he had excluded attendance from representatives of countries no longer having government autonomy. Those in attendance were all functionaries of the BIS, thereby protecting the independence of the bank and the integrity of any decisions taken by and in the best interests of the bank*

2. *The Chair announced that a submission had been made by representatives of Germany that, as the Greater German Reich had acquired the assets and exchequers of former countries which were now Reichskommissariate, the voting rights of such territories should pass to Germany.*

3. *Emil Puhl presented the case to the meeting summarising that Germany now occupied countries presently or formerly known as Poland, Belgium, Denmark, Luxembourg, Greece, Norway, Yugoslavia, Netherlands, Czechoslovakia, and France, notwithstanding their current military campaign in*

the Soviet Union and elsewhere. His country's claim was based upon the rightful ownership of assets of any territory wherein fiscal and legal governance are the criteria for international recognition of sovereignty.

4. *This proposal was seconded by Paul Hechler and support vocalised by both Hermann Schmitz and Rafaeli Pilotti.*

5. *Sir Montagu Norman raised an objection on principle that his government did not recognise the 'occupied territories' as part of the German Reich but as independent sovereign nations who had suffered military conquest; a matter over which a state of war existed between Great Britan and Germany. His objection was seconded by Sir Otto Niemeyer*

6. *Ernst Weber appealed to the Chair that the bank must remain above politics in all matters and that it was not the place of the bank to pass any judgement over, nor interfere in, the matters of any nation or customer of the bank. He stated it was imperative that such principles were adhered to absolutely to protect the Bank's international standing and global integrity. He held up the policy of Switzerland as an example of strict neutrality wherein no country would be favoured over another, and that the BIS represented such values leading other banks in Switzerland by the example set. His appeal was seconded by Per Jacobsson.*

7. *A vote was taken on the issue and the motion to allow Germany to exercise voting rights on behalf of countries now forming part of the Greater German Reich was passed by six votes to two with the abstention of the Chair.*

8. *The Chair summarised the position confirming that Germany could assume such rights with immediate effect and further confirming that Germany now controlled 64.7%*

of the voting stock. There being no further business, the meeting concluded.

Karl grunted and sighed as he replaced the document, reaching for a smaller box on which was written the word *"Verschiedenes"* (miscellaneous) He opened it to reveal a number of photographs and cuttings. The first one he picked up was a high-quality colour image with a note paperclipped to the top stating, *'Presented to Papa by Martin Bormann in 1949'*. It showed two men in SS uniform, one with his hand on the shoulder of the other who he recognised as his grandfather. The other was taller, broader, with a handsome face and a neatly trimmed moustache, although he had a long scar running down his left cheek; he had a wide, almost mischievous smile on his face; behind them, were mountain peaks. He turned the picture over and on the reverse was written, *'Wir hatten Erfolg. Es lebe hoch VVF! – Heil Hitler - Verborgene Erinnerungen – Otto S'* (We succeeded. Long live VVF – hidden memories) Underneath was printed *'Taken 08.05.1945 – Schloss Fischhorn.* Below this was written: *Presented: Alvear Palace Hotel, Buenos Aires 26.02.1949.'* Karl studied the words, ruefully reflecting that the 'hidden memories' was a clear reference to their mission at that time to hide the fortune they had removed from the Reichsbank. He jotted into his tablet more areas he wanted to explore and tapped out the name Otto S, deciding to try and establish his identity. He was not even sure why nor in which direction he wanted to take what he was discovering, but his military training in intelligence was to gather all the information, condensing this into a briefing containing essential elements. He took a call from Inge at 11:00am whom he had briefly spoken to the night before, informing her he had been attacked. He had said he could not say too much, which she had heard often in the five years she had known him. She knew he was attached to units operating on highly covert operations and had come to recognise that she could not probe too much, nor would he respond if she tried. However, she had now called him back, and, on hearing that he was in his apartment, she had insisted on coming over to make him lunch, despite his protestations. On this occasion, Inge, who was very strong willed, was not going to take no for an answer.

He decided to have a cursory look at a few other items, but resolved to begin compiling a 'brief' which would also provide a useful reference point for him in order to piece together the growing fragments of evidence from a turbulent past. He pulled out a thick accounting record book which had a title on the front, *'Transaktions Aufzeichnung des VVF 1945 -1947'* (Transaction Record of the *VVF*) He briefly glanced through the pages noting payments logged, summarising the administration of the funds. Of particular interest were entries headed 'gold shipments' but it was the destination of these which caught his attention. He flicked through the entries for 1945, noting that each had a different paying in name, presumably allocated, he thought, to mask the source of the bullion. The names of the payees jumped out at him, almost mocking in their complicity, which read like a who's who in the banking and finance sector. However, it was the value of the deposits which he found incredible. Throughout the period until 1947, deposits had been made at the Bank for International Settlements, Stockholm's Enskilda Bank, the Swiss Bank Corporation, Credit Suisse, the Vatican Bank, the Swedish National Bank, the Bank of England, JP Morgan, Chase National Bank, the Bank of Spain, and even the Bank of the Argentine Nation, together with other secure vaults across Europe. His eyes were drawn to the first transaction which noted a deposit in gold made at the BIS on 10th May 1945 in the sum of $25,000,000 – Authorised by: Otto Skorzeny with the Account Identity: *VVF* AG. He looked back at the notes he was taking and referenced the coloured photograph from May 1945 of his grandfather with another SS officer, and wondered whether Skorzeny was the same person. Looking at a valuation comparison of 2024 against 1945, he gasped when the table showed the gold deposited was worth around six billion US dollars in current values. There were entries headed United States Families, but then it dawned on him to what these referred. The names triggered memories, The Gambino, the Genovese and the Lucchese; some had an annotation in brackets of *'Meyer Lansky,'* a name which he made a mental note to check. His mind was in shock as he took in the implications of what he was discovering. *'As if there is not enough to take in, I now find this links to the Mafia! What am I getting involved in?'* Other entries were headed USA which, he realised, as it was referred to lower down in brackets, was an abbreviation for US Army. He decided that he needed to break off; there was already so much, too much, to take in. As he wandered into the kitchen area to make himself a coffee, he felt a need to translate what he had learned, into action, but what? At least, he had a start point with the meeting he had arranged. Reaching for his remote, he pointed it at a cabinet, and moments later the music of Johann Strauss began playing softly and he sat back on a comfortable armchair, trying to relax his mind as the melodic tones of 'the Blue Danube' filled the room. However, he could not resist returning to his desk to pick up the smaller box again, labelled *'Verschiedene.'* His more relaxed composure changed as he took out a series of photographs clipped together with notes attached from his father.

The first showed a blonde-haired man, dressed in a smart suit, smiling broadly as a uniformed Adolf Hitler was placing a medal over his shoulders, surrounded by others including one he recognised as Josef Goebbels. His father had written, *'Jacob Wallenberg, the CEO of*

Enskilda Bank, being awarded the Grand Cross of Verdienstorden vom Deutschen Adler (the Order of Merit of the German Eagle) – *July 1941. He sat on the Board of the Nobel Foundation, was a recipient, amongst many other honours, of the Legion D'honeur, a director of numerous global companies, including Skandia, and in the 1950's and 1960's was one of the world's most influential businessmen.'*

The second was mounted on a card, as if it had been once in a frame, and showed a thinner man, surrounded by the press, also being given a medal. The card read, *'Henry Ford, the first US citizen to receive the Order of the German Eagle, being presented at a ceremony to mark his 75th birthday in Dearborn, Michigan, by Karl Kapp, the German consul in Cleveland, and Fritz Heller, German consular representative in Detroit, on the orders of Adolf Hitler.'* The hand-written note with it stated, *'Ford Motors had secret meetings, after Pearl Harbor, with their German management. Slave labour was used within their German production plants. They were the second largest manufacturer of trucks for the German military in WWII. Payments were made to the regime, by Ford, using gold transfers. Senior managers at the German wartime plants were re-instated after the war.'*

Karl gasped, yet again, as his incredulity mixed with waves of anger at the sheer global hypocrisy of the commercial world in wartime. The next photograph was dated 9th June 1938, and showed James Mooney, the president of General Motors Overseas, receiving a similar medal. The citation by order of Adolf Hitler stated, *'For distinguished service to the Reich'*, this time being presented by Hans-Heinrich Dieckhoff, German Ambassador to the United States, at the Waldorf Astoria Hotel, New York. His father had written, *"Mooney visited Germany frequently, holding meetings with senior Nazis after the outbreak of war in Europe. GM was the largest supplier of military trucks to the regime. During the war years, extensive use of prisoner labour and slave labour was made by GM and their subsidiary Opel."* A second photograph was of Mooney shaking hands with Hitler, whilst a beaming Hermann Göring, in a flamboyant uniform complete with a sash, looked on. However, it was the date which caught his eye:- April 1940.

His intercom buzzed and it was the security concierge, stating that officers had stopped an Inge Rauff, who had taken exception to being prevented from entering. Karl smiled, as he confirmed she could have access; Inge had a reputation for being a forceful character who never 'suffered fools gladly', a trait that had drawn her to him when they first met. They mutually recognised the strength of their respective personalities which, in her case, had prevented her from ever forming a serious long-term relationship until she met Karl. If a man could not stand up to her, or, in a contradiction which she understood, respect her forceful personality, she soon lost interest. That said, she had a gentle inner side which she rarely, if ever, exposed; a defence she had learned as a child, concealing a sensitive nature, which others took for weakness. The resilience in her nature had been of great benefit during her years as a front-line officer with the *Bundespolizei*. Even though they did not live together, they had built a close relationship which, if anything, was stronger, they both felt, for the independence they enjoyed. The times they did spend together were special, intimate, in which both could let the barriers down, relishing the closeness between them. As the door chime sounded and he pressed the electronic access remote to let her in, he pushed the photographs back in the box, with a final shake of the head and decided to examine it further at a later time.

As she entered, he smiled at her characteristic failure to show initial affection or concern for what he had been through; strangely a trait he found quite attractive. Her mood had not been enhanced by being prevented from entering.

"*Scheisse, schatzi,* why didn't you let me know the *bullen* were going to be here. The *Schweine* started trying to cross-examine me. Some bullshit about membership of GVR; how much did I know, and did I know you might be involved? Never heard of that one. Is it some new kind of terrorist group?"

Karl was standing, his arms open, although his ears had pricked up as she had spoken; clearly the ebullient *Oberst* Kaufmann was fishing for more information on him. Inge was, as always, dressed immaculately in a long cream coat over matching boots, her blonde hair worn down, with one side almost covering her eye, giving her a coquettish, exquisite look.

He said nothing, as she paused for a moment, then suddenly aware of her impulsiveness, she threw her bag on the sofa and ran to him, placing her arms around him, her deep blue eyes betraying her emotion. "Oh *mein Gott, schatzi,* what is happening? Are you alright? Why have you been attacked? Here in Munich, for Christ's sake!"

He kissed her, an intimate long kiss, to which she responded; normally such passion was expressed in their lovemaking, yet she sensed his need to be close.

"Oh, *meine* Inge, you would not believe what I am uncovering. I so need to share this with somebody. How could so many people be involved in such evil? You know, I have spent my life in dangerous situations, but never had to analyse as I am doing now; and this time, it is different because my family are deeply implicated."

He was displaying emotion that he rarely showed, as dark shadows over all he had run from or hated about his background, his family heritage, were now exposed brutally to him.

"Who Karl, who?" The tone in her voice displayed a desperation. He had rarely shared with Inge his shame and anger at what he knew about his family; he rarely shared it with anyone, finding that dedicating himself to army life, discipline, and order provided him with security and certainty.

They sat down together, and she held his hand as he briefly summarised what his father had shared with him, and the documents he had left. "The Nazis, they have not gone away, but are stronger than ever. My mother and my grandmother still believe in them; even my sister, Gretchen, does not condemn them. Inge, they are everywhere. You have no idea of the enormity of this; it is almost overwhelming, but Inge, I have to act, I need to act, for the sake of all those people who suffered. I am going to piece all the evidence I have uncovered and publish it. There was a huge fortune in gold and valuables and no one knows where it all went. I want to do this. Oh *Gott*, the way these people were treated." His words were breaking with emotion in a way she had never seen before. He then unburdened all that had taken place, glad of the ability to share what was almost unbearable, yet real, emphasised by the evidence, as he showed her some of the papers. They had a snack of *Kartoffelsalat* (potato-salad) with Mosel wine, after which they viewed the documents and photographs together, and she listened, horrified by what he told her.

Later, she prepared them an evening meal of beef broth, followed by *Abendbrot* consisting of full grain bread rolls, cheese, a selection of meats and sausages, accompanied by mustard and pickles, with which they drank Reisling wine, followed by Cognac.

When they retired to bed, they both stripped naked, sharing a mutual need to belong, to share, and to savour intimacy. She reached for him, rejoicing in his arousal, loving the way his body responded, and their mouths met. Their natural craving was as beautiful, as it was passionate, seeking, wanting, desiring, needing, and when they finally lay back, their hands joined, they felt an inner peace as welcome sleep enveloped them. However, in the early hours, his was restless and troubled, his mind full of scenes he did not want to witness.

****

Now, as he sat in the small office in the *Rumfordschlössl,* his thoughts were interrupted by a call on his mobile; the voice was nervous, hesitant. "Hello, Herr Biesecker, it is Friedrich Völker; it is safe, *ja*? I am about to enter." A minute later, there was a knock on the door, and Karl opened it to reveal a tall, thin man with large eyes behind round, black-framed glasses, with a flat cap over greying hair, wearing a long dark grey coat with fur on the collar, and, rather incongruously, formal polished black laced shoes.

Völker briefly bowed, in a gesture which was clearly part of his normal business etiquette, extending his hand, "*Herr Biesecker, Wie geht es ihnen? Sehr erfreut!* (how are you, nice to meet you) You look like your father," he stuttered. He was nervous, and showing an element of being ill at ease. "I tried to ensure no one followed me, but we are all being watched. They are everywhere. How much did your dear father tell you? He was a good man, Karl, and he told me often how he regretted much and wished you were closer. I can tell you; he was enormously proud of you."

Outside, unnoticed, the two women he had seen chatting as he entered, one pushing a pram, had stopped. One of them was talking urgently into the lapel of her coat. Seconds later, they had both disappeared into the bushes, abandoning the pram which was left crookedly facing the hedging.

Völker had stopped speaking, aware his words were tumbling out, then, "*Bitte,* I am sorry; my thoughts are messed up." Karl motioned him to a seat opposite the table, then spoke slowly in a measured tone, "A *Schnapps, Herr Völker?*" He extracted a leather covered flask from his case, unclasping a lid holding two small cups. The other man nodded, removing his cap, and smiled briefly. Karl poured them both a measure, nodding to Völker, who picked his up; they touched their drinks together briefly, then both downed them in one swift movement, muttering "*Prost!*" Karl poured them another, then looked at Völker earnestly, "My father spoke highly of you; he even stressed I could trust you, but I have learned, *Herr Völker,* in my long military service, that trust has to be earned." Karl was anxious to set the tone, right at the start, that he was the one in command, and that it was imperative Völker respected his authority. "*Bitte,* tell me why I should trust you?" He looked Völker deep in the eyes and his instinct told him that he already could.

Völker was trembling, and Karl could see there was fear in his eyes yet his voice, in his answer, showed a determination or drive, or both, in a tone which demonstrated his sincerity. "Karl, may I call you this? It seems more natural, as this is how your father and I talked of you. Our families go back generations, and it was your grandfather who secured my grandfather a position on his staff where they became friends. They worked on the challenge of securing gold in the war, but my grandfather was more of a functionary, albeit with a brilliant mind. In late 1943, my grandfather met with Colonel Henning von Tresckow, who was Chief of Staff of the 2nd Army on the Russian Front. Tresckow informed him there was a plot to assassinate Hitler and seek a peace treaty with the Allies to prevent Germany falling to the Soviet Union. My grandfather was persuaded by his deeply held humanitarian values which contrasted with the viciousness of the Nazi regime." Völker picked up the cup and downed another measure, relieved at the spreading warmth and relief of anxiety. "He tested the water with your grandfather, but was rebuffed by Spacil who told him loyalty was in his blood and that he would not break the oath he had taken to Hitler. After the 20th July bomb plot on Hitler's life failed, the following day Colonel Tresckow committed suicide. Your grandfather intervened when the SS came to arrest my grandfather, vouching for him by telling them that Hauptman Heinrich Völker was a loyal officer serving the Reich who had brought the matter to his attention. He told the SS that he did not believe such reports were credible and that, in any case, they should be ignored as they undermined the authority of the *Führer*. He further stated that he had ordered Hauptman Völker to keep his ear to the ground and report any further information directly and only directly to him. Karl, your grandfather saved my grandfather's life, despite his own allegiance to the *Führer*. All my life, I have been affected by the same contradictions of loyalty, creed, and my inner sense of common decency.

"In 1945, my grandfather died from wounds received during a skirmish with the Russians in Torgau, not far from Leipzig. When he was dying, your grandfather pledged he would ensure that his wife and my father, who was only fifteen, were taken care of. He was as good as his word and after the war, my grandmother was re-housed by him. My father told me stories about how your grandfather kept his distance so that no one became suspicious about a secret they shared, which was that all was being paid for from monies secreted by the Nazis known as the *Versteckte Vermögensfonds*. You may be aware that my father was a schoolteacher but again, he was greatly assisted by the Nazi assistance network, *Die Spinne*, which he never questioned, despite being a devout Roman Catholic. We all accepted that we were fortunate and I, too, gained from our family's association with *Die Spinne*. Papa's attitude was that the past was the past and that we were, at least, making good use of our "inheritance", as he called it. He died from cancer in 1990 when I was thirty and I then met your father at the funeral. I had been working as a financial controller for *Feldmühle Nobel AG*. Deutsche Bank had taken control of this from the family of Friedrich Flick whose name you might recognise. He was a fabulously wealthy businessman whose commercial empire had been built up during the Nazi regime, in which he played a prominent role. Your father offered me a position working for what he initially described as *Die Spinne,* and the salary was very attractive. Once inside the organisation, I found I was actually working for a company called *VVF* which you mentioned during our phone conversation. It was clear from your knowledge of this, and your description about your father, that you were who you claimed to be, after which I agreed to meet with you. Your father placed his trust in me very quickly because of our long family association and because we both shared the secret of our link to the *Versteckte Vermögensfonds*. I do not know how much you know, and, perhaps, in revealing what I have just revealed, lies the reason you can trust me. From what you said over the phone, it is clear your father shared the password, '*Adler-Geldbörs*' and, I believe, therefore, he will have vouched for me." He thought for a moment, removing his glasses, before decisively replacing them, "I also know, Karl, that your father made provision for you."

Karl was taken aback, then extended his hand again, with a sense of relief. "*Ach* so, forgive me; it is good to meet with you and I think we may have much to share."

12

Aktion Bernhard

Monday 16th August 1943 10:45am
Schloss Labers, Merano, Italy

The tall SS officer with the four silver collar flashes denoting his rank as *Obersturmbannführer* (Lieutenant Colonel) was sitting next to another officer in the back of a large open-topped Mercedes being driven from the airfield at Bolzano the thirty-minute drive to his destination. His orders from both the *Führer* and the *Reichsführer* were clear, although slightly contradictory. As a military commander, he had become used to interpreting orders, rather than following them, a trait which had earned him respect from the troops serving under him, and the recognition of his outstanding ability by his friend, Ernst Kaltenbrunner, the head of the RSHA, or *Reichssicherheitshauptamt*. Kaltenbrunner had recommended him to Walter Schellenberg, the head of the SS Foreign Intelligence Service, to head up the development of a special forces unit; a move personally endorsed by Hitler. As he threw his cigarette out over the window raised to his side, his adjutant, *Hauptmann* Hans Danneberg, remonstrated with him, with an informal manner that marked a long relationship, built on mutual respect and forged in combat, addressing him with the rank of full Colonel, out of respect. "You know the *Führer* disapproves of smoking, *Herr Oberst?*" which provoked a swift response,

"Hans, if I heeded what my superiors encouraged me to do, I would be a dead man now; instead, I am a *Dummkopf* and yet, they give me the Iron Cross and keep promoting me!"

Danneberg chuckled at his commander's customary irreverence he showed to anyone in a senior position, irrespective of status. He had served in the *SS-Leibstandarte Adolf Hitler* under this man, with the long scar running down his left cheek, obtained from his student days duelling with fencing blades, since their first combat experience. They had seen action in the Netherlands, France, The Balkans, Romania, and Bulgaria, being transferred to the *Waffen-SS Division Das Reich* where they had taken part in the invasion of the Soviet Union in June 1941. *Obersturmbannführer* Otto Skorzeny was a charismatic figure, sporting a thin film-star like moustache, with a larger-than-life personality which engendered him to those who served under him, but which worried some superiors whose orders he would execute in what was described as a *'willful manner'*. However, he had become a favourite of the *Führer*, which afforded him a hidden protection, and tolerance of his cavalier manner.

Two days previously, Skorzeny had been summoned by Hitler to meet with him at his Bavarian Alpine retreat at *'the Berghof*, in the Obersalzberg, near Berchtesgaden. The *Führer* was in a deeply pensive mood, and, although he had welcomed Skorzeny with a warm handshake, asking him about the recovery from his headwound, received on the Russian front the year before, he paced his long study displaying unease. He had waived Skorzeny to a seat, before picking a phone up and ordering tea. His hands were clasped behind his back, as he walked to the long window overlooking the Untersberg mountains opposite. His field-grey double-breasted tunic was simple, displaying, Skorzeny thought, his need for little outward display of authority or decoration, despite his total command of all around him. Skorzeny admired his power of leadership, combined with an extraordinary aura which was mesmerising. The *Führer* gazed out over the alpine view, seeming lost in his thoughts for a moment, then, quietly, his familiar guttural voice held Skorzeny's attention totally.

"We need to awaken Charlemagne from his slumbers in these mountains to rise up and oppress those who threaten the Reich. The *Deutsche Volk* understand my historic mission to liberate Germany from the contamination of our blood by the *Juden und der Untermenschen*. The role that destiny has chosen for me is the deliverance of the Reich and I will not fail in this sacred task, nor allow the Bolshevik infection to spread its filthy decay. Out of the heroic struggle of Stalingrad and the sacrifices of our warriors given in blood, we must deliver retribution." His voice rang out, the tone lifting, as if addressing a mass rally, and Skorzeny was transfixed.

"Last week, I authorised the withdrawal of our forces from Sicily. They have fought bravely but our Italian allies are not united as we are by blood. I do not see the English and Americans as our natural enemies and so, it is in the east where we must concentrate our forces. The Russian inbreds and their primitive Slavik barbarity must be overcome and you, *Herr Obersturmbannführer,* have played your part in this monumental struggle. Now is the time to strike back, for the German *volk*, for German blood, for humanity, and for our great Fatherland. If we are to repel the barbarians in the east, we must strengthen our Italian front.

"I have a mission to deliver a blow to those opposing us; we must re-assert ourselves in Italy where, last month, the King intervened and stripped *Il Duce* of his powers in a gross interference in matters of state. Mussolini has been arrested but our intelligence has information on his location. We will re-galvanise the forces with whom we are allied if we can either capture and restore Mussolini, or eliminate him which shall then be seen as a decisive step taken by Germany in order to install our own regime. I will take whatever steps are necessary to show the world that we control the destiny of Europe. I want Mussolini either dead, as their captive, or, preferably, taken alive and delivered to me. There are others already allocated to this mission, but you will take a prominent role because you are uniquely admired; if you succeed, you will raise the spirit of our people and our heroic forces. I, too, admire your skills as a commander; I also trust you will execute my will and so you will carry my authority to override orders on this mission, and in another..."

Hitler stopped speaking, then gestured with his hands as if grasping or seeking alternatives. He walked slowly towards the seating area, and, with a sigh, lowered himself into a chair opposite Skorzeny, fixing him with a relentless stare.

"*Herr Obersturmbannführer,* I am a realist and, after the Bolshevik scum pushed us back from Stalingrad, the Reich is now on the defensive. We must prepare ourselves for an unthinkable future; a future where I must select those whose trust I can rely upon to execute my will, in whom I can entrust the destiny of our Reich. I want you to be part of the legacy I will leave for the Fatherland if we succumb to the forces who threaten us. We have an historic mission which must continue, no matter what the outcome, because that mission is greater than any of us; it is chosen by Providence and will never fail. We must make plans to protect our economic assets, ensuring they are not pillaged by the Bolsheviks. You will have a part to play in this epic purpose." He turned as a door opened and a white-coated figure entered, pushing a trolley on which were set out a teapot, cups, and an array of biscuits. The man snapped to attention, giving the Nazi salute, "*Mein Führer,* tea is served."

Hitler's eyes brightened for a moment, with a hint of a smile, responding, "*Herr* Linge, where are the cakes?"

In the afternoon, Skorzeny had been driven, with Danneberg, to the villa owned by *Reichsführer* Himmler at Schönau, thirty minutes-drive from the *Berghof*, accompanied by an armed escort in a small truck and two motorcycle outriders. As they approached down a thin road, they came to a barrier and a guard hut, from which two men dressed in black SS uniforms emerged, one holding a *Schmeisser* machine gun at his waist, suspended from a strap. On viewing the driver's papers, who identified Skorzeny as a guest invited by the *Reichsführer,* the man clicked his heels, extending his right arm stiffly, then barked an order to his companion who went to a field telephone notifying the security detail stationed at the lodge of their arrival. They passed a gateway on which eagles were mounted either side on posts clutching the SS runes, below which was the name of the residence in gothic writing, *Schneewinkellehen.*

As they approached the house which had the appearance of a traditional Alpine lodge, Danneberg remarked, *"Grosser Gott,* it looks like a scene from a children's fairy tale."

Skorzeny laughed in reply, "And Uncle Heine is the handsome prince; if you do not believe this, he will have you shot!" Danneberg joined in the humour, loving his commander's reputation for irreverence to superiors.

"*Ja,* well, maybe after this meeting, we will find out how we are going to live happily ever after. Perhaps, he can make the forces of Ivan retreat!"

The lodge had a timber upper half stretching to an apex roof, inset with windows with balconies from which colourful flowers spilled over, beneath which were more windows with shutters set in cream walls. In the centre of the building was a large double doorway inset with studs.

As the Mercedes swept to the door, an officer, dressed in a field grey uniform marched out, and raised his arm, as a guard driver opened the door. "I am *SS-Obersturmbannführer* Werner Grothmann, personal adjutant to the *Reichsführer*. He will be pleased that you are punctual. He desires that both of you attend the meeting he has called." He led the way down a corridor, lit with mock flaming torches set in iron supports, into a large open area, stretching up over two floors, where Grothmann stopped, gesturing with pride. There was a feeling of spaciousness, lit from windows above, and to the side was a grand staircase which wound to a balustraded upper area. On the wall were two large oil paintings. One was of Hitler standing in front of a swastika, held in a wreath, in a brown uniform, his hand on his hip and his arm outstretched, as if directing his authority, whilst below, in a valley, could be seen a column of armour moving towards the horizon. The other was of Himmler, in his SS uniform, his arm stretched out in the Nazi salute, whilst behind him, lines of men were standing to attention on parade, one of his hands gripped the base of a large black banner on which the SS emblem was displayed in silver. In gothic lettering at the base of the painting in a scroll effect were the words of the SS motto, '*Meine Ehre heist Treue*'. The entire opening was dominated by a huge round iron chandelier with more lights represented as flaming torches. There was a seating area at the furthest end and a large window opened to a lake view beyond a rolling lawn. Crossed swords and shields gave the entire area the feel of the interior of a castle, yet this was offset by the array of comfortable seats positioned in the far window area. Grothmann spoke briefly to a uniformed orderly, then announced that they were to be taken to the conference hall where the *Reichsführer* would join them at the prescribed time of 2:30pm.

The orderly marched in front of them down another corridor to two tall double doors, which opened out to a long room with panelled walls in the centre of which was a table with eight chairs either side and two at either end. The sets of dual windows at the far end gave views over the Tegernsee Lake beyond. The décor was sparse giving the sense of a military briefing room, contrasting with the area they had left. The orderly bid they sit and offered them both coffee which he left to prepare.

"This beats the barracks, *Herr Oberst;* a shame they don't serve brandy," Danneberg quipped, breaking the tension which they both felt.

"This is not a problem," Skorzeny retorted, "I have a bottle of Cognac in my briefcase to treat *die Trunkenbolde* (drunks) like you," resulting in a rude gesture from Danneberg and a grin. On the Russian front, they often shared a bottle which helped with the trauma of combat operations.

At that moment, the door opened, and *SS-Obergruppenführer* Karl Wolf entered, whom they had both met previously, and who smiled in greeting as they shook hands warmly. He had been adjutant to Himmler, and still attended most strategic meetings where important decisions were made. He cupped his hand as if breaching a confidence, speaking in a low voice, "I have divorced, with the *Führer's* blessing, but the *Reichsführer* does not approve; I think I am to be transferred to Italy." He lent even closer to them, "I can tell you, he is as ever, resourceful, and a practical man, preparing for any outcome from this war. Watch your backs, *meine Kameraden,* these are very dangerous times. Our loyalties are to no man but the Fatherland."

The orderly appeared, pouring them all a coffee, but leaving a jug of water and a glass whispering, "This is for the *Reichsführer.*"

Skorzeny glanced at his watch, it was just reaching 2:30pm, and, as if prompted, the doors swung open and Grothmann entered, "Please stand for the *Reichsführer; Heil Hitler!*"

Himmler swept in, dressed not in a uniform, but a dark grey lightly pinstriped suit, with wide lapels, on the left side of which he wore a gold nazi party badge. His hair was almost totally shaven, and he adjusted his round glasses, peering at them for a moment, before commanding in his precise, slightly high-pitched tone, "*Bitte setzen!*" His face betrayed no emotion, but his demeaner was commanding, exuding the authority that all recognised, respected and feared. Entering behind him was the towering, unmistakeable figure of SS-*Obergruppenführer* Ernst Kaltenbrunner, the chief of the Reich Security Main Office (RSHA). He had been appointed to the position following the assassination of Reinhard Heydrich by British trained Czech agents in 1942. He nodded briefly to Skorzeny, with whom he enjoyed a friendship, with a hint of a smile. Behind him, were three other officers dressed in SS uniforms but unknown to both Skorzeny and Danneberg.

As he sat, the *Reichsführer* turned to Skorzeny, "Your interpretation of the reason for your meeting with the *Führer?*" The abruptness of the question took Skorzeny by surprise, but he recognised in an instant that Himmler was fishing for information. Hitler had made it clear that he had placed his trust in him and Skorzeny respected his oath of loyalty to the *Führer,* which he would never betray. He was not inspired by the *Reichsführer; he* tolerated his directness, and aloof manner, but Himmler displayed a lack of comprehension of military tactics or logistics which was frustrating and dangerous to Skorzeny and his fellow officers as combat veterans,

"*Meine Reichsführer,* he is concerned about the outcome of the war and believes that special forces may be the key to the outcome. As you will be aware, I am now training and commanding the newly formed *SS-Jagdverband 502,* which specialises in sabotage, espionage, and intense, skilled paramilitary operations." Skorzeny knew from years of military and intelligence training, that answers he gave under scrutiny or interrogation should be as near to the truth as possible. He appeared confident as he addressed the *Reichsführer's* question. "In the light of the current military situation, the *Führer* has tasked me with building up a military unit capable of paralysing attacking forces through covert, or 'behind the lines' operations." He said nothing about the task outlined to him of capturing *Il Duce*, or in establishing a plan to remove German assets in the event the military situation deteriorated. Hitler had been utterly explicit in his words, using Skorzeny's Christian name for the first and only time as he grasped both his hands in his, "Otto, the Reich may not survive, but from the ashes, we will rise again with a new power. The brilliance of our colleague, the economic genius, *Herr Funk*, has shone a light on the future. Our might will not lie in the Panzers, our *Luftwaffe,* nor our armed forces, but in the strength of our economy dominating a Europe united by global greed in a new economic union.

"Our survival depends on gold, the security of which you will take command of in the event of our military collapse." Hitler had sunk back in his armchair, beads of sweat on his forehead, and, for the first time, Skorzeny noticed a slight shake in his left arm which he attempted to conceal by holding it behind his back.

"*Herr Obersturmbannführer*, this will be the defining mission I give to you, and in your hands, if this be necessary, will lie the future power of the Reich. If we lose this war, we will rise up, like a Titan from the deep, and our Teutonic Knights shall be dressed in suits, dominating Europe with an unstoppable financial force."

Now, Skorzeny was suddenly very aware of the letter he was carrying, signed in his presence, and given to him by the *Führer* himself that morning. He completed his response with words delivered lightly, "In short, *Herr Reichsführer*, the *Führer* has commanded that I am answerable to no one except himself in executing his orders. In addition, the *Führer* has relieved me of the obligation to take orders from anyone of any rank, if such orders may compromise my mission." He had delivered his words in a slow, serious manner; but now, seeing the fury in Himmler's face, he lightened the tone, "I have a reputation for disobeying orders, of which I am, I confess, quite proud, but I regret, *mein Reichsführer,* I am sure you will understand, even I cannot contravene the orders of the *Führer.*" Now, as he faced Himmler, he saw the normally implacable look darken, and shake with anger. Underneath the table, his hand clutched around the grip of his Luger pistol. His response had hit home, and he knew the careless manner with which he had delivered his last words would have been judged gross insubordination, if not treason from anyone else, with potential dire consequences.

The *Reichsführer* slammed his fist on the table in an uncharacteristic display of irritation, "Why does the *Führer* not consult with me before talking with my commanders? I am the strength in the Reich, providing his security and protection, which, if I withdrew, would leave him exposed, vulnerable even. I created and command the SS; the most powerful force in Germany. Only I can direct, interpret, and ensure the *Führer's* wishes are executed." He suddenly sat up straighter, as though aware he had said too much.

Himmler looked directly at Skorzeny, for an uncomfortable length of time, quietly adding, "You will not forget, *Herr Obersturmbannführer,* the motto on your dagger, and your belt, your 'honour is loyalty' and your oath is to follow the orders of the leaders appointed by the *Führer.*" There was an awkward, menacing, silence during which those present were left in no doubt that their right to live rested on the authority of this man.

The *Reichsführer* then slowly turned to the three other officers who had followed him when he entered. His voice now resumed a level tone - "Permit me to introduce *SS-Sturmbannführer* Alfred Naujocks, and *SS-Sturmbannführer* Bernhard Krüger of the *Reichsicherheitshauptamt* (German Security)." The two men bowed briefly in acknowledgment. "These officers are accompanied by Friedrich Schwend, aka Fritz Klemp, or even, perhaps, *SS-Sturmbannführer* Dr Wendig." The *Reichsführer's* eyebrows raised in a brief, and rare, attempt at humour - "I believe his SS rank changes as often as his name. I have even heard he is introducing himself now with the rank of *Standartenführer* (Colonel). Forgive me *Herr Doktor,* but there is no record of you in the SS at all." His expression suddenly changed to an icy look as he added, "You will understand that I never make mistakes in such matters."

Schwend spoke in an almost desperate stutter "*Mein Reichsführer,* forgive me, but I am involved in sensitive areas and must protect..." His voice tailed off as Himmler snapped,

"*Genug!*" (enough!), adding in a cold measured tone, "You are a crook involved in currency fraud and smuggling; you are fortunate not to be an occupant of Dachau." He then turned to address the room in his clipped high-pitched tone, "Those of you in this room have a vital part to play in the future of the Reich. We need more gold, *meine Kameraden,* and we also need to secure this in the unthinkable circumstances our forces are over-run. Gold is the passport to our future prosperity and the guarantee that the glorious will of the *Führer* is executed, *Heil!*" He extended his arm, and all followed suit, although Skorzeny felt he was acting out a part in a kind of ritual.

Himmler held his hand up, "I have taken it upon myself to put in place a strategy to secure the assets we need. *SS-Sturmbannführer* Naujocks set up a money counterfeiting operation in 1940, entitled *Unternehman Andreas* which succeeded in perfectly replicating British currency. For some months, we successfully flooded their financial system with forged banknotes which are virtually undetectable and which will, in time, have a de-stabilising effect of their economy. For political reasons, this innovative endeavour was not properly controlled or expanded. *Sturmbannführer* Naujocks had an unfortunate disagreement with the late *SS-General* Heydrich and matters were not given sufficient priority. However, last year I rejuvenated the programme and massively increased production in a new mission named *Aktion Bernhard* under the direction of *SS-Sturmbannführer* Bernhard Krüger. One purpose of this operation is to buy gold using some of our vast stocks of counterfeit currency for this purpose and help build up our gold reserves.

Sturmbannführer Naujocks will now co-ordinate with both *Obersturmbannführer* Skorzeny, and *Hauptmann* Danneberg," he paused, shooting at look at Skorzeny, "subject, of course, to the approval of the *Führer*. You will organise security for the covert transport and delivery of gold to nominated safe places for deposit, or, in the event this process is compromised by events on the ground, storage of the assets realised from *Aktion Bernhard*." He turned to Krüger, "*Herr Sturmbannführer, bitte.*"

Krüger stood up, clicking his heels. He was a youthful looking, well-groomed officer in his late thirties, with thick black hair worn slightly longer than was customary in the military. He spoke in a relaxed style, "I am commandant of Blocks 18 and 19 at Sachsenhausen Concentration Camp where we operate independently, sealed off from other areas of the camp. I have prisoners who are skilled craftsmen, and they can re-produce or forge documents with incredible precision. Sachsenhausen gives us a low-cost human resource, with the benefit of assured secrecy. In 1941, *Unternehman Andreas,* was successful in counterfeiting British £5-00 notes with extraordinary accuracy. We sent Jews on holiday to England to spend the money! *Ja, a*ll they had to do, was spend money! How can they criticise us Germans, when we are so altruistic?"

There was laughter from around the table. Krüger continued, "However, this operation lacked finesse because it was slow and agents, we sent to England, were intercepted warning the *Englanders* what we were doing. Now, we have re-directed our resources. We have established contacts all over Europe, courtesy of *Doktor* Wendig, and we can utilise this network to launder the counterfeit currency. Our agents will buy gold, jewellery, or exchange our forged notes for hard currency, smuggling this back to the Reich. We have occupied Schloss Labers, a fortress in Northern Italy, as a centre from where agents, controlled by *Doktor* Wendig, are exchanging counterfeit bank notes for US Dollars, Swiss Francs, valuables, and gold. This is a central point to where agents deliver their proceeds, which is then transported and deposited in designated banks, mainly over the border in Switzerland. Recent military events have made us re-think the future and this, *Herr Obersturmbannführer* Skorzeny, is where you and your special forces fit in. *Heil Hitler!*"

He sat down and Himmler rose, leaning forwards on the table, staring at each person in turn, pausing as he fixed Skorzeny with a penetrating look, "You will not speak of this to anyone outside this room. If you do so, I will have you shot. You will now make immediate arrangements to execute my orders and, *Herr Obergruppenführer* Kaltenbrunner, you will have a report on my desk by 6:00pm outlining what plans are in place. *Guten Tag.*" He straightened, nodded to Grothman, who marched swiftly to open the door, following the *Reichsführer* out, as all occupants immediately stood, clicked their heels, and extended their right arms stiffly.

Kaltenbrunner, the most senior officer present, took charge, announcing that they would have a twenty-minute break. Coffee was served by an orderly, as he took Skorzeny to one side, speaking quietly, ensuring that they could not be overheard, "My friend, you will understand why I ensured that the *Führer* gave you the mission of securing the assets of the Reich. I sense power-play being exercised here by our beloved *Reichsführer*. You will now enjoy the full protection of the *Führer* and I will, of course, fully brief him. My loyalty will never be called into question."

"Perhaps, he should have remained a chicken farmer," responded Skorzeny wryly, and they both laughed, relieving the tension from the meeting, but recognising the perilous path that lay ahead.

That had been the previous Saturday, after which Skorzeny and Danneberg had flown to Munich, enjoying dinner and staying the two nights in suites at the Hotel Vier Jahreszeiten, all paid for by Hitler personally. They had been welcomed by the owners, the Walterspiel brothers, who had feted them with Champagne and introduced them to some society hostesses, with whom they had spent the evening and the following day. A flight was arranged for them on a Ju52 transport aircraft out of Munich to Bolzano, Italy, at 8:30am on Monday, which had taken just ninety minutes, giving them time to arrive for the scheduled 11:00am meeting. As they wound up the hill to the entrance,

Skorzeny, slipped his Luger pistol from its holster, extracting the magazine, from which he began removing rounds.

"Was machst du, Herr Oberst?" asked Danneberg

"Just ensuring that management authority is respected," responded Skorzeny with a slightly wicked smile.

13

The Tower of Basel

Monday 16th August 1943 10:30am
The Bank for International Settlements,
Gegenüber Schweizer Bahnhof, Basel, Switzerland

Thomas McKittrick entered the panelled boardroom with a grim expression on his face, accompanied by the assistant manager, Paul Hechler, and Allen Dulles, who was recognised as a political advisor on international financial issues, and member of US Intelligence. In the room were shareholders of the bank and their representatives, together with Swiss banking executives with whom the BIS had a close relationship. Cigar smoke hung in the air and the buzz of conversation slowly silenced as McKittrick gathered his papers together from the file he was carrying, then stood to address those present, "Good morning, Gentlemen. I regret that our agenda has been kind of hijacked by events. I have just been briefed by Emil Puhl, the vice president of the Reichsbank, and, one of the representatives of the German Reich with BIS, that Germany wishes to move large quantities of gold here and deposit it here. They have agreed to smelt the gold in order to remove any identifying characteristics other than the Reich emblem. This frees the BIS from the political sensitivities which may flow from accepting gold deposits with other national markings. They have nominated a separate account for this purpose stating that their strategy will be to manage this through a trading company separate from the Reich. I am prepared to endorse this move, subject to your agreement.

We also have a request indirectly emanating from the *Reichsführer* of Germany, Heinrich Himmler, communicated to me this morning by our assistant manager, Paul Hechler, for a reserve to be set up in the name *Schwend-Fonds* on behalf of the *Schutzstaffel* into which both gold and currency will be held independently of the Reichsbank."

He was interrupted by Emil Puhl, who stated bluntly and loudly, "I have not been informed of this, *Herr* Hechler. Why not? Who gave you these orders?"

McKittrick was about to intervene, but decided to allow Hechler to reply. The assistant manager tersely responded, but with a touch of arrogance. "The orders came directly from the head of the RSHA, *Obergruppenführer* Ernst Kaltenbrunner, with the authority of the *Reichsführer*. Of course, if you wish me to inform them that you object, that is a matter you might regret."

"Gentlemen, gentlemen!" McKittrick now interjected, "I will not permit any exchanges which might be interpreted as being a threat, or, indeed, which do not benefit the management of this institution. The BIS is respected for its political independence and will not intervene or pass judgement on the internal affairs of member nations. However, we may have a problem in acceding to this request as it might be seen to compromise the Reichsbank and hence, I think, we might, have to be advised by the president of the Reichsbank, Walther Funk. As a majority shareholder, their endorsement would be essential before we take a view on this."

"Here here." the words were uttered by Montagu Norman, and echoed by Otto Niemeyer, with others nodding around the table. The anger in the face of Paul Hechler at this unexpected turn was obvious.

McKittrick turned to the respected Per Jacobsson, a founder of the BIS, "Can you confirm that my interpretation is a correct one here?"

"Absolutely, Mr President, no external authority over this bank is held by the *Reichsführer,* no matter how much authority he may wield in his country."

"A pretty odious individual, by all accounts," muttered Norman, causing Hechler to jump to his feet, shouting.

"That is unacceptable, you will apologise!"

"Order!" barked McKittrick. "Your words are not acceptable, Sir Montagu," which gained the response,

"Terribly sorry, old chap, I merely meant I was not sure he is quite the sort of fellow to invite for afternoon tea." There was laughter around the table.

"I will not stand for this and I will file a report for the *Reichsführer* himself!" Hechler's voice had risen again.

McKittrick spoke with authority, "Let us deal with the first item I raised. The receiving of increasing quantities of smelted gold from the Greater German Reich. The issue is how this bank may be judged, in the post-war climate, from trading in assets which some of the world view as being illegally obtained."

Masatsune Ogura, a thickset man in a three-piece suit with a watchchain on the waistcoat spoke, "The Empire of Japan has no objection. Surely, this is the best way to avoid any difficulties. Our strength is in our impartiality. I, myself, stepped back from government on a matter of honour. In Japan, honour is part of our culture."

"Ah yes, old boy," Otto Niemeyer interjected, "but you see, these chaps are, if reports are to be believed, taking gold from private Jewish collections, or from occupied territories."

"Oui, c'est vrais," the French General Manager, Roger Auboin spoke, "But, perhaps, we must safeguard our financial structures, without which, the markets would become impossible; there would be chaos. My country is now occupied but we must maintain financial order for the future."

"I guess Roger has a good point there," Allen Dulles added. "We gotta prepare for a post-war business strategy and, whatever the outcome, the German economy needs to be strong. I think our duty is to create a stable commercial climate. If Germany has prospered through her expansionist policies, then we must not repeat the mistakes of the Treaty of Versailles, but recognise that the future prosperity of us all rests on protecting the profits of industry and commerce; that is the fuel of the future. I can speak with connections I have in Chase National Bank, enabling deposits to go there which will spread the risk. These guys are powerful, influential people, who will assist politically, if necessary, in avoiding troubling issues for this bank."

The crisp voice of Marcus Wallenberg cut in - "I concur with Allen; our businesses supply customers on all sides without question. That is not our place. We are there to ensure supply meets demand. Expedience can serve us well; last year, whilst I was cutting deals in the United States, my brother was receiving the Order of the German Eagle from Adolf Hiter. Business does not discriminate through politics but can thrive during conflict so that, in peace, normality can return as soon as possible. My bank will be available also to assist in spreading the risk. We can all gain a little from this arrangement, whilst ensuring a rapid return to a vibrant economy after the war, whatever the outcome."

The dapper Rafaele Pilotti added, "My country is in turmoil after *Il Duce* was deposed and we need to have certainties for the future. Whether we have disagreements with Germany or not, surely it is better that we in the BIS are able to provide a safe place for their gold, or through our connected banking interests, rather than it disappearing, having been dissipated by the victors, as happened after the Great War. Let us unite in this purpose for the good of our future." A vote was taken by a show of hands and all present were in favour of the Reichsbank proposal, although Sir Montagu Norman and Sir Otto Niemeyer abstained.

That night, Thomas McKittrick wrote in his journal, *'Today in the BIS Boardroom, we rose above politics, maintaining our integrity. I wrote directly to the president of the Reichsbank to inform him that the bank could not, and should not, interfere with the internal policies of governments. I informed him that the BIS would assist with the process of accepting gold deposits or in sourcing other secure institutions. I also informed him that we needed his authority to accept funds into a new Schwend-Fonds account, relieving the bank of any accusation that we have not acted openly. I feel that I am embarked on an historic journey, during which I am making a difference, and helping to steer a safe course through troubled waters.*

****

Monday 16th August 1943 11:00am
Schloss Labers, Merano, Italy

As they neared the top, they passed through two guarded checkpoints, the first of which radioed through their arrival. At the second, there were positioned two manned *Sd. Kfz234* heavily armoured eight-wheel vehicles. Four more were parked outside the main gates to the castle, beyond which was a short driveway over a bridge to an arched entrance with four guards standing either side.

"Anyone would think they have something to hide," remarked Skorzeny as they drew to a halt. The door to the Mercedes was held open, and, as they alighted, they were met by *Sturmbannführer* Bernhard Krüger. "*Heil Hitler! Wilkommen* to the den of iniquity," giving a broad grin, after initially saluting. Krüger looked nervously around him stating, "You know I report directly to the *Reichsführer*, and he watches everything."

Danneberg was surprised by his commander's response, "Ah, *Herr Sturmbannführer*. or shall I call you Bernhard? *Mein Kamerad, Hauptmann* Hans Danneberg, and I have a business proposition to put to you. Shall we go somewhere private. Please ask your men to leave us." His uncompromising tone left no doubt that this was an order.

Skorzeny fixed Krüger with a steely look, placing both hands on his shoulders. "I am acting with the direct authority of the *Führer*. One word from me, Bernhard, and it will not just be your career that is over, although you might be spared and sent to the Russian front as a *Schütze*." (private)

Krüger immediately snapped to attention, clicking his heels, sensing Skorzeny's total authority. He spoke briefly to the junior officers behind him, then led Skorzeny and Danneberg down a dimly lit corridor to an open area in which two typists were working. They approached a door on which was the single word, *Kommandant*, *w*here he turned, explaining, "I have an office bearing the same title, at Sachsenhausen, but our somewhat eccentric colleague, Doctor Wendig, whom we refer to as Friedrich Schwend, which we believe is his real name, keeps promoting himself in rank. Having this sign here reminds him who is in command. The office beyond was sparse, with a book-case, a desk in front of a large window, and with a minimal nod to comfort, some Persian rugs. There was a two-seat settee next to a coffee table in front of which which was a leather swivel-chair. Krüger gestured to the settee, then took a seat to face them, but Skorzeny remained standing, speaking brusquely, "*Sturmbannführer* Bernhard Krüger, I am engaged on a mission given to me by the *Führer*. Bernhard, your loyalty is to the *Führer* above anyone else, *ja?*" Skorzeny paused, as he pulled a cigarette from a silver case, snapping a lighter open, and inhaling deeply.

Krüger replied, as Skorzeny raised his eyebrows stressing the question, "*Jawohl, Herr Obersturmbannführer.*"

"*Sehr gut,* Bernhard, because if you speak to anyone about what I will now say, you are a dead man, *verstehen?*" (understand?) Skorzeny's tone had become threatening, despite his relaxed pose, as he fixed Krüger with an unblinking look. "If you co-operate, you will live out this war to be a rich man; if you do not, regrettably, things may not be as good for you. From this point, you report to me directly. You will not speak to the *Reichsführer* about this, nor anyone else." He reached across to the leather document folder he had carried with him, extracting a letter which he handed to Krüger, whose eyes widened visibly as he read. He handed the letter back, slowly, absorbing the implication of what he had seen. Then he stood, in a somewhat over dramatic manor, clicked his heels, giving the Nazi salute. "I am at your service, and pledge my absolute loyalty to you and the *Führer; Heil Hitler.*"

Skorzeny continued, "Today, Bernhard, we are going to re-negotiate the deal which our friend, Schwend, has struck, the terms of which, even you are unaware. This is correct, *ja?*"

"*Mein Gott, Herr Obersturmbannführer,* these are matters which the *Reichsführer* has decided, and only he can authorise such terms." Krüger spluttered.

"Bernhard...Bernhard, you are forgetting what we have just agreed. You are now our business partner. *Wilkommen.*" He held out his hand which Krüger took, and Skorzeny slapped him on the back, and added in a warm tone, contrasting with his previous demeanour, "*Wunderbar;* now, we have an agreement, we can proceed to the meeting. Lead on, Bernhard."

After a short walk down a wide intersecting internal walkway with grand long windows overlooking the hills beyond, they came to some double doors, which, Bernhard informed them, led to what had once been a dining room. A suited man was sat with three SS officers at a meeting table, two of whom Danneberg recognised as Naujocks and Schwend, but Skorzeny immediately strode passed them to the third, placing his hands on his shoulders. "Josef Spacil, you old dog," he beamed at him, "I haven't seen you since they put you in charge of plundering the Russian banks. What the hell are you doing here? Apart from the fact that you are a bigger crook than this lot." Spacil shook both Skorzeny's and Danneberg's hand warmly, responding with,

"The *Führer* said you may need the services of an accountant, and that I should mention his letter which would attest to his approval of my involvement."

"*Gute Gott,* he thinks of everything." Skorzeny replied with genuine admiration. "I am delighted you are here."

Krüger interrupted, "*Meine Kameraden,*" he gestured to the man in a suit, "this is George Spitz, he is a crook, part of Friedrich Schwend's gang, and a Jew."

The man looked indignant, "*Bitte, Herr Sturmbannführer,* I am an art dealer from Munich."

Krüger looked at him with a touch of disdain, but without malice, "I am surrounded by them, forgers, confidence tricksters, thieves, and this one buys art, using counterfeit money, and claims to be a dealer. Only a Jew could do this."

They sat at the table, and Skorzeny took immediate charge as the person in command of the mission outlined by the *Führer*. "Today, I will inspect the work being carried out here, but first," His voice hardened, "*Herr SS-Sturmbannführer,* or is it *Standartenführer* Schwend, you will brief me on your work. Keep it short as I have little time before I report back to the *Reichsführer*. First, is your name Fritz or Friedrich?"

The smooth face of the slim, dark-haired man facing him was unflinching if not arrogant as he retorted, "I will answer to both, but change to suit my purposes. You should note, *Herr Obersturmbannführer,* that I work for the *Reichsführer,* and that he has set up a unit in my name, which I command, the *Sonderkommando Schwend*. I do not think it would be wise of you to speak to me in this way."

Skorzeny slowly drew his pistol from his holster, adopting an icy edge to the tone in his voice, as he pressed the pistol to Schwend's head. "I do not think it would be wise of you to speak at all, except to answer my questions." He turned to Danneberg, "I have no time for *dieses Kotzbrocken*". (piece of vomit) "I will ask the question one more time and if he does not answer swiftly, you may shoot him, if I do not do so first."

"My pleasure, *Herr Oberst,*" Danneberg responded, producing his Luger which he cocked with a rasping noise, before waving it in front of Schwend, with a sneer

Schwend's implacable look had changed to one of utter terror as the colour drained from his face, and his hands began to shake.

"So, Schwend, what is your full name?" rapped Skorzeny.

"Friedrich Albert Schwend," came the nervous reply.

"Describe your function here?" Skorzeny replaced his Luger in its holster and lit a cigarette as he turned to Danneberg, "Blow his brains out if fails to answer succinctly. I do hate long-winded answers." Danneberg now had both elbows on the table with his weapon trained on Schwend's head.

"Please, I will answer you..." Schwend's words were tumbling over each other. "I supervise the distribution of currency produced at Sachsenhausen through my contacts across Europe which is used for exchanging currency, buying gold, and materials needed by the Reich."

"What is the purpose of *Sonderkommando Schwend?*"

Schwend hesitated, and Skorzeny nodded towards Danneberg who lifted his handgun off the table, his finger curling around the trigger.

"I work for the *Reichsführer* who instructs me what to buy; my organisation ensures these are procured and delivered secretly to locations chosen by him."

"What kind of goods?" Skorzeny barked.

"Gold, diamonds, securities, paintings, even silk stockings and perfume."

"You are using forged currency to supply the *Reichsführer* with personal wealth when the Reich needs urgent materials for war production?" Skorzeny's voice had risen.

Schwend bowed his head, nodding, recognising his life hung by a thread.

"What part does this Jew play in your filthy operation?"

"He is a senior agent dealing in art which he procures with the currency we produce. We have agents in many specialist fields. Spitz here travels throughout Belgium and Holland. We even trade indirectly with dealers in the United States."

Skorzeny stubbed out his cigarette and stood up. "All of you in this room are witness to the information I have obtained today. I am acting on the direct orders of the *Führer* and it is my job to secure the assets of the Reich and ensure their safety. None of you will speak of this to anyone or I will have you immediately shot. If any of you do not trust my word, the controller of this operation, *Sturmbannführer* Krüger, will now confirm that I have the written authority of the *Führer*."

He looked towards Krüger who stated loudly, "This man carries a letter signed by the *Führer* and anyone of any rank must obey his orders. *Heil Hitler!*"

Skorzeny continued, "*Sturmbannführer* Naujocks will now leave this meeting with the Jew and organise the preparation of all assets held here for inspection."

As they left, he looked at Danneberg saying, "I think our colleague, *Herr* Schwend, has now appreciated that he needs to cooperate, you may put away your weapon. Schwend's deep sigh of relief was audible as Skorzeny sat beside him. "Now, *Herr* Schwend, to business. How much of the proceeds from *Aktion Bernhard* are you siphoning off for yourself?"

The expression of relief on Schwend's face froze with the question as these were matters privately agreed between Himmler and himself; the *Reichsführer* had sworn him to secrecy on pain of death. He had never shared such information with anyone.

He gave his response hesitantly, "This varies and, of course, is subject to market fluctuations in a volatile wartime situation. You must understand, *Herr Obersturmbannführer,* such matters are dictated by economic variations..."

Schwend's voice trailed off as Skorzeny took out his pistol once more, and he felt the cool metal as it was pressed it to his temple. Sweat was forming on his brow as Skorzeny spoke in a terse voice, "I think you mis-heard me, Schwend, at the start of this interview, when I said I wanted answers to be brief and succinct." He removed the pistol from Schwend's head for a moment then forced his head round face round to face him. "You see this, *Kotzbrocken,* this is a favourite of mine, the *Luger P08* and I have lost count of the number of men who have died after being at the wrong side of this weapon; the question is, will you be the next?" He turned quickly and fired; those at the table ducked instinctively, their ears ringing with the loud report, as his shot hit a brass plate over the fire mantlepiece which crashed to the floor. He turned back to Schwend who was white-faced and trembling, "I think I have had enough of you; my patience is exhausted." He raised the Luger to point at Schwend's forehead.

"*Bitte, Nein*!" his victim screamed as Skorzeni's finger squeezed the trigger. There was the sound of a click, as Schwend's head fell forward, with a sob, "*Bitte...bitte*"

"*Ach so*, Schwend, it appears we have a mis-fire. Perhaps, Providence has intervened. Maybe, I should show you mercy. Shall we try again? He looked at his pistol, rasping back the catch once more, raising it to point at Schwend's head. "What is your share from *Action Bernhard?* your last chance to live."

The voice in response was in a weak and shaky whisper, "33.3% of all transaction values...but, then, I have to pay my salesmen..."

"Salesmen?" quizzed Skorzeny sharply.

"Those who purchase or exchange the currency for assets...They can earn as much as 25%," came the shaky reply.

"Like the Jew?"

"*Ja,* he has special Reich clearance because he is a well-respected art dealer."

"So, *Herr* Schwend," Skorzeny's voice had now become amenable, almost amiable. "Thank you for your co-operation. I think we are building an understanding. I am agreeable that you should receive a share of 26%. This will encourage you to negotiate sharper terms with your, er...salesmen. The balance will come to the *Reichfonds* (Reich fund) for the benefit of the future of Germany. If the profits are good, we will, of course, cut you in for more. I think we have a deal; would you agree?"

Schwend looked aghast, "*Mein Obersturmbannführer...*" he blurted, then, seeing the look in Skorzeny's face, he finished with a weak, "Of course."

"Excellent! It has been good to do business with you," Skorzeny stated and to Schwend's astonishment, he extended his hand which Schwend shook meekly. Skorzeny then put his Luger back in its holster, turning to Spacil, "*Herr Sturmbannführer,* my good friend, please prepare confidential minutes of our business arrangement, ensuring that these are witnessed, and signed by *Herr Schwend.* I will leave the accounting for the new *Reichfonds* to you. One final duty for you, *Herr Schwend,* you will prepare and give to me a list of all the assets and their location which have been diverted by the *Sonderkommando Schwend.* This meeting is now over. After lunch, I will inspect the assets held here. *Heil Hitler!*"

After those present had raised their right arms in response, they left, leaving Danneberg with Skorzeny. "*Mein Gott, Herr Oberst,* you make a fine businessman. What the hell is in that letter signed by the *Führer?*"

"The passport to our future prosperity after the war", replied Skorzeny, handing over the letter which Danneberg read with incredulity. The letter carried the Eagle and swastika motif to the top left in gold, under which was printed simply, *'Adolf Hitler'*.

'Obersalzburg – Berghof - Den 14. August 1943

To: All Reich Military, Police, Die Beamten und Deutsches Volk
By this document which carries the authority of the Führer und Reichskanzler, be it known: SS-Obersturmbannführer Otto Skorzeny is engaged on my direct orders, and carries my authority, and shall be obeyed immediately and without question.
All military ranks, including the Wehrmacht, SS, Geheime Staatspolizei, (Gestapo) or those holding office in any capacity will obey any orders issued by SS-Obersturmbannführer Skorzeny irrespective of rank or position or status held in the Reich.
SS-Obersturmbannführer Skorzeny is to be obeyed as if I was issuing such orders myself. He has an historic duty which he is undertaking for the Reich and reports directly to me.
Each use of this authority will generate a written report which will be given to me.
If any person resists an order given under this authority, it shall be classed as treason and dealt with under the severest penalty available to the Volksgerichtshof (People's Court) *or as interpreted appropriate by any serving officer of the Wehrmacht, Schutzstaffel, or Geheime Staatspolizei.*
Der Führer und Reichskanzler
Hitler's sprawling signature appeared below this in the centre.

Danneberg looked up at Skorzeny who was sitting, in a relaxed pose, with a cigarette in his hand, "Clearly, I can never dare disobey one of your orders again, *mein Führer,"* prompting a single fingered gesture in response.

****

Four weeks later on 12th September 1943, around 80 German Paratroopers under the command of *Sturmbannführer* Harald Mors, and 16 members of the *Waffen-SS,* commanded by Otto Skorzeny, executed a daring mission entitled *Unternehmen Eiche* to rescue the deposed Italian Dictator, Benito Mussolini, from captivity. His location was established by German Intelligence, using counterfeit money as bribes, obtained as part of Operation Bernhard. A force of ten gliders bearing paratroopers and special forces rescued Mussolini from the mountain-top Hotel Imperatore, at Gran Sasso, where he was being held, without a shot being fired. Mussolini was flown, with Skorzeny, from the scene of the raid in a light *Fieseler Storch* aircraft, and was delivered by Skorzeny to Adolf Hitler at his Wolfs Lair headquarters, at Rastenburg two days later on 14th August 1943. Skorzeny was awarded the Knight's Cross of the Iron Cross by Adolf Hitler, personally, for his part in the rescue.

14

Divided Loyalties

Monday 8th January 2024 11:30am
Rumfordschlössl, Englischer Garten, Munich

Karl had listened with some fascination to Völker talking animatedly about the links with his family, his father, and his grandfather. He looked at the thin bespectacled man, who projected a studious manner, in his slightly oversized jacket, and a somewhat anachronistic waistcoat worn over a shirt and neck tie. He appeared like a caricature of an accountant or, perhaps, Karl mused, a schoolteacher.

"So Karl, you will be wanting to go to London?"

His question caught Karl off balance, and he was initially evasive. "What makes you say that?"

"Because, *mein lieber Junge* (my dear boy), I was the person who arranged it." Völker gave a self-assured smile which was in somewhat of a contrast to the nervous figure who had entered earlier in the morning. Karl began to feel that he was not controlling the way the meeting was going, and that he was being toyed with. Völker continued, "Perhaps, I need to be a little more honest; forgive me. I already knew you would make contact at some point and that your father had fully briefed you. You see, Karl, I was your father's confidante, and his eyes and ears in many situations. We both shared disillusionment towards the end; I was asking questions about my loyalty, as he was. That is why he knew he could trust me and that I would never reveal the provision he left for you. Our trust was based upon a deep friendship and a foundation with roots in the past. Now, we are involved in a dangerous game."

"We?" replied Karl, "I have to deal with this alone."

"On the contrary, *Herr Soldat-Kämpfer*. (soldier fighter) Do you have an understanding of banking or equities, stock investment, exchange rates, bank access security, financial markets or accounting protocols? Could you even speak the language of a banker? On all these areas, I am an expert; so, you do the fighting and the tough guy business, and I'll look after the math. We can act as a partnership, just like our family history This, I think would be good, *ja?*"

Karl was taken aback but, despite being slightly irritated, he could not help but warm to the eccentricity of this man, and, he had to admit to himself, he was intrigued by the long family connection. "So, *Herr Buchhalter*, (Mr Book-keeper) what are you suggesting?"

Völker pushed back the glasses on his nose, in an even more schoolteacher-like manner, Karl thought, suppressing a smile as Völker continued, "I think that, perhaps, a mix of brains and brawn may be needed. I also have inside knowledge that will be invaluable to you. So, I will return to my question. Will you be travelling to London?"

Karl now sensed that Völker was seizing the initiative, but decided to surprise him with his next words, "I may have business here first. You know, I have a document in my possession, the implications of which are beyond massive; the contents of this document, if made public, could bring down governments, major institutions, and result a political and international banking scandal of unprecedented proportions. I would describe this as my guarantee of safety to avoid, as we say, describing the nuclear option in the military, 'mutually assured destruction.'"

This time it was Völker who displayed some surprise, clearly taken aback by Karl's words. "What, in the name of God are you referring to?"

"My father left me an inheritance with the power to cause devastating consequences" Karl lent forwards, looking directly at Völker with unblinking blue eyes. He spoke slowly to emphasise the words, "I have in my possession what is called *Transaktions Aufzeichnung,* which is a detailed record of *VVF* transactions from 1945-1947. This records the disposal of Nazi assets, including an unimaginable fortune in gold, and currency after World War 2, implicating many leading figures, and some of the most reputable financial institutions in the world."

"*Oh Gott!*" Völker exclaimed, clearly shaken, "I know this record; he told me he had destroyed this. You cannot release any of it; you cannot."

"I will dwell on it," Karl responded, adding, "So, *mein Buchhalter,* maybe we can help each other, *ja?* I was thinking that first, I would like to meet Heinrich Hackmann, who I think is now controlling d*as Geheime Vierte Reich,* or maybe Niemeyer. Can you fix this?"

"Hackmann is rarely ever seen," came the reply, "and he likes to keep out of sight unlike Manfred Göring, his predecessor. He only allows those access to him from his closest inner circle, or proposed by them, and even then, it may take weeks for clearance to be obtained."

"What about that odious little man, Franz Niemeyer?"

Völker nodded, recalling, "Ah, yes of course, you met him at the funeral. I was there, but it was not the time to introduce myself. I do not trust him but, at this point, it is difficult to know who we can trust because there are divided loyalties."

Karl pressed the point, "I presume you have dealings with him if you are involved with handling their assets."

Völker looked uncomfortable for a moment then, "I am only a cog in the wheel; some months ago, a successor as controller of *VVF* was appointed, one Reinhard Funk, who took over his new post on January 2nd this year. You may have heard the name; his great grandfather was the legendary Walther Funk, who was president of the Reichsbank in the war."

"*Scheisse, Buchhalter,* do you people never disappear?"

"You are one of us, *Soldat-Kämpfer,*" came the quick retort which old instincts nearly raised Karl to anger, then he smiled, resigned to the truth in Völker's words.

Völker added, "They came to my office on my return after the Christmas holiday and said that I was to be relieved of all formal duties over the month ahead, after briefing my successor, who was Funk's assistant. I am being transferred into the investment banking division, but have no further responsibility in relation to the day-today management of *VVF*. I could try and make up a reason to see Niemeyer but I cannot guarantee where his loyalties lie, and that it will not be reported back."

"I think the power of the *Transaktions Aufzeichnung* might guarantee an audience." Karl spoke his words with an assured tone.

Völker now felt composed, matching Karl's confidence in his response, with a hint of sarcasm, "So, you will need me and, I think I like the idea of a break in England. Of course, if I take such a risk, there is a condition."

"Bankers! You lot are all the same," muttered Karl. "What is your price?"

"Well, I will trust in your generosity once we have succeeded in our mission. *Prost!*" Völker's voice had a mischievous tone; he extended the small tumbler in a triumphant gesture. Karl hesitated for a moment, then shook his head in a resigned manner, before touching his tumbler to Völker's.

"Ok, *Herr Buchhalter,* we have a deal." Karl reached down into his briefcase, extracting a folder from which he took out the coloured photograph, which his father's note stated had been presented to his grandfather by Martin Bormann in 1949, and passed it to Völker.

"Do you recognise the SS officer with my grandfather?" he asked.

"*Ja,* of course, that is Otto Skorzeny. He met with your grandfather after the removal of gold from Berlin in 1945. He was in charge of concealing assets of the Reich from late 1943, on Hitler's orders, after things started going badly for Germany on the Russian front. He had a secondary role which was to divert some of the funds generated by a counterfeit currency operation known as *Aktion Bernhard* away from the control of Himmler's SS and into the *VVF.*"

Karl stood up, retrieving his coat, before pacing to the window - "I think we should put in place a plan over lunch somewhere more private." He sighed deeply, "You know, Friedrich," he said, using Völker's Christian name for the first time, "the more I hear, the more uneasy I become. Even back then in their supposedly disciplined regime, loyalties were divided and, it appears, to echo your own words, no one could be trusted. Why did you follow these people? I do not understand what motivates a loyalty to a failed creed that should have died in the ruins of Berlin in 1945. Instead, it appears, you people have infiltrated every part of our society. Our businesses, our financial institutions, and even our political infrastructure."

"Karl, my friend, I am not a fanatical Nazi...Do I look like one?" Völker gesticulated in a mocking gesture to himself. Then, added in a more earnest tone, "But, there is another way of looking at this. There are huge forces at play in big business, powerful institutions, and organisations that are growing to compete outside the sphere of democracy. Hitler called democracies "babbling" because they could not make decisions, bound by their loyalty to factions of their electorate. He offered an alternative in which there was strength and a national pride. Of course, I do not condone the excesses of the fools that abused their position, inflicting the appalling suffering on the Jews, the Russians, the Poles, the Slavs, or the appalling atrocities committed which cast a dark shadow on what could have been a better way. Look at society today, riven by political disagreement with weak decision-making from politicians who have no real conviction, or, if they do, they dare not speak out for fear of offending people. Weak government, Karl, is the inheritance passed down to us from democracy.

"There are new powers at play; powerful factions that bypass what they see as the "unfortunate" diversion or irrelevance of elections. Have you heard of the Bilderbergers or the World Economic Forum, also known as the WEF? These are unelected bodies of incredibly powerful people whose agenda is far more sinister than anything which was envisaged by National Socialism. You think things have got better? The world is in a very dangerous place right now..." He broke off as Karl held his hand up, then moved around the walls, then back towards the centre of the room facing the door, his gun now in his hand; he gestured to Völker to carry on speaking. Holding his weapon in both hands at arm's length, Karl stepped backwards, his eyes not moving from the door, as he edged towards where he had previously been seated. Völker now began talking of his studies and experiences which had led him in his choice of career. Karl pointed to his briefcase; Völker nodded, placing the file back, closing the lid, and slipping his coat on, whilst continuing to talk, as Karl pointed towards the window. They edged back, and Karl gestured for Völker to lift the sash, and, as he did so, there was an audible squeak. Karl saw the handle turn on the door, and as it crashed open, he caught a brief sight of a figure holding a gun as he loosed off three shots, hearing the scream of someone being hit. He ducked as an automatic weapon was fired into the room from the side of the doorway, shattering glass in the windows and knocking chunks of plaster off the walls. Völker was already outside having dropped, with Karl's case, to the grass six feet below. Karl now raised himself, firing six shots in rapid succession, swinging himself into the frame and out. As he dropped a long burst of fire sent splinter shards flying from the window frame. He grabbed the case off Völker, hissing, "Stay close to the walls, then follow..." He fired again at the window, then reached in the case for two canisters, ripping the firing pins off each as he threw one back towards where they had jumped, and the other towards the corner of the building to where he was moving. There was a loud hiss, followed by another, and thick white smoke began pouring across the building. Within seconds, Völker was totally dis-orientated, as his view of all around him disappeared in the blinding fog that enveloped them. More shots were fired as Karl grabbed Völker's arm, leading him down a bank; he paused, opening his case, from which he took another cannister, throwing it with a powerful sweep of his arm in the opposite direction from which they were running. "Quickly, we have less than a minute" he urgently whispered." As they began running again, there was a huge detonation behind them, but Karl did not stop, pulling Völker by the hand until they began to emerge from the haze and buildings could be viewed through the trees ahead. Karl led the way over a small footbridge crossing the fast-flowing Schwabinger Bach to some office buildings backing onto the park. They quickly moved through a pathway which emerged onto Königinstrasse, crossing onto

Giselastrasse where Karl gestured to an alleyway which they entered and stopped. Völker's breath was coming in short rasping gasps.

Karl turned and grinned for a moment, "Don't expire on my yet, *Herr Buchhalter,* you haven't earned your keep. This is what you wanted, isn't it?"

Völker could hardly respond. He was not a man who ever exercised but he managed, as Karl peered out of the alley, "Oh *Gott,* you threw a grenade…What about shrapnel…the people?"

Karl chuckled as he responded, "You *alte Hasen* (slang term for elderly) have no idea. Do you think this is still the *Wehrmacht?* That was a *Blitzknall* (thunderflash). They make a hell of a noise creating the illusion of an explosion. We use them in training, but they don't teach you this in accounting."

The sound of police sirens could be heard and they watched as six vehicles shot passed the end of the road followed by an armoured truck. Karl looked briefly to right and left then waved to a grey Mercedes with a yellow taxi sign which pulled into the curb. As they entered the taxi, he turned to Völker with a grin, "I think you owe me your life, *Buchhalter,* so lunch is on you; where are we going?"

To his surprise, Völker gave confident instructions to the driver, appearing totally unphased by the proposal and clearly, from his relaxed response, used to frequenting the more elite venues. "*Sofiel Munich Bayerpost Hotel bitte.*"

Twenty minutes later, their taxi pulled into the cobbled approach to the hotel, slowing outside the opulent frontage, where a smartly dressed concierge opened the door. They proceeded into reception where Völker asked for a table in a private alcove in the *Délice La Brasserie* restaurant demonstrating he was at ease in his surroundings and that he knew the venue well. They were shown into an area at the top of the restaurant, away from other guest, in an alcove behind two pillars which afforded some privacy. Once sat at their table, Völker ordered a vintage 2020 Chablis, exuding more confidence than Karl had experienced since they met.

"You see, *Herr Soldat-Kämpfer,* you may have the brawn, but I am guessing you would not have selected the 2020…perhaps, you might have chosen the 2018, but, sometimes, a more excessive year of production lacks the quality *n'est-ce-pas?*"

Karl knew that his companion was playing with him, whilst demonstrating that he was sharper than might, at first impression, appear to have been the case.

"You must understand, Karl," continued Völker, "I have been right at the forefront of controlling the *VVF* for many years, including investment strategies, and total asset management. Your father trusted me, and I respected him. I brought forensic accounting skills whilst he was more entrepreneurial which made us an excellent team and for which we were well rewarded. This has been so since the formation of *VVF* and your grandfather was able to set up a supermarket chain funding the entire project from risk management capital that was readily available to him.

"The SS officer you asked about, Otto Skorzeny, also became fabulously wealthy as a result of our assets. He invested heavily in railway development in Spain, oil trading, manufacturing, and essentially buying and selling anything with markets in Argentina, Cuba, Angola, Egypt, Palestine, Greece, Spain, Ireland, Switzerland, and the U.S.

"He was typical of those our grandparents supported. They had access to unimaginable funds to set up and develop enterprises which gave them and *VVF* a highly profitable return. There were no set up or development costs for them and this enlarged our asset portfolio."

Karl interrupted, "It is almost as though the war betrayed the victors. Nazism wasn't defeated; you people just went underground and continued to build your fortunes. I cannot comprehend how you all live with your consciences. Yesterday, I unearthed information about business interests which flourished under the Nazis and they are still doing so."

"Ah, you are an idealist," replied Völker, "I admire this.

A waiter, clad in an apron, approached the table and Völker addressed him taking charge which Karl found a little disconcerting but he smiled as Völker demeanour was amenable, although, perhaps, as he spoke, Karl sensed a touch of mischievous humour - "Might I suggest the *Flanksteak Sauce Bérnaise*. I eat here regularly and I can vouch for this."

Karl nodded, noting that the meal dish selected was amongst the most expensive on the menu as the waiter bowed, and Völker adopted a serious tone, "Please understand that I do not adhere to all National Socialism stood for but, in the alternative, is it any better in the western democracies or in other systems of government? Look at the world and ask yourself if Iran is better, or Russia, or China, or India, or Saudi Arabia, all of which operate with human rights abuses, quite apart from huge abuses of power. Is Democracy any better than totalitarianism? Witness how Palestine has been treated by Israel which nearly caused World War III last year. What about the endemic corruption in South Africa, Nigeria, Zimbabwe, or the abuses of power across the entire African continent. The British Empire collapsed and left the world in a worse place than when they ruled it. Would you wish to live in Kenya, Nigeria, Uganda, or Somalia? Or maybe you would prefer Libya, Iraq, or Afghanistan. Western democracies interfered there and left anarchy. Yes, I agree that we should all reflect on how power is being exercised and we should, as you raised the point, cast our minds over the part that major businesses have played. I do not mean just German businesses, but look at Ford, and General Motors who supplied the Nazi regime and the Allies in World War 2."

The wine arrived, and Völker waived the waiter away, declining to taste it after it had been uncorked, allowing him to fill their glasses before departing. He raised his glass to Karl's. "To our partnership, because whilst I admire an idealist, I am an accountant and, in my world, we have no room for fairy tales. *Gesundheit!*"

Their glasses touched and, despite their differences, Karl found himself warming to this self-assured, yet diminutive figure with his rather large round lensed spectacles, which he had the habit of pushing up his nose, blinking, as he did so. He clearly was very individual if not somewhat eccentric which somehow seemed to lessen their very differing perspectives. He could not, nevertheless, help but agree with the logic of some of his companion's statements, yet he countered with, "*Herr Buchhalter,* I may be an idealist, but I have to employ the most ruthless methods to protect certain freedoms and basic principles which, I can assure you, would not grace the pages of any fairytale."

The wine tasted good, and he felt himself relax, despite the contrast with the threat on their lives only an hour before. This he had become used to as a combat veteran, able to compartmentalise his emotions, fears, aggression, and anger once away from areas of danger.

Völker was nodding his head, "Yes, we have the makings of a good partnership. *Vive la difference.*" He raised his glass again with a wry look. "You see, Karl, in your democratic world, business influences and guides decision-making whereas under National Socialism, business served the needs of the *Reich*. In this, our forefathers were pragmatic, I think, in that they recognised businesses all over the world want to trade, including banks, and financial institutions, especially those in

Switzerland. Here in Germany, companies such as Bayer, Mercedes, BASF, Bosch, Hugo Boss, AEG, Volkswagon, and Varta all flourished. Did that make them any worse than companies on the Allied side? Think, Karl, both Ford and General Motors employed slave labour in their German factories. Of course, I would not approve of this, but the National Socialists of the day saw the workers held in concentration camps as an incredibly useful low-cost asset. That was before all the mass-murders began which our forefathers were unhappy about because this policy removed assets, rather than utilised them.

"Assets, you call them, assets?" Karl felt his anger rising - "These were people who disagreed with your Herr Hitler, and his thugs. Political activists, certain religious believers, homosexuals, gypsies or Roma, and the vast numbers of prisoners of war, all of whom suffered brutality on a barbaric scale. Assets? How can you justify this?"

Völker held his hands up, exclaiming, "Karl, Karl, please, I was using their term, which, in pure accounting terms, I understand. I condemn all of the fanatical madness that undermined the original direction of National Socialism."

Karl's voice still betrayed his emotion, "And *der Judenfrage?* (Jewish question) Please do not tell me you are one of those who term it as "an unfortunate excess" or, the term I have heard used about the horrific butchering of Russian prisoners of war or Poles as "regrettable!"

Völker's tone changed, becoming more direct, "Karl, I am not an apologist for the past which I cannot change. There were crimes committed on all sides but would never justify mass murder, or torture, or persecution because of beliefs. I would remind you that it was the Allies who killed more civilian people in single days or nights of bombing in what is also a war-crime. In Japan, in just three days, over a quarter of a million people were slaughtered. In Dresden here in Germany, or Hamburg, the British and American bombers killed tens of thousands of people in deliberate raids to cause firestorms. We cannot change the past, nor might we agree on the present political direction, but the guilt or complicity in crimes of the past should not divide us today. *Bitte.*" He held out his hand...and, after a moment's hesitation, Karl extended his own and their eyes met, nodding in a mutual understanding.

Their meals were served an, as they ate, they reminisced over their past and the direction each of them had taken. As he finished, Karl wiped his mouth with his napkin, then, "I have to admit, that was delightful and I thank God you are paying which makes it taste even better. He sighed, thinking for a moment, then spoke in a resigned tone. "I suppose both our families were culpable in so many ways. I have wrestled with the contradictions of my father's lifestyle and that of my grandfather from which I have benefitted. My father used to say to me that Germany descended into chaos in the 1970's because of extremists on the left and that there was anarchy at one point. He said it would never have happened in what he termed 'The old days.'"

Völker looked at him earnestly, "Karl, all of Germany was caught up in the euphoria of Adolf Hitler and what he appeared to represent; order, economic recovery, the restoration of national pride, and belief in our country. Was that so bad? Our grandparents did not think so nor did millions of Germans initially. Now, we can't even solve the migrant crisis. One minute, under Merkel, we open our borders, then we say we will improve the controls, and now we say we can take no more, yet still they come. You know the irony of this? It was the Nazis who dreamed up the idea of the European Union. Oh, the hypocrisy of politics eh." They both laughed and already, all the earlier tension between them had evaporated.

Karl felt they had created a connection and was more relaxed saying, after coffee had been served, "We need to work on a plan and, on that, maybe two minds are better than one. Our first priority is to 'follow the money', as they say, but I have now been the target twice, and that makes me uneasy; so, I think we need to visit this man, Franz Niemeyer, and just put him under a little pressure. Planning and execution of that will be my department, not yours, I can assure you, although I will let you learn that what I do will most certainly not appear in any fairy-tale. My concern, as my father rightly pointed out to me, is that the gold does not fall into the wrong hands, or should I say worse hands than those of the GVR. I think, maybe, we need to establish where loyalties may lie, so to speak. Then we go to England and do some digging there. Even though I am not an accountant, even I can understand what a discrepancy is. Now, correct me if I'm wrong here, *Herr Buchhalter,* but if there were twenty 12.5 kilo bars of gold in the Hatton Garden vault in London, and only ten recovered, that means ten are unaccounted for. If we deduct six which my father managed to make disappear, that leaves four 12.5 kilo bars of gold with a value of over three million euros. Add to that thirty 1 kilo bars, of which just four were recovered, then we are left with twenty-six missing with a value of over 1.5 million euros. So, you guys are chasing 4.5 million euros."

Völker laughed, *"Zehr Gott, mein Soldat-Kämpfer,* you should have been an accountant. However, you are incorrect because no one has claimed any of the gold which was recovered from the robbery and still held by the police. The GVR is, therefore, seeking to recover assets worth over 12 million euros. There is also the small matter of the 15 million euros worth gold removed from the vaults of the Berlin Volksbank in 2013, and the 10 million we lost last year in the armoured truck attack."

"Why was the recovered gold not claimed?" Karl's face showed his incredulity.

Völker gave a rueful smile. "For the same reason we have had our debate over lunch today, my friend. All of the bars carry a swastika identifying their source. Passions still run high and neither VVF AG, nor any banks holding or handling money for them want this to go public as it may not only embarrass them, but result in claims. As you may be aware, certain banks such as the Swiss Bank for International Settlements played a huge role in assisting the Nazi regime. want to be seen to be associated with any modern-day involvement with gold from that period.

"In 2000, a US judge ruled in favour of a settlement by Swiss banks for their collusion with Nazi Germany in the Second World War. The case had been brought by the World Jewish Congress and had taken nearly five years to settle with bitter argument. Even the Swiss government distanced itself from what was being argued. The settlement is ongoing, and is still very sensitive, having stirred up anti-semitic sentiment in Switzerland. Nearly 1.5 billion dollars has been paid in compensation so far. Sensitivities are still there and we cannot risk anything coming into the public eye about this. The British government themselves have been complicit in keeping all this quiet and, as a result, you can imagine the scandal notwithstanding the political fall-out if this became public. Powerful factions are involved at the highest level and hence, we need to tread carefully."

"*Scheisse,*" Karl exclaimed in a hissed whisper, "this whole thing would bring down the British government."

"Exactly," responded Völker, "but, Karl, we have a problem. If it emerges that there were another six 12.5 kilo bars, unknown by anybody in either the GVR or the *Reichslegion,* then my life will be at risk; and your inheritance will disappear. You might imagine that the lure of an untraceable quantity of gold valued at over 4.5 million euros would be utterly irresistible."

They both sat for a few minutes without speaking as the enormity of all they faced sank in. Völker broke the silence first, "I regret there is another issue which is that, following his appointment, Funk has already raised the issue of the gold missing after the Hatton Garden break in. Niemeyer has just appointed a special unit of our Intelligence service to visit the crooks involved in the Hatton Garden raid. Time is of the essence here, Karl."

Karl's eyebrows were furrowed as he thought back, "I recall my father saying that there had been an attempt to launder some of this gold in London via a known fence who was also a criminal informer. Did anyone trace the source and interrogate him?"

"We knew his identity and that he was a police informer, but I never sanctioned any such action nor saw any action in that direction," Völker replied, "I suppose, on reflection, it might have been a wise move. I will retrieve his details from our system to which I still have access."

Karl clapped his hands, in a mocking gesture, "You see, you accountants think you know all the answers and sometimes you are incapable of even the simplest deduction. You may thank the Lord you have a *Soldat-Kämpfer* onside."

They both laughed which eased the tension before Karl stated that they should attempt immediate contact with Franz Niemeyer with a view to arranging a meeting.

15

Den of Iniquity

Thursday January 6th 1944 9:00pm
Grand Hôtel Les Trois Rois, Blumenrain, Basel

Thomas McKittrick took the call from Allen Dulles in his hotel suite; Dulles was impressing upon him that urgent, and more specific plans needed making for a strategy to ensure the smooth transition of German business interests in a post-war economy. McKittrick had been requesting guidance, via Dulles, as more German clients were becoming nervous at the prospect of a German defeat, and were seeking assurances regarding the future and their personal security. Dulles had stressed that the strategy of the financial sector was critical to ensure there was little, or no disruption to United States business interests, whilst building a new western bulwark against the Soviet Union which, he said, was the greatest threat now facing global security.

"We gotten a few problems back in the US with some goddamn voices calling for the dissolution of your bank and that anyone who has been involved in doing business with the Nazi regime should face justice. Hell, Thomas, do these guys not realise the financial sector has armed the United States, Britain, and even the Soviet Union? Sure, we did business with the Krauts, but they need to wake up to the reality of the world, and stop living in some God forsaken idealist refuge. But these guys are not all back-water hill-billies, we got a job on making the right waves with the right people. I've got the president's ear but he's up for re-election later this year and I guess even he is a little oversensitive. We need to tread carefully here or we may all end up the wrong side of the Justice Department."

McKittrick felt a sense of alarm that he might be at risk of being targeted and politically sacrificed. "Damn it, Allen, What kind of world do these jerks think we live in? I spoke of this when I came over to the US just over a year ago; I stressed the need to recognise we were in a new world economy based on global imperatives. We are surrounded by leftist radicals. Who is leading this?"

"Those two dumb asses at the Treasury Department, Harry Dexter White and Henry Morgenthau Jnr. They are both Jews so I guess we know what to expect. Listen, this is all too sensitive to go into right now; I guess walls have ears and we need to keep things hush hush, so maybe you could pop on over and I'll see you in a couple of days. Can we meet in my offices, say Saturday at 12:00? Lunch is on me."

McKittrick smiled wryly as he replaced the receiver, recalling previous visits to Dulle's somewhat diminutive 'offices', but he recognised the importance of Dulles not attracting attention to his clandestine work for the OSS. He cast his mind back to December 1942, when he had visited the United States at the invitation of major business interests. There was a growing optimism and recognition that Germany may be on the back foot, after set-backs on the Russian front, and the realistic prospect that the war could now be won by the Allies. Many US entrepreneurs were clamouring to explore the business potential in a post-war market. This had become more prevalent following the defeat of German forces at Stalingrad in early 1943, after which

McKittrick had been prevented from returning to Switzerland by those who saw the BIS as guilty of collaboration with Nazi Germany. Fortunately, Allen Dulles advanced a pragmatic argument to the US government that McKittrick was more useful to the United States back in Basel from where he fed invaluable intelligence on the internal machinations of the Nazi regime. Dulles was, by then, the OSS head of US Intelligence in Switzerland This intervention finally enabled McKittrick's return to the offices of the BIS in April 1943 at which time he was formally recruited as an OSS agent, which Dulles described as "insurance".

On McKittrick's December visit to the United States, he had been summoned to meet with Henry Morgenthau Jnr., who was Treasury Secretary. McKittrick tried to explain to Morgenthau the need for European economic stability, and the pragmatic approach adopted by the bank in standing back and remaining above politics. He had stressed that the BIS was adopting a strict policy of neutrality, without making any judgement over, or becoming involved in, the affairs of sovereign nations. He was genuinely surprised when a white-faced, and furious Morgenthau, accused him of involvement in the attempt by the Nazis to annihilate the Jewish race, storming out of the meeting after only twenty minutes.

That December, a huge dinner was hosted by leading business interests at the University Club in New York, at which McKittrick was guest of honour. Thirty-seven of the most influential financiers, industrialists, and businessmen gathered to hear him speak. He had extolled the importance of recognising emerging global markets, with massive opportunities from improved transport infrastructure, air-travel, and, not least competing political ideologies in a changing world. His speech highlighted that a new working-class was providing an exploding market for consumer items, citing that even Hitler recognised the potential and had capitalised on this by making a people's car available to the masses known as the Volkswagon. Markets, he stressed, did not discriminate based upon the views of those in power, and that business had to rise above such issues taking the higher ground as was exemplified by the BIS. He drew cheers after stressing that the military might of nations would eventually lead to a peace based upon a recognition that advanced weaponry would render warfare obsolete. This could only succeed provided that global suppliers and manufacturers did not become involved in the disputes between their customers or nations, irrespective of whether they were engaged in hostilities. Business, he said, must triumph over adversity and, in that, he echoed a phrase used by Hitler, there must be a 'triumph of the will', driven not by power, nor politics, but in securing the economic stability that would lead to greater prosperity for all. As he finished, he was greeted by a storm of applause and received a standing ovation.

Afterwards, McKittrick met with many who congratulated him on his approach and he felt it was one of the proudest moments of his life. Leading bankers, financiers, and industrialists queued up to shake his hand including the presidents of the New York Federal Reserve, the National City Bank, the Bankers' Trust, and General Electric. He was congratulated on his foresight by a former under-secretary of the treasury and the former U.S. ambassador to Germany. Chief executives were there from Standard Oil, General Motors, JP Morgan, Brown Brothers Harriman, and Kuhn Loeb. An ebullient John Foster Dulles, who was attending with his brother, Allen, had taken him to one side as liqueurs, and coffee were being served.

They had sat on a quilted crimson velvet couch, with occasional tables at each end. McKittrick had declined the offer of a large cigar from an embossed leather case, before John Foster Dulles extracted a gold lighter from his waistcoat, then, after puffing generous clouds of smoke, he had leant forward with an earnest expression, "These are dark times, I'm afraid, Thomas. We gotten Goddamned lefties, and liberals getting all wound up about so-called business ethics. These guys have no real grasp of the need for pragmatism in a changing world. They don't like your bank, and they gonna do all they can to try and pull you down. Whilst we have powerful friends on our side, these sons of bitches are using the sacrifice of American lives in this war as leverage to gain the upper moral ground. They even mobilising the church to speak out, and the president is getting rattled." He paused, as they were offered brandy from a waiter, holding a silver tray with white gloves.

McKittrick was exasperated as he exclaimed, "Do these folk not understand the critical importance of maintaining economic and market stability? After this darn war is over, who the hell do they think is going to pay to clean up the mess and re-build. I need the BIS license to operate in the US re-instating. Hell, we can't officially operate over here since they revoked it back in '41. Now they've taken my Goddamn passport away, so I can't get back to do my job, despite feeding them intelligence on stuff I know about the Krauts."

"We're both going to do our best for you, Thomas. We all need to unite on this," John Foster Dulles stated emphatically. "You need to encourage your business connections in Germany that we gonna look after them, nurture them, so to speak. I'm heading up the Federal Council of Churches in countering the opposition we getting, but these bastards want to see your bank closed. They gonna to stop you returning to Basel, citing national security issues. I'll head them off at the pass with that one in court, but it's gonna to take a little time. I cannot stress to you how important it is to the interests of the United States that we have economic stability in Germany, not just to protect our financial interests, but to avoid the Commies getting more of a foothold. The Ruskies are starting to kick ass, and if they succeed in defeating Hitler on the Eastern Front, they will try to seize German territory and expand their evil regime. Money talks, Thomas, and we need to look after our kind of people, whether they be in Germany, Italy, or Japan. We are the bastions of free enterprise here in the US. As you rightly pointed out this evening, we, representing the interests of global commerce, must rise above political or idealistic constraints, whilst, of course, defending and promoting our virtues of freedom and justice."

That had been just over a year ago and now, already, much of what John Foster Dulles had predicted, was taking a sharper focus. Although he had been prevented from returning to Switzerland or leaving the United States, Dulles had managed to overturn this by April 1943, although the bank's license remained revoked. The Russians had started a relentless offensive pushing German forces back, which were retreating in many areas, although, recognising the very real threat to Germany itself, they were putting up determined resistance, and attempting counter-offensives. In Western Europe, Sicily had fallen to the Allies in July 1943, and Mussolini deposed. By early 1944, the Allies were advancing through southern Italy, although, Mussolini had been rescued by the Germans and re-instated in the north. US forces were gathering in England, in preparation for an invasion of mainland Europe through landings in France. These were widely expected by the summer of 1944.

McKittrick was now being approached by a growing number of German contacts offering information in exchange for assurances, or in order to build bridges in readiness for a post-war scenario. Many businessmen were seeking reassurance that they would escape any retribution for their part in working for the Nazi regime, or in the exploitation of cheap or slave labour resources provided by the Reich.

Saturday January 8th 1944 11:45am
23 Herrengasse, Bern, Switzerland

The cab rattled over the cobble-stoned street on a ridge high above the river Aare, with the Bernese Alps giving a picturesque backdrop to vineyards on tiers, between the street and the river. McKittrick tipped the taxi driver, pulling his trench-coat tightly around him against the piercing cold, as the snow flurried around him. He walked through the arched double-doors of the large five-storey baroque style building, into the welcome warmth of the foyer. On the right was a panelled door on which was a simple notice proclaiming, 'Allen W. Dulles, Special Assistant to the American Minister.' He pressed the buzzer, and seconds later, a smiling jacketless Dulles, with maroon braces over a shirt and tie, greeted him with a warm handshake clasping McKittrick's in both of his. Despite his appearance being like that of an archetypal professor, with his rounded glasses, and thick moustache, McKittrick had come to respect his quick mind, backed by an outstanding analytical ability. Dulles looked around, briefly, checking no one was in sight before leading his guest up some stairs into his office. The smell of pipe-smoke permeated the air. Piles of papers littered the room with its arched window and balcony, from which there was a view across the vineyards to the river below, and the mountains beyond. A large double-pedestal desk was in one corner, behind which was a captain's chair covered with green leather. Opposite the desk was a tall-backed chair, with tired brown padding on which was a box file which Dulles removed, waiving McKittrick to sit.

"Tidiness ain't my strongpoint, Thomas, but I know where to find everything." He laughed as he lit his pipe, "I have to fight off my secretary and my housekeeper who both carp on about sorting my mess out. Goddamn Germanic mindset these Swiss have; order is everything to them. Bourbon?" He walked to a cupboard, pulling out a bottle of *Old Crow* Kentucky Bourbon. "You want a splash of Soda?" McKittrick nodded, extracting a large pad from his briefcase on which he had scribbled notes during the ninety-minute train journey from Basel he had undertaken that morning.

"I am getting a heap of requests, Allen, from the Krauts who want to know what the hell is our strategy after this shindig is over. They want guarantees, and we gotta give these guys something. My bank is also holding a heap of money on their behalf. Rumours are spreading that the BIS may be at risk; I am having to re-assure them but, hell, Allen, I'm concerned at the noises from Washington."

He took the glass from Dulles, swirling the ice in it for a moment before taking a generous drink, savouring the welcome, spreading warmth within, as Dulles re-lit his pipe, puffing smoke from the corner of his mouth. "We have a hill to climb but I'm on it, Thomas. I've got Ambassador Leland Harrison to join us for lunch and he is on our side. As ambassador, he has the president's ear, and, trust me, my friend, once we get the election out of the way, FDR will ensure we get our way. Big business is on our side in this.

"Ok, let me sum up: We got the money boys in the US Treasury ganging up against us in the form of US Secretary to the Treasury, Henry Morgenthau Jnr., and his senior advisor, Harry Dexter White. White is a radical whose vision of the future involves a de-industrialisation of a new Germany based on an enforced agrarian economy."

"Jesus Christ!" exclaimed McKittrick, he sounds like something out of Stalin's Russia. Is this guy some kind of Commie?"

"Listen, buddy, I got my friend, Adolf Berrie, who advises the president on internal security, checking him out. There have been rumours."

"And Morgenthau?" McKittrick asked.

"He's drafted some God-forsaken garbage about partitioning Germany, and creating regions which would be ceded to Poland, France, and Soviet Russia, with some areas coming under international control through a new united nations structure."

"My God, these are crazy ideas," McKittrick exclaimed. "They will destroy an economy in which we all have an interest, and one from which the US will massively gain in the dividends which flow from re-construction."

"I'm afraid it gets worse, my friend," added Dulles. "They are calling for the dissolution of the BIS."

McKittrick uttered just one word, "Hell!", before downing the rest of his drink in one.

Dulles continued, "We have one ace card to play, unless, of course, we have to get down really dirty and involve Hoover's mob at the FBI. Those guys can either make dirt which sticks, or 'remove' the problem which is not something I like to advocate."

"So...the ace card?" came the quick response.

Dulles lent forwards, gesturing with his finger to add emphasis to his words, "John Maynard Keynes, the brilliant British economist. He has the ear of both the president and Winston Churchill. He is on our side, but only if we give export guarantees and promises of immunity to the German businesses who supported Hitler."

At that point, there was a knock at the door, and a smartly dressed woman entered, "The US Ambassador's car is outside, *Herr* Dulles."

"*Danke,* Helga," he responded, turning back to McKittrick, "I think this lunch will be very interesting. I booked the Bellevue Palace. We are eating in *La Terrasse* which can be very useful as my German friends sit in one partitioned half, whilst we Allies dine in the other. This enables much, shall we say, hidden and delicate diplomacy to be conducted."

Twenty minutes later, the large black *Cadillac Series 67* limousine purred up the Kochergrasse in the medieval centre of the Old City of Bern to the ornate colonnaded entrance of the Bellevue Palace. At the entrance, a concierge marched forwards to open the door, then the under-manager stepped forwards, welcoming them both and led the way to *La Terrasse.* McKittrick had heard of the restaurant and its reputation as a covert meeting place for highly sensitive talks wherein both Allied and Axis personnel could meet in a relaxed, sumptuous setting. However, he had never dined there and, as they entered, he was struck by the elegant ambience. From an ornate plaster ceiling, crystal chandeliers added splendour to a long room with arched windows lining one side, giving a view over an external terrace with the mountains adding a dramatic backdrop to the city of Bern from their elevated location. Subtle lighting set into the wood panelled walls on the opposite side, with arched internal windows and doors leading to the lounge area, added a feeling of space. Those guests they passed as they were guided into the restaurant were expensively dressed reflecting the luxury of the hotel, and evidencing their status. The immaculately dressed US ambassador rose to greet them from a table which had been cordoned off behind crimson rope at the top of the room. "Well, howdy boys," he quipped in an exaggerated manner, "glad you could make it." He gestured to the room, "You wouldn't think there was a war on. I've ordered Champagne which will be charged to the federal government and classed as essential wartime expenditure. A fine 1943 *Pol Roger* which, I am told, is British Prime Minister Winston Churchill's favourite. The Krauts sell it to us directly by the truckload through a Swiss agency in exchange for hard currency, or occasionally gold. This is what wartime achieves, ingenuity and resourcefulness in commerce which, gentlemen, is what we need to oil the wheels towards a post-war world economy. One from which we can all share in the handsome proceeds huh?"

McKittrick felt relaxed and at ease with Harrison with whom he had spent considerable time, and they had often met jointly with Dulles. Leland B. Harrison was both a highly experienced senior international diplomat and had held government office, whilst also having worked within intelligence. He was a man who, at sixty years of age, wielded considerable influence with a knowledge of the inner workings of the White House, and was respected by the president to whom he had ready access. He had endorsed McKittrick's recruitment into the OSS, at the suggestion of Dulles, in order both to make McKittrick's position less open to criticism, and facilitate their joint strategy on sensitive financial affairs. Increasingly, McKittrick's intelligence was of considerable interest, giving an insight into the internal situation and direction within the Nazi regime. After the Champagne had been poured, Dulles took over the course of their conversation.

"Gentlemen, I represent some of the most powerful people in Washington, people who expect their investments to be protected, and that the United States will uphold and support our commercial interests, not only during wartime, but afterwards. I need to give the president a fait accompli with an inalienable plan in which he can evaluate the benefits. FDR is nobody's fool and he likes arguments or policy direction to be clearly and concisely set out which he will endorse, if he can see the benefits. He rarely, if ever, changes course and so we need to get this right. Thomas, can you outline to us the latest information you have gained from your German connections."

McKittrick took in a deep intake of breath, "Events are moving fast. German morale has sunk to a new low ebb. After their defeat at Stalingrad, they then lost control of the Ukraine and, as you know, Kiev fell to the Red Army in November; now it appears increasingly likely that the siege of Leningrad will be broken any day, and Russian forces will then drive west towards Poland. The failures on the Russian front have changed the German mindset. They no longer believe in the infallibility of their *Führer*. Instead, they are being fed with new nonsense from their deluded propaganda minister, Goebbels, which is being termed the final heroic struggle, labelled '*Totale Krieg*'. More and more people are approaching me, wanting to know what the strategy of the Allies will be if Germany is defeated or surrenders. There are talks of plots against Hitler, but he still enjoys fanatical support."

Dulles interjected, "I am in touch with some well-connected guys and there is a credible plot against Hitler's life. Those taking part are seeking assurances from us of backing for a post-Hitler government. In that way, they say they can muster support and ensure the overthrow of the regime. However, this does not suit the positive economic aftermath that the economists have projected and I have been forbidden by FDR from giving the plotters against Hitler any guarantees at all. Hell, it would sure save a lot of lives."

There was silence for a moment before McKittrick continued, "We face a situation wherein their business leaders want clarity which I am unable to give. I can tell you that my good friend, and director of the BIS, Emil Puhl, recognises not only the need for direction, but is also desperately concerned about the position of the Reichsbank, of which he is the vice president."

"But surely he must recognise that this institution will be disbanded after the war is over?" Harrison observed, pausing as a waiter attended their table, refilling their glasses, then, "There will be a totally new management structure; initially under the supervision of the Allies."

"Leland, my friend," responded McKittrick, "he is not so concerned about this, but has told me there is a King's fortune in gold held in the vaults of the Reichsbank, some of it which is not even officially traceable as it has been hidden from the records. If the Ruskies get there first, my God, they will have a field day."

"Jesus H Christ!" exclaimed Dulles, "How the hell have they managed to hide this extra gold?"

McKittrick responded. "They call it the *'Versteckte Vermögensfonds'* which were set up on the orders of Hitler to deal with the excess gold they took from the Jews and that which was looted from occupied territories. I am told that they have also managed to effectively steal some gold from their own exchequer through a brilliant accounting fraud scheme. However, Puhl does not know how that is carried out."

"Where the hell do they keep it? Surely it is not all in the Reichsbank vaults?" This time it was Leland Harrison who was looking aghast.

McKittrick looked uncomfortable for a moment, taking in a deep breath before saying in a quiet voice, "I regret, gentlemen, much of it is held by the Bank for International Settlements."

Harrison clapped both his hands over his eyes in exasperation, as Dulles slammed his fist rhythmically on the table, shaking his head in dis-belief.

"Goddamn it, McKittrick!" Dulles spoke first, "Are you crazy? Why the hell did you not speak of this before?"

McKittrick's response was given in an uncertain, faltering voice, "We have high standards of integrity, trust and confidentiality which underpins the foundation of the bank, and this is one reason the institution is held in such high regard. You attended the meeting last August when I announced this."

Dulles now sounded uncertain, "Thomas, if I recall, you stated they were merely opening an account for unmarked gold, but it was never announced that this was to hide a hidden asset; effectively this is theft from their own exchequer to cover their own theft from the Jewish people. Integrity trust, and confidentiality? My God, I think the BIS could be accused of involvement in fraud here." He ran his hand through his hair, displaying his discomfort

"If those Jews in the treasury get to know about this, the BIS is finished," added Dulles with a grim finality to his tone. "Right, gentlemen, we need a strategy and by the time we leave here, we will have one, so help me God."

The tension which had built up relaxed as they discussed direction over their lunch with a main course served of Swiss Black Angus Entrecôte, complemented by shallots and truffled potato mash. A second bottle of *Pol Roger* had been served and both Dulles and Harrison were enjoying large Cuban cigars, courtesy of the hotel manager. They accepted McKittrick's view which he now put across more forcefully that economic *'realpolitik'* demanded that the bank rise above the moral or political judgements that others might make, in order to create a new confidence for investment in a post-war world. He explained that he was walking a tightrope to ensure that the BIS maintained its fierce independence from political allegiance. The German commercial sector, he argued, were not all colluding with the Nazi regime, but were victims of circumstance and had to survive in an autocratic world where speaking out could mean arrest, imprisonment, or worse.

Before they departed, Dulles summed up their approach, after reflecting, "You know, I once met Adolf Hitler. It was back in '33 and

I thought the guy was pretty well-meaning until I began to realise their barbaric treatment of the Jews. Now, here I am, covering up for them, I guess, in the interests of mammon, God help me. You know what is crazy, we are considering giving the guys at the core of the Nazi industrial machine immunity, despite knowing that they have been involved in employing slave labour or, in some of their factories, permitting summary executions. I guess we can't always choose those with whom we do business, nor even like them.

"So, gentlemen, I think we are agreed on a plan in three parts which you, Leland, will confidentially share with the president to get him onside.

1. We give the Kraut businesses export or trading guarantees to a pre-war level, ensuring their sustainability, backed by gold reserves from their so-called 'hidden assets fund'.
2. We give an immunity from prosecution for war crimes to business leaders unless there is incontrovertible evidence proving their direct guilt in the public domain. In such cases, we ensure sentences are short, or rapidly commuted with guarantees that their business interests and personal assets will be protected.
3. We put in place a plan to ensure the safe removal of Nazi gold from the Reichsbank in the event this comes under threat from advancing Soviet forces, which, of course, will include the *VVF* or what might be termed *'Raubgold'*.

Leland Harrison's parting words gave voice to their unease at being complicit in double-standards. "I just feel sorry for those poor bastards reaching out to us for help who are putting their lives at risk in a plot to assassinate Hitler; and we turn the other way, because it is not in our financial interests."

On 20th July 1944, *Oberst im Generalstab* Count Claus Schenk Graf von Stauffenberg, a decorated army officer, attended a military conference at the *Wolfsschanze* (Wolf's Lair), Hitler's Eastern Front HQ. He placed a briefcase, containing a single primed bomb as near to Hitler as he was able, before receiving notice of a pre-arranged phone call, giving him an excuse to leave the room. There should have been two bombs but, on account of last-minute changes to the conference venue, Stauffenberg only had time to prime one. At the meeting were 20 officers and Adolf Hitler. Another officer, *Oberst* Heinz Brandt, moved the briefcase against a table leg, which had the effect of shielding the subsequent blast. At 12:42, the bomb detonated, killing a stenographer instantly and causing the deaths of three other officers. Hitler survived, with minor injuries to his leg, right eye, and a perforated eardrum. At 1:00pm, von Stauffenberg, believing Hitler was dead, flew to Berlin to action a plot to overthrow the regime in a military coup.

Hitler was able to speak personally to commanders on the ground just after 7:00pm, having first spoken to Goebbels. By 11:00pm, the conspirators in Berlin were arrested. At just after midnight, von Stauffenberg, together with other officers involved, was summarily shot outside a military HQ, in the light provided by the headlamps of a parked truck. At 12:30am, a Waffen-SS unit led by *Obersturmbannführer* Otto Skorzeny arrived and further summary executions were forbidden, pending interrogation.

In the aftermath, 7,000 people were arrested of which 4,980 were executed in an orgy of violence, many of whom were not involved, but implicated by the Gestapo, settling old scores or for other unconnected reasons.

16

Transaktions Aufzeichnung

Monday 8th January 2024 2:00pm
Sofiel Munich Bayerpost Hotel, Bayerstrasse 12, Munich

"Franz, it is Friedrich Völker, I need to see you as a matter of urgency." There was a pause; Niemeyer's voice at the other end sounded surprised, and a little hesitant "What is the urgency?"

"I have a record of extremely sensitive *VVF* transactions which, *Herr* Spacil told me before he died, must never be made public because of the information this contained about those organisations involved. He stated that the implications if this escaped into the public domain, could be catastrophic, de-stabilising the political establishment and creating a loss of confidence in the financial sector sufficient to cause a global financial collapse. He indicated that he was taking steps to ensure that the file did not fall into the wrong hands."

The reply was abrupt, "OK... *ja*, but...why have you not divulged this to me previously?"

"Because it was not until today that I came across this information again. I was not sure who I could turn to as *Herr* Spacil was very concerned towards the end, saying that no one could be trusted. I feel that I would rather deliver the documents to you in person. Are you in your offices now?"

There was a pause for a moment before Niemeyer spoke, "*Nein,* if they are so sensitive, bring them to me later; shall we say 7:00pm at another address...on Ludwigshöher Strasse, Thalkirchen, south of the city centre, near the river? Do you know it?"

Völker acknowledged the address as he scribbled the number down on a hotel pad in front of him.

"Where are you now?" Niemeyer asked, this time taking Völker by surprise, but he managed to respond in a matter of a fact voice.

"I'm just about to leave the *Ratskeller* where I've been having a catch up with friends. Is there a problem?"

"No matter." The voice was abrupt and indifferent. "I think it would be better if you do not share that you are meeting me with anyone...for security reasons...7:00pm." The line went dead.

"I think he knows what has happened," Völker said with a sigh, "His reaction seemed strained.

"And that, *mein Buchhalter,* is why you need me," said Karl raising his eyebrows as he gave Völker a wry smile, "but, I think we may bring in some additional support or, in military terms, reinforcements."

He reached into his wallet extracting the thin grey plastic card with the intersecting triangles in black, which he placed on the table.

"*Mein Gott,* where did this come from?" Völker looked incredulous.

"I thought you knew everything about my father," Karl replied laconically.

"You know then; this logo is *Die Spinne,*" Völker covered the card with his hand, "and it is not good to show this openly."

Now Karl recalled with a jolt, seeing letters bearing the same mark amongst his father's papers on his desk many years before, which, he had been told, represented a spider on a web.

"I may not like you people," Karl responded with a slight smile, "but in the military we are trained to use every resource at our disposal, so, for the first time in my life, I will call upon the assistance of the Reich." Völker shook his head with a despairing resigned look as Karl pressed the number into his phone; there was a brief pause then a friendly female voice, "Please key in your unique chosen six-digit numeric code preceded by a letter." Karl entered S080545, smiling to himself that it represented S for the surrender of Germany and the date that this was signed to end the Second World War in Europe. There was a short pause before the same voice announced, "Thank you for your patience; please now key in your father's date of birth." After Karl had done this, he looked up. "You people deservedly had a reputation for efficiency." "Perhaps, you should join the GVR," Völker replied resulting in a single fingered gesture from Karl, as they both recognised the growing camaraderie between them.

The voice in Karl's ear now said, "You are now being put through." Then, a male voice, "*Bitte,* you now need to say clearly where you were given this number?"

"I received a package from an adult male in the grounds of the Church of St Georg, *Bogenhausen,* last Friday."

"*Guten Tag, Herr Biesecker,* this is Major Dieter Metz," came the swift response.

Thirty minutes later, a black Mercedes drew up outside the hotel with heavily tinted windows, and they were greeted by the blonde-haired Metz, in his darkened glasses, as he had worn previously. They entered the rear of the vehicle, Karl furtively glancing to right and left as he did so. Metz spoke in an almost jovial tone, "I was kind of expecting your call after I heard about the drama at the *Rumfordschlössl* this morning. Your little shoot-out has caused a hell of stink, and alarm bells rang after we received a call from an informer in the *Deutsch*

Abteilung or DA saying that a hit had been authorised; I wondered whether it was you. I nipped over to the *Rumfordschlössl* and spoke to one of the terrified staff who recalled the name of a BND officer requesting a room as being Geldmann, which gave the game away, so to speak. Now, we have had no less than Chancellor Olaf Scholz, himself, on the phone to my boss demanding an explanation. The chancellor is furious, especially as he has been informed that a neo-Nazi extremist group were involved. A code has been issued warning the press that this is a matter of national security and must be passed off as an isolated incident resulting from the action of a former deranged army officer suffering from PTSD."

"My day goes from bad to worse," Karl muttered, "first, I am forced into recruiting this dummkopf as a partner, then I am shot at, and now I am written off as deranged, quite apart from suffering the accusation from a Major in the BND that I may have caused this incident." They all chuckled, as Karl introduced the former deputy financial controller of the GVR, Friedrich Völker, whom, he said, had already deservedly earned the nickname, *'Buchhalter'*.

"I knew of you by name, of course, *Herr* Völker, but I am unsure why you may wish to associate yourself with this man; you know he is armed and dangerous. Shall we dispense with formalities? Please, call me Dieter." The banter of the exchange eased the tone and there was already a sense of growing between them.

Karl briefed Dieter on the direction of his initial enquiries, his knowledge of the source of the *VVF,* and missing gold which had disappeared after the 2015 Hatton Garden robbery in London, much of which Dieter was aware. He informed him of the meeting arranged for Friedrich with Niemeyer, but that there had been a stipulation that Friedrich should come alone. However, he did not mention the bullion bars secreted by his father for the 'inheritance,' trusting in the assurance of confidence from Friedrich Völker. Dieter had not told them where they were going other than to a safe area where they could consider a strategy. It was somewhat of a surprise, therefore, after a thirty-minute drive heading south of the city, when the Mercedes turned into Heilmannstrasse, heading past bland grey walls, and turning right towards a wide entrance to what Karl knew were the BND headquarters in the Pullach area. He had a fleeting worry he had allowed himself to be drawn into a trap when Dieter stopped the car, twenty metres before the entrance barrier, turning round.

"Welcome to BND HQ. Trust me, my friends, this is about the safest place you could be right now. On a given password, no one will even look inside the vehicle. We will then proceed to a concealed entrance at the rear which is used for clandestine meetings. Many people have entered here without any press knowledge at all, including prime ministers and presidents. We had President George W Bush and Prime Minister Blair here when they met with Prime Minister Ariel Sharon of Israel for a secret briefing on Iraqi WMD just before the second Gulf war. No one even knew they were in this area at the time. Oh..." he added with a grin, "in addition, I can add a little touch of irony here that this used to be the HQ of the *Gehlen Organisation*."

"Who the hell are they?" Karl asked, almost anticipating, with dread, the type of answer he would receive.

"This was an intelligence organisation set up by both the CIA in the US and the senior former Nazi Head of Intelligence on the Eastern Front, *Generalmajor* Reinhard Gehlen, after the end of the Second World War. They became the eyes and ears of America during the Cold War era of espionage and covert operations against the Soviet Union and East Germany. Gehlen was involved in recruiting many former Nazis to work for US and British Intelligence. He was the first head of the

BND, retiring in 1968 when he was awarded the Grand Cross of the Order of Merit of the Federal Republic of Germany."

"*Lieber Gott!* Is there no end to the pervasive infection and infiltration of you people?" Karl looked askance.

"Where have you been, Karl?" was the cheerful reply. "Who do you think was helping to run government? We even had former senior *Wehrmacht* officers in NATO. They just swapped one uniform for another." He gunned the engine, heading towards the barrier, which was flanked by two guards, turning to say, "Please be silent as we clear security; there may be additional restrictions as a result of this morning's exchange of fire." He need not have been concerned although one of the guards did ask whether he had checked passengers he may be carrying for weapons. Karl smiled, as he placed his hand on the reassuring grip of his weapon.

After entering an enclosed port surrounded by blackened glass, they left the Mercedes, and Dieter pressed two fingers over a security recognition scanner. A door swung open and he led the way, leaving his vehicle access fob on a small desk as they entered a long corridor. They took a lift to the third floor, exiting onto a thick carpeted area which Dieter announced was the "executive suite." They followed him through double light wood panelled doors into a large office with a meeting table to one side, and a couch with easy chairs beneath a lamp on the other, whilst under a window a large black semi-circular desk was positioned.

Dieter pointed to the easy chairs, removing his thick leather jacket and flat cap, before taking their coats and clicking an intercom switch, calling for coffees.

"The question I have for you, Karl," he began, is why you wish to see Niemeyer?"

Karl thought quickly, realising that trust was clearly compromised within the GVR. He did not wish to give too much away, despite sensing that Dieter could be trusted. However, he decided that if he stayed close to the truth, he might probe Dieter's motives and loyalty. He was aware that, bizarrely, he was effectively protecting the organisation he had spent a lifetime hating. "The information I have is that your man, Niemeyer, may have been compromised and that he may be working for the *Reichslegion*."

At that moment, the door buzzer sounded and Dieter clicked a remote by his chair to permit entry. A rather overweight man, with a large moustache entered in a white chef's jacket, wheeling a small trolly, announcing in a deep voice, "My pleasure is to serve you *Kaffee und Kuchen*. I trust *Dallmayr* coffee is good for you? I have prepared some light sweet cakes and pastries also."

"*Danke* Johan, I am sure my guests will be impressed at your skills." The man bowed and exited leaving Karl to exclaim, "Trust the BND to get service like this; in the *Kommando Spezialkräfte,* we go to a canteen or make it ourselves."

"That is because you are the brawn, whereas Dieter and I represent the brains of this country," quipped Friedrich, causing Dieter to laugh as he poured the coffee.

As he handed a cup to Karl, Dieter's next comment both surprised and re-assured him. "Your information on Niemeyer is good, I think, as we have had our suspicions for some time. Our people are keeping a very close eye on him; but, as the net closes in, so to speak, we may have a situation where the *Reichslegion* has already decided to act decisively. This may explain the attempts on your life; however, there is another major problem which I can share with you. *Der Leiter* has not been seen in public for two weeks and although he is very secretive and rarely ever communicates his location, even to those close to him, we became concerned when emails were not being responded to in the last week. We spoke to his wife yesterday. As you may be aware, she is a *Bundestagsabgeordnete* (Bundestag Deputy) for the *AfD*, and she has confirmed that she is worried; he has gone days without communicating and has not responded to messages she has left for him. He recruits his own security people and their identity is secret. However, his private secretary told us this morning that she has a protection contact number and will attempt them to obtain information. If my worst suspicions are correct, Herr Hackman many have either been kidnapped or worse."

"Ah, *Die Nacht der langen Messer!*" Remarked Karl wryly.

"You clearly know your history," Dieter replied. "Yes, that 1934 'Night of the Long Knives' Nazi purge was extremely bloody, with over 85 murdered, and some claim double that number. However, it effectively removed any potential challenges to Hitler. I hope to God we are not yet facing anything of that magnitude; it could bring about the collapse of our government. The reaction against the right could result in a ban against the AfD, and other parties just when we are making strides to gain a greater foothold on political power. You know that in the last twelve months, our vote in the AfD has grown and the opinion polls are showing an increase in popularity. If there is open street violence, the calls for right-wing parties to be banned will gain traction again."

Karl shook his head disdainfully, "*Gott*, you people are everywhere."

"That is democracy, *mein Soldat-Kämpfer!*" interjected Friedrich, with a grin.

Karl held up a derisory two fingers, with a sigh, then turned back to Dieter.

"Are the *Reichslegion* also infiltrating the AfD?"

"Not as far as we know, but we do know they are involved in the ultra-right-wing party, *Die Heimat*. They are also anxious that the resurgence of belief in the right must not be compromised, but maybe after the success of their audacious attack last year on the armoured security convoy escorting a shipment of gold at *Gottmadingen*, they believe that they can act more brazenly."

"Who leads the *Reichslegion?*" Karl asked. Although briefed on the existence of the organisation by his father, he had not revealed any information about the leadership.

"There is not one leader as far as we are aware, but a leadership group whose identity is a closely guarded secret. This is especially so since the killings began in 2022, although we have had a truce in place right now for a year because of the political reasons I have outlined. However, if they have taken Hackman, that will end and things could become very violent."

Friedrich lent forwards, "So, the question must be, do I meet with Niemeyer or not? At least we know his location."

"I think you should attend, but perhaps carrying less than he expects, which may guarantee your safety. I have a plan. We need to wire you up for sound, and then, if things become a little tense, we go in heavy with my crack team of GSG 9" (elite special forces unit)

Karl spoke up, "I will accompany you, Dieter. You may understand I am fully trained in urban warfare, and have combat experience."

"*Verdammt,* Karl, this is not Beirut, or Afghanistan, but Munich…You have already caused mayhem on our streets," countered Dieter with an exaggerated gesture, holding his hands up, causing them to smile.

"I think you may understand that I know your background almost as well as you do. That is my job; I am an intelligence officer after all. Right, the time is 4:00pm. We need to prepare a plan. You said you had told Niemeyer you had a file of transactions. Can you explain to me why this might be of interest to Niemeyer?"

"I think I may be able to assist there," said Karl, "I have the *Transaktions Aufzeichnung* which is a record of all transactions made between the *VVF*, banks, and other bodies, covering the period from 1945 to 1947. This records the disposal of billions of dollars-worth of gold and currency looted by the Nazis. The document was left for me by my father as, what he termed, 'insurance'. If any of the information contained in there was to leak out, it would potentially bring down some the world's leading financial institutions, notwithstanding an unprecedented scandal involving not just banks, but the Papacy and the Roman Catholic Church."

"*Mein Gott!*" Dieter exclaimed in a breathless voice, "This is becoming huge. We have never been made aware of this"

"Dieter, this is my life insurance policy; if anything happens to me, this will be made public. Your people, no matter how much they have reformed, may wish to have me eliminated."

Dieter responded, "Karl, we are not like this; we have changed and we are committed to a democratic path. That is why the *Reichslegion* broke away. They are the danger to Germany now. There are many like us across Europe, look at Kurt Vilders in Holland, or the Italian Prime Minister, Georgia Meloni. We just believe in order, strong leadership, and national pride in our heritage. Is this so wrong?"

Karl reached for the electronic pad in his case on which he had been compiling a record of evidence from what he had found in his father's box.

"Your heritage; how can we balance heritage or even relate this to what happened?" Karl's voice betrayed the very real emotion he felt.

Dieter held up his hand, both acknowledging and parrying the point, "Karl, please, we must learn to commit the past to history. Do we now condemn Britain or the United States for their past? Where would we stop? When the victors became complicit in the crimes of the perpetrators, does that make them any better? I have my ideals too; dwelling on the horrors of the past does not change what happened. Surely, we should unite in protecting the future."

Karl sighed deeply, "*Ach*, you do not realise how huge this is, Dieter, or how I carry the guilt of the past because of my family. Your Nazi friends were very thorough, and, of course, in that I include my grandfather, Josef Spacil. I have records of receipts for *Judenleihgebühr,* you know what this is? Payments made by some of the leading businesses of the day, most of which still exist, for Jewish slave labour."

"Please, Karl, I do not condone the actions of our forefathers. Let us join in stopping the extremist people of today." He nodded emphatically, then extended his hand; Kerl hesitated, then shook it, with a rueful smile, saying, "Ok...ok."

"So, Karl, why would Niemeyer be so worried about what your father left you?"

"Where do I start? There are detailed records of bullion and currency deposits made at leading banks looted from the Jews and stolen from occupied territories. Vast gold deposits were transferred into the Bank of Spain, organised by the German SS commander, Otto Skorzeny, who was a friend of my grandfather. Vast shipments of gold were taken out of Germany and never traced."

Karl now referred to the notes he had made on his tablet. "Some gold went by U-Boat in 1945 to Argentina in highly secret operations to finance the foundation for a new administration under the Hitler's former Nazi Party secretary, Martin Bormann. U-977 carried Bormann to Argentina, together with huge reserves of gold on both this submarine and another, U-530. As the records show, they were organising the formation of the 4th Reich from there.

"Even American crime was involved in arranging shipments of gold from Europe to the United States which was either looted by US troops, or paid to them in bribes. American forces closed in on the caches of gold in April and May 1945, and many went back to the United States very rich men. Burial sites containing small amounts of currency and bullion were discovered by them and officially surrendered to cover up what was really happening. The Mafia became involved because of the security needed to ship the gold. Here in Germany, we developed contacts within the Genovese Family in New York City through, get this, a Jewish mobster by the name of Meyer Lansky. Imagine if any of this emerged? This is probably the greatest cover-up in history because no one dared speak out…it was just too big. The file I hold implicates some of our greatest and trusted institutions. So, you are correct, Dieter, this is huge, but it is more than huge. There is so much more but, as you say, time is short."

By 6:00pm, they had formulated a strategy; Friedrich and Karl had been introduced to a thick-set, burly man, in military uniform, by the name of *Polizeihauptkommissar* Bruno Schneider. He was to lead a *GSG 9* unit whose brief was to take the building on Dieter's order, or if Friedrich activated an alarm signal secreted inside a highly sensitive listening device which appeared to be a pen. They studied a projection of the property on the large screen on one wall of the office. "Do you wish me to authorise drone surveillance, Bruno?" Dieter asked.

"I think it will not be necessary, *Herr Major;* we will assault directly from the front with a back-up accessing the rear of the property from the lane adjacent to the woodland behind." He grinned at Karl and Friedrich. "Trust me, we specialise in shock and awe; we will not be knocking on the front door."

"I only thank God that I am on your side," responded Karl. They changed into black combat-wear, blackened their faces, and were issued with gas masks and helmets. Friedrich was to be driven to the house on Ludwigshöher Strasse in what appeared to be a taxi, driven by a plain clothes officer, escorted by an unmarked car which would follow at a discreet distance.

Karl shook Friedrich's hand as he left, saying with a wry smile, "*Viel Glück, Kamerad,* I admire what you are doing…if you are successful, I might just accept you as a true partner." The rude forearm jerk signal he received, in return, was not entirely unexpected.

Karl followed Dieter down a corridor to a lift taking them to the lower ground floor, then through a heavy door into a large open space with small windows around the grey upper walls. A group of twenty heavily armed men, dressed in assault gear, were checking their weapons.

They walked across to where the stocky figure of Schneider was standing, scrutinising bags of equipment. He looked up as they approached and spoke tersely.

"Please allow my men in first, but follow close behind just in case we have any problems from the rear." He handed Karl a set of ear defenders and darkened glasses, "We are going to use *M-84* stun grenades which give one almighty bang, disorientate, creating loss of balance, and cause temporary blindness."

"Yes, I used these in Afghanistan," Karl replied. "How will we gain entry?"

"We are using the latest version of the *Simon* breach grenade. The Israelis invented it. All we do is attach the projectile to an *M-16;* they have one hell of a punch. We can breach from 15-20 metres away and its accurate, easy to use, and causes minimum collateral damage. These mothers are the best for gaining quick entry."

A variety of weapons were either held by unit members or neatly stacked next to bags containing assault devices and explosive. Karl recognised most of them including two of his favourites, the *Heckler* and *Koch 416* assault rifle, and the *G95KA1;* the latter, a recently introduced short barrel version weapon.

Metal shutters were raised at one end of the assembly area and a truck reversed inside. The men piled into the back and the bags loaded in, as Dieter and Karl joined Schneider in the front. Karl been offered a *SIG 550* assault rifle but had opted to rely on his *Glock* handgun which he now checked as the truck pulled out for the ten-minute drive to Thalkirchen. "Be careful where you point that bastard," remarked Schneider dryly, "those things are dangerous."

On entering Thalkirchen, they pulled into a wooded parking area where a number of vans with tinted windows were waiting. After Schneider held a final briefing with his unit, they unloaded the truck, dispersing into the waiting vehicles. Schneider walked back to where Dieter and Karl were standing, directing them to enter a van with him, whilst two commandos loaded weapons and equipment into the rear. "The operation will commence from the back of this vehicle, so, you will enjoy the spectacle, and miss nothing." Schneider grinned as he spoke, his teeth showing white against his blackened face, and Karl recognised, like many he worked with on combat operations, that Schneider truly relished his work.

In the 'taxi', Friedrich was turning over in his mind how he was going to play out the scenario put to him by Dieter. He could feel the adrenalin, sensing the danger to which he was subjecting himself, but somehow thrilling to this. All his life he had spent working in accounting and administration, envious of those he often met who seemed to lead more exciting lives. As a result of working for Heinz Spacil, he had mixed with some interesting people. These included many military figures, espionage agents, and politicians including those from the former East Germany, which had united with West

Germany the year he joined *VVF AG*. At that time, he had met many of those who had once held prominent roles in the Third Reich. They were elderly by then but there was always something similar about them that he noticed. Despite their ages, they had a proud bearing, and refused to ever countenance any criticism, implied or otherwise, of the Nazi era. Some of them had even greeted each other by extending their arms in the Nazi salute. He had formed a friendship with one of them, Wilhelm Höttl, who had become fabulously rich from money laundering activities involved in secreting monies from the Reich after the war. There was almost a contradiction behind him, as he had used a considerable amount to found and endow a school in Bad Aussee in Austria, serving as director, and in which he taught until his retirement in 1980. He had been quite a genial old man, fascinating Friedrich with his stories of how he had duped the authorities, yet involved many in his dubious activities of secreting monies and valuables. Ironic, Friedrich now thought, that he should be on the trail of those who had stolen some of this which was a prospect he rather liked. Frankly, at the age of sixty-three, he had been presented with what might be his last chance of ever gaining some real excitement in his life and he was relishing the challenge he was facing.

17

Bretton Woods

Saturday 24th June 1944 11:00am
Chequers, Aylesbury, Buckinghamshire

The Prime Minister, dressed in a burgundy silk dressing gown, stood up and thundered the words - "I deem this suggestion preposterous, Mr Keynes, that we should afford financial guarantees to these Nazi perpetrators of some of the greatest crimes in recorded history, and heinous plots against our empire, notwithstanding Hitler's dastardly plans, with his loathsome gangsters, to impose his dark shadow over the peoples of Europe. This is anathema to me, Mr Keynes, anathema. "As the great bard himself warns, *"How quickly nature falls into revolt When gold becomes her object!,"* to which, I shall add, 'The folly of rewarding the vanquished, will cost the victor dearly. Here we are, within one month of launching the greatest, most noble armada in history in our endeavour to remove the curse of this evil under which we have witnessed tyranny and suffered the pain of loss as our brave men toil and give the supreme sacrifice, and you dare to suggest assisting those whose production has prolonged our struggle?"

There was an uncomfortable pause, as each of the four men sitting in front of Churchill around the dark oak meeting table in the historic

Elizabethan splendour of the Hawtrey Room, considered their response. The smell of cigar smoke hung heavy in the air, whilst the low ceiling and panelled walls, on which were hung tapestries, and portraits, gave a sense of deceptive homeliness and relaxation. This contrasted with the mood as Keynes faced the difficulty of obtaining Churchill's endorsement of a policy which he would not readily accept. Sir John Maynard Keynes had requested an urgent meeting with the Prime Minister, having received a worrying report from Allen Dulles about a post-war plan being hatched in the United States, to dismantle the German economy. He knew Dulles well from pre-war visits he had made to Washington. Keynes had first met him when giving a presentation to President Franklin Roosevelt in 1934 on his theory for economic growth that had been published in a book entitled '*The means to Prosperity*'. Dulles had come to greatly respect and support the views of Keynes which were adopted, in part, by the US government.

The figure of Major General Stewart Menzies in a black pinstripe suit, who had remained silent in the unfolding exchange which had begun some twenty minutes earlier, now spoke. "I think, Prime Minister, if I may, that we, perhaps, need to weigh up the intelligence benefits here. Jerry is on his back foot, and our chaps sniffing around are getting more and more chatter about dissatisfaction and disillusion amongst those surrounding Hitler and his henchmen. There are some benefits if we offer a few carrots to the German commercial sector; you know the type of thing, assurances of immunity or the commuting of prison sentences, and combine these with a sprinkling of commercial post-war guarantees, as suggested by my learned friend, Sir John Maynard Keynes. We can, I think, fuel the fire of the Jerry business community's unhappy plight, so to speak, by spreading a little hope, whilst also demoralising their war effort at the same time."

Churchill lit his cigar, thinking for a moment, then, in a calmer voice, "I think it was Henry Fielding who said, "*Make money your God, and it will plague you like the devil...*" I am thankful that I have paid scant attention to the value of the former in my life, yet in so doing, I have oft attempted to resist the temptations of the latter. How the devil, forgive the repetition, do you propose we de-moralise the Nazi businessman?"

Menzies replied confidently - "We destroy their hope in every aspect of their regime, sow seeds of economic confusion, depress the value of their businesses, add uncertainty to their investments, and destroy credibility in their economy. They will be grateful for our assistance, whilst we undervalue their assets; in this way, our own investors and those from the United States can profit from the conclusion of the war, and obtain stakes in the post-war economy at a lower cost."

"Confound you, Sir," Churchill responded, "you are, indeed, one devious Machiavellian with whom I would not wish to engage in a game of poker."

"Prime Minister, I am merely fulfilling the role for which I am grateful you entrusted me to perform," Menzies countered with a tone of affected shock.

"I am surrounded by those who do not shrink from performing dastardly deeds, and, whilst I have always admired those who act upon conviction, my own endorsement may, on occasion, be tempered by jurisprudence or, perhaps, by a failure to properly evaluate the outcome. I recall Lucio's words in '*Measure for Measure*',

"*Our doubts are traitors,*

And make us lose the good we oft might win,

By fearing to attempt."

"I believe, Prime Minister," the quiet but authoritative voice of Sir John Anderson, the newly appointed chancellor of the exchequer, commanded the attention of those present, "we might be well-advised to heed the words of Sir John Keynes. We have opposed his views previously, yet recognised, upon embracing his ideas, that our economy can expand and thrive with responsible borrowing and manipulation by the treasury. If he can advise us on rising out of the catastrophic effects of the financial crash of 1929 by doing what no one at the time was proposing; that being to borrow, spend, and enlarge the role of the exchequer, then, Sir, assuredly, we are well advised to take heed of his words. I conclude that he may have a very valid point. If we adopt the American suggestion of humiliating the Germans and starving their economy, as I understand they propose, we are repeating the mistakes of the Treaty of Versailles; a humiliation upon which Hitler relied in seizing power. I am utterly opposed to such a strategy which assuredly would lead to the destruction of an economy and the horrific deprivation of the people." He then removed his glasses, folding them deliberately, as if to add gravitas and a finality to his words, "Notwithstanding, I might add, Prime Minister, the opportunities which might then be lost to our own economy from those amongst us who might benefit from investing in the resurgence of a post-war German economy under our jurisdiction."

The immaculately dressed figure of Sir Anthony Eden, attired in a morning suit, with a styled and folded white top hankey set in a dark grey jacket, quipped, "Here, here. Look here, Winston, I can subdue these chaps, using what you term 'dastardly tactics', through my people at the *Political War-fare Executive.* We can leak a few letters, let it be known which names are being looked at for capital punishment, or life sentences; you know the sort of thing. Frightful business, but we can scare Jerry witless, then offer a few little carrots, whilst investing judiciously, and prepare to reap the rewards of a *Royal Flush,* to echo your reference. Might even have a little flutter myself; I did have a fine win at Ascot last May when it resumed activities, and I confess that the prospect of making a little money from these cads is not an unattractive proposition. To use another quote, Winston, might I say, *'If your enemies are hungry, feed them. If they are thirsty, give them something to drink. In doing this, you will heap burning coals of shame on their heads.'* A biblical quote from Romans, I believe, old chap"

Churchill, long used to Eden's impertinent lack of formality and deference towards him, grunted and rose from the table. He walked to the window, peering out over the rolling grounds of grass and trees surrounding the 16th century building, nestling in the heart of the Buckinghamshire countryside. He had long learned to despise the enemy, which assisted in his authorising some of the more uncomfortable aspects of the war wherein lives would be lost in significant numbers.

Churchill now turned to face them, reflecting, "Leadership is never an easy mantle to bear, the weight of which can be the cause of more discomfort than the reward, privilege, or protection afforded. These perpetrators of some of the greatest crimes the world has witnessed or imagined, my conscience dictates, reinforced by the cries of those who have perished under their cruel, barbaric savagery, must never escape justice. The men and women of our empire who have toiled these long years, many suffering the pain of loss of those dear to them, or who will endure the agonies of their injuries for a lifetime will say, 'Never parley with those responsible, and exact a revenge so terrible that the world will shudder at the consequences.' But then, does that course make the victors guilty of sinking into a dark abyss from which they will never rest, tormented by their actions?" His words, spoken to the British nation only three years before and broadcast from this very room, echoed in his ears, as he walked slowly back to his seat, "*We will never parley, we will never negotiate with Hitler or any of his gang. We shall fight him by land, we shall fight him by sea, we shall fight him in the air, until, with God's help, we have rid the earth of his shadow and liberated the people from his yoke."*

"Sir, if I might add..." the voice of Maynard Keynes had a somewhat exasperated note. "As you will know, I have many connections with associates in the United States of America which include some who advise the president. I regret to inform you that I believe President Roosevelt is currently being mis-advised by his Secretary to the Treasury, Henry Morgenthau, to dismantle the German state. Additional pressure is being applied by his very persuasive and highly influential US Treasury Department official, Harry Dexter White."

Stewart Menzies interjected, "Prime Minister, our own connections in Washington have some concerns about this chap, White; he seems to be somewhat over fond of our Soviet...er allies. Our sources in Intelligence are whispering that there is some disquiet over his associates. Dashed if I know why Roosevelt listens to him, but he has, I am afraid to say, got the ear of the president."

"I'm afraid it gets worse, Sir," Keynes continued, "my contact within the Bank for International Settlements, has picked up a highly classified US Treasury paper, drafted by Morgenthau, which drives a coach and horses through any of the post-war agreements which you have negotiated with both President Roosevelt and Soviet Premier Stalin. The paper is entitled '*Suggested Post-Surrender Program for Germany*'. Keynes reached into his briefcase, extracting a document which he handed to Churchill who stared intently at the contents through his half-moon glasses perched on the end of his nose.

"How the deuce did you obtain this and why was it surrendered to you?" Churchill's eyebrows were deeply furrowed.

"Pretty easy, actually Sir," Keynes replied in a lighter tone than was, perhaps warranted, "Thomas McKittrick, the American president of the Bank for International Settlements, is also employed by American Intelligence as an asset. His handler is the Head of OSS in Bern, Switzerland; a chap called Allen Dulles with whom I am also well acquainted. Dulles is an intelligence advisor close to Roosevelt, and has access to secret presidential briefings. He is, Sir, implacably opposed to Morgenthau's plan which, incidentally, also calls for the dissolution of the BIS, hence McKittrick's interest." His tone now became more serious again, "Prime Minister, this Morgenthau program calls for, amongst other matters, the abolition of any German army, the destruction of its entire armaments industry and the splitting up of Germany, as a country, into a number of states. The plan proposes that some of these states are administered by the United Nations, parts being taken by France, and others by Poland, with the forced de-industrialisation of large parts of Germany, including the Ruhr region. The proposal also entails the closure and destruction of all mines. Sir, this would involve turning Germany into a non-state, removing its sovereignty, and force the German people to live off the land, which is economically impossible. The result would be the death by starvation of large parts of the German population, whilst decimating its post-war industrial economic structure. The result would be anarchy, which the Soviets would no doubt welcome, reaping the benefits in the ensuing social unrest, by spreading the seeds of communism; this, whilst ensuring the wholesale destruction of any potentially productive elements of German industry or its economy."

Those present in the room sighed at the horrific ramifications of Keynes' words, and there was quiet as they absorbed the enormity of what was being proposed in the United States. It was Anthony Eden who broke the silence, "I am moved to speak very directly on this matter and I cannot stress my position on this more clearly. I will not put my name behind, nor lend nor give support to such a monstrous enterprise which I see as a betrayal of our values. This is a route to creating a slump across Europe which would spread to the world, quite apart from our nation becoming culpably involved in the mass starvation of millions of the German civilian population – assuredly a recipe for the spread of Marxism."

Churchill's face had reddened, "This is outrageous! A betrayal of the foundations of our trust in our allies and all that I have built upon in the creation of the Anglo-American alliance for a post-war Europe. I will have none of it, nor be drawn into signing off on this ill-founded strategy, the results of which future generations would rightly condemn us for accepting. The British Empire will not be subdued but its voice will be heard, as it was in the darkest days, standing up against tyranny for the cause which we know, by our historic instinct, is the right direction to take, guided by the unconquerable spirit of Britannia, and, gentlemen, destiny will be our judge, overseen by the Almighty." His voice had calmed as he re-lit his cigar, looking directly at Keynes, "I remain puzzled, Sir Maynard, if not vexed, by the question posed by your concern over the future of the accursed Swiss Bank for International Settlements, the activities of which I have had the misfortune to become acquainted with previously. Not least, Sir, when they facilitated the plundering by the Nazis of the assets of Czechoslovakia after their unprovoked invasion. Why should I wish to save this BIS?"

At that moment, there was a loud rhythmic knock on the door, and a balding man entered, dressed in a jacket with tails over grey trousers, wearing matching grey gloves. He walked briskly forwards, bowing to Churchill, then nodded his head briefly towards those round the table in a show of respect. "Forgive me, Sir, might I remind you that it is the hour of 12:30pm and that luncheon will be served at 1:00pm, as instructed. Should I serve pre-lunch aperitifs?"

"Ah, Sawyers, my good man, you may, indeed, prepare Champagne but we will wait until luncheon is served before partaking. Might I ask what the good Mrs Landemare has prepared for my esteemed guests?"

Sawyers bowed again, "I believe melon will be served, Sir, followed by beef consommé with oaked sherry, completed with a main course of roast beef."

"Ah, I think my guests would appreciate some *Pol Roger* Champagne, especially as they are from the financial sector and hence, must be treated with favour."

"Indeed, Sir." Churchill's butler stepped back a pace, nodded again, and exited the room.

During this exchange, Keynes had produced another folder from his case, from which he was leafing through papers. He then placed these neatly on the table, referring to them as he spoke, "Prime Minister, if I may continue; as you are aware, last month, the Americans proposed that a conference be convened to discuss a global post-war monetary system. My sources inform me that the Norwegians, having been briefed by this blighter, Morgenthau, from the US Treasury, will present disturbing evidence about the Bank for International Settlements. This will allege that the BIS has been involved in activities which might be adjudged as colluding with war crimes and hence, demand that the bank be liquidated, a move which you might wish to endorse. However, I beg that I may advise you on a different course, and, Sir, with good reason."

Churchill lent forwards, his mouth clasped around his cigar, with a firm resolute expression, waving Keynes to continue.

"The deputy director of the Reichsbank, Emil Puhl, is a regular visitor to Switzerland where he socialises with the president of the BIS,

Thomas McKittrick. He provides a useful conduit, feeding intelligence regarding the activities of increasingly disenchanted German business executives. As the Soviets are now on the offensive, these businesses are increasingly seeking safe places to invest their assets; the Bank for International Settlements is a well-respected institution in Germany, and it is one in which we have an interest. Indeed, one of the major shareholders is the Bank of England. If the BIS is liquidated, we in Britain will lose leverage over post-war German industry, notwithstanding the interest we must take in stimulating the post-war European economy and not strangling it, as Morgenthau is proposing."

Churchill stubbed his cigar out with a thumping gesture, and interjected, "Look here, Sir Maynard, could we ever justify benefitting from these confounded individuals who have, through their involvement and, yes, investment in the dark deeds of the tyrannical regime of the madman who presides over the evil of the Nazis?"

The reply was hesitant, yet delivered succinctly, drawing uncomfortable sighs and coughs from those in the room. "Sir, since the mid 1930's, we have benefitted from, and, might I say, participated in a financial system which has rewarded us from Nazi activities."

Churchill's voice rose again, "Explain yourself, Keynes; my patience is being tried.

"O gentle son,
Upon the heat and flame of thy distemper,
sprinkle cool patience.""

Keynes looked pensively for a moment, then took a deep breath before replying in an impersonal tone. "Prime Minister, you will recall the stink in Parliament over the Czechoslovak scandal. In summary, the Nazis marched into Prague in March 1939 and immediately sent armed soldiers to the offices of the National Bank. The Czech directors were ordered, on pain of death, to send a request which instructed the BIS to transfer 23.1 metric tonnes of gold from the Czechoslovak BIS account, held at the Bank of England, to the Reichsbank BIS account, also held at Threadneedle Street here in London. Our diligent governor of the Bank of England, Sir Montagu Norman, authorised the request, effectively endorsing the plundering by the Nazi regime of gold held in occupied territories. But, Sir, I regret matters did not stop there. Indeed, we, as a nation have been complicit through the BIS in continuing to profit from the Nazi regime.

"For bankers, Sir, the most important thing is to keep the channels of international finance open, no matter what the human cost. This, I'm afraid, is the reality of international finance. The Bank for International Settlements was founded in 1930 by our Bank of England Governor, Sir Montagu Norman, and his close friend Hjalmar Schacht, the former president of the Reichsbank, known as the father of the Nazi economic miracle. Schacht has even referred to the BIS as "my bank". The BIS massively benefited from the Nazis throughout the 1930's but particularly so, after the Czech scandal. The bank carried out foreign exchange deals for the Reichsbank; it accepted looted Nazi gold, recognising the puppet regimes installed in occupied countries. These countries, together with the Third Reich, soon controlled the majority of the BIS shares. That situation will, of course, rapidly disintegrate as we advance across Europe and restore regimes, subject, of course, to the, ah, cooperation of our, ahem, Russian allies.

"However, the BIS assisted in the funding of the Nazi war machine through loans. I can state categorically that the Reichsbank continued paying interest on the substantial monies lent to Nazi Germany by the BIS. This interest was used by the BIS to pay dividends to shareholders which included the Bank of England. Thus, through the BIS, the

Reichsbank was, perhaps by way of ironic justification, gentlemen, assisting in the funding of the British war economy."

Churchill now spoke slowly, his tone measured, "As Brutus says, in Julius Caesar, *"Th' abuse of greatness is when it disjoins remorse from power."* I must shoulder responsibility for my blindness in pursuit of goals, which, I can only hope that history will judge to be of a higher purpose, excusing any lack of moral judgment which might, perhaps, replace that expressed by Shakespeare as remorse. Sir Maynard, pray conclude your address with your recommendations in order to ensure we do not sink, 'ere we can swim, in this mire of financial probity."

"Thank you, Prime Minister." Keynes's voice now assumed a more confident tone, "We can, perhaps, sense that there might be a crumb of evidence which supports some element of integrity in what, I freely admit, might be seen as a mire of self-justification in the pursuit of monetary gain for investors. I have here a document from the Bank of England board of Director's minutes which states, and I quote, *'The primary function and policy of the bank must be to maintain our neutrality in fiscal matters and, through our interest in the BIS, to secure a stable post-war economy. This will both benefit our shareholders, and the British economy which will expand in the fertile re-development of European commerce, not least, with the rapid resurgence and recovery of the strong industrial base in Germany.'*

"In my view, if the BIS is liquidated, it would destabilise the leverage which we can excerpt now on many economies through our interest. However, of primary concern must be the protection of a post-war German economy which will assist in re-construction whilst avoiding the pervasive influence of our Soviet friends. They would, doubtless, wish to see the emergence of a communist state from the ashes of

Nazism, notwithstanding the anarchy resulting from Morgenthau's *Post-surrender Program*. At the forthcoming *Monetary and Financial Conference* being held at Bretton Woods in the US state of New Hampshire, there will be four US delegates, headed up by the assistant secretary of state, Dean Acheson. He is more pragmatic than his colleagues, being a lawyer by profession, and broadly endorses my view that we must support the German post-war economy."

Anthony Eden lifted his finger, "Ah, we know this chap, Acheson. You remember, Winston, when we were banging on Roosevelt's door in 1940, reminding him that there was a war on. Acheson was the fellow who helped put through the lend-lease package in 1941 which thankfully gave us much needed equipment and supplies. Damned good year, really; thankfully, the Japanese bombed Pearl Harbor, which woke the Yanks up, bringing them to the party rather belatedly."

"Anthony, these remarks and your reputation for good humour and wit are not best served by your ill-chosen words," Churchill chided him, before turning to Keynes, "Pray continue, Sir Maynard, I am becoming persuaded, albeit with some reluctance, that I may be forced to sanction the skulduggery which I already sense you are about to brief me upon."

Keynes cleared his throat, "Prime Minister, two of Acheson's fellow delegates will be Morgenthau, and his side-kick from the US Treasury, Harry Dexter White. Acheson, however, is a friend of Allen Dulles who, you will recall, is running US Intelligence in Switzerland. OSS have authorised a top-secret initiative known as *'The Harvard Plan,'* which I might add, is endorsed by those in the know on Wall Street, Thomas McKittrick of the BIS, and, not surprisingly, our own Sir Montagu Norman. This, Sir, is behind the reason I requested this meeting today. The *Harvard Plan* is a strategy whereby we secretly work with the powerful business factions within Germany. In effect Thomas

McKittrick is working with Nazi industrialists who trust the BIS, in what the OSS briefing describes as *'close cooperation between the Allied and German business world'*. Covertly, McKittrick and Dulles have the full backing of the State Department but even the president is not aware of this. McKittrick is, as we sit here, cutting deals to keep the Germany economy strong." There were audible gasps around the table.

Keynes clasped his hands together, leaning forwards, "Finally, Prime Minister, I can confirm there are powerful forces behind this *Harvard Plan*, Sir, not least many in President Roosevelt's own Democratic Party. They are fundamentally opposed to the route he appears to be adopting with the Morgenthau program, including, my sources tell me, a potential vice presidential candidate, Senator Harry Truman, who may well run at the Democratic National Convention next month. He has stated, off the record, that under his Presidency, the BIS will not be liquidated. Therefore, whatever is agreed at this conference, there will be moves to delay any action against the bank."

"I am somewhat surprised?" Churchill looked puzzled, "Is not Henry Wallace the sure choice as the present vice president?"

Keynes stroked his moustache whimsically, before replying "The vultures are circling, Prime Minister, and regrettably, the president's health is failing. The powerful recognise that he will probably not live through his next term as president. Power may soon change hands, and, Sir, suddenly the role of vice president has assumed supreme importance."

The voice of the chancellor of the exchequer cut in, "Dash it all, pretty dirty business, this American democracy nonsense. They should never have ditched the King and remained a colony."

Keynes sighed as he continued, "In conclusion, Prime Minister, Morgenthau will attempt to introduce his program at this Bretton

Woods conference, but somewhat hidden in the discussions and proposals being put forward for the new world economic plan. There will be an attempt to close the BIS which would be a grave mistake. Sir, we cannot allow Germany to collapse and we must support the Harvard Plan, and be party to discussions with German industry. That is my submission which I put to you for your endorsement."

Churchill stood, and walked slowly towards the map of Europe set into an alcove, on one side of which were positioned markers bearing US, Canadian, and British flags, faced by others with a swastika emblem. On the right side showing Eastern Europe, there were more flags with the swastika, facing a long line of those with the Soviet hammer and sickle emblem.

He turned and sighed deeply, pausing to light another cigar, then, in a weary voice, "*'There is no act of treachery or meanness of which a political party is not capable; for in politics there is no honour.'* Words wisely spoken by one of my predecessors, Benjamin Disraeli. I fear that we say soon be facing an enemy in the East, and that thought persuades me, together with your wise words, Sir Maynard, that pragmatism may override all my instincts. I will authorise only one delegate attend this wretched conference at Bretton Woods which shall be you, Sir Maynard. Indeed, I will lend you my aircraft, *Ascalon,* for the purpose, a rather delightful *Avro York* fitted with a few niceties to make your journey a little more pleasant. I want a full briefing immediately upon your return. However, in the interim, despite what may be taking place, I will continue to authorise the pulverising of German Industry from the air. Conscience dictates my duty, but destiny demands that I must remain blind to that which every instinct within my soul cries out against, which is, negotiating with Nazis."

At that moment, a loud knock preceded the entrance of Sawyers, announcing, "Luncheon is served, Sir."

"Then we must not tarry," Churchill announced in a lighter voice, "nor, indeed, must we keep the good Mrs Landemare waiting."

Saturday 1st July 1944 9:30am
Bretton Woods, New Hampshire, USA

Sir John Maynard Keynes was finishing breakfast, complemented with the luxury of real oranges and bananas which he had not seen since 1939, in the colonnaded dining room, overlooking fountains on the grass terraces that dropped below the hotel in tiers. He nodded thanks to the waitress as she poured coffee, then rose as the familiar smiling figure of Allen Dulles approached the table, puffing his signature pipe. "How the hell are you? I hear tell you the only one coming from England. Seems to me your Mr Churchill might be in two minds about what is happening here. Am I reading too much into this?"

They shook hands warmly and Keynes gestured Dulles to another chair at the table. As they sat back down, the waitress returned and Dulles accepted the cup of coffee being offered.

Keynes began in a light tone, with a touch of mocking reproach, "Perhaps I should inform you, Sir, that I am here representing His Majesty's government over Great Britain, and the dominions of the British Empire, of which England is only part, notwithstanding Scotland, Wales, Northern Ireland and associated islands."

They laughed as Dulles responded, "You Brits sure know how to swing for the fences considering your size."

"My dear chap, might I remind you that you are one of our former colonies, secession from which might yet prove to have been your greatest mistake."

Dulles threw his head back in laughter. "Thank God we are on the same side, Sir John. Turning to pressing matters, we gotten problems here and my guys in OSS are telling me that we are at a pivotal moment. If some of the crackpots in the treasury and their cronies get their way, we gonna lose one heck of a lot of money, and the Krauts will have no country to return to. We gonna try and get Senator Harry Truman in position for vice president at the forthcoming Democratic Convention, but there are dark forces at work here. McKittrick at the BIS is telling me that German businesses are getting more nervous by the day. First off, we need to re-assure these bastards, but we also gotta keep our friends on Wall Street with us. Then, there is a need to maintain the reputation of the United States for keeping integrity and justice uppermost in order to keep the folks back home happy."

"Time is on our side old chap." Keynes was relaxed and reassuring as he spoke. "Money does not take sides, nor does it have any loyalty, nor incidentally, in economic terms, do I. Let politicians worry about justifying their actions, whilst we put in place the foundations for the future. My life, Allen, has been spent advising others, including the United States, on balancing the books, borrowing wisely, and investing with prudence, without relying on such old-fashioned measures such as the gold standard. Hence it is merely a question of manipulation and timing. I will accept what is proposed at this conference, with reservations which will need substantive further Parliamentary consideration. In other words, we play for time which will result in change. The war will end, German business assets will deliver returns through the BIS, and political posturing over unfortunate issues from the past will fade. I saw this with the last lot, old boy; human avarice has a natural way of erasing from memory the carnage of war. Look here, I have Churchill convinced and he will not accept any interference with areas where Britain has an interest. You work your political misdeeds and I will lever the economic machinations. Delay,

Allen, delay which is the friend of bureaucracy, and the joy of democracy."

"Hell, you're worse than we are in OSS, but we got bastards like Hermann Schmitz, the CEO of IG Farben, to worry about. These guys had firing squads in their factories, employed slave labour, and manufactured Zyclon B, used in the gas chambers of Kraut concentration camps.

"Yes. Pretty unfortunate business that. Tell your chaps negotiating with the Nazis that if they've been involved in more, shall we say, regrettable activities, but want their businesses to survive, then they may have to serve sentences. However, the PM has reluctantly agreed that we can get them commuted to short terms on which he has obtained the acquiescence of your Mr Roosevelt. You can assure Thomas McKittrick that our future German business colleagues will not need to face the hangman's noose."

"We have another issue to face, John, over which your undoubted skills or influence may have no sway. If the goddamned Ruskies reach Berlin before we do, they will seize the massive stash of gold which is held in the vaults of the Reichsbank. The last thing we want is Uncle Joe Stalin to get his paws on that, cos he'll never surrender it or admit to having possession. We gonna have to figure out a strategy for dealing with this."

18

Die Reichslegion

Monday 8th January 2024 6:45pm -Wolfratshauser Strasse, Thalkirchen, Munich

The taxi pulled into the curb by the entrance to the Martha-Maria Hospital on Wolfratshauser Strasse which ran parallel to the house on Ludwigshöher Strasse where the meeting was scheduled to take place. They waited for the signal to confirm the SG 19 unit had deployed to their positions. The officer driving the vehicle asked Friedrich to test his pen which had a top that could be turned anti-clockwise triggering a signal. As he turned it, a light flashed on the vehicle dashboard surveillance monitor. The officer then activated the hidden vocal monitoring system, giving him a thumbs up with a grin. They had opted not to attempt video surveillance using a concealed briefcase camera to avoid any possibility of detection.

The radio announced that all units were in position and the taxi swung out, turning left onto Josephinestrasse, where the road narrowed as they entered a secluded neighbourhood in a wooded area. They took another left passing a number of large older-style detached properties, facing the trees opposite with enough room for parking on one side only. They pulled in just before a double fronted white painted house, built in a traditional Alpine style, with double iron gates to the front, beyond which were steps leading up to arched doors with decorative brass handles. The officer driving muttered, "Destination reached. Gates open. Package being despatched," then he turned to Friedrich, "Be assured, this unit is the best; on alarm activation, we will be there in seconds. *Viel Glück*!" He shook Friedrich's hand, who picked up his briefcase, and walked towards the gates as the taxi pulled away. Friedrich was trying to affect a calmness, despite his heart beating fast, and an ache of nervousness. He had never done anything like this before, and yet, despite his nerves, he felt a thrill of almost boyish excitement; an exuberance he had not experienced in many years. As he approached the doors, they swung open, and a man in shaded glasses dressed in a leather jacket, asked to see his identity card. He looked briefly to right and left down the street, before the door hummed shut, with a click of multiple locks. "Wait here, *bitte*." The man motioned him to a bench style seat, leaving Friedrich alone in a large hallway, with square marble tiles on the floor and very little decoration, apart from a classical chandelier, inset with multiple candle effect lighting, in an antique gold finish. A stone staircase, with an iron balustrade wound up to the right, whilst on the left was a corridor from which the man re-emerged, handing him back his ID card. He bid Friedrich to follow him down the corridor past a number of varnished oak doors, to a double framed doorway on which was a light panel which turned green as they approached.

Both automatic doors swung open, revealing a large, luxuriously appointed room around which were pillars, alcoves with inset lighting, comfortable chairs, and, curiously, Friedrich thought, tapestries on the wall depicting classical scenes, some of battlefields. Niemeyer was sitting behind a curved desk, with a huge lamp one side, scribbling notes, without looking up. Behind him, on the wall, was the large Nazi gold eagle clutching a swastika which surprised Friedrich as the GVR had adopted to abandon such symbols in the early 1960's. The decision had been made in the wake of renewed threats of prosecution in West German courts of former Nazis for war crimes and those openly displaying any symbols associated with that era. The floor was covered with rich, thick, luxuriously woven rugs with exotic floral patterns, although he noted that by the desk, the floor covering had a circular runic pattern he had seen previously, adopted by the SS in the heyday of Himmler's control.

"Friedrich Völker, *mein Gott*, it has been too long since we last met." The smiling figure of Franz Niemeyer rose and walked forwards, dressed in a dark business suit and blue silk tie; his darkened glasses hid his eyes, beneath thick neatly parted wavy grey hair. His appearance, as always, was immaculate. He extended his hand, clicking his heels, as he did so, in a military fashion. Friedrich accepted the handshake which was firm, purposeful, and business-like.

"Please, shall we sit?" Niemeyer gestured to two settees set at a 45-degree angle facing a low coffee table, beneath a frame, in which was a white military baton, with a gold tip at either end, decorated with black crosses, and golden Reich eagles."

"Ah, I note your interest, Freidrich. We are proud to have this baton which belonged to *Reichsmarschall* Hermann Göring. *Die Amerikanischen Dummköpfe* think they have the only one at their national infantry museum in Georgia, but this was the original presented to him. We had many friends, in strange places, after the war and, with a little persuasion and reward, our friends in the mafia offered assistance in retrieving this. Our former leader, Manfred Göring, loaned this to us, in recognition of the work we carry out to support our movement. You know many of the old guard from the *Reichsmarschall's* era would, as they say, be turning in their graves if they saw the weakness in direction from our leaders today. *Gemeinschaft Kraft durch Freude* (Strength through joy) bred loyalty to our cause from the workers. We had great spirit then bound by a strength of leadership and a clear message. These days, our members have lost their way - *Einig seid und True...* (Be united and loyal) What happened, Friedrich to such great slogans?"

Friedrich felt he was already being tested, and, as coached by Dieter, he was well prepared with his response, "*Ja*, I feel this; the principles we once stood for are being diluted. Many people, even those who are the grandchildren of those who carried the torch, are walking away, subdued into a pathetic liberal mindset. This is one of the reasons why I wanted to see you. This morning, I was made aware of a document so dangerous in the wrong hands, I knew I could only share this with someone I felt could be trusted."

The reply was quick, and delivered rapidly with a cold enquiring tone, "I thought you said this had been in your possession for some time, *Herr Völker*?"

Friedrich felt Niemeyer's eyes stare at him sharply, and the adrenalin pumped within, but his mind was prepared, "I knew of its existence, but I was not aware of its whereabouts until today. You may know of it by name, *Die Transaktions Aufzeichnung.*"

The reaction in Niemeyer's face was instant, which betrayed both shock and alarm, "But how is this possible? That was destroyed on the orders of *Der Leiter* years ago."

"That was my understanding also, *Herr Niemeyer,* until today when I was shown the original. It was not even a copy."

"Then, you will please now give this to me."

Niemeyer's face was set in a ruthless expression and Friedrich knew that the way he delivered his next words was critical, not least to his safety. "*Weh!* (Alas) I had it in my hands this afternoon, but that

Schwachkopf, Biesecker, took it back off me just before I left to come here.".

Niemeyer showed no reaction but his hand reached inside his jacket, and Friedrich, in turn, slipped the pen from his top pocket, and had his fingers around the top, but Niemeyer hesitated, then seemed to affect a more relaxed tone. "*Ach,* no matter, all in good time. Did you study the *Die Transaktions Aufzeichnung?* I have never seen it. Forgive me for being remiss. Will you join me in a drink of Cognac?" Friedrich's tried not to let his relief show in his voice, "*Danke schön, Das wäre gut.*" He lent down to pick up his briefcase as Niemeyer walked to an inlaid mahogany cabinet in one corner, with a rounded front; a light came on as he opened the door to reveal a mirrored interior laid out like a small bar. As Friedrich reached for his briefcase, his thoughts were focussed on one immediate revelation, 'H*e knows about Karl so he must be involved!'* Dieter had told them there was a complete top-security news black-out on the shooting that morning on the orders of the chancellor himself, and no names had been released, even within BND briefings, apart from a high-ranking internal security specialist. His mind raced as he sensed a dual of wits developing in which Niemeyer, at very least, would attempt to extract as much information from him as possible, whilst assessing how far he could be trusted. He took out a large notepad nonchalantly, aware that Niemeyer was watching his every move from the mirrored cabinet as he fixed the drinks.

"So, this man, Biesecker, where is he now? Ice?"

"*Bitte!* He was returning to his apartment, then to a safe house, owned by a friend of his, where he was going to lie low. I convinced him that I could help protect him and fooled him into giving me the address. He will be of little use to us as he is anti-anything which might have Nazi connections. Apparently, he detested everything his father stood for. Such a pity because Heinz Spacil, and his father before him, were geniuses."

Dieter had stressed to him in the planning of this operation that it was imperative he stayed as close to the truth as possible, whilst, hopefully, drawing out any further intel he might obtain on the *Reichslegion*."

Dieter had drummed into him, "Your job is first and foremost to establish whether Niemeyer is involved with the *Reichslegion*." Friedrich felt confident that he had achieved the first objective, but whether he succeeded in other aspects of his mission, he was conscious might depend on the next few minutes.

"Why did Biesecker want to see you?" Niemeyer asked, looking him deep in the eye, as he handed him his drink in a crystal tumbler.

"He said he had important information he needed to give to me with which his father stated I could be entrusted. Also, he was seeking further information on some of our reserves held in UK banks and secure facilities. However, after the attack this morning, he decided that he might need to hang on to it for what he described as "life-insurance."

"So, Friedrich, why did you choose to contact me? "

Friedrich thought quickly; *'he did not react to the mention of the attack,'* confirming Niemeyer's complicity.   He chose his words carefully "I think it was after listening to you at the funeral oration. I have been unhappy with the direction we have been taking for some time and your words were the most striking I have heard. We have become caught up in euphemisms, political and social niceties, and there is a betrayal of what our movement originally stood for. I have not spent a lifetime supporting the finances of a project that I can now see losing its way, even becoming politically correct. *Mein Gott*, the next thing we will be doing is announcing we are becoming inclusive, welcoming homosexuals, immigrants, slavs, or even Jews."

He had not expected the reaction he got as Niemeyer guffawed; then, rising from his seat, he walked over to Friedrich, his glass extended, "I have misjudged you – I think you should work directly for me. *Heil Hitler!*" Their glasses touched, and Niemeyer held his up, "To the resurgence of the 4th Reich!" He downed the remains of his drink in one.

Friedrich followed suit; the warm feeling spreading inside him was welcome and he referred to his notes on the table next to him as Niemeyer took his glass. Suddenly, and swiftly, Niemeyer had turned and was holding a pistol at his forehead, the cold barrel pressed against his skin.

"Give me a reason not to kill you *Herr Völker;* you had better make it good. Whether you live or die is of no consequence to me. My life is dedicated to the Fatherland. Speak!"

Friedrich's pen was out of reach, and he trembled with genuine fear as he spoke, "What reason did I have I to contact you? I need not have done so; nor did I even need to tell you of *Die Transaktions Aufzeichnung*, or even inform you that Biesecker has possession of it...Then, in a desperate tone, "I have his address at the safe house and will give this to you!"

The gun remained pressed against his temple and Niemeyer's eyes seemed to penetrate his, as though he was reading his inner thoughts. *'Why had the GSG9 unit not appeared?'* He was shaking visibly now, his mind went blank, and then, curiously, he thought of his mother. The pressure was increased, and his muscles tightened as he waited for the inevitable.

The next words he heard were delivered in a voice which was cold and impassionate, "The address *bitte*."

The incongruity of the affectation, *'bitte'* seemed, somehow, bizarre to Friedrich, despite his predicament; but, the absence of the expected shot resulted in a flood of relief which swept through him as the pistol barrel was removed from his head.

"I have it in my phone." Friedrich said weakly, his voice still shaking from the experience. Niemeyer motioned him to move, still keeping the Luger trained on him. *'Should I activate the signal?'* His hand hovered over the pen for a second but some sixth sense told him to risk continuing to play the role and complete his mission. *'I am crazy,'* he thought, as he reached for his mobile from the table, reading from a text entry he had been given by Dieter. "Biesecker told me he was taking refuge in a house owned by a friend, on Alsterkrüger Kehre, just off Alster Krugchaussee. I convinced him that I was disenchanted with the movement, and we agreed to meet up again in the coming days. My parents were friendly with his and so we already had an association."

He reached for his pen, scribbling the address down on his pad, ripping the paper off and handing it to Niemeyer.

"Thank you for your cooperation." Niemeyer's voice now assumed a more measured, relaxed tone. "Do you have his mobile number?" Then, in response to Friedrich's nod, "Please text him to ask if you can meet him there, say, in one hour. Perhaps there is something you want to add to what you gave him before."

Friedrich tapped out a brief message and, in seconds, a reply was received confirming Karl would be there which he showed to Niemeyer, who walked to his desk, replacing his pistol under his jacket, much to Friedrich's relief. He pressed an intercom, *"Militärbesprechung sofort!"* (Military briefing immediately)

Niemeyer now spoke in a genial manner, "So, *Herr Völker*, we can now relax because either I can trust what you have told me, or I kill you here, in this room. I can now speak freely because I think, as they say, I hold all the ace cards. Another drink I think?" Friedrich felt disorientated by the contradictions in Niemeyer's behaviour, as his 'host' took his glass. The situation had become almost unreal, yet the reality of the danger he was in, he found both daunting and exciting. There was a staccato knock at the door and a man marched in, wearing a field grey uniform buttoned to a collar in black, with silver patches; on one side were the letters D A in a German Gothic font and on the other oak leaves denoting rank. The uniform was very similar to those used by the SS which Friedrich had only seen in photographs and archive footage of the Nazi era.

The man halted, clicking his heels, giving the extended right arm Nazi salute. "Ah, *Standartenführer* Kessler, I have an address which I want raiding. You are looking for a Karl Biesecker; get his photograph from our intelligence team. Take him alive, if possible. He has in his possession a large secret document identified as *Die Transaktions Aufzeichnung*, the seizing of which is your primary objective. You may use lethal force as I do not wish there to be any witnesses. We must not allow to anything to jeopardise '*Unternehmen Langen Messer*'. (operation long knives) I want this attack to take place within the hour. Communication by secure, encrypted channels only. Report back immediately on the success of your mission. *Danke.*"

The uniformed man stiffened to attention, "*Jawohl, Herr Reichskommissar.*"

Niemeyer handed him the address, and the officer clicked his heels again, executing a smart about turn, and left.

Niemeyer now turned to Friedrich, briefly smiling with his mouth, yet his eyes showed no humour. "Many of the finest dedicated former soldiers are volunteering to join the growing ranks of our secret crack military unit, the *Deutsch Abteilung*, after leaving the *Bundeswehr*. In this paramilitary unit, old standards of discipline are maintained, with the emphasis on loyalty to the Fatherland. There is none of this politically correct garbage that undermines order and stability. We have active service units operating in Ukraine, Latin America, Africa, and in the Arabian Gulf where we also supply maritime units to protect ships; very lucrative business, I might add. You, by now, may have guessed, *Herr Völker*, that I am a proud member of the *Reichslegion*." He retrieved the glasses from where he had previously left them on the cocktail cabinet and handed one to Friedrich. "Now, you have one hour to either impress me or die, because this time, together with the report from *Standartenführer* Kessler, will determine whether it will be the former, or the latter."

On the street outside, a number of vans had arrived at intervals, parking separately in order not to attract attention. Inside a black *Mercedes Benz Sprinter Welfare* with darkened glass on the rear windows, positioned opposite the house, Karl sat with Dieter and Schneider. Behind them were two commandos, one armed with the *Simon* breach rifle grenade which was now armed facing towards the rear doors. The atmosphere was tense as they listened to the conversation between Friedrich and Niemeyer. "Perhaps, now we go?" Karl said, for the second time, having urged the operation be commenced fifteen minutes earlier when Friedrich's life was being threatened. Whilst he was a highly trained urban warfare commander, his specialist skills were in direct assaults, fighting in both tough terrain environments, and street combat. Now, he was constrained by, but respected, the assessments of both Dieter, and the seasoned burly figure of Schneider. "I say, wait." Dieter responded, "Your *Buchhalter* is doing well. If we had gone in before, we would not be able spring the trap on the *Deutsch Abteilung* assault, nor would we have the intel on Niemeyer."

Schneider added, "We can be through that door in seconds. I concur with you, *Herr Major*." Then, into his collar mounted microphone, "All units, check in: prepare for imminent assault." The screen on the tablet brightened as four separate boxes displayed a green tick.

Karl now had his pistol in his lap, and was aware of the familiar feeling he always got on active service in the pit of his stomach, together with a sense of heightened awareness. He felt his phone vibrating and on retrieving it from his jacket pocket, there was a message from Inge. The text read, '*Urgent…I have unearthed some information worth its weight in gold. Call when you can. Lieber Dich*' (Love you) He wondered for a moment, then replaced his phone, as he listened intently to the conversation through the speaker.

Niemeyer was talking, "The GVR lost its way years ago, under the direction of the former leader, Gunther Roche; he was too old and had lost his grip. That oaf, Manfred Göring, was on the right path but he lacked direction. We would all have been old men before he achieved his goal. After the movement was betrayed in 2021, [1] many began coming over to us, seeing that we portrayed the true values of the *Führer*. Now, we are ready to move and take control of the Reich."

Friedrich had recovered his composure and was thinking fast as he looked at his notes, knowing that he might be poised on the edge of discovering much more. Then, taking up his pen, as if using it as a pointer, he stated, "I was disillusioned also and this is why I brought this information. We could weaponize what I have seen. I recognise you may not trust me, but look at the information I have briefed you on." All the while he was speaking, he was aware the clock was ticking, and that his life was under threat. "If those in positions of power knew we might release this into the public domain, we would have enormous leverage.

[1] Covered in previous book, 'The Barbarossa Secret'

"*Herr* Niemeyer, within *die Transaktions Aufzeichnung*, there are post-war transactions recorded in Nazi gold, involving leading banks and institutions across the world; evidence of deposits made by wanted war criminals, donations to the US Army, the involvement of the Mafia, and even the Vatican. The exposure of this would trigger the loss of confidence in financial institutions and the collapse of markets, notwithstanding the fact that governments have been implicated in hiding this for eighty years. Now, you see why I wanted to only share this with someone who could be trusted; and, perhaps, that is why you can trust me."

"The record could be decisive." Niemeyer, acknowledged, showing real interest in what he was hearing. "That, Friedrich, may prove to be the case in the next 30 minutes. So, you wish to be part of the true National Socialist movement and join us?"

"*Natürlich, Herr Niemeyer*. So, this *'Unternehmen Langen Messer'*, is this your plan to move against the GVR? This is splendid. Who will be *Der Leiter?*"

A triumphal look came into Niemeyers mid-blue eyes, "If only they knew, *ja?* He is a true National Socialist, one who upholds our traditions, and values of order; one who is committed to a restoration of pride in our Fatherland, and the promotion of an Aryan race free from Jewish or immigrant contamination. First, we shall strike the GVR, removing the leaders, and any we suspect may threaten the will and direction of *Der Leiter*. We shall be the masters in the replacement of the GVR with the *Reichslegion*. We shall not stop there, but join the swelling right-wing movement across the world. We will sweep to power, as the *Führer* did, through the ballot box, but then, the German *Volk* will awaken, as if from a deep slumber and witness as we strike, not with tanks and stormtroopers, but through our economic domination of Europe. Italy, Holland, Switzerland, and Spain are all swinging towards the right as the people recognise that democracy does not deliver decisions or security. This, *Herr* Völker, is our moment. Our *Leiter, Oberst* Konrad Kaufmann, is a trusted member of the German security services, and many have already pledged their loyalty to him."

"What about the current leader of the GVR, Heinrich Hackmann?" Freidrich asked.

"*Ach*, he is right beneath our feet. We have him under guard in the cellar together with his predecessor, Göring. When the moment comes, I will gladly put a bullet in both their heads."

Friedrich nodded his head in understanding as he twisted the lid of his pen.

Outside, in the van with the darkened windows, Deiter spoke, "Christ, I have heard enough from this crack-pot," just as the screen in front bleeped and the words flashed, '*Achtung! Aktion! Achtung! Aktion!*' Schneider spoke into his mic, "Go, go, go… *Schnell!*" The rear doors were kicked open, as figures in black battle dress, darkened faces, and masks ran across the narrow street; Schneider then leapt from the vehicle, followed by Dieter and Karl. There was a flash from the van, a loud report and the doors to the house disintegrated with a thunderous roar as the first commandos, now crouching, reached the entrance. A stun grenade was thrown in as they threw themselves to the floor, then, half crouching, half running, the first were through the entrance, with two remaining at the doorway, their assault rifles held to their bodies, as they peered right and left pivoting. There were two more explosions at the rear of the house and the sound of glass crashing.

Inside the property, as the first deafening explosion impacted, causing the building to shake and Friedrich's ears to ring, Niemeyer had thrown himself to the floor. In the corridor outside, there was the sound of automatic fire, then staccato shots, followed by shouts of "room clear", then, "On the stairs!"....more shots, and the pepper-like smell of tear gas, as Niemeyer, his pistol now drawn, screamed, "You will die, Völker." His first shot hit Friedrich in the upper arm, as he threw himself at Niemeyer, feeling a searing hot pain, without any forethought other than the instinct of survival. Behind, a door opened, and a grey uniformed man entered, and fired a burst of shots at the double entrance doors. Friedrich's eyes were running, and his breath coming in short gasps, as he wrestled for his life with Niemeyer, gouging at him with his fingers, tearing, straining; he had never been a fighter, but now he was desperate to hold on. He frantically tried to roll their bodies so that Niemeyer was facing the soldier who screamed, "Get back! Get back!" Another entered, and tried to pull Friedrich off as suddenly the doors exploded, disintegrating, and smoke poured into the room. Friedrich was beginning to lose his grip, feeling the other man starting to force his arms back, as Niemeyer's superior strength began to tell, then, more shots; Niemeyer was wrestling his gun hand slowly downwards with the barrel pressed against Friedrich's stomach. Friedrich shut his eyes, but, in a last frantic wrench, he had one hand free and, for a moment seized by hatred, he hit as hard as he could into Niemeyer's contorted face; a shot rang out, and there was nothing...

Out of the mists, his mother was calling to him; a bizarre sense of well-being seemed to surround him as he drifted towards the sound of her voice. There was no fear, or sense of foreboding, yet, the mists were clearing, and his mother's voice fading, and from the comfort, he felt anxious, as his name was called. This time, it was a more pressing tone, "Friedrich, are you with us...Friedrich, *alles ist gut.*" Now there was disorientation; the mists faded although he wanted their comforting blanket to return. "Breathe deeply...you can do it." He was breathing, wasn't he? He tried lifting his arm, but it flopped down, then he was aware of a mask on his face, and he could hear muffled, murmured voices. Sleep beckoned but, as he began to breathe in shallow breaths, the voice was more insistent. "Friedrich, come on, we are all waiting for you. Breathe!" Then, a voice he almost recognised, "I need you with me, *Herr Buchhalter.*" There were people in the room in white coats, masks, lights, a tube in his arm, and two from a mask on his face. His eyes shut and opened again. "What is happening?" he managed, his voice hoarse, and weak.

"You are in the Bundeswehr Medical Academy Hospital at the *Ernst-von-Bergmann-Kaserne,* (military barracks) my friend." He looked up to see the smiling, yet reassuring face of Karl Biesecker.

"I think meeting you was a mistake..." Friedrich said weakly, his breath coming in sharp intakes. "I am remembering being shot at more than once...for the first time in my life." He coughed, and his mask was removed to give him some water.

A doctor leant over him, shining a torch into each of his eyes, "You are very lucky, *Herr Völker.* You have been administered a large, potentially lethal dose of *flunitrazepam,* which you might know as Rohypnol. You were on the verge of a coma; you must concentrate on breathing deeply, and take in some oxygen."

Suddenly, Friedrich's mind focussed on the evening earlier, and his dual of words with Niemeyer. It all seemed a long way away, yet he knew it wasn't.

"What happened? How did I get here?" he gasped.

"Niemeyer is dead," Karl responded. "Sadly, for me, not from my weapon, but a well-aimed shot from our friend, Schneider. He saved your life; but you were incredible. We were listening to you as you succeeded in exposing all the intel needed."

Consciousness was now returning a sharper awareness to Friedrich, as he absorbed Karl's words, trying to remember, but so much was missing; then, a recollection, "But why did you not come sooner? He had a gun at my head."

"*Ach,* I thought it might be a way out of the deal we made plus, well, you were doing quite well. I felt this would be a good, ah… practical for you on your pre-operational training before we depart for England, *ja?* Unless, of course, you have lost your nerve?"

The single fingered gesture in response brought a smile to Karl's face as Friedrich weakly muttered, "Already, I have proved myself indispensable, *Soldat-Kämpfer;* let us enjoy a vacation in England, '*old chap*'", speaking the last two words in English. Karl grinned, as he left the room. It was 4:00am, and he suddenly felt very tired having spent hours waiting as doctors attended to Friedrich. Dieter had arrived at the hospital 15 minutes before, having attended an immediate post-op de-briefing, chaired by the deputy head of the BND covert operations division, Wernher Schultz, who had arrived by helicopter from Berlin. Schultz was a member of the GVR, whereas his immediate senior, the vice president, *General Major* Dag Baehr was not. Schultz had informed Baehr that he would take the briefing and report directly to him once it had concluded. The meeting had been interrupted by a call from the German chancellor who was apoplectic with anger at what he termed "cavalier operations by security forces bringing anarchy to the streets of Munich."

Schultz had been able to inform him that investigations were ongoing, but they had averted an attempt by Neo-Nazis to carry out a number of assassinations of leading figures. The chancellor's response was,

"*Lieber Gott,* we have not seen this sort of thing since Baader-Meinhof and the Red Army Faction in the 70's and 80's. This must be stopped." He became calmer as Schultz told him that covert operations were continuing but public safety would increase daily as a result of ongoing security measures following an intelligence coup which, he trusted, the chancellor would understand needed to be kept confidential.

Dieter informed Karl in a quiet voice, as they sat in a corner of the hospital canteen, having a coffee, that there had been ten *Reichslegion* casualties on the raid including two fatalities, one of which was Niemeyer. Two members of the assault force had also suffered gunshot injuries, with one being hospitalised. Heinrich Hackmann and Manfred Göring were released without harm but were being questioned in a secure, hidden location.

He was also able to inform Karl that *Oberst Konrad Kaufmann,* together with five other suspects, had been taken into custody, with further arrests pending.

"What about the unit they despatched to obtain *Die Transaktions Aufzeichnung?*"

"Karl, this was a great success, thanks to our friend, Friedrich. Twenty members of the *Deutsch Abteilung* were surrounded, with no escape route, as the street in which our safe property was situated is a cul de sac. The officer in charge of the *Reichslegion* assault, *Standartenführer* Wolf Kessler, was wanted in connection with the attack on the armoured security convoy escorting a huge shipment of gold at *Gottmadingen* in October 2022."

"Ah yes," Karl put his cup down, nodding his head, "another piece of the jigsaw fits into place."

Dieter looked at him with astonishment, "You know about this? It was all hushed up. I should not be surprised; your father was so thorough and I'm sure you know more than I do. Tonight, we have cut off the head of the serpent, but I regret the organisation will continue, albeit much weakened. The operation has been incredibly successful which is down to you. Your father would be very proud of you."

Despite his discomfort at being associated with a covert right-wing faction, Karl could not suppress a warm glow at the thought that, for once, he had achieved something of which his father would have been truly proud.

Returning to the welcome calm familiarity of his apartment, now securely guarded by a fresh detachment of police, he suddenly remembered the message from Inge. He tapped her name on WhatsApp, and a sleepy voice answered, "Oh *mein Gott,* Karl, it is five in the morning...*Was ist los?*"

"Your message...weight in gold?" he replied, with a tired, yet slightly curt tone.

Her voice softened, "Oh Karl, I'm sorry; I was sleeping. I could not rest after you said you had to find out what happened to the gold at the end of the war. I called up old colleagues in the *Bundespolizei* who hold senior intelligence authority to access classified documents in the Military Archives Division of the *Bundesarchiv* (German Federal Archives). They checked records made by the Nazi administration, many of which, incredibly, are still classified. Government records carried on being maintained after Hitler's presumed death in the bunker at the end of April 1945. In fact, the records department continued operating for over a month, even after Hitler's successor, Admiral Dönitz, was arrested in late May 1945. The Nazis, as you know, were very thorough record keepers and Karl, you would not believe this..." her voice was excited now, "There is a log recording the journey of the final shipment of gold and valuables after their removal from the Reichsbank in April 1945, together with information on something called *'Der Raub-Gold-Zug.'* (The stolen gold train)

19

The Heist

Saturday 21st April 1945 10:00am
The office of the *Führer*, Reich Chancellery, Wilhelmstrasse 77, Berlin

They waited nervously, apprehensive, if not fearful, hearing the booming sounds of distant explosions from the front, as the Russian Red Army continued its relentless advance. Their one bond was absolute loyalty to National Socialism, the *Führer,* and the Fatherland. They all felt the heavy weight of impending doom, yet they retained faith in his leadership. They were in the ante-chamber, outside the tall double entrance doors to his study. They had been summoned, at short notice, that morning. and each had undertaken a journey that now carried some risk. There were the daily bombing raids from the Americans, and from the British RAF at night, plus occasional daylight raids by enemy fighters who would dive on the city, picking targets out at random, especially moving vehicles. The raids had left large craters in many of the main thoroughfares, and vehicles had to swerve to avoid such hazards which included masonry from bombed buildings now strewn across the streets. Arriving at the Reich Chancellery was very different that day, although they were all familiar with the building, having attended many meetings and occasions there. When they had turned off Wilhelmplatz to enter the *Ehrenhof* courtyard (Court of Honour), unusually, they were stopped by SS guards in full military battledress who demanded to see their identity papers. They proceeded towards the portico entrance with its four great pillars, some now pock-marked with bullet strikes caused by Allied aircraft strafing, beyond which, in the wall above the doors, was an eagle and swastika set into the stonework. There were the scars of shrapnel all around which were now commonplace in a Berlin suffering daily poundings from air-raids. In front of the entrance, there was a hive of activity as men, standing in lines, were loading files, paintings, carpets, furniture, and tapestries into waiting trucks.

As the door to the Mercedes was opened from an attending guard, *SS-Standartenführer* Josef Spacil could hear the shouts of *"Schnell, schnell..."* from the Officers and NCOs adding to the sense of urgency. Behind him, another car had pulled in, out of which the tall figure of *Obergruppenführer* Ernst Kaltenbrunner emerged, waving his arm in greeting to Spacil who walked over, clicking his heels, *"Heil Hitler!"* Then asking, in a quiet voice, "What is going on, Ernst?" Their relationship allowed an unusual familiarity between them, although Spacil secretly loathed the man who had come to regard him as a friend and confidante.

"I think it is best that the *Führer* informs you, Josef, but be aware that it was I that put you forwards for what will probably be the greatest mission of your life." He pulled Spacil to one side of the steps below the large bronze statue of a naked classical figure, clutching a sword, known as *Wehrmacht*. Kaltenbrunner spoke in a low voice, "I shudder to think what will happen here, but I know there are major plans for a last great stand. Then, if we are not successful in negotiating with the

Western Allies, an exodus to South America where preparations have already been made. If all fails, plans are in place for the safe transport of the *Führer,* but he will not leave the *Führerbunker* until he is certain there is no other way. Yesterday, we all celebrated his birthday with him, and he informed us that if we were unsuccessful in uniting with the Allies against the Bolshevik scum, then this would amount to the greatest betrayal in history. Some of us were puzzled by his words; Josef, he also stated that he would never be taken, alive or dead, but that his work was done and that he would soon relinquish the office of *Reichskansler*."

An officer walked towards where they were standing in the courtyard whom they recognised as Hitler's adjutant, *SS-Obergruppenführer* Julius Schaub, who glanced upwards, nervously. "*Meine Kameraden bitte*, it is not safe to be here. They send fighters over who shoot at anything that moves. Come, please; follow me, and I will inform the *Führer* of your arrival." He led the way through the doors, into a reception room, then through more towering doors which were five metres high, into a hall with walls clad in mosaic, where men were passing materials down a line towards the exit. Then, up some steps through the round ante-room with a curious domed ceiling and into the *Grosse Marmorgalerie* (grand marble gallery) the sight of which shocked Spacil. He recalled first seeing this when summoned to meet the *Führer* in 1940. He had been totally awestruck by the size of the gallery stretching 150 metres in length, with red marble flooring, and cream marbled walls with, on one side, at symmetrical intervals, magnificent classic style doorways over which were Germanic shields. On the other side, floor to ceiling windows, whilst ornate gold candle effect lighting was set into both walls with comfortable seating provided by baroque style chairs positioned around occasional tables on exquisite rugs. On the walls had been sumptuous tapestries depicting mythical classical scenes, many showing powerful figures brandishing swords, or spears. He had been told that the gallery was twice the length of the Hall of Mirrors at Versailles and, he recalled, that the impression he had then was one of power, majesty, and insurmountable strength. Now, the scene was very different with dozens of men moving rapidly, carrying papers and furniture, whilst the gallery shutters were closed. Gone were the chairs, tables, floor coverings and tapestries, leaving the gallery with a dark, depressing feel. As they passed one window, they saw the effects of a bomb blast which had torn down the structure around it and men were working to put in a temporary covering. Spacil felt that he was now witnessing the collapse of the unstoppable might which he had felt the Reich represented, yet he forced these thoughts from his mind as he had total faith in the *Führer* to whom he had dedicated his life.

They had entered through double doors to the right into the less grand, yet still ornate gallery which led to the *Führer's* office, outside of which, they shook hands with the short, portly figure of Walther Funk, dressed in a dark business suit, and were introduced to *SS-Obergruppenführer* Gottlob Burger, a tall imposing figure, wearing the Knight's Cross of the War Merit Cross with Swords, at his neck. He appeared quite genial, smiling and relaxed, despite the pervasive, imposing dark feeling which felt almost suffocating. Now, as they waited, they were silent, reflective, and were not moved to speak. Somehow, with all they had witnessed, and with the constant sound of exploding artillery shells in the distance, it would have seemed, somehow irreverent.

Suddenly, the doors opened, and the figure of *Obergruppenführer* Schaub appeared, stepped backwards, clicking his heels, and extending his arm stiffly in salute, "The *Führer* will see you now. *Heil Hitler!*"

They filed in to the enormous office which was 25 metres long and 16 meters wide, with walls in red marble where, on previous visits, there had hung paintings which had now been removed. The large rug covering most of the floor area remained although much of the furniture had also gone. The shutters in front of the Chancellery gardens were partially closed and light came from the wall lights and remaining standard lamps around the room. The former central crystal chandelier had been taken down and all appeared sparse and cold, although an enormous eagle and swastika in gold remained above one central entrance door. As they each entered, they came to attention, giving the Nazi salute, but if it had been the state of the Reich Chancellery which had shocked Spacil up to that point, it was nothing compared to that he felt at seeing the appearance of Adolf Hitler. The icon representing the faith in National Socialism, the figurehead of their creed, the almost godlike figure who had inspired millions, held rallies, and resurrected the pride of the *Deutsches Volk,* was shuffling towards them, his figure stooped, and his military tunic seeming to hang off him.

His face was deeply lined, sallow, with dark shadows beneath his eyes which appeared bloodshot, looking more like an elderly man than one just aged 56. He returned their salutes with his right arm bent at the elbow, flattening the palm of his hand backwards, although there was evidence of a tremor which he tried to hide by then clasping his hand behind his back. Behind him, stood Josef Goebbels, in a double-breasted brown uniform, and wearing a red swastika armband, who smiled at each of them warmly. He was standing with Martin Bormann, also in a brown uniform, who bowed his head briefly to each of them.

Hitler shook hands with them in turn, pressing both his upon theirs as if to emphasise the gesture, and Goebbels followed suit, before waving to some chairs and a settee in matching mid-blue upholstery, opposite a round table facing more easy chairs by a log fire crackling in a marble fireplace. The setting was comfortable yet contrasted with the unrelenting feeling of impending disaster. The atmosphere felt awkward, but also unreal as though they were suspended in a void over which they had no control or direction. Each person took their place, without speaking, but waited until the *Führer* bid them sit. Hitler stood behind a tall chair, resting his hands on either side. His eyes, as he met theirs, were still piercing blue, his direct look seemed to absorb their inner thoughts. His voice was tired, but retained the command, and uncompromising purpose to which they had each pledged their loyalty and, for which they would carry out his will, to the death.

"*Meine deutschen Kameraden*, the time has come for great decisions; decisions which I must take now to protect our heritage. What happens to me now is of little matter; my heart beats for the Fatherland which has been in my blood and to which I have dedicated my life. The task remains to build a future for *das deutsche Volk*. Our destiny will not be shaped by the storm-trooper or further blood sacrifices, but by powerful economic forces."

He stopped, looking upwards, as if seeking celestial inspiration, then waived his finger, "History will record our heroic struggle and rue the day that nations failed to respond to our call to confront and fight the filthy creed of communism. The Russian barbarians will release their bloodlust, not only on Germany, but will threaten the world for years to come with their cancerous creed, and insatiable desire to conquer; no one will be safe from the primitive Bolshevist mire. The post-war world will also face a new threat from the fanatical *Jüdischer Parasit*, driven by their Zionist greed for land and money. Here, in Germany, we pledged that we would stand against these forces and were betrayed by those who did not have the will or the strength to join us, or remain with us.

"Now, *meine Kameraden,* in what may be the final days of the Third Reich, I am liberating a financial force for the future, which others may direct and, heed my words, Germany will dominate Europe financially, until we are, once again, admired and recognised as the bastion of the future, re-capturing the will and purpose that began with my leadership. I have prepared the way and planned the final steps in which each of you will play a critical role. Our financial assets must be liberated from the possibility of being plundered by the Russian *Untermenschen,* or by American gangsters. For that purpose, some months ago, assets from occupied territories started being collected and transferred by train to secure destinations near Berchtesgaden and around Salzburg.

"The gold and currency held here in Berlin will now come under your command, Herr *Standartenführer* Spacil. You will gather the remaining assets in Berlin, travel to Berchtesgaden, and rendezvous with a force, which is already in position, under the command of the man sitting next to you, *Obergruppenführer* Gottlob Burger. This will be the location of what the Allies believe will be our final stand, aided by false intelligence which we will leak. In reality, we have very different plans, and we have contacts amongst *die Amerikaner,* to whom certain assets have already been pledged. They are a nation of gangsters who will do anything for money. If we do not join forces with the Allies against the communist vermin, then, from the ashes of the 3rd Reich, the 4th Reich will rise triumphant controlled from the centre we have established in Argentina where we will re-group and to which we will direct our resources. All of this will be under the control of the Chief of the Party Chancellery, SS-*Obergruppenführer* Martin

Bormann." He nodded towards Bormann who jumped to his feet, extending his arm in salute, uttering just two words, *"Mein Führer!"*

"My plans for the security of all assets from the Reich will be executed under the direction of *SS-Obersturmbannführer* Otto Skorzeny whose orders are to be obeyed without question. His orders are my orders! He carries a written authority to that effect. Anyone failing to carry out his orders will be executed. *Verstehen Sie meine Herren?"* His voice rose to emphasise the question in a manner which made it clear that it could only be answered one way. As one, all rose to their feet, stretching their arms out, *"Jawohl, mein Führer."*

Hitler seemed to relax a little as he added, *"Standartenführer* Spacil, your mission commences now. Tomorrow, you will pay a visit to the Reichsbank, and remove the remaining gold and currency assets; Herr Funk, our Reichsbank president, will brief you. The future of the Reich depends on the success of this mission, and I feel the hand of Providence guides my will. *Heil!"* Hitler now turned, and shuffled towards the door, as if in a daze, yet turning, just before he walked out, fixing them with one last look of defiance.

Sunday 22nd April 1945 9:00am The Reichsbank, Jägerstrasse, Berlin

There was the sound of explosions as the city was rocked by artillery shells fired by the advancing Russians. Few people were on the street as the convoy of twenty trucks rolled into Jägerstrasse, and men jumped out, dressed in the uniforms of the SS, belonging to the *Leibstandarte SS Adolf Hitler* guard, many armed with *Schmeisser MP40* submachine guns. Two trucks were pulled across the road, blocking it, and soldiers climbed out, lining the street to bar access. *Standartenführer* Spacil, together with his long-trusted comrade, *Oberfeldwebbel* Artur Schmidt, walked in front of twenty men towards the sombre looking edifice of the Reichsbank, holding his *Walther P38* pistol by his side. The long classical style building had suffered considerable bomb damage in preceding weeks; the top storeys on one side were partially collapsed, whilst the pillars to the main front had chunks missing, although the entrance remained relatively undamaged. As it was a Sunday, the heavy double doors were closed, although the president of the bank, Walther Funk, had briefed Spacil that some administrative staff were working during the current emergency which had been declared. Spacil turned the handle, pushing the heavy door open, revealing a small, tiled entrance way with a wooden hatch to the left and a bell push. The twin doors opposite were locked, but there was light coming from a glass panel over the top. He smiled to himself at the bizarre situation as he pressed the bell for a couple of seconds, then again to add emphasis.

The hatch on the left was unlocked and a white-haired woman, with pince-nez glasses peered up at him. "We are closed!" She said emphatically, "What do you want?"

"Oh, everything you have in your vaults *bitte*. Open the door, now, *schnell!*"

"I need authorisation," replied the woman, brusquely.

"*Frau Bankerin*, I am here on the direct orders of the *Führer*." He lifted his pistol and pointed the barrel into her face. "You will have these doors opened now, or I will immediately execute you for treason; then I will blow the doors off and shoot the first five workers I see. Open now!"

Fear came into the woman's eyes, and the colour drained from her face; the SS had a reputation for summary executions. She called out, "Heine, unlock the doors. Do it quickly."

As they heard the locks click, *Oberfeldwebbel* Schmidt, kicked the doors open, shouting, "On the floor now!" He lifted his Schmeisser and fired a burst into the ceiling, sending showers of plaster onto those

below. A man in a dark grey suit with a winged collar, and thick lensed round glasses, held his hands up, addressing Spacil, "*Bitte,* I am the Manager, and no one has informed...." His voice trailed off as Spacil thrust his pistol against the man's forehead, "*Halt den Mund!*" (shut your mouth) then shouting,
"If anyone fails to comply with my orders, I will shoot this man first, then execute them. No one will move unless we tell you to." He turned his head to the manager, "Kneel on the floor...now!" The terrified man, now white-faced and shaking, did so. Spacil held his pistol to the man's temple. "How many people are working outside this room?"
"Please, I will cooperate. There are eight in the document room, and four working in the accounting office."
Spacil looked across at *Oberfeldwebbel* Schmidt and nodded. They had studied drawings of the bank before embarking on the mission, and now Schmidt left the room, taking four men with him. Shortly afterwards, there was another short burst of gunfire, followed seconds later, by another. Spacil smiled to himself, recognising from years of active service with Schmidt, his signature method of putting the fear of God into any group of unarmed people The other SS men were now checking round the large open room, their weapons held at the ready with the occasional shout of *"Kopf nach unten!"* (head down). Spacil walked slowly and deliberately down the length of the room, his jackboots echoing off the tiled flooring. Minutes later, Schmidt re-appeared with a group of bank employees, all with their hands held behind their heads. Spacil walked back to the manager,
"Today, *Erbsenzähler* (bean counter), we will be making a large withdrawal from your bank." There were guffaws of laughter from the SS men positioned around the room. "You will now open the vault, and form a work party who will carry all the contents and load them into the trucks outside." Then, in a louder voice, "If you co-operate,

you live; if anyone fails to do so, this man will be shot first, and two others will be executed." He lifted his pistol, giving a wink to Schmidt, and fired a shot into the oak panelling lining one side of the room." There was a whimper, and someone cried out as Spacil barked his instructions, "You will load valuables, and currency into the front trucks, and gold into the rear trucks. My men outside will direct you." He spoke to the manager again, "Now, choose your work party. *Schnell!*"

Spacil accompanied the Manager with Schmidt and two other men to the vault. They descended stairs to a thick steel door leading to further heavy meshed sliding doors, beyond which the floor split into two corridors. Each led to entrances controlled by combination locks, and large wheels to draw back the stout locking bars. As they entered the first vault, Spacil was struck by the enormous stacks of paper currency. The Manager explained, "We have mainly US dollars, British sterling, and Reichsmarks. There are some other currencies…Italian lire, Spanish pesetas, and Japanese yen. The currency in the black packing is counterfeit, the majority of which is Sterling but there also some US dollars. This is used by the *Sicherheitsdienst*." (Reich Intelligence agency)

"We will take it all." Spacil said in a matter of a fact tone.

They proceeded down the second corridor but, this time, at the other side of the main vault, there were further locked mesh entrances, but it was what was beyond which made their eyes open wide. There were stacked bars of gold in varying sizes, behind which were row after row of packing cases, all of which, the Manager stated, were full of bullion bars. "The ones at the front are awaiting packing. These are from the smelting room, where we take the gold sent to us by units of the SS across the Reich, especially that which is collected from the inmates in the camps. Here, we melt it into bars, which are then used as security for our transactions with banks outside the Reich."

When they returned to the central office, the entrance doors of the bank swung open, and a young officer entered, with dark hair and thick round glasses, holding a briefcase, which he placed on the floor before removing his leather gloves, and slapping them into his hands. "I should have you arrested, *Herr Standartenführer*, I believe you are robbing the Reichsbank."

Spacil grinned briefly, "Ah, *Hauptman* Völker, always late, but we need your skills. Everything we remove must be documented, accounted for, and valued. I think counting money is your primary skill, because I am told you are a lousy soldier."

Their greeting was warm and informal, based upon mutual respect and years of working together. "*Herr Standartenführer,* I would rather be accused of counting money than falsifying accounts and fraud, skills in which I am told you are the unsurpassed master."

They shook hands and Völker had a table set up next to the access corridor, extracting a large accounting record book from his case.

Four hours later, the last of the crates of gold and currency were loaded, but Spacil had had to organise, and requisition, against much resistance, five further trucks for the purpose. Four *Schwerer Panzerspähwagen* heavily armoured vehicles, with tank cannon barrels pointing menacingly forwards, mounted alongside deadly *MG 34* heavy machine guns, had now moved into position at the head of the large road convoy, their commanders sitting in the upper turrets. A further two *Puma Sd.Kfz 234* armoured cars were positioned at the rear, armed with the latest *PaK 40* heavy duty anti-tank armour piercing weapons. A fuel bowser had also drawn up, although they were to rendezvous with fuel trucks at various points on their journey, the first of which would be waiting at the Berlin Tempelhof Airport.

At 1:30pm, Spacil checked that he had radio contact with all vehicles in the convoy, and, as the retaining flaps on the trucks were being fastened, he walked back to the bank with Schmidt. The sound of explosions from incoming artillery fire were already closer, and every few minutes another salvo came in, shaking the ground. Spacil hurried into the bank where Völker was standing by the doors; he looked at Spacil, with an open-mouthed expression, shaking his head, then beckoned him to join him in a small side-office out of earshot. He spoke with a sense of restrained excitement. "Oh *mein Gott,* Josef, you know the value of what we are removing? In those trucks is at least 200 million Reichmarks worth of currency and gold, excluding the counterfeit currency." He whispered, "This equates to 80 million US dollars before current exchange rates collapsed!" (Equivalent to 1.4 billion US dollars in 2024)

Spacil thought for a moment, then replied, patting him on the back, "We had better take good care of it then, Wolfgang...*Kommen!*"

In the bank were still positioned a number of SS troops guarding bank staff who had been permitted to sit at available desks and tables, some of whom had been commandeered to make and serve coffee. As Spacil re-entered, the hum of chatter ceased and the soldiers by the door jumped up, saluting as he walked to the centre of the room. He spoke in a measured, but commanding tone. "You will not speak of what has occurred here today to anyone, or you will be shot." He paused as Schmidt lifted his weapon, cocking it with a deliberate move, before pointing it ominously around the room, his eyes darting menacingly from one person to another; then Spacil continued more loudly, "You will attend work normally until you are relieved of your duties. On behalf of the *Führer,* I thank you for your service to the Reich." He straightened to attention, giving the Nazi salute, *"Heil Hitler!"* clicking his heels, before executing a smart about turn, and marching out, followed by the men under his command. As they left the building, he turned to Schmidt, "You do love to be a little over-dramatic, *Oberfeldwebbel,*" betraying a slight smile.

"I don't like to disappoint my audience, *Herr Standartenführer,*" came the good-natured response.

They were elated with the success of their mission thus far, and, especially so, as there was a substantial additional gold bullion cargo in newly smelted bars with no identifying marks or numbers; this had not been accounted for either the day before by Walther Funk, or included in Volker's figures, As they were leaving, the wail of air-raid sirens sounded, and Spacil spoke quickly into the radio, "We will proceed at speed to the Schloss Britz estate southeast of Tempelhof Airport, and park in the wooded area, until this air raid has ended. If the convoy is hit, split up and re-gather there." The engines roared, and the convoy moved away, sounding horns to warn other vehicles to move, picking up speed as the sound of anti-aircraft fire could be heard. Smoke was everywhere and people were now scurrying to find shelters with available space. They heard the first bombs, but it seemed they were concentrated in the area beyond where they had left five minutes before. However, as they were passing Tempelhof, there were huge explosions as the airfield was hit, and the shockwaves rocked the convoy, with some trucks being hit by flying debris but, although shaken, they continued. Arriving at Schloss Britz, the armoured vehicles slammed through the gates, and they pulled into the relative shelter of the thick wooded area bordering the estate.

As the bombing eased, Spacil contacted the commander of Tempelhof, *Oberst* Rudolf Böttger, by radio, who confirmed that he had executed Kaltenbrunner's orders and organised two aircraft. The front of the convoy doubled back, leaving the rear heavily guarded under the trees, and sped back towards Tempelhof Airport.

On arrival at Tempelhof, the large gates were opened, and as the trucks pulled onto the tarmac apron, *Oberst* Böttger walked over to meet Spacil with a handshake, although he did not return the normally expected and customary, *"Heil Hitler"*, limiting himself to a military salute. His face looked strained, and tired, as he took a deep breath before saying, "I think it is all over, *Herr Standartenführer*. I have just heard, the 9th Army have lost Cottbus; the Red Army is advancing from the South East, and although being resisted from the North, they are in the outskirts of Berlin. They will overrun everything within days; God help us all. The *Führer* has given me orders to blow this place up but I cannot. I would get on those *verdammte* aircraft, and get out of this hell. We have become very efficient at filling holes within hours of them bombing. The far runway is clear." He pointed to the far-left side of the airfield, "You have two *Ju 52* transport aircraft waiting. They are fuelled and ready to go; we will need to record your consignment and who is travelling. Your wife is already here."

When Spacil asked where Kaltenbrunner was, Böttger responded that he had already left the day before. Kaltenbrunner, he said, had arrived unexpectedly in a state of some panic, stating that Berlin would fall imminently, and had been flown out with some other members of Hitler's staff. He had left a message for Böttger to pass on that he would rendezvous with the convoy when they reached Berchtesgaden. Spacil thought for a moment; "I had no idea it was this bad, *Herr Oberst*. I cannot leave my men and just fly out after we load the aircraft. I am on a mission which may secure Germany's future when this war is over about which I am sworn to secrecy. You can help; please log that I was on the flight out today, and I would ask that you record the freight as records and files from the Reich administration. I am sorry it has all come to this; I think the world will condemn us, but rue the day they did not join us in resisting the communist

Schweine." Böttger looked at him, seeing the sincerity in Spacil's eyes, and nodded, extending his hand. Then, they briefly embraced, before the trucks traversed the airfield and bag after bag of currency and lighter valuables were loaded into the two aircraft.

After a tearful farewell to his wife, Spacil returned to where *Oberfeldwebbel* Schmidt was waiting. "That was tough," he remarked simply, as he climbed back in the cab of the truck.

"That is why I never married, *Herr Standartenführer,* and because I am single, still available, and good looking, the ladies want me even more."

"God above, have I got to put up with this *Blödmann* (dumbass) for the next 750 kilometres!" came the reply, as the trucks raced back through the pall of smoke now hanging over the whole of Berlin.

Oberst Rudolf Böttger did not execute the *Führer's* orders to blow up Tempelhof Airport, and three days later committed suicide as the Soviet forces closed in.

20

The Final Journey

Monday 23rd April 1945 12:30am
Outside Potsdam, Twenty-five kilometres south-west of Berlin

They had rested under the trees the previous night until 6:30pm, when Spacil summoned a meeting of NCOs, one of whom was assigned to each truck, together with the commanders of the armoured vehicles. He had commandeered a room in Schloss Britz, which was being used as a *Wehrmacht* HQ by elements of Army Group Vistula, and had been established as a field command post by General Helmuth Weidling, the commander of the Berlin defence. General Weidling was happy to grant Spacil's request to use the facilities and took the opportunity to ask him about the *Führer's* demeanour. Weidling had been given conflicting messages; the first that an order had been issued that he be executed for retreating in defiance of Hitler's orders, then another, summoning him to meet with the *Führer* the following day. He had heard that the *Führer* had suffered a breakdown the preceding day, after being briefed on the collapsing military situation, and he was concerned that he might be held as a scapegoat for the failure of others to stand their ground. Spacil had informed him that when he saw Hitler in the morning of the day before, he was entirely in command,

and further, that he had fully briefed Spacil on a mission to transport material to a secret location down south. However, he did not inform Weidling about the nature of his mission, nor that his trucks were packed with gold. He had heard that, in the wake of the Russian advance, some German units were suffering from indiscipline and disaffection, not something that he had encountered from any within the SS. Spacil knew that his success depended on the highest levels of secrecy being maintained, hence he posted guards outside the operations room he had taken over for his briefing. Weidling warned him that the situation on the roads to the west and south of the city was fluid, and that the routes were clogged with refugees fleeing the conflict. He further informed him that German defensive lines were barely holding, and were suffering from regular Red Army breakthroughs. He finished by shaking Spacil's hand, saying, "The *Ivans* fight like dogs, rarely take prisoners, and never surrender. However, their weakness is that they do not think for themselves. They are never prepared for surprises and believe the poison their Communist masters feed them. If they are told we are attacking from the North, they do not reinforce their western or eastern flanks. If they are told we are retreating, they fail to prepare for counter-attacks. Also, they are starving; these primitive slaves of the Bolshevik *Schweine* will do anything for food. Get them in a crowd around food, then shoot them. If they offer to talk, or surrender, kill them. I have fought these *Untermenschen* since 1941 and I have no respect for them." Weidling saluted, then executed an about-turn, before marching away.

In the briefing, Spacil issued orders that two lead trucks and two at the rear were painted with red crosses on a white circle, denoting they were part of the DRK (*Deutsches Rotes Kreuz* – Red Cross). He instructed them to obtain white coats and red cross uniforms from a medical unit operating in the Schloss. "I want the armoured vehicles to have their gun barrels covered by tarpaulins because," he said with a wry smile, "we do not wish to alarm Ivan as we prepare to give him a very warm reception", drawing laughs from the assembled SS. He outlined the strategy he had discussed with *Hauptman* Völker telling them to get some rest and prepare to leave at midnight. His parting words were received enthusiastically. "*Meine tapferen Kameraden,* we are embarked on a momentous mission given to me personally by the *Führer*. I can promise that, if we are successful, you will be given substantial financial reward immediately upon our safe arrival at our destination in Berchtesgaden, so that when this war ends, which I think will be soon, you will be able to build new lives; lives in which you enjoy a prosperity you never had before. *Das ist alles. Heil Hitler!*" The convoy had stopped outside Potsdam, south-west of Berlin, as a radio message had been received warning them that Soviet forces were closing in on their previous chosen route. They opted to take a more westerly direction and then swing round to the east and head south once they were well clear of Berlin. Progress had been slow out of Berlin, despite their constant hooting and shouting at the lines of people trudging slowly away from the city, even though it was the middle of the night. Some walked with handcarts, others with nothing, whilst many desperate looking mothers with distraught children by their side, were caught, wide-eyed, in the beams of vehicle lights. They carried lost expressions on their faces of people who had seen too much and who no longer cared, driven by nothing other than the primeval instinct to survive. Searchlights added an awful drama to the scene, that were periodically lit to assist with the limited luminescence provided by the hooded vehicle lamps, making them less visible from the air. There were bodies too of both civilians and soldiers along the verges, but no one noticed in the pitiful lines of despairing humanity.

As they entered the outskirts of Potsdam, they were faced with a roadblock, and a barrier manned by *Wehrmacht* soldiers.

An officer walked over to the lead vehicle, in the front of which Spacil and Völker were sitting, together with a driver.

"*Papiere!*" he grunted at Spacil, then noting his rank, he added, "*Bitte Herr Standartenführer.*" As a seasoned career military man, Major Wolf von Lieben had little time for the SS and their reputation for brutality, despite holding some admiration for their unswerving discipline and loyalty. He was not prepared for the response from Spacil who was anxious not to reveal his identity nor have any record of the convoy logged. "*Herr Major,* I am on a mission which has been given to me personally by the *Führer*. You will let me pass...now." Then he paused, before adding, a sneering, "*Bitte.*"

Major Lieben came from aristocratic roots, and found taking orders from anyone distasteful, even less so, some Nazi upstart. He beckoned his men, a dozen of whom walked forwards, raising their weapons to waist height. "*Herr Standardtenführer,* the Russians are less than thirty kilometres from here; they have taken Cottbus, and are now attacking Königs Wusterhausen. The *Führer* has ordered that anyone who retreats must be executed. So, I will ask again, *Papiere!*"

The microphone on Spacil's vehicle had been set to transmit to the convoy throughout the exchange, and now he uttered the phrase with which he had briefed his men, "*Ein Reich!*" Major Lieben looked puzzled for a moment, then spoke his words more harshly, "I will waste no more time; you will step down from your vehicle and my men will conduct a search. *Schnell!*"

From the side of the vehicle came a harsh voice, "*Sofort aufhören! Achtung!*" (Halt immediately) followed by the ratcheting sound of multiple catches being pulled back on machine guns. Searchlights from the convoy now flooded the scene as *Oberfeldwebbel* Schmidt strode into view. He shouted, "I have two hundred highly trained members of the *Leibstandarte SS Adolf Hitler* with me. If you resist my orders, you will be shot. You will all place your hands on your heads, now! I report directly to *Reichsführer SS* Himmler. I will not mention this in my unit report if you do as I say. Remove the barrier; *Schnell!*"

The look in Lieben's face had now turned to fear as his eyes struggled to see in the dazzling light. "I think, *Herr Major,* you should do as he asks." Spacil now had his pistol pointed at Lieben's head, who turned, blurting out over his shoulder, "Lift the barrier!"

Spacil added in an icy tone, "*Herr Major,* if any mention of this incident is made anywhere, my men will return and you will die, *verstehen?*"

Lieben nodded, his hands now held behind his head.

"Now walk slowly back and stand with your men," Spacil commanded. Moments later, Schmidt appeared and saluted, saying, "Good plan, *Herr Standartenführer!*"

"I thank God it was not Ivan," Spacil responded, then, "What is this 'unit report,' and since when did you report directly to *Reichsführer* Himmler?"

Schmidt gave a brief smile, "The answer to your second question is, I don't, and in answer to your first, I think you called me 'dramatic' at the Reichsbank. *Heil Hitler!*"

Spacil spoke through the radio stating, "The Russians are closing in; we will take a westerly route to Werder, then re-join the road to Leipzig, swinging east once we reach Wittenberg."

The convoy rolled through the countryside, until the first streaks of light could just be discerned. The roads were clearer now but Spacil had made it clear that daytime travel was too risky because of the dangers of air-attack from marauding Allied fighter-aircraft that were searching for any moving targets; plus, daytime travel would attract more attention as it was unusual for long convoys to be seen at this time.

At 4:30am, they had approached Linthe, a small town seventy kilometres south-west of Berlin where they were stopped, this time by a *Hauptsturmführer* in an SS uniform by the side of a small armoured troop carrier. He looked exhausted, and drawn, his eyes reddened as he approached the open window of the lead truck, but still managed to click his heels and extend his arm, "*Heil Hitler!* They are everywhere, these *Russische Bastarde;* we killed so many of them, but they just kept coming. They are maybe seven or eight kilometres to the east of here in Luckenwalde. They took Cottbus yesterday and I think they are trying to encircle Berlin. Leipzig fell to the Americans three days ago so God be with you; God be with all of us."

The trucks rumbled on until 6:00am when they reached the cover of some trees outside Wittenberg. They had only managed 110 kilometres since leaving Berlin, mainly as a result of painfully slow progress, not only because of refugees, but debris and abandoned vehicles which had suffered attack, littering or blocking the way. Spacil announced they would rest until 12 noon but had changed his plans because of the rapidly deteriorating military situation. He now decided they should risk travelling in daylight, separating into six separate groups, five minutes apart, each escorted by one of the armoured vehicles and regroup at their scheduled fuel stop at Hof, near the Czech border. At 12 noon, he departed in the lead truck, followed by three more and an armoured vehicle. One hour later, as they reached the outskirts of Torgau, they stopped, seeing a huge column of smoke over the town. Spacil decided to wait until proceeding, allowing the other parts of the convoy to catch up, giving them added safety in numbers. As he waited, a lone aircraft swooped over where they were parked, before looping back to dive low over them. They all awaited the inevitable sound of machine gun fire, or cannon shells, but then felt a wave of relief as the aircraft roared overhead, and disappeared over the horizon. "I am pretty sure that was a Russian *SU-2R* fighter aircraft," remarked Völker, "I spotted the Soviet star on his wings."

"*Ja*, but they are also used for reconnaissance. We may have trouble ahead," replied Spacil grimly.

The column, having re-grouped, made its way slowly forwards, maintaining a ten-metre gap between each truck, whilst two of the armoured vehicles positioned themselves behind the lead trucks which now bore the red cross on the front and sides. Entering the town, the streets were deserted, although smoke arose from some buildings, many bearing the signs of combat with smashed walls or roofs; Spacil felt the familiar tightening in his stomach which normally preceded moments of action.

As they approached the main crossroads, a large lone tank, in camouflage green and yellow, rumbled into view and stopped, its turret turning ominously towards them. "*Verdammt,* that's a Soviet *T-34*," said Spacil as the radio crackled and the voice of Schmidt came through who was in the truck at the rear. "We have a little trouble back here. Ivan is behind us; around thirty men, just walking."

"Do not engage unless you have to, *Oberfeldwebbel*," Spacil responded, adding, as a small number of soviet soldiers began walking towards them, "I think we may be bargaining with the *Schweinehunde;* it looks like a delegation. Armoured, do not rotate your turrets, but load and prepare." They donned white coats over their SS tunics as the Russians approached with their weapons at the ready, stopping about 25 metres away. The Russian commander walked slightly ahead of his men, dressed in an open khaki double-breasted greatcoat with red-piped collar patches, and blue breeches tucked into black boots. On his head was an officer's service cap with a crimson band and piping, and a large red star in the centre. He shouted in broken German, "I am Colonel Aleksandr Vasilievich Rokov of the 1st Ukrainian Front. You are surrounded. How many are in your convoy and what is its purpose?"

Spacil shouted back, "We are carrying urgently needed medical supplies and food for the city of Leipzig. The Americans have approved our consignment because they need help after taking the city." Then, in a quiet voice, towards the radio, "Are they still behind you, *Oberfeldwebbel?*"

"They are stopped around twenty metres behind us," came the quick reply. "We have the *MG42* machine gun prepared and in position."

"When I give the password, not until," Spacil replied.

The Soviet officer had summoned a radio operator who was now crouched by him with a headset speaking into a microphone. Spacil muttered to Völker, "The mention of the Americans will have confused them because there is already tension between Ivan and Uncle Sam".

The officer now shouted, "How many personnel in your trucks?"

"There are forty-five of us. Drivers, doctors and medical orderlies." Spacil answered. "We have supplies of blood also. There are many wounded in Leipzig after the battle there. The war is over for us, Colonel, and we wish to save lives." Then quietly, *"Hauptman* Richter, how close are you to getting a target line on that *T-34?"*

"We need to swing by 5 degrees, *Herr Standartenführer*; but we also have to loosen the covering. We are loaded with the *PaK 40*. One shot should take him out."

Spacil shouted, "*Herr* Colonel, we can share food supplies with you as a gesture; we have more than enough."

Rokov turned to his men, and, after a few exchanges, he gave his reply - "You will bring some to me here, but if I see anything suspicious, I will open fire." He drew his weapon from its holster, pointing it at the truck.

"We are unloading now," Spacil yelled to the Russian, then spoke quickly into his mic, "Six men unload food rations; three from this truck, and three from the one behind; slam doors, make noise. Richter, as they do this, unfasten your covering and train your weapon. Fire upon password. You go as if supervising, Völker. Stick that Kepi on your head; your SS cap might frighten them!"

Völker grinned as he doffed the cap, and shouted to the trucks behind, "*Raus, Raus,* unload food." Doors slammed, as men tumbled out, there were accompanying noises and crashes as food crates were taken down whilst behind the second truck, the tarpaulin was loosened and the turret moved a fraction at a time, almost imperceptibly. "Target sighted," the voice of Richter announced. Three crates were now being dragged to the front of the truck. Spacil tensed as he uttered the words, "*Ein Reich!*"

Almost simultaneously, there was a loud thump from behind, followed by an enormous flash and explosion as the *T-34* turret received a direct hit. The loud staccato noise of the rear-mounted machine gun started, as Schmidt had thrown up the canopy, taking the Russian soldiers behind totally by surprise, many of them pirouetting as they fell to the floor, their arms flailing. To the front, the *Panzerspähwagen* began firing cannon shells as the Soviet troops ran in disarray, desperately seeking cover. The Russian officer had fired twice before being hit, and Völker cried out as he tried to climb in the truck, being pulled in by Spacil with blood pouring from his chest and shoulder. Smoke was spreading across the road and there was shouting and screams from the injured, mixed with the deafening sound of the armoured vehicles spraying the street in front with deadly effect. The noise of gunfire was everywhere, and the glass shattered to the driver's side of Spacil's truck as it lurched forwards, leading the convoy and picking up speed, with soldiers shooting from inside the trucks, adding to the deadly firepower being unleashed. There were more bangs as the truck was hit but they continued past the tank with thick black smoke pouring from where the turret had been as part of it had blown clean off. Minutes later, they hit open countryside and the sounds of the shooting died away.

Völker was lying against Spacil, his breathing laboured. "Are we clear?" he asked weakly, then adding, "I feel so cold, Josef, using Spacil's Christian name which he had only ever done in private. Spacil spoke into the radio, "Medic to me as soon as we halt." He turned back to Völker, speaking softly, "We gave Ivan a good beating, Wolfgang; they should never have come into the Fatherland. Thank you for what you did." He desperately applied a field dressing to the wound, telling Völker to hold his hand over it.

The convoy sped through the countryside for a further ten minutes, but, after passing trucks packed with German soldiers heading the other way, they slowed to a stop as they came to into a wooded area. Völker was slipping in and out of consciousness as he was lifted from the front of the truck and placed on a stretcher. Spacil walked with him to the rear where room was made for them. After examining him, the medic applied a further dressing to his chest, injected morphine, and patted Spacil on the shoulder as he walked away.

Völker tugged at his sleeve, "Please tell Helga I love her. I am going, my friend."

"You are not leaving us, Wolfgang, but I swear if anything happens to you, I will take care of her, and your son."

"Oh *Gott,* Josef, let this not be in vain." His voice was fading.

Spacil placed his hand on Völker's. "You are a wonderful friend, and I will never betray what we have fought for."

"I wish I could see...the dawn once more." His breath came in deep gasps, and he was gone.

They buried him in a clearing, forming a cross out of two crate pieces, then fired a salute, before resuming their journey. There were a further six casualties from the action, but all suffered minor injuries and were able to continue with the convoy.

They reached Hof at 5:00pm meeting up with a fuel bowser, commandeered by the SS. During the re-fuelling operation, Spacil was briefed by the local commander on the military situation. He was informed that Nuremberg had fallen to American forces three days previously, Stuttgart had surrendered to the French the day before, and that the eastern-most route, through Regensburg to Munich was still open, although the US front line was moving eastwards daily. Alternatively, he was told that he could divert through western Czechoslovakia, where the German 7th Army had a strong presence but, he was warned, the roads were not good and subject to rogue partisan attacks. Spacil opted to risk the quicker route hugging the Czech border, via Regensburg to Munich.

After a three-hour rest, the convoy departed under cover of darkness at 8:30pm. Unlike Berlin, the route was clear and there was little sign of any traffic or battle damage to the roads or towns they travelled through. They passed occasional groups of soldiers who cheered them as the trucks rolled by, some giving the Nazi salute. Schmidt had now joined Spacil in the cab of the lead truck.

"What is the plan when we reach Berchtesgaden, *Herr Standartenführer?* I am already thinking of some fine Bavarian beer with all the riches you are bestowing on us."

"The reward is for the lower ranks only *Oberfeldwebbel;* we do this out of loyalty to the Reich," smiling as he turned to see Schmidt display a single fingered gesture. Their long service together had brought an unusual lack of formality, although Spacil trusted him with his life. "Our job is to ensure the freight is concealed from both the Russian and Allied invaders, which we will do under the direction of a man the *Führer* has entrusted with this task. You may have heard of him, *SS-Obersturmbannführer* Otto Skorzeny."

Schmidt nodded his head. "Ah *ja*, he is the one who rescued Mussolini from the mountain fortress; then last December, he drove the Americans crazy by leading a group in US Army uniforms behind their lines in the Ardennes offensive. I think I will enjoy meeting him."

"He has a reputation for drama, so you should get on fine, but, unlike you, he has a successful reputation with the ladies."

"I think being with you is a drama, *Herr Standartenführer*," came the quick response. "Under your command, I have learnt many skills, but I did not expect bank robbery to be amongst them,".

The banter between them helped lighten the mood after the trauma of losing a close comrade and had often been used previously.

They drove without incident until they passed a sign for Schwandorf when they saw two heavy vehicles blocking the road ahead. They were half-tracks, with white star logos of the US Army on the side, and both turrets were pointed directly at them. They halted, as Spacil spoke tersely into the radio; "Prepare for action; enemy roadblock." The speaker crackled and the voice of *Feldwebbel* Hoffman from the rear spoke. "We have a *Sherman* tank which has rolled into the road behind us." At that moment, searchlights lit up the entire area, positioned in the trees either side. A loudspeaker blared, "This is the United States Third Army Infantry Scouts. No one need die here. The war is nearly over, lay down your arms and exit your vehicles. If you do not, I will order the armour to open fire."

"Armour ready?" Spacil hissed.

"*Jawohl, Herr Standartenführer*," came the reply

"I will distract them, and as I do, sight your targets." He turned to Schmidt, "We may have to fight our way out. Lay maximum fire to a line 25 metres either side of the armoured to the front, rear armour will take out the *Sherman* with similar field of fire. If I do not succeed, commence firing. *Viel Glück!*"

With that, he took his pistol off, donned his cap, and exited the truck, with his hands held high. He shouted in English, "I am *Standartenführer* Josef Spacil – I agree to surrender but I ask to briefly speak with your commanding officer."

A voice boomed back, "This is Captain Henry Dexter Calhoun of the 6th Corps of the US Infantry Scouts. What do want to say Kraut?"

"Please, a quick private word – I am unarmed and will come to you; I will then command my men to surrender. I agree there should be no deaths."

"Come forward, Kraut, but one wrong move and you will no longer exist."

Spacil walked towards the armoured vehicles, looking down to shield his eyes from the dazzling lights, until he was 10 metres away.

"That's far enough – we'll come see you."

Seconds later, one searchlight swivelled slightly, allowing his eyes to adjust, as an officer in a helmet, flanked by two men with their weapons raised, walked forwards.

"Speak, you sonofabitch, and it had better be good." His tone was harsh. "I have 50 guys with me who are dyin' to kick your asses. We all serve with General George Patton's Third Army and no one messes with us, Kraut."

"Captain, I am carrying gold in my trucks. If you let us pass, I will leave sufficient quantity to make you all wealthy men. No shots will be fired. No one need know, and no one gets hurt. If you do not, I have two hundred highly trained SS combat veterans with me who will fight to the death for the Fatherland, plus four armoured vehicles with armour piercing shells. However, if you let us through, we will pay you, gold with a value of $275,000 US dollars." (Equivalent in 2024 to $5,500,000)

There was a whistle from one of the US soldiers standing next to Calhoun, whilst the other muttered, "Jesus H Christ!"

"So, Captain, if I die, there will be a lot of deaths here today, but, if you accept what you Americans call 'a deal', you are all, as you might say, a hell of a lot richer and everyone goes home. So?"

Calhoun paused, shook his head, then was about to speak, but uttered an expletive before lighting a cigarette. He took a deep draw, as his Sergeant said, "Er, Captain, Sir, we need to talk some."

Calhoun waved him away, and spoke to Spacil, "Holy Mother, Kraut, you got balls," he exhaled sharply between his teeth, adding more forcefully, "Ok, here's the deal, you unload the dough, we check it, and you walk away. You pull any funny business, you history, *verstehen?*" Then muttering, "I must be crazy. Sarge, bring the Goddamned prisoner truck up here."

Spacil shouted orders back and boxes were soon piled up by the verge just in front of the convoy which Calhoun checked with his Sergeant, whilst others looked on. He then walked back to Spacil, his pistol still drawn, with four men behind him, nervously holding their weapons at the ready. "Well, hell, Kraut, I guess you kept to the deal. You better get your asses outa here. Good luck boy." He extended his hand, which Spacil shook, then stood back and saluted.

"It's been a pleasure doin' business with y'all," Calhoun stated, with a wry smile, then shouted commands back to his men and the two half-tracks moved to the side of the road, the soldiers waving to the convoy as it passed.

In the early hours of the following morning, as they rested in the Munich barracks, Spacil sent a signal to Skorzeny.

21

The Raub Gold Train

Tuesday 9th January 2024 1:00pm
Braunstrasse, Harlaching, Munich

The phone was vibrating on the cabinet by the bed and, despite his normal ability to return to an instant state of alert, part of him did not wish to; his subconscious thoughts were to flee from the past in which he was now involved. Despite this, he had slept deeply since returning to his apartment, exhausted from all he had been through the day before, followed by the stressful period at the hospital in the early hours with Friedrich. He was relieved to hear Inge's voice. "Karl, I want to come over plus I need to see you." There was a hint of desperation in her voice. Then, in a much softer tone, almost as an afterthought, but typical of her, Karl thought with a smile,
"Are you OK, *Schatzi?*"
"*Ja, ja, mir geht es gut, mein Engel,* but I fly to England tomorrow."
"Karl, there is more incredible information I have from the archives;" her voice was almost breathless, "and I want to see you. Maybe, I could come with you."
"Inge, no, this has become dangerous and I do not want you involved or exposed."

"Pah, typical man! What the hell did you think I did for ten years in a police special unit; powder my nose? Well, I'm coming over – see you at 4:00."

He was about to reply but she was gone, leaving him shaking his head, but it was her impulsive and very individual nature that had first drawn him to her.

He arose, had a shower, then, clad in just his dressing gown, he made a cup of coffee and wandered over to the box full of documents by his desk and began sifting through the papers. There was more corroborating evidence reinforcing much of what he had previously discovered, especially relating to a recurring term, *Judenleihgebühr*, recording fees paid to the Reich by business for the provision of Jewish slave labour. The same names came up time and again, some haunting him such as IBM, Ford, BASF, Porsche, SIEMENS, and, suddenly, he felt re-motivated on his quest. He singled out a document folder, yellowed with age, on the front of which was written *Die Ehrenarier* over an eagle and swastika in German gothic script. There was a note attached in his father's handwriting. '*Die Ehrenarier* (Honorary Aryans) *were those of non-German, or 'impure' German blood, who gave loyal service to the Fatherland which, incredibly, did include Jews. After the war, this grew as more people of Jewish origin and other institutions were prepared to do business with us. This spawned a further secret organisation, named die Ehrenarier Treuhänder Deutschlands (ETD) (honorary Aryan Trustees of Germany), which were those who were happy to accept our assets which included gold, currency, and valuables such as art treasures and jewellery. There is a record which lists details of who assisted us in this process between 1945 and 1960. On this list are senior figures in some of the most reputable global institutions, including the Vatican. I placed this in a file, as your supreme guarantee of safety, and put it with your unofficial 'inheritance' in London. Our people were unable to obtain information on this after the robbery at Hatton Garden because of the security clamp down. I used to keep your grandfather's SS ID card with these documents, so please look out for this if you recover the file. After all, I would not wish my position or my reputation to be compromised.'*

Karl could not help smiling; was this an attempt at humour by his father? He studied the list in the honorary Aryan's folder which meant nothing to him other than the odd entry which caught his eye including,

'All those of Japanese blood;
Helmuth Wilberg (Luftwaffe General - Jewish origin)
Amin al-Husseini (Palestinian Mufti of Palestine in the British Mandate)
Princess Stephanie von Hohenlohe (Abwehr agent - Jewish Origin)
Emil Maurice (Chauffeur to the Führer – Jew)'

There were a couple of sheets listing those similarly awarded this 'honour' but Karl discarded them as having little value. However, he added a note about *'die Ehrenarier Treuhänder Deutschlands'* into the record he had started compiling of key information on the Nazi regime days previously. There were more photographs of his grandfather with various people, many of whom he recognised, including Hitler and members of his inner circle. There was a colour photograph of him standing in shorts, holding a drink with the man he now knew to be Otto Skorzeny. On the reverse was written, *'Our lives are blessed, with Otto at Es Barcarés, Alcudia, Majorca, August 1965.'*

At 4:00pm, as he expected, the door buzzer sounded; Inge was always punctual. She entered carrying a thick document folder and a shopping bag. "Ok, lover boy, as you are so concerned about my safety,

I can't possibly go into the kitchen; it's far too dangerous. So, I have brought the ingredients for you to make *Sauerbraten;* (Pot meat roast stew with spices) that is, if is not too challenging a mission for you tough guys in the *KSK*."

He strode over to her, slapping her backside, as he pulled her to him; they rocked together in a long hug, both aware of, and delighting in, the enormous emotional bond between them. As Karl moved into the kitchen area, Inge pulled out a bottle of Champagne from her bag announcing, "So, Mr Tough Guy, as it appears you are leaving me yet again, I thought we should celebrate our time together, but before you depart on your little jaunt, you might reflect on my input which, despite the, er, 'danger,' I can give because of the years I spent powdering my nose in the police. Since I last saw you, I have been to Berlin and met some former colleagues who, like me, were never exposed to danger." As she pulled her coat off, she was pulling faces at him, finishing by sticking her tongue out.

"I have brought with me, at great risk, some highly classified material which you, as a tough guy, would never be trusted with. This includes..." she looked up triumphantly, "the travel record of the convoy carrying the *Raubgold,* after it left Berlin in 1945. This contains reference to the first record we have of bribery involving the American forces. But, my little hero, I have much, much more to tell you, but you are not hearing about it until you open the Champagne which, I might add, is a wonderful *Bollinger.* We ex cops from the *Bundespolizei* know how to party because we love danger!" She giggled playfully as she leant over the back of the sofa, coquettishly, handing Karl the bottle.

As he poured the Champagne into crystal flutes, she began, "So, how much do you think was removed and concealed by the Nazis?"

"I am not sure but my father said it was a huge amount, but he was never specific."

"Karl, it was so huge, that no one has ever released the information, because no one knows exactly, and, also because, no one dare release the estimated figure. The secret documents in the Federal Archives contain estimates, which, in today's value, equate to $100 billion."

"*Lieber Gott!*" Karl gasped. "That is incredible. I recall father saying that there were official records of the *Versteckte Vermögensfonds* placing the figure at around $25 billion, but this..."

His voice trailed off with a hiss through his teeth.

"Champagne please, tough guy. This tough lady has uncovered much more, but I'm thirsty."

He handed her a glass, then they kissed before touching their glasses together, and he moved to sit next to her.

Inge continued, "This was all covered up at the end of the war by agreement between US President Truman and British Prime Minister, Winston Churchill. The problem was that forces on both sides had become involved in stealing some of the gold and valuables, whilst there was evidence of complicity involving senior Allied military officers in doing deals with former high-ranking Nazis. Further, a huge amount of the gold was unaccountable and not included in the official accounts as it had been either looted from the Jews or seized from countries that had been occupied. The records showed that all such 'requisitioned commodities' should be listed and forwarded for processing to an office of the *SS-Wirtschafts-und Verwaltungshauptamtes* (Economic and Administration Office) at a section headed by, wait for it, *SS-Standartenführer* Josef Spacil, your grandfather!"

Karl grunted, then sighed, shaking his head, adding, "Yes, he was supposedly a genius in 'concealing' assets through creative accounting."

Inge now referred to notes she had prepared, "There was also the issue of the involvement of banks and financial institutions which could have caused a financial crisis at a time when recovery was the priority. In addition to this, they wanted to conceal what was happening from Russian Premier Stalin with whom tensions were already running high. So, matters were left there which meant that theft and corruption did not get properly investigated and that was a gift to organised crime. The Allies put out some story about recovering the missing gold in a mine at Merkers which kept the press quiet until the 1980's." She took another sip of her Champagne, adding, "This is making this girl hungry, so, into the kitchen, tough guy."

As Karl busied himself preparing the meal, Inge spoke animatedly, "Rumours began circulating in 1981 when Hitler's former architect, and armaments minister, Albert Speer, began talking to the press, saying he had many secrets to reveal. In Germany, he gave an interview to *Der Spiegel* in which he hinted at financial dealings with international banks during World War 2, and referred to missing gold that had disappeared after the war. This prompted our chancellor, Helmut Schmidt, to launch a highly secret investigation. Reportedly, he was astonished by what was unearthed, but decided to classify the report as 'top secret', effectively burying the findings and consigned this to documents that could not be released for at least a century. The notes attached state that the chancellor considered that the report opened up highly sensitive issues which, if made public, would put the spotlight on former Nazis who held prominent positions, especially those in business. Further it would reveal the existence of a secret Nazi enclave which was established after the war in Bariloche, Argentina.

Apparently, this was the nerve centre of a new organisation which many called 'the Fourth Reich' run by Hitler's former National Socialist Party boss, Martin Bormann."

"Yes, my father's notes confirm this and we were told he had died in 1945." said Karl.

"Never believe history told by the victors…" She was shaking her head ruefully. Then she added in a more serious voice, "So, there was nervousness at this time regarding any talk about Germany and the war. The 1980's was a period for the resurgence of the new Germany, free from the past which was rarely spoken about. However, in September 1981, that was all being put at risk; Albert Speer was due to give an interview to the BBC's Newsnight programme in London on the plundering of art treasures by the Nazis, where he had promised a scoop. Prime Minister, Margaret Thatcher, was briefed that he was a loose cannon and the dossier states that, having discussed the sensitivities of the situation with Helmut Schmidt, it was necessary for "appropriate" measures to be taken on the grounds of national security. The British PM assured Helmut Schmidt that British security services would deal with the matter. On 1st September 1981, Speer suffered what was described as 'a sudden stroke' at his Bayswater hotel, and died a few hours later."

"*Mein Gott,* this gets worse," Karl said. "But how do you know all this?" Inge picked up her document case, and extracted two sheets of paper. "It was all in the report prepared for Helmut Schmidt and I have in my hands;" she held up papers, pausing to add drama, then speaking with a triumphant tone, "a copy of a confidential British Intelligence briefing on the death of Albert Speer, together with a telex sent by Prime Minister Margaret Thatcher to Chancellor Schmidt. The telex reads as follows:

'Dear Helmut, my understanding is that the Speer issue has been dealt with in the appropriate manner considered, and approved, during our discussions. Thank you for your support and consent for the removal of this threat from the past to the security of our present social fabric.'"

Inge looked up sharply, "Karl, you cannot quote this, nor can you say that you have ever seen it." Then, she changed her demeanour to a playful, "Is dinner ready yet?"

"You are one incorrigible, irrepressible woman," he replied, looking at her with admiration.

"This is what I get for powdering my nose," she retorted, "There's much more, but I like a little anticipation, so, food first," she added in a sing-song voice.

As they sat at the table, having dinner, Karl related to her the events of the previous day, the attempt on his life, his meeting with Friedrich, and his part in the subsequent police raid on the house used by Franz Niemeyer and the *Reichslegion*. As he spoke about the raid, she placed her hand over his arm, shaking her head in dread at what might have happened, her eyes meeting his, with a knowing, caring smile. They finished the Champagne, opted to have some more wine, and settled on a large glass of Chablis. Karl lit the wood stove, dimming the lights as they sat together on the couch, her hand reaching across to clasp his.

"So, my handsome tough guy, you want to see what else I have to show you?" She angled herself provocatively as he sighed and shook his head in mock disdain.

"*Spielverderber!*" (spoilsport) she exclaimed as she reached for her document wallet. "As part of the enquiry ordered by Helmut Schmidt, there were a number of classified reports generated but my friends in the *BND* are very loyal and I had to use feminine wiles to get whatever I want."

Karl sighed, lifting his eyes upwards as if exasperated, and pulled his hand away as she giggled.

"My boy-friends always remain loyal, and like to give me what I want. So, here we have a document which is classified, but my guess is that we can easily trace references to it in publicly accessible records or via the internet which will add a fabulous addition to your book."

"What book?" Karl replied

"Well, you said you wanted to publish what you were uncovering, so, I know it will make a fabulous book and I will be your researcher, whilst you take all the plaudits. The document I have here is entitled, *'Der Raub-Gold-Zug'* or *'The Werfen Train'* which is the name given to it by the Americans who claimed to guard it. The information in here is just incredible, Karl, and it implicates the British, French, and the Americans in seizing a fortune in valuables and gold which were looted by the Nazis in the Second World War."

"This just gets deeper and deeper," Karl was shaking his head, his voice was despairing, "but please go on."

"So, in 1944, the Nazis knew they were losing the war and plans were being put in place to safeguard and hide their assets. Clearly, what you are uncovering was a major part of that strategy. This was being repeated all over the Reich. In March 1944, Hitler ordered the invasion of Hungary, despite it being an ally, because the Germans discovered the Hungarian government were secretly negotiating with the Allies. 800,000 Hungarian Jews were forced to hand over all their assets. The Nazis even issued official receipts, carefully recording the owners' identities and labelling containers accordingly. Most of the Jews were shipped off to the camps and very few survived. By late 1944, the Red Army was closing in and the Nazis needed to remove the vast amount of gold, silver, paintings, gems, diamonds, and precious jewellery they had amassed. They had also stored booty in Hungary plundered from other parts of the Reich. A plan was drawn up and authorised by Adolf Eichman to ship the valuables out by train and take it to safe locations for concealment." She looked up from the record in front of her which she was following. "You may have heard of Eichman; he was a senior Nazi who organised much of the meticulous planning for the transportation and management of the Jews, in what the Nazis termed 'The Final Solution.' He was hunted down by the Israelis after the war, kidnapped by their intelligence in Argentina, taken to Israel, and hanged after a trial, in 1962."

"Justice, I suppose," muttered Karl, "but I do not approve of the death penalty."

"Ooh, my tough guy shows his soft side," she teased, leaning over to give him a quick kiss, which served to lighten the moment. She looked back down at the record, turning the page over, "The goods train that he authorised left Budapest on December 15th 1944, after being loaded with 1,560 cases containing gold, precious stones, paintings, and other valuables collectively worth around $3.5 billion dollars in today's value. There were smaller shipments, but no record exists of their destination or what happened to the valuables they carried. The consignment despatch note for the biggest train is here; I have it." She pulled out a sheet of paper and passed it to Karl.

As he read, his eyes widened in astonishment and horror at what the document represented in terms of both state sponsored cruelty, and human suffering. At the top of the paper was the Nazi eagle emblem, and a heading in gothic script, denoting its secrecy, under which was a neatly typed list:

Steng Geheim
Reich Versendung

Authorisiert: SS-Obersturmbannführer Adolf Eichmann

Ausgabedatum: 14-12-1944

Endziel: Salzburg

Güterwagen: 32

Anzahl an Boxen: 1560

Versendung:

9,200 kilos gold bullion

3,500 kilos silver bullion

708.44 kilos diamonds and pearls

8,750.25 kilos gold rings

914.5 kilos miscellaneous gold

1226.25 kilos miscellaneous silver

3,275,000 US dollars currency

2,600,000 Swiss francs currency

42 cases miscellaneous coins

2,023 pieces furniture

1,652 paintings

3,970 rugs

17 gathered bundles of silver-topped walking sticks

200 cases fine porcelain

243 cases of assorted dinnerware

322 cases of crystal glasses

75 cases fine linen

8 cases rare Stamps

150 cases furs

9 cases watches

72 cases miscellaneous clocks, cameras, typewriters

100 cases top-coats

3 cases silk underwear

50 cases miscellaneous art – sculptures/statues/cultural artefacts

Karl handed the paper back muttering darkly, "You might as well call it a pillage record."

"I think we need another drink" Inge responded, "In fact, we deserve a strong Daiquiri; can I suggest a touch of the *crème de banane* liqueur. Come on, my hero, let me show you how to live dangerously."

She carried on speaking, paraphrasing from perusing the report, "The train was commanded by *SS-Standartenführer* Arpad Toldi, who was a Hungarian Nazi administrator with special responsibilities for policing. There were 213 people on board, including Toldi's family, SS guards, and a unit of miners in case they needed to bury the consignment. The train had 24 carriages with accommodation for officers, and escorting guards, plus 32 freight cars. During the following days, the train endured no less than ten robbery attempts on its journey which were repelled by the SS guards aboard. The first stop was Zire, south of Budapest where it took on more precious cargo. The report says that it is impossible to quantify the value of the new consignment as it was not properly inventoried. A significant quantity of gold and precious stones was loaded which had been stored secretly at the nearby Obanya Castle. This was repeated on its journey, as Toldi was ordered to other unscheduled locations to pick up more gold and valuables. The train was then halted in a place called Brennbergbanya. Here it not only took on more cargo, but a thorough re-categorising of the freight took place. Everything was carefully sorted here into categories but, strangely, not evaluated. As Soviet and Allied forces were advancing through Europe, they waited several weeks until they knew they had a reasonable prospect of safe passage, before leaving to make the next leg of their journey in March 1945, with the Soviet army now only a few miles behind them.

"As the train entered Austria, it made more unscheduled stops, but this time for cases to be unloaded into trucks. Little is known of what happened to these, but it was later revealed that on more than one occasion, the officer in charge of the trucks was identified as the German commando, Otto Skorzeny. Under questioning, after his capture by the Allies, Toldi stated that Skorzeny carried a letter of authority signed by Adolf Hitler giving him the right to give orders which carried the authority of the *Führer*. Am I getting this drink or not?"

Karl had made the drinks but had stopped at the edge of the bar, transfixed by what he was hearing. He walked over to her as she said, "Karl, the most extraordinary bit is yet to come; you will not believe it."

"You certainly know how to keep a man interested," Karl replied, as he handed her the generous measure of mixed liqueur."

"Oh, I intend to keep you very interested tonight," she teased, "but first, a toast to us...*prost!*" They touched glasses again, and she kissed him, squeezing her arm tightly around his body, as if seeking safety. Then, she pulled back, wanting to reveal everything she had discovered.

"Now, to the interesting bit, which is incredible. On 30th March 1945, Toldi left the train with his family, unloading a substantial amount of the treasure onto a truck convoy. The official story put out later was that he abandoned the train, but we discovered something very different. Toldi sought the assistance of a senior influential colleague, *SS-Sturmbannführer* Wilhelm Höttl. He served in the *Sicherheitsdienst* (Intelligence) and was acting Nazi head of Intelligence and Counter Espionage in Central and South East Europe. Höttl had offered his services, and been accepted, as a double agent working for American Intelligence. He was in regular contact with the Head of American OSS in Switzerland, Allen Dulles, who had an office in Bern. A deal was struck with Toldi, brokered by Höttl with Dulles, for Toldi to be given safe passage, and a guaranteed release after the war with a new identity in exchange for 10% of what was on the train. Dulles and Höttl organised the removal of boxes from the train into trucks, which were given an escort by US forces into Switzerland. No trace of what was removed from the train was ever discovered."

"*Oh mein Gott,*" Karl exclaimed, "Was everyone corrupt? How much more is going to come out? Did no one have any scruples?"

"Oh, Karl, you have no idea. There is much more. It was Allen Dulles who helped Germany rebuild its Intelligence service after the war, incidentally under the control of a former high-ranking Nazi, Reinhard Gehlen."

"Yes, I recall that rat, Niemeyer, talking of this at my father's funeral."

"Ah, yes, of course, I remember this now too," Inge responded. "Well, Dulles was very close to the US president and had enormous influence through powerful friends in business and political arenas. So, he now reveals to Roosevelt that the Germans are trying to shift gold and other valuables so that these were safe from the advancing Soviet forces. President Roosevelt is adamant that the Russians must be prevented from seizing former Nazi assets. He authorises German forces be given assistance, or, at very least, left unhindered in removing gold and other assets in order to ensure it did not fall into Soviet hands. Of course, this was all unofficial, which meant that it could not be admitted to even after World War 2 ended."

"In April 1945, Dulles put in place a plan whereby Höttl became an intermediary between US forces and the Germans moving the treasure. Unofficially, US commanders took some of the boxes by way of 'compensating' them for turning a blind eye. As the Germans removed the freight off the train, US and British forces looked the other way, and did not attempt to interfere. Even four-star US General Lucius D. Clay, one of the most senior Allied officers in Germany, having been appointed as the Deputy Commander of Military Government, was in it up to his neck. His HQ was in the Bavarian town of Garmisch-Partenkirchen which acquired the name "Sin City" amongst Allied soldiers because of the looted goods openly traded amongst the troops, including priceless artworks. Clay was known as the Commandant of *'the forces of lawlessness and disorder,'* and oh my goodness, Clay himself was not immune from corruption; even his wife was shipping loot back to the US using the General`s private airplane. Regular trips were made to Miami bypassing customs checks by declaring these trips a "Classified Mission".

"Many others were involved in the so-called co-operation between Nazis on the ground and Allied forces, including one Major General Henry Collins, the commander of the 42nd Infantry Division in western Austria. The train ended up in a place called Werfen, where the French forces looted two of the carriages, before Collins was assigned responsibility for its security. He was an uncompromising officer and few ever dared question his orders. Vast amounts of gold and valuables disappeared from the train at this time, but no records exist of how and when this was removed, although, curiously, military records were scrupulously maintained of other items being 'requisitioned'. Those involved included the most senior US and British officers serving with SHAEF (Supreme Headquarters Allied Expeditionary Force). Our intelligence records that these matters were considered too sensitive to investigate after the war as too many prominent figures were involved and there was a need to face the Soviet threat. There is credible evidence that some items were removed under the orders of General Patton, and presented to the Supreme Allied Commander, General Eisenhour, who, of course, subsequently became president of the United States."

Karl rose to fill their glasses with a final nightcap, his head reeling at the implications of what he was hearing. Inge was looking back at her notes, "The file records that this Major General Henry Collins officially 'requisitioned,' certain items whilst undertaking his duties to guard the train, and I quote:

'China dinner service for forty-five settings, thirty sets of table linens, twelve silver candlesticks, sixty bath towels, thirteen rugs, fifty crystal wine glasses, sixty crystal Champagne glasses, eighty crystal goblets, thirty crystal tumblers, sixty silver dining pieces, eight paintings, sixty sheets, sixty pillow-cases, and sixty large bath towels.'

"However, this was just that which was recorded because other senior officers were also involved in what was effectively looting, and by the time an inventory was prepared of the goods the train was carrying, over four hundred paintings had disappeared which were never recovered whilst most of the gold was missing. Some of the paintings turned up at auctions many years later. Our files record that an American Jew, by the name of Meyer Lansky, had become involved in May 1945 in supervising, monitoring, and transporting shipments of recovered Nazi gold and artworks back to the United States for what was termed "processing." He had built powerful Mafia connections throughout the United States and pledged to ensure that Jewish people would be compensated and looked after."

Karl put his glass to hers, as he muttered darkly, "Yes, I came across him in *Die Transaktions Aufzeichnung* which my father left for me." He sat back trying to put all he was hearing in order.

Inge referred back to her notes - "This man Lansky was a real big Mafia boss, who together with his associate, Lucky Luciano, was running the Manhattan Mob. Our file shows they expanded their interests, post-war, across the entire United States in what was known as the Jewish Mob."

"*Ach Scheisse!*" Karl exclaimed, "Is there nothing of virtue amongst this mire? Wait, you said, the owners' identities were recorded by the Nazis. Why did we not return the looted valuables?"

"After the war, the Americans did not wish to admit they had been involved in, or seen to be turning a blind eye to, the stealing of plundered Nazi gold or other valuables. Nor did they want to be seen to have had any involvement with the Mafia who were controlling a lucrative market with huge sums changing hands for gold and precious stones. Then there was the embarrassment of works of art being sold off at auction, many of them by the families of former senior US military officers. There were repeated requests from Jewish organisations and the Hungarian government for the return of the looted items which fell on deaf ears. The United States falsely claimed that it was impossible to trace the owners and eventually what was left on the train, after that which was taken by the Germans, the Americans and the French, was sold off for auction. Some of the proceeds was finally given to the International Refugee Organisation, but... the balance was absorbed by the US state.

"I cannot believe that so many were involved in this orgy of greed and corruption." Karl blurted out in a desperate tone.

Inge sensed the very real personal anguish that her revelations were uncovering about the past; a past in which Karl's grandfather had played a large part. She spoke more softly, "The imperative agreed at the time was that none of the looted items should fall into the hands of Soviet forces. The intelligence briefings record that post-war planning envisaged that Germany would become naturally aligned with Britain, France, and the United States. Stalin's Russia was already seen as the future enemy by the Allies."

"Ok, so what happened to Toldi.?" Karl asked.

"Oh, he disappeared for a while at war's end, but he was arrested and interrogated in August 1945."

"And?" came the reply.

"He was released without charge, disappeared, and was never heard of again."

"What about *Sturmbannführer* Höttl?"

"Ah, yes, he testified against leading Nazis at the Nuremberg war crimes trials before continuing to serve as a US Intelligence agent, operating in the Soviet part of occupied Austria. He then founded a school which he ran until 1980, passing away in 1999. Oh, and he received a Cross of Merit from West Germany for his work as a historian and as a school director, despite the protests of surviving Nazi victims."

"Ach, I do not think I can be shocked further...and this influential OSS man, Allen Dulles?"

Inge was almost reluctant to utter the words, "He became Head of the CIA…oh and later served on the Warren Commission investigating the assassination of President John F. Kennedy."

22

Honour Amongst Thieves

Wednesday 10th January 2024 8:00am
Flight BA947 Munich to London Heathrow

Karl had his portable ultrabook mini laptop open, preferring the larger display to his notebook, and was running his hands rapidly over the keys, even before the flight had taken off.
"I wish you had been there last night, Friedrich, that woman of mine is incredible, and her brain is so sharp; *ach*, but maybe it is better you were not there; she asked me to marry her, and you would have been working out the cost of the wedding."
Karl had been picked up by Dieter at 6:00am, and they had proceeded to the hospital at Ernst-von-Bergmann-Kaserne, where Friedrich was waiting, before Dieter drove them to the airport where he bid them farewell. He informed them that they would be met at Heathrow by a trusted agent, attached to the German embassy, who had excellent connections within British security. Intelligence protocol was that the agent would not be named to them until they were approached. At Munich airport, they were whisked past all security, although secret regulations required that a declaration was signed by them covering any weapons or ammunition being carried, before boarding the aircraft. Karl surrendered his *HK P30L* to a uniformed BND officer who checked it was not loaded, before asking if there were any further

weapons in their luggage. Karl confirmed that his case held both a *Walther PPK* with 40 spare rounds, and a service issue knife, whilst Friedrich stated his bag contained a *Ruger LC9* with 56 rounds.

"Have a nice holiday," the officer quipped with a grin, as he snapped the mechanism closed on Karl's pistol, handing it back to him. As they exited from the security office, and were escorted through the boarding gates, a man in a set of worker fatigues, carrying a tool kit, stopped, and spoke into his lapel.

Now, as the aircraft climbed, Friedrich reacted sharply, "She asked you to marry her? Herr *Soldat-Kämpfer,* she must be crazy."

There had been no hint the night before, other than the usual closeness they shared from their ten-year relationship. Somehow, however, recent events seemed to have brought them closer; Karl had found her support wonderful during his difficulty absorbing the revelations given to him by his father, and the realisation of his own emotional bond with him after his death. Now, it was as if, in many ways, he was seeing her as never before. The respect and admiration he held for her had deepened with her self-directed energy to assist him on his private mission that she recognised had become a driving force in his life. This had reached a climax as she had shown him a document, signed by British Prime Minister, Margaret Thatcher, addressed to the German chancellor, dated 18th August 1987.

10, DOWNING STREET
The Prime Minister
18th August 1987

His Excellency Helmut Kohl
Chancellor of the Federal Republic of Germany

Dear Helmut,

The regrettable potential impediment and security threat to progress in our ongoing discussions with the Soviets, has, I believe, now been removed. Mr Gorbachev has been, as you know, quite receptive to discussions on détente, dis-armament, and the liberalisation of Europe, which our friend and ally in Washington, President Reagan, has striven so hard to achieve.

Clearly, our aim is to achieve a new free Europe which, of course, we hope could lead to the unification of your country and the lifting of the scourge of communism which has blighted your people since the end of the War.

All of the great strides we have made in the cause of freedom were threatened by just one last source from that dark era, and that could not be permitted. The risk associated with the possible impending release was one which could have impacted the entire free world.

I made the decision to excise that risk, for which I take responsibility, and I am grateful for your understanding in our telephone conversation today, and your co-operation in the matter of subsequent security arrangements. I have also discussed this at length with President Reagan who has, unreservedly, endorsed the action taken.

Please accept my sincere thanks, and, I am sure I can express those on behalf of the free world.
Yours sincerely,

Margaret Thatcher

At first, he did not grasp the enormity of what he was reading until Inge said slowly, "Remember Hess?" He reached for his phone, tapping the date and name, his eyes widening, exclaiming, "This was the day after Rudolf Hess, the 93-year-old former deputy *Führer* of Nazi Germany, supposedly hanged himself in Spandau Prison. Of course, he knew about the laundering of Nazi assets."

"And much more," Inge added. "He knew that the Allies had considered entering into a treaty with the Nazis against Russia, which would have almost certainly delivered Hitler victory." [1]

Karl had looked at her, and in the meeting of their eyes, there was a deep unspoken bond, as she had reached for him, and he for her. Papers cascaded to the floor as they were devoured by their desire for one another, and as she held him, feeling his arousal matching her need, she pleaded for him to take her, crying out as they joined, yet yearning more as he sought to give and take, and give again. Their bodies moved in unison, and then her words were uttered, gasping as she shook with her release, feeling his, "Oh *Gott*, my beautiful Karl, marry me."

Now, as they sat on the aircraft, Karl was briefing Friedrich on all that Inge had uncovered, some of which Friedrich was already aware. "I told you, Karl, there is so much; you have no idea what you are on the

[1] Covered in previous book, 'The Barbarossa Secret'

edge of, or who is implicated." Then, as they were looking through some of the documents Inge had forwarded to Karl, Friedrich added, "I have memories of meeting this man, Wilhelm Höttl, who helped ensure the safe passage of the train and organise the disappearance of *SS-Standartenführer* Arpad Toldi. He was a good man. Not all of them were demons, you know. Arpad Toldi and his family settled in the new German community which we had established in Argentina. He was given a job in our police and security service with a new identity but kept his head down, and was never traced by post-war Nazi hunters or investigations. When Dulles became head of the CIA, he helped conceal the whereabouts of many Nazis who the US perceived as useful, or because they knew too much."

However, it was the record Inge had obtained, documenting the journey of the convoy of gold escaping Berlin that really took Friedrich's interest. He read the bland account recording the death of his grandfather, feeling a painful connection with the past. As the aircraft touched down, Friedrich turned to Karl, "There is no honour amongst thieves, but we must try to somehow justify or, at very least, understand the sacrifices of those who went before."

As they entered the arrivals hall, proceeding to immigration, they were approached by an official looking man, dressed in a jacket and tie, "Mr…er…Timothy Warren, and Mr Bernard Shekel?" Friedrich winced at the identity Dieter had created for him. "My name is Graham Henshaw from the Foreign Office; would you come with me, please." He led the way down a corridor to a door. They entered a bland office with grey walls and a curtain running down the centre. "Please don't worry, this is where strip searches are conducted but we won't be requiring you to undergo that today." He attempted a smile. "Would you wait here a moment please?" He returned moments later accompanied by a woman, in her mid-forties, smartly dressed in a dark suit, and an older man in a checked sports jacket, and an open-neck shirt. They introduced themselves as *Stabshauptmann* (Captain) Ilse Göttner, from the German Embassy, and Major Howard Kent, liaison officer between the Foreign Office and MI6 Intelligence.

Major Kent began, "Welcome guys to the UK; don't worry, I am on your side," he smiled disarmingly. "The reason we have asked you to pop in, is that our boss, Cameron, is a bit of a stickler, and, as foreign secretary, he does not like hush hush operations without him being briefed. We call it ex-PM syndrome!" He half laughed as though mocking the system. "So, before I let Frau Göttner lead you astray, can you give me a version of why you are here? Something I can placate Uncle David with."

Göttner turned to Karl, her penetrating eyes betraying her resolute, uncompromising nature. "Tell him what you wish without compromising national security. After all, we are, as he says, all on the same side."

Karl appeared relaxed as he spoke, "We are here to investigate the infiltration of extreme right-wing elements into our international financial sector, and also, on behalf of the German state, to trace and seek the return of gold reserves stolen by the Nazis during the war. Some of this, we believe, may be held in UK banks or may have been seized by UK law enforcement agencies. You will understand, under the agreement between our countries and the EU, that we hold diplomatic immunity and the right to secrecy in relation to our activities."

"Can I ask why you did not use the usual channels; you know, Europol, that sort of thing?"

"Major Kent..." Karl assumed a military bearing, his voice calmly but unmistakeably displaying his authority. "Might I remind you that your country dropped out of the EU and that co-operation between us on security matters is tangled in red tape, despite the so-called TCA (Trade Cooperation Agreement) which has so many pre-conditions embedded within it, it requires a lawyer to request a file on a shoplifter. Major, I think we are both military men…the politicians have created a complete pigs-ass of this, so please, word your report to Mr…or Lord Cameron how you will, but we have a job to do."

"I will add," Ilse Göttner interjected, "that later today, we have a meeting scheduled with your home secretary, and Sir Mark Rowley, the Metropolitan Police commissioner. Perhaps, I might suggest you approach Mr James Cleverly after our meeting for a de-brief." She stood up, clearly designating that the meeting was over.

"As I said, you are welcome here," Major Kent seemed unruffled, as he extended his hand. "Enjoy your stay in the United Kingdom."

Ilse led the way to the exit from the building where a white '*S' Class Mercedes* was waiting, guarded by an armed UK police officer. On the door was written, *Embassy of the Federal Republic of Germany*, underneath which were the words, *United Kingdom*. A driver held the rear door open, and Ilse followed them inside, where the rear seats were aligned to face each other. Ilse's voice assumed a friendly tone, "Get used to it, boys, because we have allocated something far less ostentatious for you to drive after today. Now, I will introduce myself less formally, I am Ilse, attached to Defence Attaché staff at the embassy. My real job is with BND Intelligence and I report directly to Major Dieter Metz. Also, it is important that you know I am a loyal member of the GVR, so we can speak openly. I suggest first names, if you agree. You have a video brief from Dieter awaiting at the embassy but I will fill you in. Today, you meet some important people, including the home secretary."

Friedrich's voice cut in, "*Heiliger Strohsack!* (Holy crap) Can you please explain how we have progressed from a minor issue which we are investigating, into a meeting with one of the leading members of the British government? I have never met anyone important in my life, apart from former Nazis."

"Forgive him, Ilse," Karl stated. "He is a *Buchhalter,* and has no imagination."

She laughed as she replied, "I have learned that with the British, you start at the top and work your way down. They are still steeped in the past, with rank and respect, and nothing gets done because of the bureaucracy they create. We start at the top, and then you go underground but we have doors to open, sensitive police files, and, trust me, they are obsessed with preventing anyone from looking too closely into the War."

"How far is the embassy?" Karl asked,

"About 25 kilometres from here so, about an hour away."

"An hour? *Verdammt,* why so long?

"You have a lot to learn about the British. They can't organise anything, especially their transport. You should try seeing a doctor or a dentist. Thank God we make our own arrangements."

During the journey, Ilse explained that, whilst she was their case officer, she had been instructed to step back and allow them complete operational independence. This was something Karl had demanded, in return for his reporting back to Dieter his success in investigating and penetrating the criminal world surrounding the laundering of gold in London. He had explained to Dieter that his father had private investments in London, which formed part of his estate, and that they had been compromised during the Hatton Garden raid of 2015. He had agreed to undertake a mission to both investigate this, as the British Police had long since suspended their enquiries, and attempt to trace the gold taken in the robbery, thereby preventing this from falling into the hands of the *Reichslegion.* Ilse made it clear that all resources would be available to him, including armed back-up agents; she also stressed that she had contacts inside both MI6 and MI5, who could give support where required. On the political front, there were MP's that could be relied upon to provide pressure, should it be needed, both from within the government and the opposition. Ilse explained, with a smile, that 'favours' were sometimes 'called in', especially where there had been indiscretions by members of parliament in relationships that they may wish were not made public. As she spoke, Karl felt numbed now by such revelations after all he had been exposed to in recent weeks.

When they arrived in Belgrave Square, the car swung past the smart Georgian frontages displaying the flags of various embassies, down a smaller street in which was a very modern frontage, flanked by blocks with tinted windows and an angled access up a floor to the entrance. "Don't tell anyone," Ilse said, cupping her hand in a mock gesture, "but we have more BND operatives here than in most major German cities. This is where we conduct much international business out of the sight of prying eyes, especially the *schweine* from the Russian Federation although, God knows, they have approaching $2 billion invested in property in the city. However, since the invasion of Ukraine, things are not so easy for them."

In the comfort of Ilse's office, Karl sat in front of a secure connection, and, within seconds, he was watching the smiling face of Dieter in a recording.

"Hello Karl, and Friedrich; well, I have some surprises for you. Yesterday, Wolfgang Schmidt, our Minister for Special Affairs made urgent contact with the British home secretary requesting a high-level security meeting. The Right Honourable James Cleverly is new in post, and was most anxious to please. I might add, he was also anxious not to be implicated in any scandal which may result from matters surrounding the Nazi gold achieving publicity. I think the British government have enough difficulties with the press at the moment. He has agreed to organise a meeting with the Metropolitan Police Commissioner, Sir Mark Rowley; however, his role will be to enable, rather than become involved. Ilse, as part of the German Embassy, will introduce you, as a formality. You merely need to brief them that you are engaged on a highly sensitive mission on behalf of the Federal Government of Germany into the activities of extremists infiltrating the financial sector; you will say little more, nor will this be expected, other than to justify the covert request for approval and authority to access sensitive areas without question. Our chancellor has also been briefed that we are engaged on this mission, which he endorses, as part of ongoing investigations into far-right groups. However, neither he nor the British PM have been given any details which is the norm for sensitive intelligence operations; only a handful of us within the GVR know the real purpose of this assignment. The Met Commissioner will recognise the protocol of being briefed on a 'need to know basis,' so there will be no awkward questions. The meeting will take place at 2:00pm today UK time. We need to secure access to Belmarsh Prison, where the last of those arrested in connection with Hatton Garden is being held.

"We have a senior contact at MI6 who we have requested to attend. His credentials are impeccable; he was seconded by Israeli Intelligence to MI6 four years ago and he is now head of the Jewish-Arab affairs department. Interestingly, he is a member of *Na'amod*, a Jewish group committed to ending the Israeli role in the occupied territories and the establishment of equality and justice for both Israelis and Palestinians. Despite raising the hackles of many in Israel, he has high-level contacts within Israeli Intelligence and a reputation for being a little 'cavalier' in his methods; however, he has an outstanding reputation for operational efficiency coupled with an excellent military record. He was involved in helping to avert a coup in Israel in 2022[1] and is held in very high regard despite his pro-Arab sentiments. Recently, since the Israeli attack in Gaza, he has been involved with *The Jewish Voice for Peace*, an organisation which speaks out against the war. We have selected him because he takes great interest in historical issues, especially those relating to the holocaust, and hence, he could be an invaluable asset to us. He has worked in tandem with the *World Jewish Restoration Organisation* or WJRO, which attempts to recover Jewish property seized by the Nazis.

"Various Jewish organisations seek to recover gold, stolen by the Nazis, and they will want to prevent our recovery of any gold held by the UK government, or by UK banks. However, if they know that we, in the GVR, are prepared to do business with them, and that the *Reichslegion*, who the Jews detest, are also trying to get their hands on it, they will work with us in preventing this. If we commit to a deal with the Jews, this will assist us in persuading the UK government to release the gold and other valuables, that they have impounded, to us. Karl, as you know; your father did so much to safeguard all of this. As a result of the Israeli assault on Gaza, the British government are falling over themselves to pacify the Jewish lobby, whilst on the public stage they show sympathy for Palestine, and call for a ceasefire. At this time, I think we can use the Jewish connection to lever the release of the gold.

"The name of this Jewish agent is Benjamin Weiss; he's an idealist who identifies with the Arabic cause in a way which is too much for some in Israel, hence his secondment. He is a little larger than life, popular with the ladies, and I think he fancies himself as a bit of a James Bond.

[1] – **Covered in previous book, 'Fission'**

So, now, as promised, I will not interfere further, but I hope you like the car I have organised for you." Dieter waved with a wry smile as the screen went blank.

"*Gott,*" Karl muttered dryly, "That's all I need; first a *Buchhalter* and now a British secret agent who is Jewish and thinks he's a film star."

"Without me," Friedrich countered, "You would not know who you could trust, nor would you be here. Remember, I organised this trip and I have helped you with information no one else could have given you."

"But remember, *mein Buchhalter,* it was I who saved you from the assassins in the Englischer Garten," Karl responded.

"I think, *Herr Soldat-Kämpfer,* it was my brains that exposed who was trying to kill you, and, I might add, without any weapons. I think you may need my skills when we negotiate with this 'James Bond'; you would probably just shoot him."

Ilse, Karl and Friedrich were picked up from the embassy in the white Mercedes at 1:30pm, and taken the 15-minute drive to the Home Office which took up a large ultra-modern complex, within walking distance of the Houses of Parliament in Westminster. Friedrich noted that it appeared like blocks of venetian blinds which, he said, was entirely appropriate as it concealed so many hidden secrets. They passed security with Ilse's German Embassy authority, and, with the two temporary diplomatic passes she had issued to Karl and Friedrich, they were excused from a weapons scan. A young woman approached them, dressed in a black trouser suit, introducing herself as Edith, permanent assistant to the home secretary, taking them to a private lift which whisked them up two floors. Seconds later, they were shown through tinted glass doors into a generous office, lit by a chandelier which seemed a little out of place. There were a number of windows giving a view over some gardens to the embankment of the River

Thames beyond. The room was sparsely decorated, although a portrait of a smiling King Charles in a red uniform hung on the wall beyond the large light oak desk, behind which James Cleverly was sitting. He was sifting through some papers, whilst peering at a computer monitor in front of him, one of four situated at intervals. Their escort announced that his guests had arrived from the German Embassy. As they approached across the thick beige carpet, the home secretary looked up, and immediately stood, smilingly shaking them each by the hand. "Delighted to meet you," he stated; his bearing was charming, and his appearance impeccable in a dark-blue business suit, complimented with a silk matching striped tie. He appeared, Karl thought, like an ebullient host, rather than a man who headed up UK policing and security. His smartly short cut greying hair, black framed glasses and neat trimmed beard added to the image, yet, they had been briefed that behind his urbane manner was a man who was enormously knowledgeable, with an eye for detail and a reputation for efficiency. Despite this, he had a relaxed manner which communicated well to those who worked within the Home Office, before which, he was equally well thought of in his previous position as foreign secretary. He bade them sit in the comfortable leather chairs spaced in front of the desk, asking if he could organise coffee, whilst they awaited Sir Mark Rowley, who had messaged that he was running ten minutes late.

As they waited, the home secretary spoke warmly about his visits to Germany, and they exchanged pleasantries about where they had been brought up. He was particularly interested in Karl's military training, explaining that he had been to Sandhurst, and had been commissioned into the reserve, smilingly adding, as though a discreet aside, "They must have liked me, because I'm now a lieutenant colonel."

At that moment, the door swung open, and Edith entered, accompanied by a tall, well-built man with lightly shaded glasses and short cropped blonde hair, carrying an attaché case. He was dressed in a tan leather jacket, pressed trousers, in an open neck shirt with a cravat, and had a confidant self-assured manner as he spoke, "Thank you, Edith, no need for introductions, I know Mr Cleverly well; we are actually opponents in *Warhammer 40,000*, but shhhh, don't tell anyone." As Edith closed the door behind her and the home secretary waved his hands in mock exasperation, the man advanced into the room, adding cheerfully, "I believe you two guys are from the dark depths of the BND. Benjamin Weiss, representing British Intelligence, despite my being an Israeli; although, right now, I am not a happy bunny with my country."

"Benjamin please!" The home secretary's voice was authoritative, as Weiss shook hands with Karl and Friedrich.

The doors opened again and Edith announced, "Sir Mark Rowley, Sir," withdrawing as the Metropolitan Police commissioner entered in full uniform, followed by a waiter in a black waistcoat, pushing a trolley on which were cups, a coffee jug and an assortment of cakes and biscuits. After the waiter had served each of them and withdrawn, Cleverly spoke briefly, "I am here on behalf of His Majesty's government, but other than receiving a minimal briefing, I will require no further operational detail. Subject to being re-assured about the nature of your mission, I will take no further part, nor share this with colleagues. The request I received for this meeting suggested that you would need access to prisoners held in UK prisons, and some police records from a dormant case. Sir Mark will facilitate in whatever way he can, as per agreements between our two countries, although we may need to rise above the red tape caused by the post-Brexit so called EU Co-operation Agreement. So, over to you."

Ilse spoke, "Sir, a primary concern within the Federal Republic of Germany is to monitor, and where necessary, to restrict the activities of far-right organisations. We know that there have been attempts by right-wing extremist elements to infiltrate our financial sector. In addition, we need to resolve the delicate matter of the gold and valuables, which may have Nazi origins, currently held by the UK police; this can be traced to German accounts. You may recall the robbery at Hatton Garden in 2015, from which this property was recovered as evidence. As you will be aware, all investigations into the origin of property with wartime German sources falls under our investigative responsibility. Our intelligence suggests that there may have been more gold than that which was recovered; we are seeking to trace this and ensure that, where appropriate, some restitution is made to those parties who may have a claim to this. We want to operate with the utmost secrecy, because you will understand that there would be some unrest, or diplomatic fall-out, if this matter was not kept under wraps. Also, the state of Israel may attempt to intervene, claiming that much looted gold was taken from Jewish people, and that, therefore, they should have an interest in its ownership and restoration."

"That makes sense to me," the home secretary nodded, "I think we may be relieved to offload this to you."

Benjamin Weiss cut in - "If I can, perhaps, speak in support of Ilse. You know that within Israel, we have a hardline government under Netanyahu, and it is underpinned by many Zionist motives. Some Jewish organisations do not believe that the Israeli government would handle the restitution well of valuables seized by the Nazis. Our concern must also be that intelligence sources reveal extremist factions within Germany will attempt to gain possession of whatever is recovered. In addition, there are hardline Jewish organisations, notwithstanding the Israeli state, who will wish to take control of any former Nazi valuables with Jewish links. I have connections who will ensure that the latter does not happen which, of course, is why I am here. I can also ensure that influential Jewish factions work with our friends here, subject to assurances given for some restitution to deserving survivors, and the families of former survivors of the Holocaust. As I work as within MI6, you will understand that we will guarantee there is no publicity."

Sir Mark Rowley spoke, his eyes behind black framed glasses, fixed directly on the home secretary, with his face set in a serious expression. "My remit is to ensure that the integrity of law enforcement is protected. Of course, I can arrange that every assistance is given to our European partners in both their investigation, and in restoring any property we may hold to the rightful source. I concur, Home Secretary, that we should avoid any unfortunate publicity which could cause a civil dis-order situation. I suggest that our friends from German Intelligence outline their requirements or where we might assist, and then we should step back, enabling them to investigate unhindered. Benjamin Weiss here, can act to avoid any difficulty affecting either the reputation of the UK, or the Metropolitan Police, which carried out the original investigation into the Hatton Garden heist."

An hour later, as they drove away from the meeting, Ilse summed up, "So, we have authority to visit Belmarsh prison, speak to investigating officers, see the evidence obtained, including crime-scene photographs, examine that which was impounded by police after the robbery, and transport this, subject to a review by the home secretary, back to Berlin. I would say we have had a good day. So, it is only 3:30pm, what now?"

"I think we are going to prison." replied Karl sardonically, prompting Friedrich to remark,
"Why is it I never like your jokes?"

23

Deal the dough

Tuesday 24th April 1945 8:00am
Kaserne München-Freimann, Munich

"I have *Obersturmbannführer* Skorzeny for you." There was a click, a crackle, and then the relaxed voice of Skorzeny, "Josef, good that you have made it to Munich; but we may have problems now." Spacil had been woken in the officers' quarters by an SS orderly only minutes before saying that he had *Obersturmbannführer* Skorzeny on the landline from Berchtesgaden. Now, as Spacil sat in an office listening to Skorzeny, despite having just woken from a deep sleep, he was totally alert. Skorzeny spoke earnestly, "*Die Amerikaner* are everywhere, spreading south. Stuttgart has fallen, and their forces are now positioned outside Augsburg. We are running out of time. You need to leave Munich because their main forces will reach there by the end of the week. However, they have forward scout detachments south of where you are and they are setting up road blocks."

"*Ja*, we came across one of these detachments north of here last night but they preferred a little gold to fighting. I think we left them very happy."

Skorzeny chuckled, "These *Amerikaner* love to do business. We have already opened unofficial discussions with them and secured safe passage for transport to get through but it is becoming more difficult. Some of these bastards are trigger-happy cowboys but, thank God, most of them are greedy. Josef, I need to do a little business myself to secure you safe passage; however, communication is difficult, and negotiations can only take place with a trusted few. I will hope to have news for you by the end of the day; do not move from where you are until you hear from me."

9:00am 23 Herrengasse, Bern, Switzerland

Allen Dulles received the call in his Bern office and his attention was immediately focussed as the password was given, "*Adlerflügel*" (Eagle wings) "You may speak freely," he stated, lighting his pipe, whilst switching the phone to speaker. The voice, with the heavy German accent, he recognised as being that of Wilhelm Höttl.

"We have another consignment which requires safe passage, but this will be a large convoy travelling by road from Munich to Berchtesgaden. The number of trucks is twenty-five plus four armoured vehicles."

"Goddamn it," Dulles retorted, "What the hell is it this time? You got Adolf Hitler in there going on vacation?"

Höttl's voice had an urgent tone, "*Raubgold*... but more than you can ever imagine. You have units all over the south-west and transport needs to be secured. If the convoy heads east, it will fall into the hands of the Soviets. If we stop the trucks, then all will be inventoried, and no one gets any benefit."

"We can resolve the position; I will obtain the authority of US President Roosevelt, but there are costs. How the heck are you gonna deal the dough?"

"I have an exchange of two caches of major value, the location of one which I can give you now, and the other will be released on safe transit of the convoy."

3:00pm – Paderborn, Former Luftwaffe Airfield, North Rhine-Westphalia, Germany

The Dakota aircraft touched down at Paderborn, on the edge of which were littered German aircraft, most damaged or burnt out, whilst debris was piled in intervals by the perimeter, cleared from the Allied bombing and strafing attacks which had hit the airfield only four weeks before. Major General Henry Collins dismounted, accompanied by two officers and eight men, some carrying spades on their backs; a truck was waiting at the airfield entrance, from where they were driven the short distance to Schloss Wewelsburg.

Collins was a thick set well-built man, aged fifty, with a reputation for no-nonsense soldiering; he placed himself, he claimed, in the same camp as General Patton who enjoyed public recognition for a similar approach. He was known as 'Hollywood Harry' for his flamboyant ways which included arranging for military escorts with flashing lights and sirens. As they reached Wewelsburg, he turned to his ADC, Brigadier General Henning Linden, "You know what, Henning, these sons of bitches deserve gettin' the crap kicked out of them, and we deserve some reward for giving our lives to kick their asses. I say better in our hands than some God forsaken sharing out or reparations bull. We earned what we take; and we support the United States by spending what we gain back at home."

Linden, a military combat veteran in his early fifties, responded, "I'm with you, General, but I believe we need to make sure some of what is recovered goes back to aid refugees."

Collins was uncompromising in his reply, "Charity begins at home, and we all suffered here. Never forget that."

At the gate house, they were checked before being waved through to the castle courtyard where an officer approached with a guard accompanying a man in an SS fatigue hat with the death's head insignia on the front. He was wearing his SS uniform but the insignia had been removed and he had no belt. The officer spoke, standing to attention and saluting, "Major Ronald Dexter, sir. This is *SS-Hauptsturmführer* Erich Schneider, who has been given a special pass allowing his release subject to cooperation with you guys today. If he does not, in my view, you can shoot the bastard. Er…sorry, Sir."

"No need to apologise, soldier; if this Kraut wants to live, then he's got this afternoon left to impress me; if not, you will be removin' his ass on a cart within the hour."

The German spoke out in broken English, "Please, I am happy to assist you. I have received orders to give you information. I was in charge of security here when the *Reichsführer* was creating this as a military training centre. This was also a place representing the so-called Teutonic values of the SS as knights of the Reich. I did not join for this nonsense, but wanted to be a proud soldier dedicated to the Fatherland. I think you should have joined us against Russia; you may rue the day that you backed Stalin's Bolshevik *schweine*."

Collins guffawed, "Well boy, we got one thing in common; guess I might not shoot your ass after all. Let's see what you got to show us."

They followed Schneider through the castle doors over which the SS runic letters were displayed, underneath which was the motto, '*Meine Ehre ist treue*' in silver lettering. The ceilings were vaulted, and the walls lit by mock torch lamps. "We are going to the heart of the *Reichsführer's* creation of an almost religious dedication to principles that he justified on an historic narrative which I thought was preposterous. I was a student of history before the war in Hamburg, and I knew his conclusions were nonsense. None of us could argue with anything he said, nor even dare debate it with him. I hope your people do not negotiate with him because I hear that is what he has been attempting."

"Worry not, son, that sonofabitch will end up danglin' off a rope." Collins put his hands to his neck, giving a mock grunt to emphasise his words.

Schneider led the way down a long passage with sturdy timber doors set in Norman arches on either side. "So, we are heading to the North Tower, which was the epicentre of the Nazi folklore that was being created for the chivalric image of the SS as the knights of the Reich. In late March, we knew the Americans were closing in and on 30th March, my commander, *SS General* Siegfried Taubert, left here, saying that the war was over but that I should remain at my post and ensure that nothing was looted. A day or so later, an SS detachment arrived under the command of *Sturmbannführer* Heinz Macher, who was in Himmler's inner circle of trusted commanders. He had been sent with orders from the *Reichsführer* to blow up the castle, but not the North Tower."

They now encountered a large door which Schneider opened, revealing a circular room beyond, with white pillars encircling a polished stone floor which surrounded a central area in which was a sun pattern. Schneider explained, "We in the SS were the light of the Reich, and here we held ceremonies with the most senior officers to invite the blessing of history and Providence on our noble cause."

"Jesus H Christ," Collins interjected, "you guys really take the biscuit swallowing this bull-crap."

"*Ja*, but at the time, we dare not even think it, although, very privately, some of us knew this was all crazy. But you must understand, the regime relied on anyone informing on anyone, even children against their own parents for the good of the Fatherland. None of us dare admit what we may be thinking."

"So Kraut, you know why we here," Linden stated, "and you need to understand we are supported by orders from Otto Skorzeny, carrying the authority of your Mr. Hitler. So, what you got for us, boy?"

"Skorzeny...?" Schneider looked surprised, "He is something of a legend within the SS. He is working with you?"

"Let's just say we co-operating to protect the assets of the Third Reich. So, get your ass in gear and show us what we came for." Linden responded.

Schneider betrayed a look of annoyance for a moment but replied calmly, "Please, follow me down these steps." They descended to a lower level which, unlike the plastered room above with the neat pillars, was a cool rounded area, forming the base of the tower, with no décor apart from the windows, set at roof height above stark stone walls. As they looked up at the domed ceiling, they saw a circular capstone containing a runic version of the swastika. In the centre of the area was a low circular wall with another smaller circle in the centre.

As they took in the low-lit area, Schneider explained, "This is the crypt, and considered to be the sacred heart of the SS. Three weeks ago, *Sturmbannführer* Macher said he had orders to ensure the North Tower was preserved, which is where we are. The *Reichsführer* had ordered that the *SS – Ehrenring* must remain here until he returned."

"So, what the heck were these *Ehrenring?*" Collins demanded.

Schneider explained, "These are silver rings, taken from the bodies of SS officers and men who have died in combat, which were gathered here, providing a sacred centre for our SS-Order of loyalty, based on the sacrifices of others. They were personally awarded only by

Himmler, and were greatly prized. His signature was on the inside, together with the name of the recipient. We had to wear them on the left hand but, alas, mine was removed when I was taken prisoner. I think they swap hands for a lot of money."

"Goddamn," Collins growled, "Is there no end to this crazy crap? How many of these Goddamned rings were there and where the hell are they?"

"Right under your feet, *Herr General,* and there are 11,743 of them."

"Sonofabitch!" exclaimed Collins. You mean you bastards hid them right here?"

Schneider nodded, "*Ja,* Macher had been ordered to place them in a hole in a hill near Wewelsburg, and blast seal them inside, but he had very little explosive which was in short supply. This, he needed to destroy the castle, but even that was insufficient to complete the task. The castle, as you see, is only partially damaged. So, we decided to dig below the centre of this central circle, about 2 metres, then place stones over the upper level making it appear as if it was part of the construction.

"Now, we hear, the *Reichsführer* is no longer in favour with the *Führer;* we are told he has betrayed the Reich by talking to the Allies. So, my honour and loyalty lie with my wife and two children in Hamburg. I need to be there helping them."

Collins barked out orders, and four men began removing stones in the centre of the circle before digging. Within ten minutes, one called out, "We got an ammunition box here, Sir." Linden peered over the hole, ordering his men to dig carefully around the wooden box bearing stencilled lettering indicating the source and former contents. As they cleared more earth away, they discovered another box beneath. Linden ordered that two soldiers ease the first one out, pulling it up by woven carrying handles at each end. There was a central metal clasp securing it and the men stood back as Collins stepped forwards, "I must thank the *Reichsführer* when we catch the bastard," he said dryly as he released the catch, and opened the lid. He flicked the black velvet covering back. "Holy cow! We hit gold, boys, or should I say silver?" He pushed his hands into the box extracting handfuls of rings which he allowed to fall through his fingers. "Every one of these mothers will be a collector's item, and worth a lotta dough." He picked one up, showing it to his men, "Not very pretty boys, just a Goddamn skull, with some fancy patterns."

Schneider spoke, "These rings, called by many of us, *Totenkopfring* (skull rings), symbolised camaraderie, loyalty, and the sun represented power; other symbols depict the word *Gott,* salvation, and the superiority of the Aryan race."

Collins muttered, "Not very superior now we whooping your butts," to which Schneider replied, "Forgive me, *herr General,* but if we were not fighting the Bolsheviks to the east, it might be a very different story." Collins shrugged his shoulders, retorting,

"I think you bastards invaded their country first; but hell, I can't say I blame you for that."

An hour later, ten boxes containing the rings were being loaded onto the truck taking Collins, Linden, and their men back to Paderborn airfield. Collins walked over to where Schneider stood, flanked by two guards in the courtyard. He took him to one side, then shook him by the hand, saying, "Good luck boy, I hope your family are OK. I will personally see to it that you guys are taken care of but you gonna need to keep all this under your hat. I gotta hot line to General Lucius Clay, the deputy governor of Germany under Allied control, so all will be well. You report to the US commander in Hamburg and inform him that you have been asked to identify yourself by Major General Henry Collins."

Schneider nodded, thanking him, then clicked his heels and saluted.

6:00pm 23 Herrengasse, Bern, Switzerland

Allen Dulles had just taken a call from Collins, confirming that the goods were in safe hands. He was now speaking to Wilhelm Höttl, "All has been secured which is great, but you better listen, and listen good. Tomorrow, at midday, Allied bombers will be over the Obersalzburg where your friend is situated. They gonna bomb the hell out the area. My advice is that they get their asses out of there by dawn."

At 7:00pm, he received a wire from Leland Harrison, the Envoy Extraordinary or, as everyone recognised, the US Ambassador to Switzerland. The wording was concise but it was what Dulles had sought from President Roosevelt, who regarded him as a friend. *'In the interests of securing safe passage, the president has authorised that the Axis convoy codenamed 'Adlerflügel', must not be impeded. However, he has decreed that the US will use every means to detect the whereabouts of the freight when US forces take the area, expected within one week.'*

Wednesday 25th April 1945 5:00am
Kaserne München-Freimann, Munich

Josef Spacil walked down the line of trucks in the half-light of the approaching dawn, accompanied by *Oberfeldwebbel* Artur Schmidt and, as he did so, the soldiers standing in front of the vehicles raised their right arms in the Nazi salute, and came to attention. He felt a sense of pride in these men who had fought with him, and whom, he recognised were the cream of the German forces, highly trained, and loyal to the Fatherland. The news from the front was depressing, with German forces squeezed by both the advancing Soviets, who were now on the outskirts of Berlin, and from Allied forces who had crossed the Rhine a few weeks earlier at Remagen. Despite the fact that Germany still either occupied or held on to swathes of territory in France, Holland, Italy, Denmark, Norway, and even the British Channel Islands, Spacil recognised that if Berlin fell, it was unlikely that the regime would survive. He had heard that Hitler had stated that he would stay in Berlin until the end, but also knew that preparations had been made for his escape.

He had taken a call from Skorzeny at 7:30pm the night before who had confirmed the convoy could leave at 5:00am, giving time for all American and British fighting units to be contacted. Although it appeared that the advance had slowed to the south-east, there were Allied scouting patrols and skirmishes reported, some only 20 kilometres north and west of Munich. It was reported that Augsburg, containing a German military stronghold, would not hold out for more than a few days. Ulm had been taken by US forces that day, and there had been clashes with both British and American forces to the west of Munich, that were sweeping south, probing German defences. Skorzeny's voice had an urgency to it; "Josef, we have a week, at most, not only to conceal our assets, but to ensure they are safely deposited. I am in close contact with the former head of the Reichsbank, Hjalmar Schacht, and Emil Puhl, the deputy head, both of whom are in touch with senior banking officials in various countries who are prepared to receive our assets, especially in Switzerland. I will brief you, when you arrive. We are expecting trouble here from bombers in the morning, and we are moving to Bischofsweisen."

Now, as he climbed into the lead truck, where the driver awaited, he turned to *Oberfeldwebbel* Schmidt, "You know, Artur, the war is nearly over; when we have safely concealed our shipment, you may leave; perhaps take a new identity so you are not identified as SS, and make your way to your home in Hamburg or surrender to Allied forces."

The reply was swift, "*Herr Standartenführer,* I have suffered your command for five years, during which time I have often wanted to shoot you, this being one of them. I do not understand surrender, and, I am not leaving you in charge of all the loot. In any event, I have no wife, and my parents were both killed in the Allied bombing of Hamburg in July 1943. So, please do not suggest this again, because I would prefer not to kill you." The two men shook hands and the driver joined in the laughter as the convoy began its journey.

An hour passed before they saw anything unusual, then, as they approached Irschenberg, fifty kilometres south of Munich, two aircraft approached from the front at low level. As they roared over, at around 100 feet, Schmidt identified them as RAF *Mosquitos*. The aircraft banked, turned, and swooped back over the convoy, and they braced themselves for the inevitable machine gun fire but, as the aircraft flew past, they were rocking their wings, then climbed and disappeared. "I think the Englanders were saluting us," Spacil remarked incredulously.

They had passed German soldiers, marching northwards, with some riding on tanks and in trucks, but the journey was uneventful until they reached a crossroads outside Rosenheim. Parked by the side of the road ahead were some American armoured vehicles, but, as they approached, an officer stepped out beckoning them, and they could see soldiers carelessly leaning against their vehicles, many smoking cigarettes. To their astonishment, the American officer continued signalling for them to proceed and, as they passed, some of the soldiers waved, others held guns to their shoulder in a mock firing gesture, whilst others gave rude gestures with their fingers, shouting obscenities.

Two hours later, they pulled into a square opposite the domed Herz Jesu Bischofsweisen church, with the long line of trucks lining the approach road. The smiling bulky figure of Otto Skorzeny approached in SS uniform with a fatigue cap; he stopped, raised his arm out stiffly, then gave a salute, clicking his heels, before shaking hands with Spacil. "*Willkommen,* we have much to discuss, but over Cognac, I think." As they walked towards the church buildings, there was a growing droning noise in the skies, which grew louder and louder, the vibrations seeming to shake the ground, and as they looked up, they could see the vapour trails of formations of bombers. Suddenly, there was the sound of heavy guns as anti-aircraft fire erupted from batteries positioned close by. "They label us war criminals," muttered Skorzeny, "but the Americans and the British have engaged in the deliberate slaughter of civilians. I hope those poor bastards back at the *Berghof* are deep in their bunkers."

As they entered an outbuilding which Skorzeny was using as his office, they began to hear thunderous explosions, which made the ground tremble even though they were fifteen kilometres distant. Some plaster came off the ceiling, whilst the building shook, as Skorzeny calmly lit a cigarette, and poured out three glasses of Cognac from a bottle on a table he was using as a desk. The room had a wooden floor and was sparsely furnished with plain cream walls on which were pictures of the Virgin Mary, Christ on the Cross, and a framed photograph of Pope Pius XII. Spacil sat on one of the six iron chairs positioned around the table, whilst Skorzeny sat behind it. The door opened, and a smartly dressed officer entered - "Ah, *Hauptmann* Danneberg, we were just about to start without you," Skorzeny remarked, with a hint of a smile. "Hans, have you met before? This is *Standartenführer* Josef Spacil, and I can vouch for the fact that he is a bigger crook than me, and an expert at laundering money."

"I think the drink has gone to your head already, *Herr Oberst,* it was you who introduced us in August 1943, at Schloss Labers, when we re-negotiated terms and took charge of the counterfeiting operation under that *dummkopf* crook, Friedrich Schwend. I presume this drink is for me." Danneberg picked up a glass, downing the contents in one as Skorzeny raised his hands in mock despair, pouring him another, before turning to Spacil, "You see how standards of discipline are failing; even my most trusted officers are stealing Cognac from me." Then more seriously, "Josef, we have a monumental task ahead of us, both in creating a huge deception, and in transporting the gold and valuables to safe places."

Thursday 26th April 1945 9:00am
Auerbach Airfield, Saxony, Germany

Major General Henry Collins, accompanied by his ADC, Brigadier General Henning Linden, dressed in combat uniforms, were met by a young officer holding a clipboard, as they exited the Dakota followed by twelve heavily armed men. "Sir, I am Lieutenant Mervyn Cunningham of the US Transportation Corps. If I could request you sign for the trucks, drivers and the accompanying military escort."

Collins gave him a withering look, as he strode towards the trucks behind which were four *M8 Greyhound* armoured vehicles with their turret mounted machine guns and forward 37 mm guns pointing up at 45 degrees giving them a menacing look. "Son, you just fill in the blank spaces and enter who the hell you want on those forms. I am engaged on a mission authorised by the president of the United States."

"But Sir, I need someone to authorise this requisition."

Collins ignored him, and strode over to the vehicles, briefly telling the crews he was in command, and that they were moving out and travelling to the nearby town of Plauen, 30 kilometres away.

As he approached the lead truck, Cunningham tried again, "Sir, I need a name to go on the official requisition."

"Just enter the words Franklin D. Roosevelt, boy; that should do the trick. We taking these mothers to Frankfurt; you can have them back tomorrow." As Linden climbed in beside him, Collins, spoke to the driver, "Move on out, son."

He was not in the best of moods having been woken by his orderly to take a call from the deputy military governor of Germany, General Lucius D. Clay at 5:00am. "Henry, I got another little stash of dough for you to collect. The Krauts have given us the location in exchange for letting a convoy through unhindered; Washington call it post-war diplomacy; I call it good business." The words were spoken in an uncompromising gruff southern US accent, from the general whose nickname was 'The Great Uncompromiser'. "I want you to get your ass up to a small town called Plauen, some God-forsaken place up near the Czech border, and, er…liberate a little contribution to our…er reparations fund. You getting' my drift? You need to organise two trucks and four armoured vehicles right now to be ready for you; requisition what the hell you want under my authority, and then fly up there this morning. Henry, only you and those in on our mission need to know what we doin'. We all gonna live a little better when we finished whooping the Krauts and compensate ourselves a touch."

"Why all the hurry, Sir? Can't it wait a bit?" Collins did not like being given direct orders, and even less so at this time in the morning.

The response from Clay left him in no doubt and especially when he took in the General's briefing, "You need to go this morning afore the Soviets get wind we there. Plauen is meant to be part of their territory but we just got wind there is a whole heap of gold stashed there in the post office vault, left behind by Heinrich Himmler it seems. Henry, I'm talking about gold bars, silver ingots and over a million dollars-worth of cash. If we get in quickly, we can save them poor Soviet bastards the trouble of transporting all that weight."

At 10:30am, the convoy arrived in the small square in the centre of Plauen. They went straight to the senior commander's office which had been set up in the police barracks, where Collins shook hands with Lieutenant Colonel Armstrong, the officer commanding. Collins briefed him that he was on a covert mission to recover secret documents and material which were held in the local post office vault. He requested that Armstrong place a cordon around the area and that no one be permitted entry. Fifteen minutes later, he walked into the post office, together with his men who took up positions inside and around the entrance. Four men accompanied Collins and Linden as they were taken through to the office of Klaus Bauer, the postmaster. After shaking hands and introducing himself to the silver haired man, who was dressed in a waistcoat, winged collar, and black tie, Collins pulled his *Colt M1911* pistol from his belt holster, and pointed it at the terrified man's head - "I know what you have stashed here in a secret vault; you will take us to this and open it. If you do not, I will kill you and blow it open with dynamite. Your choice. Do we have a deal?"

The man, shaking uncontrollably, spoke in a quivering voice, "If the *Reichsführer* hears of this, I am a dead man."

"I got news for you; it has leaked out that Himmler has been talking to the Allies behind your Mr Hitler's back. I think it is he who is a dead man walking. Berlin is about to fall, so if I were you, I would cooperate and do as I ask."

Bauer pulled his jacket on, taking some keys from a cupboard, and led them through a reinforced steel door down steps to an underground area where he opened a further heavy door giving access to a vault entrance with a large wheel on it. There were some numbered and lettered dials on the vault door, and the postmaster's hands shook as he tried to input the numbers, beads of sweat forming on his forehead. Finally, he turned the handle and there was a series of clicks before he announced the vault was unlocked. Linden nodded to the two men with them who began pulling the thick shiny metal door open and, as they did so, Linden gasped, "Mother of God, I think we struck gold this time!"

In front of the entrance to the left, were dozens of gold bars of various sizes, neatly stacked, whilst on shelves were piles of banknotes. Linden walked in, examining the currency, then flicked a wad of notes in his hand as he spoke, "We got a whole heap of US dollars, British pounds, and German Reichsmarks." To the right, past the shelves, were bags containing cash, behind which were more bars of silver.

The men who had accompanied Collins and Linden now began filling boxes which they carried to the waiting trucks, returning with more men as others stood guard outside holding their weapons at the ready.

Later that night, Wilhelm Höttl placed a call to Otto Skorzeny, "I have spoken to my contact in the OSS here in Switzerland, and he says that all deals with the Allies are now off as the Soviets advance deeper into Berlin; they are now only a mile from the *Führer's* bunker. Otto, I think it is all going to be over so quickly." His voice choked with emotion for a moment before continuing, "Officially, my contact says US and British forces will now do all they can to find and seize any assets of Hitler's regime. Special units are being formed for this purpose. However, they will continue to maintain contact with us in the interest of what they are calling post-war diplomacy and commercial imperatives."

24

'Thieves have authority...when Judges steal'

Wednesday 10th January 2024 4:00pm
Belmarsh Prison, Thamesmead, South-East London

Benjamin Weiss had driven Karl and Friedrich to the prison in his Jaguar XK8, apologising to Friedrich, who sat in the rear, for the lack of legroom. "I need this car to maintain my image with the ladies," he explained, with a wink, as they climbed into the silver, streamlined sports car with the number plate BW1 EIS. As he drove, he explained a little of his background. He had been brought up in Nahsholim, north of Caesarea, in Israel, and had enjoyed a comfortable upbringing, courtesy of his parents, who ran a successful clothing and cloth trading business. He had served in the military, seen active service, and been drafted into Intelligence. However, he explained he had fallen foul of his superiors for his involvement with movements sympathetic to the Arabs. "You know, Arab and Jew are closely related genetically, yet it seems some in Israel think we Jews are the Master Race. Now, where have I heard that term before? We have much in our short history to be ashamed of, especially how we treated those Arabs who were living on the land which became Israel. I regret we were guilty of ethnic cleansing, not something which goes down well if you speak of this at cocktail parties in Israel. So, they had a problem with me; I was a decorated IDF veteran who associated with the Palestinian Arab cause. So, I was offered the opportunity of heading up a section in British Intelligence dealing with Middle-East issues." Benjamin laughed as he spoke, "You know the great irony, I helped save Prime Minister Netanyahu's neck by quashing an attempted coup in Israel. I even met him and he thanked me and my cousin personally. Now, I almost wish they had succeeded. Ah well, *kismet.*"

"How well do you know Dieter Metz?" asked Karl, reflecting on Dieter's allegiances.

"Ah, I know him well; he is a rogue but I respect him despite his connections with the GVR."

Karl turned to look sharply at Friedrich, who shrugged his shoulders.

"You see," Benjamin continued, "You may be surprised to realise I know all about the GVR which I discovered during the investigation into the Israel coup attempt. We uncovered evidence of Nazi covert operations after the war, their links with organised crime, and involvement with the Kennedy assassination in the USA. There is more I cannot talk about, but I can say that JFK was treading on a lot of toes. He and his brother were taking action against the Mafia and investigating former Nazis some of whom held powerful positions. Kennedy had pledged to ensure the Nazi stronghold in Argentina was removed, whilst Sam Giancana of the Chicago mob and a prominent leader of the Jewish mafia, Meyer Lansky, were involved in trading in Nazi treasure seized in the Holocaust. I work with organisations trying to return this or to gain reparations from those who benefited from it...in so doing, sometimes you have to do business with the devil."

"You are an idealist." Karl stated, warming to this man who seemed to embody so many contradictions, yet embrace ideals that he shared.

"No, my friend, I am a realist," countered Weiss as they drove towards the long, tall, grey foreboding walls surrounding Belmarsh Prison. They proceeded slowly towards the first security barrier, where Benjamin Weiss showed his MI6 ID, declaring he was on a mission of national security authorised by the home secretary. The guard saluted and they passed through to a further barrier where another guard entered the password they had been allocated at the Home Office on a screen before directing them to a side courtyard reserved for staff and special visitors.

They were met by a cheerful lady, dressed in a black zip-up uniform jacket over a white shirt, who introduced herself as Prison Officer Anna Roberts in a cockney accent. She took them through a heavy door into an interior area, where another prison officer was seated at a desk with an electronic weapon detector gate next to him. He looked at his screen, seeing that they were authorised to carry arms. "No point in you walking through that; we'll have half the bleedin' Met breathin' down our necks thinkin' we're under armed attack. I do need to remind you that firearms are prohibited in His Majesty's prisons. I would prefer it if you don't point any at the inmates and would remind you that discharging a weapon would be an offence. Right, you have the highest security clearance, but you will be accompanied at all times, except, I understand it, that you have authority to hold a private meeting with Mr Michael aka Basil Seed in our secure interview room. That means no audio surveillance, and even we can't hear you. In the case of an attempted assault on your person, there is a red bell which will summon guards for restraint action. Personally, I doubt if Mr Seed is capable of doin' anything to anybody other than, maybe, nickin' a few million squid."

"In that case, he is no different to many powerful people," quipped Karl laconically.

"A typical cynical view, *Herr Soldat-Kämpfer*," remarked Friedrich dryly.

"Gentlemen, if you would follow me." Anna Roberts placed her hand over a security recognition reader, and a side door hummed open. They followed her into a well-lit open area off which there were changing rooms and showers, and a barred door through which they could see a corridor with rooms off on either side. "This is one of our new prisoner reception areas," Roberts stated as she clicked a combination keypad announcing to an intercom that she was entering, accompanied by three male visitors. The corridor lighting was recessed behind round metallic fixings and the walls were completely devoid of any decoration. The doors on the right had 'Interview Room' on a sign with a number above, and an eye level viewing window with a slider cover, whilst there were fixed metal benches positioned to the side of each entrance. At the end of the corridor was a door facing them on which was written, 'Secure Interview Suite', giving it all a sense of the absurd; *typical of the British*, Karl thought. Roberts unlocked the door with a key, revealing a room with a table fixed to the floor around which were padded chairs, and, curiously, a large wall-mounted screen which Anna explained they could link to via wi-fi to their laptops or tablets. She then spoke into her radio, requesting escort for an inmate giving his number and asked them if they would like a drink, before leaving the room.

Karl opened the small case he was carrying, set up his ultrabook laptop, and was studying a pad on which he had written some notes. Friedrich opened a tablet, whilst Benjamin stated he would intervene if he felt he had anything useful to contribute. There was a somewhat incongruous knock on the door which Karl felt added to the already surreal elements of their visit. A prison officer entered, announcing, "Mr. Michael Seed" and a slim man, with sparse, close cropped grey hair entered in a dark blue tracksuit, with an open neck shirt beneath, followed by another officer.

"Thanks Gents," Seed nodded to the officers, as if dismissing them. One spoke up, "Gentlemen, are you content to be left with the prisoner, unescorted?" to which Benjamin responded, "Thank you, if we need you, we know what to do."

As the door closed, Seed spoke, "Visiting time was over at 3:45pm boys; 'somefin' tells me this ain't a social visit. 'Ow can I be of assistance?"

Karl replied in a casual, friendly voice, "I am Karl Biesecker and this is Friedrich Völker. We are from Germany and we are investigating the disappearance of gold stolen during the Second World War by the Nazis."

Seed interrupted, "Cor blimey, you took your bleedin' time; I told Brian, I said I thought the Jerries would get involved eventually."

Karl smiled as he continued, "This is Benjamin Weiss from Israel who works for British Intelligence. He is also with the World Jewish Restoration Organisation which seeks to recover gold stolen by the Nazis."

"Stealin' gold; that's a terrible fing to do. 'Eaven protect us from people who could do that." Seed retorted, with a hint of a twinkle in his eye.

"Mr Seed, or Basil, if I can call you that?" Karl started.

Seed interrupted, "Karl, my son, let's start again. First, me name ain't Basil. That's what the Old Bill tried to pin on me. My name is Michael. You are 'ere cos you want to know where all the *suit* (loot) is from Hatton Garden. I'm doing *porridge* 'ere 'cos I am unable to give the Met more info, for which I got an extra six bleedin' years added to me sentence last year. What makes you fink I am goin' to 'elp you?"

Karl replied calmly, "Michael, we are not investigating the robbery, merely trying to obtain some information as there are inconsistencies in the police records of the investigation. If you help us, my friend, Benjamin, here can put in a good word for you and he has very powerful connections. In addition, we can reward you without anyone knowing the source, nor any records being kept of our arrangement. Finally, because our visit here is official, this guarantees no harm can befall you."

"Nah you talkin' turkey, me old fruit," Seed responded, "You've made a better start this time." He put his hand out which Karl shook. There was a brisk knock on the door, and Roberts entered carrying a tray with four coffees on it. "Coffee is served," she quipped, adding, "and Mr Seed, I've made it extra strong as you like it."

"That's me girl," Seed replied, quickly adding, "I mean, 'fank you Ma'am."

Roberts smiled, waving her finger in mock admonition as she left the room. Karl began, "Michael, can I return to your words, "*thought the jerries would get involved eventually.*" What made you say that?"

Seed leant forwards, shaking his head, "You know what, I'm sorta glad to get this off me chest. I've been 'finkin abaht this for too long. In that vault was all sorts, but there was a bleedin' fortune in gold wiv swastikas on it which we geezers left well alone. I warned 'em, I said we don't want to touch this, cos I knew you lot didn't mess abaht. I can't speak for the others but I don't fink any of us *half inched* any of the German gold cos we fought it was too hot to handle."

Karl responded, "My colleague will go over some of the inconsistencies from the police report but, Michael, can you recall anything else that was there with a link to Nazi Germany?"

"Nah, nuffin' of any value. I fink there were some papers in a file…oh and I remember like some kind of military identity card with some geezer's picture on it."

Karl's attention suddenly became more sharply focussed, and he felt a pang of inner adrenalin, hardly daring to ask the question, "You mean a German officer military ID?"

"Yeah, he 'ad one of them high peaked caps like wot you see in war films."

"And do you remember the file?"

Seed thought for a moment. "I fink the card was inside it. The file was a black like A-4 size wiv a whoppin' great Nazi eagle on the front. I left it there 'cos we fought that the Old Bill would not publicise too much abaht the robbery if there was Nazi connections."

Karl's heart was beating fast as he replied with a sigh, "You were right there." He turned, "Friedrich please."

Friedrich lent across the table and shook Seed's hand. "Good to meet with you. Please understand, I am not here to investigate the robbery, nor do I work with the British police. I have some figures here from the police report on items recovered from Hatton Garden. I would like to compare these with your own recollections. Can you recall how many 12.5 kilo gold bars there were in the vault?"

Seed paused, "It's been a long time and 'cos we was more interested in the other stuff, we didn't take a lot of notice. Wait a minute, there was two bars per crate, and we joked about what we was leaving. I fink there was fourteen boxes; yeah, I remember now… twenty-eight bars. Could have been less, but don't hold me to that."

Friedrich entered the number on his tablet, noting to himself that Seed must be lying as the total deposited and recorded by the GVR numbered twenty-four, whilst a further six were 'hidden' by Heinz Spacil for his son and daughter's inheritance. If the thieves did not remove any, then the total number of bars they left that day should have numbered thirty. He carried on, "Ok, thank you. Can you tell me how many one kilo bars were there?"

"Yeah, I remember that. There was thirty of 'em."

"You seem very sure about that figure?" Friedrich looked quizzical.

"Yeah, 'cos we said if we 'alf inched the gold, we'd likely be treated like the Great Train Robbers with all the publicity around Nazi loot, and, if we got nicked, we'd end up wiv thirty years, or a year for each kilo. Hence, me rememberin' thirty. Not worth the aggro."

"Mr Seed, can you explain to me why the police report recorded that only four 1 kilo bars were recovered from the scene?"

Seed looked genuinely surprised, sitting up straight in his chair, "Christ almighty, Guv, wot you sayin'? I can tell you. I've been guilty of many crimes, but I swear we never touched that. Bleedin' 'ell, seriously, I'm shocked."

"Mr Seed, if you are telling us the truth, then, we will reward you for your assistance, but, we are German, and we don't suffer fools gladly; so, you will understand that if you are not?" Friedrich removed his glasses in a dramatic gesture. "I want to believe you, but..." He let his voice tail off in what he hoped was a menacing manner.

"I swear on me Muvver's life." Seed responded. "I'll help you but don't threaten me; just ask me politely." Despite the arrogance of his reply, Friedrich could see that Seed was unnerved.

"So, Mr Seed, what conclusion do you think we should reach and who can we trust?"

"Not the Old Bill, that's for sure," came Seed's quick response. "They tried to fit me up by callin' me 'Basil' to get them off the hook 'cos they was getting' nowhere clearing up the Hatton Garden investigation. Now everyone calls me Basil. I'm tellin' you son, we've got bent clodhoppers on our hands 'ere."

"What is this term 'bent clodhopper'?" Friedrich asked

"Bent copper, my son, crooked police officer…they do exist you know," came the reply.

"Ok, If I was to tell you that there was an attempt by someone to cash-in on a gold bar with a swastika via a 'fence' or to have it melted down, what would your reaction be?"

"The same…bent clodhopper 'cos we wouldn't 'ave needed 'em. We melt our own if we have to. Don't need no one else. If I were you, my son, I'd check out the *bottle and stoppers* (coppers) who was on the case; first responders maybe. Won't be the first time. You might also want to 'ave a chat to my mate Ron Reader. He was the real brains behind the whole job, helping his brother, Brian, plan our little heist. Brian was always the front man with all the contacts, whilst Ron planned everything. Ronnie is a real villain but always got away wiv it by getting' others to do the dirty work whilst he stayed in the background. He's a clever geezer but never done time 'cos he's never been nicked; he don't ever go on any jobs. The Old Bill could never pin anything on him for the Hatton raid 'cos, as usual, he wasn't at the scene. Poor old Brian died last September, and to be honest, I don't think Ron will be far behind; he's not a well man. He's had some geezers round from your neck of the woods in the last couple of days asking questions. Go easy on 'im; poor bleeder's 86 now and he tends to forget things, but mark my words, he's as sharp as a button upstairs for those who matter. Tell 'im I sent you, and you might find he has an attack of clarity. Now, 'ave I earned me crust, or what?"

Karl stood up, closing his tablet, answering with, "I think it is time for a review of your sentence and, subject to a successful conclusion of our investigation, some compensation for your assistance." He lent across to shake Seed's hand, before walking to the wall and pressing the buzzer.

In the car, Friedrich spoke, "I think our Mr Seed, or his colleagues, have, to use his phrase, *half-inched* at least two of the 12.5 kilo bars. He tried to put us off looking by saying there were twenty-eight when we have records to show thirty were there."

"*Ja, mein Buchhalter,*" Karl added, "Even I picked up on this. So, this means that if the police recovered ten, together with four 1 kilo bars, that we may be uncovering a further theft of eight 12.5 kilo bars, and twenty-six 1 kilo bars."

"*Bravo, mein Soldat-Kämpfer,*" Friedrich responded, "I'm impressed by your ability to count. However, my concern is that someone else is taking a renewed interest and is that linked to our raid on Franz Niemeyer?"

Weiss cut in, "When you two Krauts have stopped your mutual admiration, can I suggest we obtain the police report on the robbery, then visit the secure evidence storage facility of the Met and examine what evidence is held there. We might also go through the National Crime Agency and check their files, as this would come under serious organised crime and they may have recorded sensitive intel that they don't want the plods to know."

"Excuse me," Friedrich replied, "What are plods?"

"God preserve me from you gentiles," muttered Weiss, "Did you never read Enid Blyton books in Germany? Never mind, clearly over your heads. Plods are policemen, my friend, and I think we are now going to have to bring some in for questioning. This, I am delighted to say, falls within my powers."

Thirty minutes later, Weiss drove into the secure underground carpark at the SIS Building, Vauxhall Cross, in the Lambeth area of London. After walking down a corridor, and entering a lift, they were whisked up to the third floor with the doors opening to reveal a smart area with a marbled floor, under a chandelier which Karl remarked was more like a hotel reception than the headquarters of UK British Intelligence. Weiss led them through darkened glazed swing doors to a further numbered door on which was written *Middle-Eastern Section*. They walked past a busy office in which a number of people were sat at computers, or engaged in quiet conversation, some acknowledging Weiss with a wave as he passed; large screens were positioned around the walls displaying news headlines from a variety of Middle-Eastern nations. At the far end was a passageway and Weiss approached a door, keyed in a combination, adding his fingers to a security pad. The door swung open to reveal a spacious office, a large desk with a meeting table adjoining it at right angles, around which were chairs, and a picture window stretching across the wall with a view over the Thames, twenty metres beyond. To the right they could see the iconic Big Ben and Houses of Parliament on the far bank, whilst Vauxhall bridge lay to their left through which the river flowed in a wide bend.

"You people in intelligence always bag the best locations," Karl observed, adding, "It is the same in Germany. In the army, we live in barracks, whilst people like you lord it up in fancy offices."

"Remember, my friend," Weiss replied, "I was a special forces officer too once; I learned to use my head instead of my weapon, huh!" His words were spoken with humour reflecting their mutual camaraderie and respect. "I think it is time for something to eat, no? Now, my short visits to Germany dictate that you might like *Abendbrot*." He spoke briefly into an intercom, giving instructions to prepare a bread buffet with cheese and a variety of meats, pausing to check that his choice suited them. He then sat in a swing seat opposite a computer, tapped some keys and a moment later, the wide screen set in the wall displayed an initial crime scene briefing report dated Tuesday 7th

April 2015. Their eyes were immediately drawn to the enlarged bold capital letters in red at the top, "CLASSIFIED – TOP SECRET"

Weiss drew their attention to the top left, "Note those on this report circulation list, Prime Minister David Cameron, Home Secretary Theresa May, Sir Bernard Hogan-Howe, the Commissioner of the Metropolitan Police, and, well, well, my former boss, the director of MI6, Sir Alex Younger. We will examine the MI6 file in a moment. They read the briefing:

'On Tuesday 7th April 2015, Officers attended at 88-90 Hatton Garden, in the Holborn District of the Borough of Camden, following a 999-call received at 8:10am from a Mr Keefa Kamara, a security guard at the premises, which operates as a safety deposit vault. Mr Kamara reported that there had been a break-in at the premises and that it appeared the vault had been compromised. He was advised not to touch or remove anything from the scene. First response officers arrived at 8:14am. Those attending were Sergeant Derek Knowsley and Constable Mark Pearson who were joined by a number of other uniformed officers shortly thereafter and the building was secured and cordoned off. At 8:25am, two officers arrived at the scene from the Flying Squad, Detective Inspector Keith Anderson, accompanied by Detective Constable Rodger Bentham. No officer attending entered the vault prior to the attendance of the Flying Squad

DI Anderson inspected the vault, and, observing that holes had been bored into the walls and that there had been evidence of a robbery, he alerted forensics.

DI Anderson interviewed the senior member of staff present, a Mr Abdul Kareem, who is the Sudanese under-manager. Mr Kareem confirmed that the premises was owned by a Sudanese businessman named Mr Manish Bavish, who is currently in Sudan spending time with his father, who also has shares in the business. On questioning, Mr Kareem could not confirm the value of items stored at the premises as such information was confidential and not recorded by the facility. Typically, he stated that items of high value were stored such as gold, jewellery, precious stones, and cash. He stated that only a proportion of the deposit boxes had been smashed open, but he anticipated that the value of stolen property could run into tens of millions of pounds, and may exceed 100 million.

Preliminary reports from the scene confirm 75 of 500 standard boxes have been forced open but that there are some larger containers also, typically used to store quantities of gold or bulky items, which have also been broken into.

During a brief inspection of the crime scene, DI Anderson witnessed that deposit boxes had been broken open and that jewellery and precious stones littered the floor together with some cash. He further ascertained that there were a number of gold bars, amongst valuables left behind by the perpetrators, upon which were the eagle and swastika emblem of Nazi Germany. In accordance with standing instructions relating to the discovery of sensitive evidence, he declared it to be a 'major incident', heightening its priority to PIP 3, and recommending that it be reported to NATIS. The head of the Flying Squad, Detective Superintendent Craig Turner, was immediately alerted who, in turn, notified the Metropolitan Police commissioner.

An initial report by forensics and officers assigned to catalogue sensitive items recovered lists ten 12.5 kilo gold bars, and four 1 kilo bars all bearing the swastika and a unique number. The 1 kilo bars are annotated 'Deutsche Reichsbank'. A black file also bearing the Nazi emblem was discovered together with a military ID card issued in the name of an SS Officer, SS-Standartenführer Josef Spacil.

Officers are contacting all the registered owners of the boxes which have been broken open, but there is no guarantee of obtaining accurate information regarding the contents or value thereof, or to whom some of the valuables recovered may belong.

It appears the alarm system was disabled as there is no sign of forced entry and the initial enquiries may suggest insider involvement. CCTV at the premises has also been disabled although some has been obtained from adjoining properties. Initial investigation shows the perpetrators, but they cannot be identified as they are wearing masks.

Further enquiries are pending but all officers involved have been instructed that this has been declared as 'classified' and that no information is to be communicated to the press. Any public communication or press releases are being issued via the office of the Met Director of Communications, Martin Fewell, sanctioned under guidelines agreed with the home secretary.

A supplementary report to this is being prepared by colleagues in MI6'.

Karl spoke out first, his heart quickening as he was reminded of the ID card; "We need to gain access to evidence recovered from the crime scene. That card belonged to my grandfather."

Friedrich added, with a note of excitement, "But the file, *mein Gott*, that will be the *Ehrenarier Treuhänder Deutschlands (ETD);* those who were prepared to authorise the acceptance of deposits taken from Nazi Germany after the war, many of whom assisted in the management of funds set up. That file is even hotter than the *Transaktions Aufzeichnung* which Franz Niemeyer was so anxious to get his hands on. So, now we potentially have not only a record of where the monies went, but who was trusted to deal with, and manage these assets."

"And," Karl stated, "We have the names of the first officers in the vault at the robbery."

Benjamin added, "I can feel some very persuasive bargaining tools coming into our possession which will ensure more reparations for the families of those who suffered. It will never be enough." He looked down for a moment, then distantly, a deep sadness in his eyes. Then, nodding with a determination; "Right, just one element I need to check." He tapped the keys on his keyboard, "Ok, just so we know, the two officers inspecting the vault, Detective Inspector Keith Anderson, and Detective Constable Rodger Bentham, have both retired from the Met. I can soon have their addresses off our database.

"So, let's have a quick look at the MI6 report, then I suggest we plan a strategy to follow the leads we have. I think we may have a busy day tomorrow." He turned back to his keypad,

"Oh God, there are so many entries here but if I can just find the ministerial briefing summary. Wait, we have the minutes of a Joint Intelligence Committee meeting here just days after the robbery. The screen on the wall blinked, then showed a document with the government coat of arms at the top left. "I think we've struck gold," Benjamin muttered, "If you will forgive the pun." They were transfixed as they read.

TOP SECRET

Minutes of Restricted Meeting of the JIC
Subject: Recovered Nazi Linked Assets
Date: 13th April 2015

In attendance:
The Rt Hon David Cameron - Prime Minister
Jonathan Day CBE - Chairman of Joint Intelligence Committee
The Rt HonTheresa May – Home Secretary

The Rt Hon Michael Fallon - Secretary of State for Defence
General Sir John Houghton - Chief of the Defence Staff
Sir Bernard Hogan-Howe - Metropolitan Police Commissioner
Sir Alex Younger – Chief of Secret Intelligence Service (MI6)
Andrew Parker – Director General of the Security Service (MI5)
Jonathan Thompson – Permanent Secretary of the Ministry of Defence

1) *The Prime Minister thanked the Chairman of the JIC for convening the meeting, stating that he and his parliamentary colleagues were there to be briefed and advised on what he understood to be critical intelligence issues. Whilst he acknowledged that other members of the cabinet might have been invited such as the foreign secretary, he was anxious to maintain as much secrecy as possible pending the outcome of the intelligence briefing.*
2) *The Chairman of the JIC identified the key issues:*
   (i) *Publicity surrounding the Hatton Garden heist*
   (ii) *Questions arising from identification of the owners of recovered Nazi gold*
   (iii) *The UK position on the ownership of the gold*
   (iv) *Historical sensitivities regarding Nazi financial trading*
   (v) *The complicity of British armed forces in the Nazi operation to hide assets*
   (vi) *Establishing claimants with an interest in assets plundered by the Nazis*
   (vii) *German political considerations*
3) *The Met Police commissioner stressed that he advised a complete clamp-down on publicity both of the amount stolen*

in the robbery, and on any mention of Nazi gold. The former would result in more criticism of policing, whilst the latter could trigger civil unrest from competing quarters to their right of ownership of assets looted by Nazi Germany. An anti-semitism backlash may result, and open past wounds.
Decision: Unanimous to accept the commissioner's recommendation.

4) *The chief of MI6 confirmed there was evidence that the volume of German assets not recovered after WWII was deliberately concealed and downplayed on the orders of Prime Minister Churchill who considered this could cause more friction with the Soviets. The wartime PM also believed the sheer value of these assets, if known, would result in a destabilisation of financial markets and post-war currency values. The information MI6 had uncovered was that authorities did not actively pursue those responsible for the stolen assets and valuables after the War, whilst there was evidence of involvement amongst Allied forces before the war ended in financial dealings with Nazis. Sir Alex confirmed that a major German investment group, VVF AG, had assets held in Hatton Garden and that this group were linked to a right-wing faction. They were known to have been involved in post-war money-laundering activities of former Reichsbank assets. If they laid claim to the gold, and could prove ownership, then preventing this being returned could be a difficult issue politically and legally.*

5) *The PM indicated that his government could not, and would not, sanction the release of the assets without a thorough investigation and that the National Crime Agency should*

involve Europol, but stressed that the matter should be conducted in the utmost secrecy.

6) *The defence secretary stated that it was imperative the UK was seen to be establishing whether there could be claims from other parties which should be pursued, or Britain may be seen to be supportive of those with Nazi connections.*

7) *The chief of the defence staff made it clear that any slur on the British armed forces must be avoided at all costs. The damage to the reputation of the UK resulting from the actions of a minute number of individuals would be incalculable, notwithstanding which, he stressed he was aware that US forces had played a far greater role in such collaborative activities.*

8) *The home secretary concurred, making the point that sensitivities were already high resulting from claims against British forces following their recent withdrawal from Afghanistan. However, she made it clear that criminal investigations into the robbery at Hatton Garden must not be compromised nor should there be any barrier to the prosecutions of those responsible. She stressed that there was high public interest in this.*

9) *The director general of MI5 indicated that there was clear evidence of financial collusion with the Nazis during WWII involving respected UK institutions. In his view, the approach to all issues outlined by the chairman should be that a shroud of secrecy be placed over the entire episode and that, in time, the matter would fade from having any major public significance.*

10) *The chief of MI6 concurred, stating that in Germany, there was a growing right-wing faction gaining traction*

politically and that Chancellor Merkel would take a dim view regarding any return by the UK of assets belonging to a neo-Nazi group, or the carrying out of any public enquiry or investigation which may serve to promote or highlight right-wing factions.

11) *The chairman concluded the meeting by summarising that it appeared there was a consensus to effectively do nothing, and ensure that the matter was declared 'Top Secret.' In addition, all aspects surrounding further investigation other than the pursuit of the criminals should be deemed 'Classified.' The meeting concluded with unanimous support for this policy.*

As they finished reading the minutes, which had prompted audible gasps of surprise from both Karl and Freidrich, Benjamin spoke, "'Thieves have authority...when Judges steal themselves.'" As his colleagues looked at him with puzzled expressions, he responded, "My goodness, don't you Germans know your Shakespeare? Perhaps, we Jews are better educated in Israel. *'Measure for Measure'*, my friends, Act II, if I'm not mistaken. So, tomorrow, I think we need to ask some former police officers if they will assist us with our enquiries, visit the mastermind behind the Hatton Garden job, Mr Ron Reader, and have a butcher's at the evidence removed from the crime scene by the Met. Karl spoke, "I think we may have another social visit to make, Benjamin. We know the identity of a 'mule' used to approach a 'fence,' who organised the melting of some gold taken in the Hatton Garden robbery. You will recall Friedrich raised this with our Mr Seed in Belmarsh. If we find this 'mule', we might just uncover gold at the end of the rainbow."

25

"They Say Crime Don't Pay"

Thursday 11th January 2024
InterContinental London Hotel, Park Lane, Westminster

Karl was awoken at 6:00am by his mobile phone buzzing on the bedside cabinet. Inge's voice was pressing, and he smiled at her typical failure to even enquire how he was in her pre-occupation with what she wished to communicate. "Karl, despite being the person you considered not able to handle danger, I have decided I will give you more intelligence to help you complete your investigation into the disappearance of the Nazi gold..." Her voice was petulant which he loved.

"Inge, just because I said, 'Yes', after you seduced me into agreeing to marry you, I have yet to consent in writing."

The response was a not entirely unexpected expletive before her voice assumed a serious tone, "*Mein Liebling*, I have an email here from my colleagues accessing the *Bundesarchiv*. Please understand, for obvious security reasons, they could not send the document, and you cannot quote the source. In 1949, when the first post-war Federal government of West Germany was established under Chancellor Adenauer, an investigation was undertaken to establish the whereabouts of the assets of the former Nazi regime. A highly secret report was generated showing that a bishop at the Vatican met with Nazi bankers in 1945; that bishop later became a cardinal. He facilitated the transfer of huge amounts of Nazi gold and currency into a secret account held at the *Istituto per le Opere di Religione* (Institute for the Works of Religion), more commonly known as the Vatican Bank. Funds were siphoned from this account via a bank closely associated with the Vatican, which was the major shareholder, known as the *Banco Ambrosiano*.

"I can feel our wedding may not be a Catholic one," Karl commented dryly.

"Perhaps, even more so when you hear this," Inge responded with a hint of unrestrained excitement at what had been unearthed. "The ties between Nazi assets and the Vatican continued long after the war, with financial transactions including transfers of monies and gold all over the world being undertaken via the Ambrosiano Bank which, like the Bank for International Settlements, became a major asset to the post-war GVR. That was, until the 1980's, when all nearly unravelled.

"This Ambrosiano bank was involved in all kinds of shady dealings including some linked to the Mafia. In 1978, the *Banco D'Italia*, which was the officiating financial authority at that time, produced a report for the Italian government which implicated the *Banco Ambrosiano* in fraudulent activities, triggering an investigation.

"I am almost frightened to ask what comes next." Karl stated.

"Oh you should be, *mein Lieber*, you can trust a police officer who never knew danger. So, the investigation revealed that the Ambrosiano was undertaking illegal monetary transactions involving the mass movement of assets to the US, off-shore companies in the Bahamas, and to various South American institutions including those controlled by the GVR. Those involved in the investigation were targeted by the

Mafia, some being killed, others silenced by threats, or suffering false imprisonment for trumped up corruption charges. Powerful interests were being threatened and the reputation of the Church had to be protected

"I kind of knew where this was going," Karl sighed, "I should say nothing surprises me anymore, but…"

"Karl, it is incredible and if it were not true, you would label it the fantasy of a fiction writer or a conspiracy theorist. The bank was being controlled by a man, nominated by the Vatican, by the name of Roberto Calvi, who was known as *'God's banker',* because of his close ties with the Vatican. He was also heavily involved with the Mafia for whom he managed assets. Any more uncomfortable or sensitive financial dealings authorised by the Vatican were handled by the *Banco Ambrosiano*. During Calvi's tenure of office, for example, the bank helped finance the *Solidarity* movement in Poland which was working to overthrow the communist regime, and gave financial support to the right-wing *contra* rebels who were trying to oust the Marxist regime in Nicaragua. In effect, the bank was a massive money laundering operation for any transactions which the Vatican could not be associated with. Simon Wiesenthal, a holocaust survivor, who ran a Nazi hunting operation, identified to the Italian authorities that he suspected the *Banco Ambrosiano* was acting as a conduit for the transferring of monies looted by the Nazis at the end of World War II. This was dynamite as it implicated the Roman Catholic Church in handling monies stolen by the Nazis."

"I was going to say, *mein Gott"* muttered Karl, "but, somehow, it seems inappropriate. So, this investigation…what happened?"

Inge replied in a playful tone, "Ooh, you are so impatient, but I like it when you crave more."

"Inge, please!" he said with exaggerated irritation, although he was gripped by her revelations.

She spoke then in an earnest tone, "Calvi was sentenced to four years imprisonment in 1981, but released after a short period, pending appeal, after pressure from the Vatican. The *Banco Ambrosiano* collapsed in June 1982 after evidence emerged of massive fraud and an inability to account for billions of dollars of payments. Calvi wrote to Pope Jean-Paul II warning of catastrophic consequences for the Church if certain matters were not concealed. Days later, his body was discovered hanging off a bridge over the Thames in London, whilst his secretary supposedly committed suicide by jumping from a fifth-floor window of the bank."

"This all gets murkier and murkier," stated Karl, as he shook his head.

"One other little gem in this story," Inge responded. "The Pope gave a personal assurance that he would pledge total transparency over the Vatican's involvement with the Bank and establish a full-scale investigation. You will not believe who the Vatican selected to head up this operation? They brought in supposed independent experts, under a man by the name of Hermann Abs. He, *mein Liebling,* was the senior commercial banker in the Nazi regime from 1938 to 1945 and a shareholder in organisations employing slave labour from the concentration camps. When Simon Wiesenthal heard the news, he was furious and demanded that the Vatican give open access to its accounts which, at first, they said they would do, but later retracted. No one has had access outside those sanctioned by the Vatican ever since, despite numerous requests from those seeking answers about the activities of the Church during and after the Second World War. Abs had been prosecuted at the Nuremberg war crimes trials, but the British recognised he was useful and knew too much, so he was reprieved and never faced justice. Incredibly, he then became a director of the

Deutschebank, joining a number of other former war criminals. Our records indicate that he was part of a major cover-up sanctioned by the Pope because of the damage the enormity of the scandal would do to the Church. Abs was still active protecting the interests of the GVR and worked closely with, I am sorry to tell you, one Heinz Spacil, your father."

"*Oh nein, mein Gott, nein,*" Karl's voice was full of suppressed anger.

"Are you OK, *Schatze?* I just had to tell you."

"Of course, Inge, you are amazing, and I am so grateful for all you have done."

Inge responded in a playful tone, "I have to look after you, Karl, that is the only reason I realised I needed to marry you."

They both laughed, lightening the atmosphere, then her voice became more serious again. "I am afraid, in one final twist, that the story gets even worse. In September 1978, Pope John Paul II's predecessor, Pope John Paul I, had just been elected to the papacy. One of his first acts was to declare a commitment to reform the Vatican finances which had come under criticism for being involved with organised crime and corruption. In less than a month, he was dead, purportedly of a heart attack, but intelligence files implicate Roberto Calvi and his accomplices in the Mafia. He had been Pope for just thirty-three days."

"*Verdammt!* You mean, they killed a Pope?" Karl was incredulous. "Are there no limits depths to which people have sunk in their greed.?" Exasperation shook his voice.

"You are an idealist, Karl, which is why I love you. Please be careful."

At 7:30am, Karl joined both Friedrich and Benjamin in the hotel Cookbook Café for breakfast where Benjamin insisted they try the full English, to which he had become partial since moving to Britain. Champagne was on offer but declined by them. Karl related to his open-mouthed colleagues the intel that Inge had given him regarding the involvement of the Vatican bank.

"When I was a boy, Simon Wiesenthal was a hero of mine," said Benjamin. "You know he was a survivor of the camps then spent his life hunting down former Nazis. Most were never held properly accountable for their crimes and, in Germany, many, like Hermann Abs, ended up in positions of influence and power. I'm afraid I have come to believe the adage, *'all power corrupts, absolute power corrupts absolutely.'*"

They discussed a plan of action, and it was decided that Benjamin would visit Ron Reader, the mastermind behind the Hatton Garden robbery, whilst Karl and Friedrich tried to trace the whereabouts of the fence who had organised the melting of gold bars bearing a swastika. Friedrich flicked open his tablet, referring to notes he had made. "He is William Samuel, and we know he resides somewhere in East London. He is known as *'Billy the Yid'*; sorry, Benjamin but apparently, he is Jewish."

"That is not offensive to me." Benjamin laughed - "In Yiddish, it is a compliment and, my friend, if you call me, *'Reb Yid',* you are calling me 'Sir'. So, let me help you; we can find almost anyone on the MI6 database." Minutes later they had an address and an image of the man they were seeking. A waiter approached the table announcing that the concierge had taken delivery of a vehicle for Mr Timothy Warren. For a second Karl hesitated, having almost forgotten his pseudonym allocated for use in England, before nodding to the others as they rose from the table, agreeing to meet at back at the hotel at 1:30pm for a de-brief. They planned to follow this by a visit to the police secure evidence storage.

Ten minutes later, Karl appeared back in reception dressed in a black leather jacket, where Friedrich was waiting, polishing his glasses in the same dark grey coat with fur collar and flat cap he had worn when they first met. "I have to say, *Herr Buchhalter,* somehow, you do not look convincing as a British citizen called Bernard Shekel, despite how apt your name is." Friedrich's one fingered gesture was ignored as they approached the concierge's desk.

"Ah yes, Mr Warren, have you any ID please?" He glanced at the passport, then in a slightly demeaning tone, "We don't get many of these vehicles to look after here; allow me…er, Sir. He retrieved keys from a hook, and walked with them to the doors, "I believe this red *Fiat Panda* is yours, Sir," handing the keys to Karl in an almost disdainful manner. Karl now recalled the text he had received from Dieter stating, *"Vehicle will be delivered at 7:00am. Note privacy glass. No expense spared."* The rear windows of the small car were tinted! As they climbed in, he was surprised that it actually felt reasonably comfortable although at 6' 4", he had the driver's seat as far back as it would go. Shaking his head, as he looked across at a smiling Friedrich, he noted that, at least, a sat nav was fitted and, within a minute, they were weaving their way through the traffic heading for South Woodford.

The address they had been given on Beechcroft Road was a narrow street about half a mile from the centre. They parked opposite a row of small terraced houses which had clearly been modernised in a uniform way, facing small commercial premises, and some older style semi-detached properties. As they left the vehicle, a young boy, wearing a baseball cap, on a bike stopped by them, "Lookin' for someone are yer?"

Friedrich replied, "Yes, we are visiting Mister Samuel. Does he still live at no 8?"

"Oh, you mean Billy the Yid, miserable old sod. That's his 'ouse there wiv the red door. He don't go out much. Where you from then?"

"Oh, I am Swedish," replied Friedrich, conscious of the fact that he should maintain some caution to protect their identity.

"You want your motor protecting?" the boy asked, with a sudden concerned look. "There's a lot of thievin' and vandalism round 'ere. Give us a fiver, and me and me mates will keep our eyes on it." Friedrich looked across at Karl, who smiled, pulling out a new five-pound note which the boy took deftly, giving a thumbs up to other two boys sitting on bikes at the top of the street. He then rode off with a parting, "I 'ope Billy don't owe you any dosh, he's as tight as a gnat's chuff."

"The world is full of crooks," muttered Friedrich. "What is a gnat's chuff?"

Karl waved the comment away, shaking his head as they approached the door, pressing a bell attached to a camera lens. A voice came through the speaker, "Who are you looking for?"

Karl spoke, "Mr Samuel, we are part of an investigation into handling of stolen goods. May we come in please?"

"He's not in; he's gone away," came the reply.

Karl decided to adopt a direct approach, "We are armed officers from the Home Office and work with British Intelligence. Either you come to the door and identify yourself, or we will force entry. We will use lethal force, if necessary. You have ten seconds to open this door before we place an explosive charge and detonate it. If you attempt to escape, you will be shot."

There was a brief pause then, "'Old your 'orses, I'm coming." The sound of internal bolts was heard, and the door opened just wide enough for them to see the face of a man in his late sixties, with tinted glasses and thick grey hair, whom they immediately recognised as William Samuel. Karl pushed the door open wide.

"Thank you for your cooperation, Mr Samuel, and for inviting us in. Now, somewhere we can talk please."

"'Ang on a minute, ain't you guys meant to 'ave ID and a warrant?"

Karl pulled his *Glock* pistol from inside his jacket, pointing it at Samuel's head. "Do not screw me around, Mr Samuel. If you obstruct this enquiry, which is a matter of national security, you will be eliminated. Is this clear?"

Samuel looked shocked, then shrugged and led them through a narrow vestibule into a lounge with aging, faded wallpaper, a three-piece suite, and a large flat-screen TV mounted in the corner.

"Sit down, Mr Samuel," Karl spoke with a ruthless edge. "Now, I will place my weapon on this table, and if I sense you are not being forthcoming, I will retrieve it, and use it. The first bullet will take out your knee, so you will never walk properly again, the second will smash your elbow, and, the third, if necessary, will end your life. So, as the saying goes, three strikes and you are out! Is this clear?" As he spoke, he checked the magazine on his pistol in a dramatic gesture. "I said, is this clear?" His voice sharpened.

Samuel's initial look of defiance melted and was replaced by one displaying real fear.

"Ok, first question, Mr Samuel. You have overseen the melting of gold bars bearing the swastika logo. Who were you acting for?"

Samuels eyes betrayed a terrified look and his voice was shaking, "If I give you this, they will have me killed. They have the connections."

Karl spoke more calmly, "Mr, Samuel, we are aware they are former serving police officers. Is that correct?"

Samuel hesitated, then slowly nodded his head, before placing it in his hands.

Karl said, in a more re-assuring tone, "Thank you for assisting us with our enquiries. Without asking you to give us any information, please nod or shake your head to confirm whether the following names should be of interest to us. The first name is former Detective Inspector Anderson of the Flying Squad... Mr Samuel?"

Samuel's voice was weak, "Oh my God." Then he nodded.

"The second name I shall give you is former Detective Constable Bentham."

"Please, have I not helped you enough?" Samuel's voice was pleading. Karl leant forwards moving his hand towards his pistol as Samuel spoke, "Ok...Ok..." He then nodded his head in a dramatic manner.

"Thank you, Mr Samuel, your cooperation is appreciated," said Karl, as he stood up, placing his pistol back inside his shoulder holster.

The deafening sound of automatic gunfire suddenly erupted, accompanied by the shattering of glass with pieces of plaster flying off the walls, as Karl threw himself to the floor, dragging Friedrich with him. "Into the hall," he shouted, as he re-drew his weapon, firing six shots in succession through the opening where the windows had been. His eyes darted towards where Samuel had been sitting; his head was bowed to his chest which was already covered with blood.

In the hall, they crawled across the floor to the tiny rear kitchen as more gunfire erupted followed by an explosion in the room they had just left. "*Scheisse,* that was a grenade," hissed Karl. "We need to be in the open, come." As he said this, the front door glass collapsed with the firing now directed into the hallway. Plates and crockery crashed to the floor as the shelving collapsed above their heads. Screams could be heard in the street they had left only half an hour before; Karl now opened the back door, descending the steps, and through the gate into a rear alley. "Two blocks and we take an exit alley back to the street." Friedrich's breath came in short gasps as he nodded. He, in turn, now extracted the *Ruger LC9* handgun which he had never used except on a range when it was issued to him five years previously. "Can you use that thing?" Karl asked.

"Not really, but I know how to point and fire it?" They ran the forty yards past the first two alleyways taking the third, as the echo of more gunfire could be heard behind them. They moved stealthily through the darkened enclosed alleyway which ran between the houses, and then Karl peered around the edge. There were three armed men in black combat gear, with balaclavas, on the street, with another two emerging from the front door of Samuel's house, one shouting in German. A Range Rover was parked at an angle opposite, blocking the road, as the three men advanced down the street. "It is time to point and fire, *mein Buchhalter,*" Karl muttered tersely. He set his pistol to auto, then extending his arms full length, he let loose a one second burst which sounded like a machine-gun as two of the advancing men fell. The other threw himself to the ground and began firing wildly in their general direction. The sound of police sirens could be heard as the Range-Rover was driven down the street, picking the man up, speeding past as Karl emptied his pistol, and Friedrich fired six rounds from his own at the escaping car. Karl tapped a message identifying the vehicle used by the assassins to Benjamin on his mobile, "*LL21TXE blue Range Rover contains three armed assailants... We been attacked... Apprehend. We OK.*" They ran to their vehicle which now had bullet marks on it. "Look what you've done to my car," Karl quipped, reflecting his experience in lightening the mood during combat operations. They drove away, dodging down a number of side streets to avoid police interception, which Karl knew would add pressure in an operation which had now become much more difficult. The prospect of a gun attack in London during broad daylight with potentially three fatalities would cause major political waves, notwithstanding the fall-out from the publicity.

10:30am Rowhill Grange Hotel, Dartford Road, Wilmington, Dartford

Benjamin swung his Jaguar up the drive and into the car-park of the impressive hotel, a large 19th century converted house set in expansive, well-tendered gardens. He had earlier called the number obtained from the online Met Police files through which Ron Reader could be contacted. All contact was via his nephew, Paul, who was listed on the file as a suspected accomplice in the Hatton Garden robbery. A voice with a thick cockney accent confirmed his identity as Paul Reader, and initially, he was evasive when Benjamin explained he worked with British Intelligence. However, when he added that he wished to arrange an 'off the record' meeting with Paul's uncle, which had been suggested by 'Basil' Seed when he had met him in Belmarsh Prison, Paul Reader relented. He pointed out that his uncle was now an elderly man of 86 years of age with severe health problems, including cancer, dementia, and mobility issues. However, he stated that his uncle loved to talk about 'the old days' and enjoyed being taken out for trips; despite being frail, he still liked to act very independently. He agreed to a meeting, subject to it not taking place within the home, that it was not recorded, and also provided it did not involve the Old Bill.

At 10:35, a red *Porsche 911 Carrera* pulled up the drive, its motor being revved, as Benjamin exited his vehicle and waved; the Porsche leapt forwards with a roar swerving in beside him. The window whirred down and a man with silver hair, and alert blue eyes, dressed in a smart zip-up suede jacket, spoke as he nodded towards the Jaguar. "Not a bad motor that; I've shifted a few of them. Better than the *F Type* in many ways; they look smarter and had more of Jaguar's old innovation. Blimey, they must be payin' you lot too bleedin' much, that's all I can say. I'm Paul, and this is me Uncle Ronnie."

Benjamin shook his outstretched hand, and looked across at the elderly man sat with him in the passenger seat who nodded in greeting, half waving his hand.

"You go on, my son," Paul Reader stated, "Find us a nice place to *chew the fat* in the Elements Bar, and me and the old man will join you shortly."

Benjamin entered the hotel, seeking out the lounge-bar where he found a table in front of a blazing fire set in a deep grate; a low ceiling, with inset spotlights, gave the room a modern, clean, and comfortable feel. There were very few people there, mainly staff, wandering through with trays, or with cleaning implements. He ordered coffee for three before Paul Reader entered, slowly guiding his uncle who had a stumbling gait, walking with two sticks towards where Banjamin was sitting. He had a faraway look in his eyes, as he lowered himself in his seat; then he looked up at Paul, "Right, piss off and leave me with this geezer or else you will start yacking for me."

"Alright," Paul replied, "I am surplus to requirements so I'll run a couple of errands; you got my number."

As he walked away, Benjamin shook Ron Reader's hand saying, "Just to confirm, Mr Reader, this is strictly off the record. Anything you say will remain confidential unless you authorise its use."

"Yeah, *cobblers*, me old fruit," Reader responded, "I've 'eard all that tosh before. Why is you 'ere and I 'ope you make this worthwhile. I don't concentrate for long so if I start talking bollocks, just stop me, and ask again. You know, I planned the entire thing for me bruv, God rest 'is soul. His gang ain't got 'alf a brain between 'em. He warned them it weren't right after the first night. I should never 'ave met or listened to them German bleeders. My old queen used to say, "the only good German, is a dead German" cos, you know what, you lot 'ave no idea what it was like for folk back then. You stick your 'eads in mobile phones, 'ave no bleedin' conversation, and can't think for yourselves. In my day, if you was out of order, you got a clip round the ear; none of this namby pamby bullshit that we have nah. I made a million squid before a I was 40, and they say crime don't pay; leave it off."

Benjamin realised that he needed to interrupt what was becoming a monologue. "Mr Reader, as you know, I have spoken to your friend, 'Basil' Seed, and we are working to get him an early release. He said we should approach you with his blessing if we needed information."

"Christ, get on with it," the old man responded. "I spoke to him earlier. Stop goin' all the way round the bleedin' houses and ask me what you want to know."

"Er, these Germans you mention…when did they appear?"

"What Germans?" Reader looked confused.

"You said you should not have listened to them."

"I told you that, Cor blimey, son, listen out," the old man replied

Benjamin tried again, "So, Mr Reader, these Germans, what did they want?"

"Them what came a week ago, or the other ones what gave me the idea back in 2014?" Reader looked up sharply this time.

"Perhaps the first ones in 2014?" Benjamin persisted patiently.

"You pourin' that coffee or what? Cor blimey, I'll be a bleedin' gonna soon, 'avin died of thirst."

Benjamin obliged, trying to suppress laughing out loud at Reader's comical belligerence.

"So these Germans?" Benjamin attempted.

"Yeah, never trust them, I say; they started it all with that Charlie Chaplain lookalike."

"The ones that saw you in 2014?" Benjamin tried to hide his frustration.

"How did you find that out?" Reader replied, then, after reaching for his coffee, "You lot in intelligence must be brighter than the Old Bill. They still don't know how much we nicked, nor where we stashed it." He tapped his nose, his eyes brightening for a moment with humour. "So what was it you wanted to see me about?"

"The Germans who approached you in 2014. What did they want?" Benjamin knew he was on the edge of something, and tried not to sound exasperated.

"You should have said that in the first place," Reader replied. "You don't 'alf beat around the bush. I got approached by this Jerry geezer who said he would give me all the gen on how his lot had successfully done a vault in Berlin exactly the same as the one in Hatton Garden. He wanted someone to do the same here, using people who had local knowledge, and then see if we could open the door for them, so to speak. He told me there was gold bars there that we should leave well alone, but we could 'alf inch whatever else was there which, he said, was worth a fortune. They was going to follow our lot in."

"So what happened?" Benjamin asked.

"The Jerries scarpered when the kit broke down on the first night; scared stiff they was. My bruv and our boys got nicked, me old son, and they all served time. But, on account of Brian's medical needs, they let 'im out early, bless 'is soul."

"Did the Germans come back?"

"Yeah, I told you, Christ, ain't you been listening? They came a few days ago asking where the gold was? This geezer offered me ten grand for information, but I didn't like the bastard; shifty, he was, so I said I would let 'im know if I thought of anything. I told them Brian pulled out of the raid before they broke in but, in any event, he instructed our lot to leave the gold. Brian didn't stay around to watch when they was doin' the job. This German was a bit uppity, and Paul told him to sling his hook and piss off. You know what, Brian left the scene of the crime, took no bleedin' part, and was still prosecuted. That was a miscarriage of justice, that was. Needs sortin' wiv that TV programme wot deals with that. Have you watched it?"

"So why didn't your brother join his colleagues on the night of the robbery?" Benjamin pressed

"He told them they was pushing their luck goin' back. Bleedin' equipment broke down. I told Brian to get out. I'm the brains, and planned this; I didn't want him takin' no more risks. The boys said they was still givin' us our share, but might make deductions, cheeky bastards."

Benjamin felt he was not going to obtain much more useful intel and so he texted Reader's nephew that the interview was over. He ordered two more coffees as he waited, listening to Reader talk of his successful career during which he stated he had made a fortune without ever being caught. Then, as Paul Reader arrived, and Benjamin stood up, shaking Reader's hand, the old man looked distantly saying, "He told them they should have left it there; Perkins and Seed. Well, they could not resist, silly bastards. We had more than enough. Besides, don't want no bleedin' Nazis on our tails." Then, as Paul was helping him up, Ron Reader added, "I've 'ad a nice chat with this gentleman; he's not as sharp as he looks and keeps forgetting what I've told 'im. Are we goin' out for lunch in your motor? Might pick up a couple of tarts if we's lucky."

Paul smiled at Benjamin, shaking his head, as Benjamin's phone began buzzing, alerting him to a text from Karl.

26

History is coming back to bite us...

Thursday 11th January 2024 1:00pm
Studios of GB News 'Good Afternoon Britain Show'
hosted by Tom Harwood and Emily Carver

The producer spoke hurriedly to Tom Harwood, as Emily Carver continued to present a segment on the case at the International Court of Justice being brought against Israel by South Africa for genocide in Gaza, having beckoned him frantically to leave his seat and join him off camera. "Tom, I think we can justify breaking in to Emily's slot. We might have a scoop here before the others if we get this out quick. Just had it from my contact in the Met. Cost me a lunch at the Savoy this, so let's make it good. There has been a shoot-out in London with fatalities; the Met are saying they reckon it will be subject to a press gagging order but, if we're quick...Geronimo! Apparently, some members of a far-right neo-Nazi group in Germany are involved; an entire house has had the front blown out in South Woodford; bodies on the road and in the house to boot. Bloody marvellous, my old friend; sometimes, I love this job." He had a gleam in his eyes, as Tom scanned the unofficial briefing given by officers of SO15 operating within the Counter Terrorism Command or CTC. He returned to his desk, nodding to the monitor, as Emily stopped in mid-sentence being alerted by a flash on her autocue, then in a pressing tone. "Apologies to viewers for interrupting our transmission from the Hague, but I think we have an urgent news-flash about an incident taking place in London, Tom?"

The presenter's face took on a grave expression, "Breaking news just coming in of a multiple shooting incident in South Woodford, in the East End of London. There has been an exchange of automatic fire on the streets and there are reports of explosions. Police sources have confirmed that there are fatalities from what is described as a multiple shooting incident in the South Woodford area of London. Armed police units are at the scene and the area has been cordoned off. Police are advising that no one should enter or leave the South Woodford area whilst their operation is ongoing. Residents are being advised to remain inside their houses. No arrests have yet been made although sources confirm that there may be a link to a German ultra right-wing neo-Nazi terrorist group." He paused for a moment, then added, "I hope viewers will forgive me, but we are getting a further update. The Prime Minister and the Home Secretary have been briefed and an urgent COBRA meeting has been convened. Downing Street have not issued any formal statement and have declined to comment other than to state that as there is an ongoing police operation in progress, it would not be appropriate to comment further at this time. We will here, at GB News, of course, keep you fully briefed as events unfold, but clearly, this is very worrying indeed, and may reflect some of the concerns which our colleague here, Nigel Farage, has been voicing about Britain's security being compromised through poor immigration controls."

Emily's autocue had now been updated and she spoke, "These are unsettling times with threats coming from many quarters. There have been recent reports of a growing right-wing faction in Germany and, indeed, there has been an upsurge in support for the right in their polls. I know that Nigel Farage warned about this too. The swing to the right has been linked to the flood of migrants that they have freely taken in, resulting from the policies of Angela Merkel, the former chancellor."

Tom Harwood picked up his lines, "Those who are old enough, will recall that there was substantial street violence in Germany linked to international terrorism in the 1970's and 1980's emanating from the activities of various groups including Baader Meinhof, and the Red Army Faction. Many members of these organisations, and others, including anarchists, in more recent times, have allied themselves to right-wing militant organisations with an agenda seeking to overthrow the political regime." He added a comment of his own, "Clearly, to see this manifest itself into violence on our streets would be very worrying indeed, and add to the many head-aches the Prime Minister is facing at this time, not least from those members of his own party who are disillusioned with the failure of the Rwanda policy."

2:00pm Cabinet Room, 10, Downing Street, Westminster, London

For once, the Prime Minister looked a little dishevelled; his tie was loosened at the collar over his white shirt, and his dark-blue suit jacket was hung over the back of his seat as he ran his hand repeatedly through his thick dark hair. His voice was at a higher pitch than normal, betraying his frustration and emerging anger. "I am trying not to swear, James, I really am; it is not in my nature, but Christ, man, why was I not briefed? It seems to me that half the security forces are in the know, and the last person to be briefed is the bloody prime minister." His voice had now risen which was even more unusual as he looked around the room staring at the uncomfortable faces of the home secretary, the Metropolitan Police commissioner, the foreign secretary, the secretary of state for defence, the security minister together with the heads of MI5 and MI6. "Why wasn't a 'D-Notice' issued? Do we have any democratic accountability left? Twelve months ago I gave five pledges to this country, and they are saying I haven't delivered on any of them. That is because my ministers do not have the balls to do what is damn well required. God help us if we lose the election and that idiot Starmer gets elected, then this country will see what real chaos and anarchy can bring."

James Cleverly intervened, "Prime Minister, if I may; might I point out that it is not unusual for matters, deemed to fall outside issues threatening national security, to be decided without involving your office. Furthermore, Sir, the 'D-Notice system is not that simple. The old D-Notice system was replaced by the DSMA notices. These are obtained through the Defence and Security Media Advisory Committee, and my colleague here, Grant Shapps, as secretary of state for defence, would normally request such a notice from the secretary of the committee." His voice was slightly patronising in tone, but, before the prime minister could respond, the youthful-faced Grant Shapps spoke, dressed in a dark blue pin-striped suit, looking down at his tablet and referring to notes.

"The committee can move quickly and I have already requested that there is a pause before further detailed news bulletins are given. We cannot expect the media not to report, nor do we have that authority. The role of the DSMA notice is advisory and, whilst the press normally abide by them, that is not guaranteed. Clearly, the important thing is that we are perceived by the electorate to be acting decisively which may also have the benefit of reversing the trend in the polls."

"Prime Minister, if I may?" Sir Mark Rowley, wearing his uniform as Metropolitan Police commissioner, interjected, "The press can only report on what we give them and, in this case, it appears GB News obtained the story unofficially. However, my press office will co-ordinate with my colleagues here in MI5 and MI6 in relation to what we can say to the media. Incidentally, I can report my latest briefing is that armed officers have surrounded a building in Wimbledon which we understand has recently been rented by some individuals of German origin. As you are aware, there are three fatalities at the scene of the incident in South Woodford; one in a house and two on the street, all of whom we have identified. The two bodies discovered on the street had multiple gunshot wounds. They are Reinhard Sturge, and Gerhard Klein. Both are wanted in Germany in connection with terrorism offences linked to a far-right faction. I presume that the foreign secretary may consider what action will be necessary politically in dealing with the German authorities."

"Thank you," muttered Lord Cameron who was jotting notes on an A-4 pad.

The Commissioner continued, "Such sensitivities fall outside my remit but, I must stress, and I am sure that my colleagues, Kenneth McCallum from MI5, and Richard Moore from MI6 will back me up on this, that we must concentrate on the very serious issues of national security here rather than political sensitivities at home."

The Prime Minister's voice now calmed and took on a more business-like tone, "Indeed, of course, quite right; we need to co-ordinate on any areas which may prejudice our national security and, of course, the safety of the public must be a major concern. Who was the other victim in the incident?"

Sir Mark Rowley looked at his notes, "Ah, he is well-known to us; a villain by the name of William or 'Billy' Samuel. He's an old-school crook, involved in a number of robberies over a lifetime in crime, often employed as a getaway driver and as a go-between dealing with a number of 'fences.' In recent years he has turned informer, mainly to avoid more stints in prison, whilst earning himself pocket-money."

"Could it be some gangland motive then?" The Prime Minister asked.

"If I might contribute here?" The voice of Sir Richard Moore of MI6 cut in. "I regret, Prime Minister, there are significant national security issues here, some of them highly sensitive with historic roots. We know that Samuel has recently laundered some gold which we believe was stolen in the Hatton Garden robbery in 2015. We suspect that a substantial amount of gold from that robbery was never recovered. Our contacts in Berlin confirm that this is part of the fortune in gold looted by the Nazis which disappeared at the end of World War II."

There were audible gasps of astonishment around the table.

Lord Cameron spoke, "I recall that robbery very well; it happened in my last year as PM when I was trying to get a deal with the EU to prevent Brexit. I do recall the German connection being raised at the time but, quite frankly, it was not a good moment for our Anglo-German relationship to start banging on about gold from the Nazi era with Chancellor Merkel. Quite apart from which, old wounds would have raised the hackles of the damned French who were being most difficult at the time. I'm pretty sure I suggested we keep things under wraps for a while whilst investigations continue as there were very serious political considerations, notwithstanding your point, Sir Mark, that such matters are, of course, trumped by issues of national security. I recall there was an amount of gold which was impounded bearing the swastika. We managed to keep that quiet from the public."

Sir Richard Moore continued, "Our files confirm that a number of major reputable institutions were involved in accepting the looted Nazi gold and currency at the end of the war. In addition, many in the US and UK administrations wanted to turn a blind eye in the interests of rebuilding the German economy. I regret to say, Prime Minister, that we have evidence of the involvement of British bankers and financial institutions playing a role at the centre of these activities, not only during the war, but subsequently. The important considerations at the time were that we preserved the economic structures in Germany and ensured that certain key German personnel were protected, or shielded from prosecution. We were up against a new era wherein the communist threat was the priority and we needed a bastion of economic strength in a newly reconstructed West Germany to make East Germany a poor neighbour. Many senior Nazis were offered protection, whilst others were given help to travel to Argentina via what was known as *Ratlines*. One part of this was the so-called *Godline*, where the Catholic Church helped influential Nazis escape until things cooled down. I'm afraid, Sir, that we know the Vatican were implicated in this."

"You mean the Pope was involved?" Rishi Sunak's voice was incredulous.

"Not directly, Prime Minister, but two of his leading bishops were, and it appears the Vatican, shall we say, looked the other way. We know that Bishop Antonio Caggiano, of Argentina, was a key player in organising the escape of many leading Nazis, together with the Austrian bishop, Alois Hudal, who resided in Rome. Caggiano was elevated to cardinal in 1946 by Pope Pius XII, despite his activities assisting many war criminals to escape being well known; hardly indicative of the position now being presented by the Roman Catholic Church that the Pope was fervently anti-Nazi."

"So, what is the relevance of all this to the street shootings today?" The Prime Minister asked.

Sir Richard Moore referred back to his tablet, flicking his fingers across the screen, "We have intel from our colleagues in the BND that two opposing far-right factions in Germany are trying to trace the stolen gold which was held in an account belonging to *VVF AG* at Hatton Garden. *VVF AG* is a large German investment group with a very murky past linked to many senior former Nazi bankers who helped finance much of German industry after the war. We shielded Nazi war criminals in the business sector from prosecution who we and the Americans felt were essential to the rebuilding of the German economy. I think many of us may be aware that some of the largest international corporations have, what might be described as, a difficult history being involved in using slave labour etc. These include many who now have UK and US production and distribution facilities. Of course, this was all hushed up after the war in the light of the need to restore German business interests. Now it appears there has been a split between a moderate right-wing group, known as the GVR, which holds a substantial interest in *VVF AG,* and a more extreme split-off faction, known as the *Reichslegion,* run by fanatical Nazis who uphold Hitler as their inspiration. Both organisations claim ownership of *VVF AG* assets and we understand a number of robberies have taken place where gold belonging to *VVF AG* has been taken. Our colleagues in the BND state that the *Reichslegion* is behind the thefts. They even have a para-military faction known as the DA or *Deutsch Abteilung* who seem to be modelled on the *SS*.

"I am afraid, Prime Minister, that we believe a unit of the *Deutsch Abteilung* are operating here in London right now. It seems they are on the trail of the missing gold. I have, of course, fully briefed my colleague, Kenneth McCallum of MI5, on this but we had not considered that it posed an imminent threat to security. The intelligence briefing we have been given from friends in the BND is, I regret, unofficial, and we cannot quote this in discussions with the German government, or my sources would be compromised. My thoughts are that if any of this comes into the public domain, the press would be on it, and it would not be long before the links I have spoken of would trigger all this being represented as a monumental financial scandal."

The Prime Minister held his head in his hands for a moment uttering a deep sigh, then, in a resigned voice, "It seems that history is coming back to bite us."

Kenneth McCallum spoke, "I can tell you, Prime Minister, that we have been loosely monitoring the movements of this group, but certainly would not have anticipated that they would have so brazenly carried out an attack on a London street. I can confirm that both the deceased, Reinhard Sturge and Gerhard Klein were members of the *Deutsch Abteilung*. They are on a list of suspects involved in a robbery at the *Volksbank* in Berlin, not dissimilar to that carried out at Hatton Garden, which took place in 2013."

Lord Cameron now stated with authority, "I believe this puts us in a very awkward position and my opinion is that this is a critical matter affecting not only our national security, but also that of Europe. We cannot permit militant right-wing factions to take root nor be given publicity which could cause a loss of confidence in our financial sector, notwithstanding which, this could encourage a re-emergence in Britain of right-wing extremism. Street violence of this nature cannot be tolerated and our reaction must be swift and ruthless. Above all, taking Sir Richard's point, we cannot possibly allow leaks about British financial institutions being implicated in activities to conceal the looted assets of Hitler's Germany."

The Prime Minister turned to Tom Tugendhat, "I don't suppose you knew about all this either, Tom, despite being Security Minister?"

"I am afraid not, Prime Minister, it comes as quite a shock to me."

"It seems," the Prime Minister continued, "that in our democracy, the last people to hear of anything these days about national security are those elected to be responsible for protecting it. Right, decision time. My view is that we arrest anyone faintly connected with these German groups and have them deported under a strict cloak of secrecy."

"Forgive me, but if I may add something of importance, Prime Minister?" Sir Richard Moore interrupted. "We have an agent working with a group, operating on behalf of *VVF AG*, seeking to recover the stolen gold. In my defence, Sir, I might add that we did give a preliminary briefing on this issue to the home secretary."

James Cleverly responded, "Yes, I did give your operation the nod of approval but my understanding was that those involved sought to seek answers about missing gold, not become embroiled in a street battle. Anyone who is part of this appalling affair needs to be removed and repatriated to Germany forthwith. I think that if ownership of any gold held by the British police can be verified, then it should be returned. We have held onto wartime spoils of Nazi Germany, without this ever being admitted, which could become an embarrassment."

Sir Mark Rowley's phone issued a bleep and he immediately placed it to his ear, nodding gravely, as the others in the room knew that such an interruption meant a serious issue. "Understood; keep me briefed." He replaced the phone to a clip on his jacket; his voice assuming an icy tone as he spoke, looking down at his tablet as he did so. "I regret, gentlemen, the situation has deteriorated considerably. My officers have surrounded a building in Wimbledon and we are in a stand-off situation. The briefing I have just received is that the suspects have taken two officers as hostages and are demanding that an aircraft is made available to fly them to Cologne."

Tom Tugendhat now leant forwards, his words uttered earnestly in the manner of a military briefing, "We need to nip this in the bud, Prime Minister, I can have our permanent London based SAS standby counter-terrorism unit in position within two hours. I propose an incisive operation to remove this problem, rescue the officers, backed by authorised use of lethal force. There is little likelihood that there will be any terrorist survivors. Sir, we must demonstrate that we will not tolerate attacks of this nature on British soil."

"Do it!" The Prime Minister responded, standing up. "Ok, no press briefings, and no private, off the record, conversations. I stress to you all that this is a solemn moment when we must take action decisively and act together for the good of this country." He looked across the table, "Grant, as Defence Secretary, do whatever you damned well have to with this D Notice committee or whatever they are called. I'll organise some story for a Downing Street press briefing, when the SAS operation has been concluded. Let our prayers be with those involved in the mission to free the Police Officers. Keep me fully briefed, Tom; minute by minute if necessary."

3:00pm The Wellington Lounge, InterContinental London Hotel, Park Lane, Westminster

The call came on Benjamin's phone, as they were completing their lunch on a secluded table under an ornate chandelier set in the bright airy room, which successfully blended traditional with modern. Square white pillars with wall-lights sat below a suspended ceiling in which were inset spotlights over tables with crisp white cloths surrounded by comfortable seating in a cream upholstery. Karl had stated that there was little doubt in his mind that at least one of the crooks involved at Hatton Garden had taken gold but, in the light of the intel Benjamin had obtained, two former police officers were certainly involved in removing a substantial quantity. When Benjamin took the call, his face betrayed disquiet as he listened, giving a shrugging gesture with one hand as spoke into the phone, "I understand, Sir, but if we can wait 24 hours, we can nail this..." The others looked on as he continued to listen, in what was clearly an uncomfortable call. Then, Benjamin's voice took on a persuasive tone. "Yes, Sir, I appreciate this, but we need just a few hours and I am confident we can complete our enquiries. If you leave the authority open to access the police security vault, then all will be resolved. Trust me Sir Richard, would I let you down? Yes, OK, the last flight, tonight; I will personally see to it..." there was a pause as he turned to them, his first two fingers crossed, finishing with, "thank you, Sir."

He put his phone down, saying, "The head of MI6 is not a happy bunny, and says the Prime Minister, himself, has stated you must leave the country now, or you will be arrested and deported. The Foreign Secretary seems to be getting his own way and has authorised that all the gold in the police vault is to be returned to *VVF AG*, if they have sufficient evidence to prove ownership. However, I have bought us time; despite him saying I am utterly untrustworthy, he has agreed you can depart on the last flight to Munich which, he says, leaves at 8:25pm. We have to move quickly."

The leading BBC news bulletin was broadcast at 11:00pm. *"News just in: A terrorist shooting incident in London was intercepted today and successfully dealt with by police and security services. At around 11:30am, armed terrorists attacked a property in the South Woodford area of East London in what appears to have resulted from a split between two rival factions. It is understood that a 69-year-old UK national with links to the terrorists died at the scene. Armed Police were deployed and cornered the terrorists in a property in Wimbledon where shots were exchanged resulting in terrorist fatalities. No further details have yet been given. Police have confirmed that they are not seeking anyone else in connection with the incidents and that there is no further cause for public concern. Investigations are ongoing but for security reasons, no additional information can be given at this time. Police have issued a statement that this is not linked to Islamic extremism, but that it was an isolated incident resulting from rivalry between foreign far-right terrorist groups with links to organised crime. Downing Street have confirmed that this is a police matter and that no statement will be issued at this time. The Prime Minister will give a full statement to Parliament once police have completed their enquiries. A press briefing will follow this."*

27

Friends in High Places

Monday 7th May 1945 10:30am Hotel Post, Radstadt,
St Johann im Pongau, Salzburg

The day was warm, and *Obersturmbannführer* Otto Skorzeny was leaning against the wooden rails outside the traditional Alpine building, smoking a cigarette and talking to his adjutant, *Hauptmann* Hans Danneberg, both dressed in SS uniforms.
"Who would have thought it would come to this, eh Hans. Berlin fallen to the Russian *Schweine*, the *Führer* dead, although some say he has escaped, Goebbels dead, and Göring under arrest for treason."
Danneberg interrupted, "*Nein*, the *Reichsmarschall* is free. I had a conversation with a colleague I know who was in an SS unit based at the *Berghof* before it was bombed. They were told to arrest Göring on the orders of the *Führer*. Although they did so, they were reluctant to do this as he was popular with them. He told them they could be his 'guests,' safe from the bombing, at his Castle at Mautendorf, despite him being the prisoner, and so they took him there. A large unit of Luftwaffe soldiers arrived under the command of the Chief of the Luftwaffe, Karl Koller, demanding his release and he has been freed. He is now seeking to negotiate with *die Amerikaner*."

Skorzeny gave a laughing grunt, "*Ach,* I always liked him; full of hot air, but good company. These are strange times, Hans, when we turn on our own; I also hear our beloved *Reichsführer* Himmler has been declared a traitor."

"'Beloved' *Herr Oberstrumbannführer?*" Danneburg responded in a surprised tone.

Skorzeny slapped him on the back, "*Mein Gott,* Hans, how long have we served together and you still miss my sense of irony and cynicism."

"*Herr Oberstrumbannführer,* I think you misjudged my wit and sarcasm, Of course, I knew you meant 'odious.' Is it time for a drink?"

"Good idea," replied Skorzeny, lighting another cigarette. He was in good humour, despite the prevailing situation, knowing that his plans were well underway. "I need one after hearing the depressing news that we surrendered to the Allies in France in the early hours of this morning. Now, I hear Kaltenbrunner is hiding up a hill near Totes Gebirge, nearly two hours from here. I think his fate is sealed; you know, I never liked him but suffered him as it served my purpose. The war may be over, Hans, but I have not surrendered." He walked to the arched doorway of the Hotel, calling out, "*Frau Lisl, Eine Flasche Brandy bitte.*" Then, turning back to Danneberg, "You see, my old friend, we have the gold, and they don't. We know where it is, and they don't; and tomorrow, we will arrange for much of it to miraculously disappear...with God's help."

He sat at a chair on the veranda, as a bottle and two glasses were brought out by a stout middle-aged woman, who raised her right arm in the Nazi salute, after serving them, which Skorzeny and Danneberg returned. As she left, Skorzeny gestured towards her, "There you go, Hans, National Socialism is engrained in the people. They like order and that is what the *Führer* gave them. Our movement will continue, but we must complete our mission and our guests will assist us in this. Prost!"

The meeting was scheduled for 11:30 and, at 10:45, a Mercedes drew up to the front of the hotel; a uniformed driver opened the rear door from which two figures emerged, both in SS uniforms. "What is my friend, Josef Spacil, doing with that *verdammter Metzger* (damned butcher), Erich Naumann?" muttered Skorzeny darkly as the two men approached them, clicking their heels and raising their right arms stiffly.

Spacil spoke earnestly, "Herr *Obersturmbannführer,* before I give my report, I regret to inform you that *Obergruppenführer* Gottlob Burger cannot join us, as planned; he has opted to surrender to the Americans and will do so today."

Skorzeny exhaled deeply, blowing cigarette smoke in the air, "*Ach*, he always was a pompous bastard; so, that will be the end of our plans to resist to the end. So be it; I will concentrate all my efforts on the future. Please continue, Josef."

"I can report that the first part of the mission has gone well. I met with *SS Hauptsturmführer* Franz Konrad two days ago and he is arranging to remove the art treasures we have stored at *Schloss Fischhorne*. He is preparing to leave for Switzerland tomorrow with our largest convoy to date. I understand that safe passage is guaranteed, thanks to *SS Sturmbannführer* Wilhelm Höttl, and his powerful American friends. Concealment has nearly been completed and dummy places have been successfully mapped to provide our victors with something they can appease their people with. Our daily trips to Basel continue and the operation should be concluded within the week."

"*Das ist gut*, Josef" Skorzeny interrupted, holding up his hand, "Although, we may not have a week. I will go over all this at the briefing, but you have brought a guest?"

"Forgive me, *Herr Obersturmbannführer*," the shorter, swarthy faced Naumann spoke in an icy, but somewhat conceited manner, "I have just finished overseeing my last duty on the orders of the *Führer* two days ago. I have always executed my duties to the letter. We set fire to the *Berghof* just before the Americans arrived. They were on the way up there as we did so." His voice now assumed an arrogant tone, "I believe that I, as SS *Brigadeführer*, hold the senior rank here and, therefore, I will naturally assume command of all operations. *Standartenführer* Spacil said that he could not, or would not, brief me, until I had met you, and that is the reason I have accompanied him here today, as he informs me that you are…" His voice trailed off as Skorzeny's Luger pistol was now levelled at his head, whilst Danneberg drew his own weapon, a *Walther P38,* which he cocked, watching the fear on Neumann's face, as Skorzeny spoke, "Listen, you piece of filth, I believe your skill lies in locking people up in vans and gassing them, and the mass shooting of civilians. I have no doubt that the Allies will hang you, if I don't kill you myself. I carry the overriding authority of the *Führer,* and all ranks are required to obey me, *verstehen?*" It was more a threat than a question. He pressed his pistol against Neumann's temple who was now shaking visibly, with trickles of sweat running down his face. "Anyone who disobeys my orders will be shot. *Herr Hauptmann*, educate this *Arschgeige*" (arse violin).

Danneberg spoke quietly, but with a commanding voice, "I am witness to a document that confirms *Obersturmbannführer* Skorzeny carries the written and signed authority of the *Führer* to issue orders which are to be followed as if the *Führer* had issued them himself. His orders are to be obeyed by any rank, or any person, on pain of death. *Alles Klar?*"

"Have you anything to say, *mein Hosenscheisser,* or shall we save the Allies time by executing you now?" Skorzeny stood back holding his pistol in two hands pointing at Neumann's head."

Neumann was trembling, "Please, *Herr Obersturmbannführer,* I had no idea, I have always and will always serve the *Führer;* that is why I carried out all my orders without question, but even I was not happy because..."

"*Schweiggen!*" (silence) Skorzeny barked loudly, cutting him off. "*Herr Standartenführer,*" he turned to Spacil, "I will give this man a mission befitting his rank. Give him an escort to pay and reward our remaining *SS* units. I suggest you send *Oberfeldwebbel* Schmidt and brief him that if this *Brigadeführer* does not cooperate, he is to be shot. When the mission is completed, you may allocate him a sum sufficient to give him the chance of bribing any *Amerikaner* in order to avoid capture. He is to remain under guard until he leaves." He put his Luger back in his holster, looked at Neumann, clicked his heels, and raised his right arm, "*Heil Hitler,*" then turned his back and walked into the Hotel. Spacil beckoned to *Oberfeldwebbel* Schmidt, who had been observing matters unfold, as he lent against the Mercedes ten metres away. As he approached, Spacil spoke, "Look after the *Brigadeführer;* if he does not treat you with respect, shoot him."

"That will be my pleasure," Schmidt responded, with a wry smile, followed by a salute, before leading Neumann away.

Spacil was about to enter the hotel when an open topped *Kübelwagen* arrived, and *SS Sturmbannführer* Bernhard Krüger emerged, accompanied by *Sturmbannführer* Friedrich Schwend. Spacil walked over to them, shaking each warmly by the hand, "Ah the master counterfeiter and his salesman. How are you two rogues?"

"We've been dodging capture for days," replied Krüger, "but we managed to buy our way out of a few scrapes. It is good paying people off with fake currency."

Schwend added, "We have tons of counterfeit currency concealed in locations all over Germany and in Italy too. Our friends in the Mafia have been most helpful."

There was a roar of a heavy diesel engine as a half-track Sd.Kfz 251 armoured personnel carrier rumbled into the square, and two officers in SS uniforms jumped off the back, waving to the remaining occupants, thanking them for the lift. They walked towards Spacil, Krüger, and Schwend, both stopping to execute the Nazi salute.

The taller man, with neatly parted black hair spoke, "*Guten Tag*, I am *Oberstleutnant* Wilhelm Höttl, and this is *Oberst* Árpád Toldi."

At 11:30am, all those who had gathered were led by Spacil into a bright airy room with a large window overlooking the green valley expanse beyond, stretching to the majestic, rugged mountain backdrop of the Eastern Alps. There was one man in a suit and six men dressed in SS uniforms, some showing signs of the stresses they had endured escaping from advancing Allied troops, or in combat. Despite the formal surrender of Germany to the Allies, they all retained a fierce loyalty to the creed to which they had dedicated themselves. Mosel wine bottles were placed down the centre of the table with carafes of water. *Hauptmann* Hans Danneberg entered, stretching his right arm out in salute, then shaking hands with each of them before taking a seat. Although they all knew Skorzeny, there was a palpable air of expectation, raised by the dramatic news of Germany's surrender.

"Come on Hans, what is happening?" *Generalleutnant* Reinhard Gehlen raised his arms in an open gesture. He was a slim diminutive figure who had arrived minutes before the meeting was due to start. He had announced to the others present that he had formerly been in charge of Anti-Soviet intelligence in the conquered territories of Russia.

Danneberg looked at them, with a pang of emotion because he recognised what they had been through, what they were all going through, and what was coming. He knew that he must not say too much in order to create the drama, just as the *Führer* had done so many times, building tension and theatre, giving speeches about which he had not briefed even his closest followers.

"All I am permitted to say is that we have a plan to open safe routes of escape and ensure the foundations are in place to secure our future."

Hermann Abs, with a neat moustache and dark wavy hair, dressed in an expensive looking civilian suit spoke, "As some of you may know, I have been a banker behind much of our economic success; my work has ensured that businesses have greatly profited from National Socialism, which gave us the fiscal discipline and courage to create an economic miracle. We are the engineers of the future, gentlemen, and I have entrusted my friends here to be in charge of our financial assets, not easy for a banker, I can tell you. Let us be patient for a moment longer."

The door opened and Skorzeny entered; as one they all stood giving the Nazi salute. He responded with one of his own, and waved his hands for them to sit. He exuded an air of authority and all felt the power of his presence.

"*Deutsche Kameraden*," he began, "Today, the forces of the Reich surrendered, but our great task continues as we follow the contingency plans initially envisaged by the *Führer*. In recent days, we have been burying currency and gold in various locations which will be...er...discovered, or surrendered to the Allies. Some of this will be declared publicly, and proclaimed as the recovery of the assets of the Nazi regime. Other elements are, shall we say, to, compensate our

American friends for assisting us in our endeavours. This arrangement shall, of course, never be made public. We have many American friends in high places including the head of OSS in Switzerland, Allen Dulles, and his brother, John Foster Dulles, a senior figure in the US Church, and an advisor to President Truman. John Dulles is also a leading figure in setting up a new international body to replace the League of Nations, which will be called the United Nations. They both work alongside John McCloy, the US Assistant Secretary of War, and the Secretary of War, Henry Stimson. These gentlemen have persuaded the new US president to ditch a programme to weaken post-war Germany in favour of one to strengthen us to become a bulwark against the Russian communist *Schweine*. John McCloy wants German business interests to re-emerge, become more powerful, and dominate a post-war European economy. They want leading figures from the fallen regime to return and re-assume controls in key areas of business, the economy, security and even within the military. Meine *Kameraden*, we will emerge triumphant from the catastrophe of the fall of the Reich with a new and more powerful *Dieutschland!*" His voice had risen and his fist slammed down on the table to emphasise his last words, as those in the room stood, their right arms extended stiffly.

Skorzeny held his hand up, "We have three key roles to play as our new 4th Reich is established. The first is to organise lines of escape for loyal colleagues, irrespective of what excesses others may judge they may have been involved in. I have been setting these up with friendly governments. These are called *Rattenlinien* (ratlines) and the first takes escapees through Spain, where we still have a friend in the leader, General Franco, plus many friends amongst the clergy. From there, the line will go to Argentina where we are organising the new administration under the command of Martin Bormann. The Allies think he died in Berlin, but he is en-route to Argentina as I speak. We don't share everything with our new friends, eh?"

There was a murmur of laughter around the room as Skorzeny continued,

"The second line we are trying to set up will be via Rome, where we have senior members of the clergy within the Vatican who are offering to help us, and we have much support from other areas of the Catholic Church. We have already been assisted by them using a route we have named the Monastery Line although some are calling it 'God's line'.

"Our second key task is to move the currency, gold and valuables we have in our possession to places of safety in order that we can then utilise this to invest in our post-war economy. In this, we have the support of powerful friends in Washington and so, perhaps, it could be said we are on Federal business." Skorzeny shot them a mischievous quizzical look, drawing more laughter.

"Our third task is to secure the 4th Reich, based on a new economic foundation, recognising that we can eventually gain politically, what we may not have succeeded in doing militarily. Germany must dominate Europe economically, and this we will aim to achieve through a new European superstate, first proposed by our Reich minister, Walther Funk, way back in 1940, but which many across Europe are now calling out for.

"Each of you will perform a role in this great enterprise for which you will be generously rewarded. Your job is to do all in your power to frustrate the Allies, yet be seen to be willing to reveal places of concealment where we have left caches of gold or currency. I am organising the setting up of an organisation called *Die Spinne* which will help protect you and your families in the uncertain post-war era, and also provide support in the event you are prosecuted.

He turned to Reinhard Gehlen. "*Herr Generallieutnant,* your mission, already mapped out and agreed with our American friends, is to work with them in setting up an intelligence network in which members of our former regime can obtain positions. The aim is to create the largest intelligence network in Europe here in Germany, working with the United States against Russia; an intelligence network that you will head up. *Ja, meine Kameraden,* this we have already agreed."

There were gasps of astonishment around the room.

"Finally, my friendly crooks, *Sturmbannführer* Bernhard Krüger *and Sturmbannführer* Schwend, we need to build bridges with the Jews in this new era. You already work with Jews in forging and laundering currency; so, you will do business with the new emerging Jewish forces seeking the creation of a Jewish state. You will offer to pay for the transport of Jews to Palestine, utilising the forged currency under your control.

"*Meine Herren*, we are on the verge of a new era; and as we work with our Allied friends, we can say we have lost the war because of the failure of the Allies to back our crusade against the Bolshevik scum, but we have won the peace. With our friends in the Vatican, it could be said, we have achieved this because it is God's will. *Heil Hitler!*" He sat down, as those in the room broke into spontaneous applause, amidst cries of "*Zeig Heil.*"

28

God's Will

Thursday 10th May 1945 10:00am

Rome

As they approached the outskirts of Rome, passing American and British military vehicles, Skorzeny turned to his companion, Hermann Abs, "To think, only a year ago, we were in charge here. You know that we proposed to *die Amerikaner* that Rome be classed as an 'Open City', pledging we would not fight in the city, or shelter our forces here? I do not think that this will be given any publicity now the war is over. They will want to paint us as demons and vilify what we stood for. History is that told by the victors at the expense of the vanquished. We could have made a stand here but entered into secret talks through the offices of the Vatican in order that the city did not suffer any damage. So, when the Allies advanced towards Rome, after they had broken through our defensive lines at Anzio and Monte Cassino, we removed all our forces from in and around the city without a shot being fired."

"These are strange times, *Herr Obersturmbannführer,*" Abs replied, "and here we are, carrying out what you termed 'Federal business.'

Skorzeny chuckled briefly, "I think I call it cooperating, or, perhaps, collaborating; they are not aware of all we are here to achieve. Perhaps you should call me Otto now, especially when we meet our hosts who may have certain sensitivities." They were both wearing dark glasses and dressed in smart business suits; their papers showed their nationality as Swiss VIP's with assumed identities having been obtained via the OSS office of Allen Dulles. Their primary mission, declared by Wilhelm Höttl to Dulles, had been to ensure that there was a route for funds held in Switzerland to be smoothly traded in the international banking sector without attracting undue scrutiny. The gold held in the Bank for International Settlements was in a tenuous position with competing factions in the US government, one side of which had already attempted to close the bank. The secondary mission was to establish an alternative escape route for prominent members of the former Nazi regime, or those who might be pursued for war crimes, giving them either sanctuary enabling them to disappear for a while, or a secure travel route to Argentina.

Allen Dulles had told Höttl that the United States could not be seen to be involved in this process and would look the other way as these escape lines were established. He emphasised the importance of creating a means whereby German scientists and other useful Nazis in security, finance and the business sector could be moved or shielded from prosecution, and that the US may need to covertly use such escape routes. However, despite the liaison between them, Dulles was neither aware how vast the value of the gold was which had been concealed, nor how much had been transported to Switzerland. The operation of the ratline to Spain was already functioning and many of those whom Skorzeny had assisted to escape via this route were now being sought as war criminals; others were being hidden in safe houses.

Skorzeny and Abs had been flown from Ainring Flughaffen that morning in a *Focke Wulf Fw 200 Condor,* which had RAF roundels and markings covering the more familiar black crosses, although their pilots were from the USAF. As Skorzeny had reflected on the two-and-a-half-hour flight, their world had changed massively in the space of the last month, but now their minds must be dedicated to the future of Germany. Their American driver swung the khaki-coloured Cadillac, displaying a stars and stripes pennant, into the Via Della Conciliazione, taking them into the Vatican City, and then turned off down a side road, emerging into St Peter's Square. Skorzeny exhaled deeply with an expression of awe at the semi-circle of beautiful majestic buildings, fronted by doric columns with statues of Saints and Popes giving way to a magnificent palatial edifice, beyond which the dome of St Peter's Basilica could be seen. "Pretty Goddamned awesome huh?" the driver remarked, adding, "There you go, boys, you in God's city; and I hear tell the Holy Father is at home so don't you go sinning y'hear."

They pulled up by some steps leading up to an archway between more colonnades, and a Priest in a black cassock, wearing a square *Biretta* cap descended, raising his hand in greeting as he approached the vehicle. Their driver jumped out and spoke briefly to him before opening the door and saluting as Skorzeny and Abs exited. The priest shook their hands and spoke in German with a pronounced East European accent.

"Bless you, you are welcome to the spiritual centre of the Church, and the home of the Holy Father." He made the sign of the cross before introducing himself - "I am Father Krunoslav Draganović. I am Bosnian Croat, please follow me." They approached a huge archway, with bronze doors, where a guard dressed in a colourful striped medieval costume, carrying a halberd, snapped to attention. "He is a

Swiss guard," their host explained. "We have had them here since 1506. Do not be fooled by the halberd axe he is carrying; these men are crack, highly trained troops. Until a few days ago, they were openly armed with sub-machine guns." As they proceeded down the various marble, stone, and mosaic floored walkways, both Skorzeny and Abs were stunned by the magnificence of the surrounding paintings, murals, sculptures, and statues, with soaring vaulted ceilings painted with vivid, dramatic, biblical scenes. Ornate stonework, arched entrances, or palatial rooms gave way to towering columns, surrounded by exquisite carvings, gilded with gold. The walls were covered by countless artistic masterpieces reflecting and projecting the dedication of man to God, images depicting scenes from the life of Christ, the crucifixion, or reflecting the compassion and purity of the Virgin Mary; some contained huge floor to ceiling scenes. Abs exclaimed, "*Lieber Gott,* I have never seen anything so incredible; it is beyond belief, Otto. I have been to Rome before but never here. I am overcome by the sheer majesty of this; and the value would be beyond belief."

The Priest spoke in mock remonstration, "Ah the words of mammon, putting such earthly notions before our Heavenly Father. As the Messiah says, *"You cannot serve both God and mammon,"* but, just maybe, in your profession, it might be forgivable." He laughed as he uttered the words, adding a welcome touch of informality to the reflection of religious splendour surrounding them. They mounted a staircase, set in white marble, on which were balustrades mounted on ornate pillars whilst magnificent candelabra were suspended from the domed ceiling above. In the walls were insets in which were figures of angels and crucifixes, above which was an alcove containing an ornate statue of the Virgin Mary, clasping the baby Jesus, her head surrounded by a golden halo. Draganović explained, "Our meeting, which will be held in strictest secrecy, will take place on the second floor. The Holy Father has his private apartments on the third floor. He knows you are here, but he cannot condone your presence, or give your reasons for being here his blessing. However, he recognises that the realities forced upon us by war require solutions in which he cannot play a part. His words to His Excellency Bishop Caggiano this morning were that we should remember that our Lord said, *"I have not come to call the righteous, but the sinners to repentance."*

Skorzeny reflected how crazy his life had suddenly become as he took in the surroundings. Only just over a month previously, he had been in the midst of an attempt to blow the bridge at Remagen in order to stop the Allies crossing the Rhine into Germany, and now, here he was in the home of the Pope!

Draganović led the way through an arched doorway which opened into a corridor containing less decoration, although there were large windows overlooking St. Peter's Square on one side, with paintings of cardinals, monsignors, and bishops on the other, interspersed with doorways. A huge gold crucifix was on a far wall under which was a plain timber door. The Priest knocked, before entering and announcing, "Your Excellences, may I present *Herr* Hermann Abs, formerly of the *Reichsbank,* and *Herr* Otto Skorzeny, representing those who served the former regime of the Third Reich." As they walked forwards, Draganović introduced them to Bishop Antonio Caggiano from Argentina, and Bishop Alois Hudal of Austria, together with Count Franco Ratti, the Chairman of the Banco Ambrosiano whom, he added, was the cousin of the former Pope. Skorzeny clicked his heels and restrained the urge to extend his right arm in the Nazi salute, instead bowing, as Abs did likewise before shaking the hands of the bishops. Both bishops were dressed in black cassocks with wide purple waist sashes or *fascia* and matching skullcaps. Caggiano was in his mid-fifties, portly, with thick-lensed rounded glasses, whilst Hudal was thin, taller, and a little older, but with dark greying hair. Ratti was in a pin-striped suit with large lapels, sporting a red silk top hanky worn a little flamboyantly. Skorzeny thought he looked like a gangster with his swept back black hair and neat thin moustache.

The room was bare of decoration apart from a crucifix on one wall, and a portrait of the current Pope Pius XII on another. There was a bookcase and a meeting table around which there were padded chairs covered in red velvet. One window gave a view across the square to the buildings opposite whilst to the right the dome of St Peter's Basilica framed the skyline. After Bishop Caggiano waved them to take a seat, he began, making it obvious that he was the senior person present.

"Gentlemen, we have considered your requests and the submission you have made to us over the last month as matters have become, shall we say, somewhat more…er pressing. Perhaps, we should put our position in context. I am Bishop of Rosario in Argentina but I have very close ties with Rome and I have worked closely with the Holy Father on a number of delicate issues. In 1942, the Holy Father sought help from Argentina in preparing the way for the possibility that the Allies may prevail, after secret discussions he held with others in your former regime. He intervened in exchange for a guarantee that the sanctity of the Vatican state would be preserved, free from occupation, and obtained assurances that the Church would not suffer further interference or persecution in Germany. Your Party Secretary, Martin Bormann, wanted to create a safe area for Germans in Argentina and a sanctuary for an escape if it was ever needed. The Holy Father approached the Argentinian Ambassador and pressures were bought to bear in the right places. The Holy Father believes passionately that the Soviet Union and its vile communist philosophy represents the epitome of Satan, and that this evil threatens the world. Secretly, whilst observing strict neutrality, he saw Hitler as the bastion against the Bolshevik threat. In the post-war era, gentlemen, that threat has increased. Our Pope recognises the value that many former members of your regime can bring to the future of Europe, defending mankind from this evil. I have been approached by many colleagues in Rome to see what help we can give. This includes his Eminence, Cardinal Eugène Tisserant of France who is deeply concerned about the French, who collaborated with the Nazis during the occupation. These people are now in great danger and some have been murdered in revenge attacks. I have personally already intervened to assist some to escape, with the help of my colleague here, Bishop Hudal.

"We also have His Eminence, Cardinal Theodor Innitzer of Austria who is calling out for help because we are the sanctuary of the persecuted. Many of those in the former German regime are being pursued as war criminals. We are not the judges, but we are agreed that punishment can be a dangerous road leading from retribution to persecution.

"We can confirm that we have met with the United States presidential representative to the Vatican, Myron C. Taylor. He has indicated that there are a number of German people who can assist in the post-war era of re-construction and in combatting the Soviet threat, but many are being sought as so-called war criminals. Others have scientific know-how that would be of great use to the Americans. The United States will, therefore, wish to secretly make use of your ratlines, as I believe you call them, and we in the Church have agreed to assist in order to avoid the publicity that certain names with political sensitivities might attract. Once these people reach South America, US Intelligence will escort them by air or sea to the United States. So, there are various reasons why, *Herr* Skorzeny, we positively responded to your request that we assist in opening these lines of escape. However, I think there are many needs that can be satisfied here today. Your Excellency, please?" He turned to Bishop Hudal, who now addressed them. He spoke in an earnest manner with a passion which came from deeply held convictions.

"I am from Austria and during the Great War, I was a military chaplain. I know about codes of loyalty, the stresses of combat, and the importance of patriotism. My heart is with the German people who now face grave threats from Soviet Russia. The world had the opportunity of uniting against communism, but the one leader who dared, was left isolated. You know why? Because this war had nothing to do with the aims of the *Führer,* but was about a rivalry of economic interests, combined with concern over the National Socialist doctrine overthrowing the tired outdated regimes of Europe, and the weakness of democracies. I have striven to unite the Church with National Socialism; this is a matter for history to judge.

"You want a secure line for those escaping Allied persecution. I will co-ordinate this via my connections through the Vatican. We will not ask awkward questions about the purported misdemeanours of those we assist; our business, as taught by our Saviour, is forgiveness. I have been appointed by the Holy Father to visit the camps where Axis prisoners are being held. I can arrange for new identities to be created for those wishing to escape, and organise the issue of papers by the *Pontificia Commissione di Assistenza.* (Vatican Refugee Assistance) These are trusted documents; if they are issued by the Church and signed by a Priest, they will be accepted and used to obtain ICRC (International Red Cross) passports for displaced persons. These can then be used at embarkation points to Argentina and elsewhere."

Skorzeny enthusiastically exclaimed, "This is excellent, and we are grateful for the compassionate stance you are adopting that will assist us in rebuilding Germany and resisting the Russian threat. Thank you, your Excellency."

"The Church, as epitomised by our Lady, is the seat of compassion, my son," Hudal responded, "and now to my friend, Father Draganović."

The priest who had been their guide spoke briefly, "Many of my brave Croatian countrymen fought with you and now we suffer the threat from the Soviets who demand that these people are given to them. They will be murdered in the same way they massacred your soldiers who surrendered at Stalingrad. There is no justice under communism. I can organise the Franciscan monasteries as places of sanctity for those escaping from Croatia but we will help any who call upon us. God would not forgive us if we turned away. Our Order can assist those fleeing to cross from Yugoslavia into Italy where we can ship them via the port of Genoa to South America." He made the sign of the cross as he finished speaking.

Bishop Caggiano now spoke, "So Gentlemen, the Church will not turn away in your hour of need, but there are other ways we can help each other, I think. Your Excellency?" He nodded to Count Franco Ratti.

Ratti spread his arms, thrusting his chest forwards in a gesture of self-aggrandisement,

"My friends, you seek a bank that understands your needs and we, at Banco Ambrosiano wish to be of assistance. Hermann Abs and I are old friends; we respect him, hold him in high esteem for his integrity, and we like to do business with friends. But, of course," he waved his finger in the air dramatically, "you must remember, we are God's bank and our costs are levied to assist the great work of the divine mission. We will accept your deposits and transfers from Swiss banks; but these transactions must be conducted in strict secrecy and, of course, in our trusted position, you would expect the highest levels of confidentiality and discretion. Today, we will accept the transfer of $25,000,000 from the Bank for International Settlements, which, because of sensitivities, will be placed into an investment account in the name of the VVF Re-construction Fund. This will be underpinned by gold transfers within the banking system. Your friends in the United States have requested that this is classified as a matter carrying national security implications and, as with other Swiss banking arrangements, this will not be publicly recorded or made available in the public domain. You and I can sit down, after this meeting, Hermann, where we can negotiate terms. You will understand that our strength lies in both our ties to the Church and our independence from it. For example, my cousin was the former Pope, but he left decisions to me, based upon the key principle of banking; trust, my friends, trust. In granting your request, I am mindful that the protection of certain sensitivities may incur extra costs, but let us consider these separately." He turned to Bishop Caggiano, and bowed.

The bishop stood, stating they should split into two separate meetings to consider details; one between Otto Skorzeny and Bishop Hudal, and the other with Count Ratti and Hermann Abs. He concluded by saying. "In all things, we must remember that we are striving to carry out God's will and, in our endeavours, we must remember his words as expressed in Ephesians 2:10, *"For we are God's handiwork, created in Christ Jesus to do good works, which God prepared in advance for us to do."* Then, he raised his hand, making the sign of the cross, *"In nomine Patris et Filii* et *Spiritus Sancti",* nodding to Skorzeny and Abs as he departed.

Two hours later, in the staff car taking them back to the airfield, Hermann Abs remarked, "So, we have the escape lines; we have the bank, and we have the blessing of the Almighty. I think Providence is truly with us."

29

'A tide in the affairs of men...'

Thursday 11th January 2024 3:30pm
Metropolitan Safe Deposits, Chavel Place, Knightsbridge, London

Benjamin had called his office from the hotel, requesting a van and a luggage trolley, specifying his preference as a *Mercedes Vito Tourer*, both of which were delivered within 30 minutes. He now drove the van with tinted windows, down the narrow one-way street, pulling up beside the building of Metropolitan Safe Deposits, with both Karl and Friedrich next to him on the front seating which catered for three. Benjamin approached the external wall intercom, calling through to reception and giving a password; a shutter door raised over a vehicle access bay into which he reversed. They were met by the senior security manager who introduced herself as Lydia Thorson; she was carrying a tablet, and dressed in a smart mid-blue business suit with a body-cam and radio mike attached. Benjamin showed his MI6 credentials, stating that they had Home Office approval to access and retrieve any evidence required relating to a specific case for which he gave her a security code. She tapped her pad, and looked up sharply with an exclamation of surprise.

"Ooh, must be important," she said with a good-humoured shake of her head, "You have the highest level of clearance, signed off by the home secretary and the Met commissioner. You also have evidence removal authority from 'C' himself, Sir Richard Moore. So, you two must be Mr Timothy Warren, and Mr Bernard Shekel? Can I see your ID please?"

They each produced their passports which she placed over the scanner on her tablet and then she nodded as Benjamin unloaded a fold-away trolley from the back of the vehicle. "Follow me please. We don't get many visits from the Met these days. I think they're keeping most of their evidence in their central storage. We tend to get the high value items they don't want leaving around for light-fingered bobbies."

"Many a true word," muttered Friedrich as Thorson put her fingers on a pad, and a heavy barred door hummed and swung open. "We have rooms especially reserved for larger Met deposits, and then there are storage areas for police boxes, but you guys have access to a larger strong-room."

"We won't be nicking much," Benjamin stated, then flirtatiously, "but you can body-search me, to check, if you wish."

She shot him a withering look, "You know it's people like you that make the harassment laws necessary." Then, she added coquettishly, "More's the pity; I used to like the odd wolf whistle. For gawd's sake, don't report me for saying that. You can't say nuffin' these days without offending somebody."

They arrived at a heavy metal door with a keypad, into which Thorson entered a combination number, then stood back to allow Benjamin to enter his own unique code. The door clicked and opened, the lights beyond coming on as it did so. It was a long deep passage with both lockers and boxes lining the walls, interspersed with numbered doors.

"You have authorisation to enter storage area 49A," Thorson confirmed, adding with a note of sarcasm, "A word of warning, our on-site guards are licensed to carry torches and hand-cuffs, just in case you are planning to rob the joint. Press the intercom buzzer when you are ready to leave." She flashed a dazzling smile at Benjamin, before turning in a somewhat exaggerated, provocative manner.

Karl looked at Benjamin, in a derisory manner, "We are on a serious mission; what do you think you are doing?"

"I think it's the James Bond image that does it, plus my extraordinary charm, and poised demeanour," came the nonchalant reply from Benjamin.

"*Um Himmels willen!*" (For Heaven's Sake) Friedrich exclaimed, "Let us open the damned door then, Mr Bond, and find out what we have been risking our lives for."

As they approached the wide door to 49A, Karl could feel his heart beginning to thump, knowing that he was uncovering a bridge to the past, almost sensing his father's hands placed on his, as he had done in his final days.

Benjamin input the combination and the screen bleeped with a message, 'Access Approved'. He opened the door, revealing a six-metre-long narrow walkway, with shelves on one side, an inspection ledge, and a tall storage cabinet at the far end. The whole area was brightly illuminated from an LED batten above. There were evidence boxes on the shelves labelled with the crime date of 2/04/2015 and the title: '*Hatton Garden*'.

"I'll take the cabinet," stated Karl, "if you two split the shelves between you." As he walked inside, his eyes were caught by a box on the shelf at the far end which was labelled, '*Nazi Papers.*' "I think I should just take a quick look at this first..." He pulled the box out, and placed it on the inspection shelf, undid the retaining cord and pulled the cardboard flaps open, gasping audibly, at the first item he saw. "*Oh mein Gott,* this is my Grandfather!" His voice was in a choking whisper as he stared at the open yellowing card with the picture of a smartly uniformed SS officer with a cap bearing the death's head insignia, above which was written, '*Schutzstaffel der N.S.D.A.P.*' and in the line below '*1 SS Panzer Division Leibstandarte SS Adolf Hitler*' and his service number. The name, *Josef Spacil*, was printed, and the rank shown of *SS-Standartenführer;* his photograph bore the circular stamp of an eagle and swastika. However, his eyes widened as he looked on the other side, under the date, 20. April 1944, where there was another circular stamp, with the eagle unusually looking to the right, under which was the signature of *H. Himmler,* followed by the words, *Der Reichsführer SS*. He gingerly picked the card up which was in a black leather holder, on the front of which were just the *SS* runes in faded gold. He reached for the file below on the front of which was the Nazi eagle emblem, but it was the title which really caught his attention, '*Die Ehrenarier Treuhänder Deutschlands*' (Honorary Aryan Trustees of Germany)

"I think I have something extraordinary here," Karl announced to the others who were sifting through evidence boxes, as he pulled the file out. "This file, *meine Kameraden,* contains details of every organisation and every person which accepted Nazi gold from 1945 until 1960. My father described this in the papers he left me as 'the supreme guarantee' of my safety. I did not reveal that I was looking for this because I knew it was so important that if anyone found out, it could be the greatest guarantee of my demise." Friedrich peered over his shoulder as Karl opened the file, inside which were neatly typed records, separated by file tabs which were annotated by years from 1945 to 1960. In each section were dates, amounts, names, organisations, and notes.

Friedrich exclaimed, sounding shocked, "This was the file I knew your father once had, and which we all thought had been destroyed together with the *Transaktions Aufzeichnung*."

Karl looked at Benjamin, "I am afraid there are Jewish names on this list, my friend."

Benjamin's reaction surprised him, "That does not shock me; my cousin and I discovered, eighteen months ago, in the Intelligence operation I told you about, that even former SS officers were recruited by the Israeli Intelligence services, including one of their most celebrated commanders, Otto Skorzeny."

"*Was, nein?*" Karl gasped incredulously, "That name crops up again? This is incredible because he is in my grandfather's records as being one of the men entrusted with the *Raubgold* at the end of the war, and implicated in concealing this from the allies. *Ach,* so many coincidences linking this together"

"Coincidences, or, perhaps more, my friend," Benjamin responded, "*'Whether you turn to the right or to the left, your ears will hear a voice behind you, saying, 'This is the way; walk in it.'* Sometimes, I like to feel there is some reason behind all we do." He looked at Friedrich who was shaking his head. "Isaiah 30:31 in case you are wondering, old chap," he added with an exaggerated English accent.

Karl was now examining the file, "Look at this; it records £250,000 sterling currency being given to a Jewish Brigade by a *Sturmbannführer* Schwend, authorised by my Grandfather. The notes record the transaction was in part exchange for an amnesty agreed by Skorzeny with one Israel Carmi of the *Tilhas Teezee Gesheften*."

"Oh wow! Now that is interesting," Benjamin responded - "I know of them. That translates roughly from Hebrew into the 'Kiss my Arse' Brigade in English. They were secretly formed to assassinate former members of the Nazi regime after the War, whilst running a covert operation for illegal emigration of Holocaust survivors to Palestine."

"At least, I can, for once, empathise with the actions of my grandfather for his part in this," muttered Karl, with some relief.

Friedrich interrupted, "I am sorry to disillusion you on this, Karl, but I know of these transactions. They were all paid for with fake currency. After the War, we flooded Europe with counterfeit UK sterling and US dollars. You have no idea of the massive amounts involved. An SS officer by the name of Bernard Krüger ran a huge forgery operation at the Sachsenhausen Concentration Camp where skilled Jewish forgers, draftsmen, and engravers were used to create incredible forged banknotes. Even experts could be fooled by them. After the war, the Allies colluded with those involved to cover up how much was produced because of the destabilising effects it would have on international markets. The ripples from this contributed to British inflation which were felt for decades after the War."

"The more I look into all this, the worse this nightmare becomes," Karl sighed as Benjamin suddenly sounded more business-like.

"We are on limited time and need to move quickly; let's check the locker; I think the boxes on the shelves are mainly court records and trial evidence."

Karl opened the double doors, and inside were six plywood packing cases, of around 60 by 30 centimetres stamped with 'Sealed evidence – Authorised Access Only'. He pulled one out, with some difficulty because of the surprising weight, then, taking a penknife from his pocket, he slit through the red plastic seals. As he opened the lid, pulling back the covering paper beneath, they each gasped at the sight which greeted them. The gold seemed dazzling, reflecting the light, mesmerising them. Each bar was engraved with the Nazi eagle emblem clutching a wreath encircled swastika, beneath which was written, 'DEUTSCHE REICHSBANK' then the words, '12.5 KILO FEINGOLD 999.9', followed by the serial number. Karl shook his head in disbelief, yet also feeling an eerie sense of connection with the past. He looked at the faces of Benjamin and Friedrich who gave rueful smiles, nodding their heads.

Thirty minutes later, a smiling Lydia Thorson met them at the doorway, as Benjamin wheeled the luggage trolley, covered with a sheet, into the corridor.

"Robbing the vault are we?" Thorson remarked with a cheeky tone, to which Benjamin responded, "All authorised by the home secretary, Lydia," using her first name flirtatiously as he pulled a card from his pocket, handing it to her, "Dinner is on me; just call when you free," resulting in a loud sigh of derision from Friedrich, and a chuckle from Karl. Thorson looked at Benjamin, shaking her head, then with a disdainful look, she took the card, and led the way to the exit.

In the car, Friedrich turned to his companions, with a shocked voice, "We have just walked out of a police secure evidence centre with nearly £2 million worth of bullion. This is crazy...completely crazy."

"It does not belong to them," responded Benjamin, "but, with a bit of luck, they will not miss it for a while. Shall we say, this is just a deposit and I intend that some of it returns to where it came from. Remember the *Shoa,* my friends and never forget it."

"The *Shoa?*" Friedrich said, "What is this?"

"It is the Hebrew word for catastrophe," came the reply. "That is our word for what you call 'The Holocaust.' My great grandfather, both my grandparents, and three of their children, including a baby, perished in Auschwitz; but two more, my father and my aunt, escaped on the *kindertransport* organised by the great British humanitarian, Sir Nicholas Winton. They called them '*Winton Trains*' that rescued so many from Prague. He was a wonderful man and I owe my life to him.

…Then, later, my parents met here in England; my mother, also from Prague, had been a baby when the Nazis came for them. She was hidden by neighbours who fled to Britain after the War to escape communism. All her family were murdered; parents, grandparents, and three siblings. Sometimes, it is all too much to think about." His voice was breaking with emotion; tears were in his eyes and the journey continued in silence until they neared Kilburn, twenty minutes later.

Benjamin took a call from the Met, en route, over the loudspeaker,

"Bravo Juliette November, this is central; attending officers confirm Kilburn suspect in residence with his wife; armed plain-clothes will be close by, but will not interfere unless you request. We are awaiting confirmation on Hammersmith suspect; officers attending; standby."

"Queen's Park is our first stop," announced Benjamin, his voice now much brighter. "Let's try not to cause an international incident this time, boys, or should I call you, *Kameraden?* We are looking for Kingswood Avenue…" He glanced at the sat nav screen, "Just one minute away."

"Can I suggest I take over at this point," Karl spoke, pulling out his handgun, checking it was fully loaded, as he automatically did before all combat operations. "I am skilled at interrogation, and bent cops really annoy me which will add an interesting edge to my line of questioning."

"Try to exercise some restraint, please." Benjamin's voice pleaded, but with a mocking edge.

"*Gott,* why did I ever get involved in this madness?" Friedrich muttered, "You people in security are all madmen."

They pulled up outside a row of substantial Victorian terraced properties facing the hedges bordering Queen's Park opposite.

"That's our target with the blue door," stated Benjamin, who now pulled out his own weapon, a *Beretta Bobcat 21A*.

Karl looked at it with derision, "Is that thing a toy? Don't MI6 give you boys proper weapons?"

"Size isn't everything," came the good-natured reply. "Besides, this was issued to me by Mossad. We are a little more subtle in our Intelligence."

"Heaven preserve us," commented Friedrich, "I think I'll leave mine in my holster."

"You just bring your calculator, *mein Buchhalter*," Karl replied, "I think you might need it."

They exited the vehicle and Karl entered the small front garden with Friedrich, approaching the door, whilst Benjamin paused by the gate, his eyes darting up and down the street, with his hand inside his jacket clutching the grip of his weapon. There was a door-cam bell which Karl pushed, saying quietly to Friedrich, "I've just promoted you," as the intercom crackled and a voice said, "Yeah, how can I be of assistance?"

"I am Chief Inspector Karl Geldmann," Karl held up his BND identity card, "and this is DI Bernard Shekel from the German division of Interpol. We want to speak with former DC Rodger Bentham."

"Yeah, that's me, who's the geezer by the gate?" came the reply.

"We are accompanied by a member of the British SIS, who works with MI6. He will decide if he can reveal his identity; I think, as an ex-cop, you know how this works. Mr Bentham, we will be brief, but we think you can help us with our enquiries. We have authority from the Home Office at the highest level on a matter of national security…please may we speak?"

"How do I know I can trust you?" came the response.

Karl quickly replied icily, "You don't…" but then, on a hunch, he added, "But, if you want to avoid what happened this morning in South

Woodford, and your place being ripped apart by the plods, you will speak with us."

"Jesus Christ almighty," came the response, before security bolts were pulled back. The door was opened, revealing a man in his early fifties, with thick dark hair, greying at the sides, wearing an open-neck shirt under a smart black suede jacket. In the hall-way behind were travel-cases.

Karl spoke in a friendly but business-like manner, with a touch of sarcasm, "Going on holiday, Mr Bentham?"

"What, oh yes, we are leaving tonight for Spain...Puerto Banus; too bloody cold 'ere this time of year. We have an apartment there." The reply was nervous, but he extended his hand which Karl shook, entering the house with Friedrich; Benjamin followed slowly, walking sideways to the door, checking the street. Bentham led them down a corridor and into a lounge, speaking all the time, Karl sensed, with a slightly nervous edge. "I think I'll trust you; nice to meet some cops in what is a very dangerous world. I tell you, I'm glad I took early retirement. Bleedin' Met ain't what it used to be. First, they cut the numbers, then we got all namby pamby, and now, we daren't arrest no one, especially if they black, or gay, or one of these new nutters who identify as whatever they bleedin' want. We got people walkin' the street shouting, *Jihad!*...We can't send messages with any 'near the knuckle' humour any more. Christ, it's a bleedin' joke. Cup of tea boys? I tell you, it's all bloody pc and woke now..." The words were tumbling out.

Bentham waved them to a long cream soft-leather sofa, as Benjamin went to the window, checking the street from behind net curtains. Friedrich sat down, but Karl remained standing; he spoke slowly, looking directly into Bentham's eyes.

"Is that the reason you stole the gold at Hatton Garden, Mr Bentham?"

Bentham stopped moving, clearly shocked, then tried to recover his composure. "That's crazy mate...stupid talk."

"Your friend, William Samuel ...he did not think so." Karl's eyes were staring at Bentham, unblinking.

"Oh Christ, yeah, I heard, poor old Billy the Yid."

"I have very little time, Mr Bentham, and I want answers."

"I can't tell you nuffin'," Bentham replied, "We nicked the gang that did that job. They stashed the loot; we could never find it. I'm bloody shocked you accused me; twenty-five years-service I gave."

"Get his wife," Karl spoke coldly to Benjamin, as he pulled his handgun out, "Either he speaks, or she gets the first bullet." As Benjamin left the room, Bentham's voice became high-pitched

"Jesus Christ...Jesus, leave Enid out of this. You can't do this; this is British law...My lawyer will have you."

"I'm German, Mr Bentham, and I don't play games, nor do I play by your British rules. Do not screw around with me; my patience is exhausted." He cocked his weapon...sweat was pouring off Bentham's forehead and he began shaking. "You see, Mr Bentham, your friend, Billy, was very forthcoming, and we have met two of the villains who carried out the Hatton Garden job. I would trust them any day above you; I despise bent cops. To-night, I leave for Germany; in the secret service, people die; it happens all the time. We accept it; no one gets prosecuted, and we preserve, er, democracy with all its freedoms, but there is a price, Mr Bentham, and I do not care whether you live or die." Karl's face was cold, expressionless, almost aloof as he spoke.

At that moment, a woman in her late thirties entered in front of Benjamin, who had his gun in his hand. She started sobbing, "God almighty, Rodg, what is happening?"

"This is very simple, Enid," said Karl, adopting a slightly softer tone, "your husband took gold from Hatton Garden which did not belong to him. Now, it appears, he would rather you die than tell us where it is. If he cooperates, we leave immediately; we tell no one, and, no one goes to prison but, if not, you both die here and we leave anyway. Also, if you cooperate, you will keep a little of what was stolen in exchange for your silence, by way of demonstrating our gratitude. If not, we are with intelligence, and you will have been killed in a robbery; a little ironic, but that is life. So? I told your husband that my patience is exhausted but he does not seem to care about you." He raised his weapon, pointing it at her head.

"Tell him Rodger..." she screamed at Bentham, "I told you this would happen..."

Twenty minutes later, Benjamin loaded the luggage carrier back into the *Mercedes*, and gave a brief wave to the special branch officers standing outside, as they pulled away.

Friedrich spoke, in a shocked voice - "What will happen to them? Would you have shot them? *Gott,* I thought my people were ruthless."

"They will be held by Special Branch until we have verified that Bentham told us the truth," replied Benjamin. "If so, they will be released, and our little sweetener will guarantee their silence, but I cannot speak for Karl's actions. I am deeply shocked myself."

"You called me the *Soldat-Kämpfer,* Friedrich, so, I thought I would live up to your expectations," said Karl, with a chuckle. "Not very bright, hiding it under the floorboards; but that's the plods for you, a little short of a shilling, I think, is the British expression."

"I'm only glad I was a military man, and not a cop then," quipped Benjamin.

"I think I want to go back to being a *Buchhalter,"* Friedrich replied. "You are all crazy. We are now carrying around 5.25 million US dollars-worth of gold bullion in this vehicle, without security...*Oh Gott!*"

"We have police protection," Karl responded calmly.

"The *verdammte* police nicked it in the first place; this is all crazy ..." Friedrich replied, waving his arms.

At 5:00pm, as they approached Hammersmith, Benjamin spoke, "We have less than three and a half hours. I think we may be in need of diplomatic containers." He pulled in, checking his contacts, then announced he was calling the Israeli Embassy. Seconds later, he began speaking, "Aaron, Benjamin Weiss; I need to remove some items from the UK, my old friend, and we will have more good news for the *World Jewish Restoration Organisation*. What weight limits are there on diplomatic pouches? Excellent! Can you meet me at the security car park at Heathrow at 7:45? Inform Lufthansa airline that there will be a diplomatic package weight of around 120 kilos."

"How in God's name will you explain that away?" Friedrich gasped incredulously after the call.

"You need to understand the Jewish mind, my friend." Benjamin responded. "In our culture, pragmatism gains understanding, and even more so, if there is a good motive, or where money is involved. *'Justice, and only justice, you shall follow, that you may live and inherit...'* Deuteronomy 16;20..." He looked up with a thoughtful expression, holding his forefinger in the air, then, "or, as your bard would say, *'There is a tide in the affairs of men, which, taken at the flood, leads on to fortune; omitted, all the voyage of their life is bound in shallows and in miseries.'* So, my view is I'd rather the fortune, than the misery...good Jewish pragmatism, eh?"

"God protect me from a gun-carrying philosopher," Friedrich responded.

As they pulled off the Hammersmith flyover, Benjamin called the Met controller and the reassuring voice responded, "Bravo Juliette November, armed officers in position. We believe target alone and is in residence. Access via two entrances as property borders a corner on Ravenscourt Square. Surveillance reports white van occupied by at least two males in proximity; arrived around thirty minutes ago and parked 50 metres from property, facing Ravenscourt Park. A further four Special Branch officers have been despatched and are in position; maximum caution advised. Out."

Karl spoke with a smile, "I think, *Herr Buchhalter,* you might be advised to check your weapon; just remember to point it in the right direction."

Benjamin eased the Mercedes down the side street off Ravenscourt Square, passing a variety of luxury cars, and pulled up alongside a large square white Regency style property. A side-door faced the street with a door-bell push and an intercom.

"A tidy-sized house for a retired Detective Inspector," Benjamin remarked dryly, as Karl snapped the safety on his weapon, before slipping it back into his holster.

"I think," Karl stated, "One of us should approach the side-door in case those men in that van try to carry out a re-run of this morning and attempt to jump us."

"My turn then; shall we try a more subtle approach? It is more suited to my style. Leave the talking to me," Benjamin said lightly as he left the vehicle, and walked up the three steps to the door. He pressed the intercom button, and seconds later, a voice spoke, "Who is it?"

"Good afternoon," Benjamin started, "Am I speaking to Mr Keith Anderson, formerly Detective Inspector with the Met? My name is Benjamin Weiss, and I am here from the Home Office Security Surveillance team."

The answer was a little brusque, "Yeah, but I'm very busy right now. What's the issue?"

"Ah, we have been alerted that there have been threats against former Police Officers from organised crime syndicates."

"I've heard nothing..." There was a pause, but Benjamin sensed interest in his voice. "What's going on?"

"A former partner of yours, DC Rodger Bentham, has received a threat from criminals linked to a major crime syndicate; some of the villains involved were those you investigated. So, if we might have a word? I've just been interviewing Mr Bentham who sends his regards."

"Cor blimey," came a warmer response, "He's a bigger villain than any of them. I'll let you in, 'ang on."

In the van, Karl and Friedrich had listened to the conversation through Benjamin's body mic. "You stay here," Karl muttered, "We don't want to spook him if we are to try, what Benjamin calls, 'a more subtle approach'. Personally, I think I would rather rely on my weapon. Watch our backs; I never trust the police."

The sound of a security chain on the door being slipped, was followed by the appearance of a smartly dressed man, in a jacket and tie, with somewhat unruly grey hair. Benjamin waved to Karl, as he exited the vehicle, before turning to Anderson, offering his hand. "Pleased to meet you Sir; my colleague from the Home Office, Karl, is joining us." They entered a foyer with an ornate chandelier hanging above a marble tiled floor.

"I'll take you into the study." Anderson appeared relaxed as he walked ahead of them to open a brightly polished panelled door leading into a room with modern furniture which seemed a little out of place, Karl thought, within the style of the house. There was a light oak desk and a number of matching easy chairs and two book-cases, one on either side, whilst the window beyond gave a view over the trees and grass of the park. "Take a seat, boys; sorry I was a bit uptight, I'm off to a reunion dinner tonight; nothing too formal. A retirement of one of the desk-Sergeants I knew well at Holborn Nick. Fancy a whisky?" They declined, as he poured one from a decanter, mixing it with dry ginger, before sitting at his desk. "So, what's been happening, gents?"

Karl sat back, observing, as Benjamin spoke - "Mr Anderson, or can I call you Keith?" Anderson gestured with his hand, and a smile. "We have a problem. Now, we take threats against former Met Police officers very seriously. That is why we want to ensure you are protected. You are under a very serious threat, Keith, resulting from your investigations into crime, not least the Hatton Garden job."

"Christ, we nicked them; never saw that lot as threatening; they were called the diamond wheezers because they were all old codgers."

"Here's the thing, Keith, you may have heard of William Samuel?"

Anderson lent forwards, his eyes suddenly alert, "Yeah, poor old Billy...mixed up with some foreign gangs, so I heard. He was a class grass. I'll miss the poor bastard."

Benjamin's voice was relaxed, "Dreadful business, Keith, that is why we wanted to speak with you. You see, he was an excellent informant and told us that you wanted to launder some gold you had removed from Hatton Garden."

Karl watched as Anderson's expression changed from one of benign interest to one of horrific shock and realisation.

Benjamin continued, "Now, Keith, we respect your long service and we want to protect you, and reward you. If you reveal the location of the gold you removed, we will make you a substantial offer, and avoid all that unpleasantness surrounding a criminal prosecution. You know how it is, Keith, those crooks you banged up and their friends are not very pleasant to former officers. It's a travesty really and we want to ensure no harm comes to you. So, here's the deal; we allow you to keep five 1 kilo bars in exchange for the rest. In other words, you get over three hundred thousand pounds, your freedom, the money you have already laundered, and the ability to lead a life as a respected former officer of the Met. That's why we are here, Keith, because we want to take care of you. Now, shall we shake on this?"

Karl watched in astonishment as Benjamin outlined his terms in the manner of a close friend and colleague.

Anderson looked stunned, the colour draining from his face, then spoke in a trembling voice, "Can I have time to think this over?"

"Absolutely, Keith, no problem. I think two minutes will be sufficient, don't you agree? Oh, and by the way, your colleague, Detective Constable Rodger Bentham has accepted our offer and he was most helpful; he informs us that you both decided to spend four 1 kilo bars, so no need to worry; we won't tell anyone if you don't. We'll call that a fee for…er…looking after the assets. Just one other thing; our agreement is subject to silence from you; regrettably, if you break that commitment, we will be unable to protect you, and your life will then be at risk. Now finish your Scotch and relax; you are amongst friends."

Five minutes later, Karl emerged from the house to collect the baggage trolley, saying to Friedrich, "I've wasted my time all my life; I think I am converting to Judaism. Friedrich, that man is a legend; no threats, no guns, no violence, just a silver tongue…and we have our gold."

Friedrich was still smiling and shaking his head as he watched Karl re-enter the house, when he heard the first shout from a vehicle he could see across the road, bordering the park. "Armed police! Lay flat on the floor and put down your weapon…Now!" His heart thumped as he saw a police officer behind the front door of the car, his arms out-stretched holding a pistol. Two more policemen were at the rear, crouched on the roadside. The shout, almost a scream, came again, "On the floor…Now! Put down your weapon!" A police siren was sounded from a vehicle out of site, as he heard shots. The two officers at the rear of the car ran further back and were on the floor, as there was the sound of an automatic weapon being discharged. Friedrich decided to seek safety in the house, leaving the vehicle and reaching for his gun, his hands shaking, as he heard an engine loudly revving followed by the shriek of tyres. He dimly heard an officer scream, "Discharge weapons!" as a white van careered into the police vehicle. More shots rang out; the van now headed into the street towards Friedrich who crouched, aimed his handgun and loosed off six rounds in rapid succession, as the van kept coming towards him, then sped past. He was in a daze as he heard a huge metallic bang, seeing a cloud of smoke from the direction the van had taken, dimly aware of a voice saying loudly; "Lay on the floor and put down your weapon!" Seconds later, he was being roughly frisked as he heard the voice of Benjamin, looking up to see him show his ID to a police officer, "I am Colonel Weiss, and I am with SIS; he's with us; let him up."

The voice of the officer seemed ridiculous as Friedrich heard him say, "Sorry about that, Sir, but we need to stay down until the incident is cleared."

Benjamin spoke again, "We have to go, officer; I am on a covert mission, with clearance at the highest level, and authorised by Sir Alex Younger of MI6; we need to be at Heathrow by 7:00pm. I don't think the occupants of that van will give you too much trouble." Smoke was still rising from what they could now make out was the white van which had hit the wall of a building 75 metres down the road.

More police were now on the scene as Karl emerged from the house, lowering the trolley, laden with boxes, down the steps, which Benjamin helped him load into the back of the Mercedes. Friedrich was led to the front where he sat, white faced, trembling from his ordeal. Benjamin spoke to the senior police officer at the scene. "You will be told how this is to be reported and under no circumstances will you make mention of the building we have just left, nor will you enter it. I trust you understand this is a matter of national security. You have not met with me, nor the men accompanying me, and no statements, whatsoever, are to be given to the press. That will be handled by the Met Press Office and No 10. Any police casualties?"

"Just bruised and shaken, Sir, especially their egos, as I think your man might be the hero of the hour."

Minutes later, they left the scene with a police car ahead of them, its blue light flashing as an escort. Karl turned to Friedrich - "We leave you alone for five minutes, and you turn the streets of London into a battleground. Thank God you were pointing your gun in the right direction."

Friedrich responded, his voice still shaking, "You can always rely on a *Buchhalter* to keep you out of trouble."

On the aircraft, in business class, both Karl and Friedrich accepted a welcome pre-take-off drink of Champagne. Karl requested two further Pear Brandies and they touched glasses together with a smile of relief that they could, at last, relax. Their drive to Heathrow had been shortened by the police escort which remained with them until they arrived at the security area. They had met with Aaron, from the Israeli embassy, who supervised the packaging of the diplomatic bags, which were marked with the blue Star of David on a white background, under which was written, '*VCDR, Article 27.4 - State of Israel – Diplomatic Bag*'. Benjamin had then turned to Friedrich and Karl, bidding them farewell, stating that he had some more business to do of a "subtle" kind, with a wink, and that he would rendezvous with them the following Monday in Munich.

They were then whisked directly to the aircraft, accompanied by plain clothes officers, bypassing security, and escorted on board the waiting Lufthansa *Airbus A320*.

As the aircraft took off, Friedrich was doing some calculations on his tablet; he tried to suppress his excitement as he stated, in a whisper, "We have recovered gold to the value of 8,525,566 US dollars, and 5 cents."

Karl took a sip from his Champagne, "As our Jewish friend quoted, *"There is a tide in the affairs of men, which, taken at the flood, leads on to fortune"*"

Friedrich countered, "He also said, *'Justice, and only justice, you shall follow,"* to which Karl responded, "and that is exactly what I intend to do..."

Epilogue

Sunday, 14th January 2024 11:30pm
Hotel Bayerischer Hof, Promenadeplatz, Munich

Karl and Inge were staying the night, and now, as she lay in his arms, warmed by their exotic after-dinner cocktails, he said, "I think we should celebrate our marriage here, in this hotel. Somehow, after all we have shared, and discovered, it seems almost providential." He laughed, then sighed, "I think my grandfather would love the choice of venue, but would never understand why we chose it." Their meeting was scheduled for lunch the following day; however, they had decided to have a night away from the apartment where they kept being drawn back to the box which had unlocked so many secrets. They had taken their cocktails in the unique Falk's Bar, situated in the hotel's historic Hall of Mirrors. The bartender had explained to them that it was the only part of the hotel to escape damage in the Allied bombing of Munich in 1945, which had all but destroyed the hotel. He had leant forwards, as though sharing an indiscretion, speaking quietly, and looking round to see if anyone was listening. "They loved this hotel, the Nazis; they were all here, Hitler, Göring, Bormann, Goebbels, Himmler, Speer …I know this because my grandfather was a chef here in the war. We have photographs of them all taken in this place. He used to say the boss; that was the owner, Hermann Volkhardt; he would mix with them, but for only one reason, to keep the hotel in the family because the Nazis wanted it. He and his son, Falk, who this bar is named after, re-built the hotel after the war and Falk, he dedicated his life to this place creating the extraordinary venue you see today. The recovery of Germany was miraculous; heaven knows how they had the means or the money." Karl could only nod, and listen politely to the irony in the man's words, but reflecting that it was as if he could never achieve freedom from the burden he felt.

They had sat in the bar area admiring the beauty of the exquisite, ornate, baroque styling, with surrounding mirrors, above which a detailed stucco ceiling captured the magnificence of a bygone age. In the adjoining room was a fabulous dome, inset with glass, and they had then taken a seat by pillars which all somehow mixed well with the modern concealed lighting. Inge had looked earnestly into his eyes, "What are you going to do, Karl?"

He knew to what she was referring, and spoke softly, "What I believe is right, because, if not, we inherit the guilt of those who went before. Of course, I cannot speak for my sister, or Friedrich, who is part of their organisation. I want you to tell them about what you discovered."

Now, as they lay together, she whispered, "Love me." Their thoughts were lost in the passion they shared, and in the restful sleep which followed.

Monday 15th January 2024 12:30pm
Osteria Italiana, Schellingstrasse, Munich

The choice of the Osteria Italiana had not been on a whim; they all knew it had once been the favourite Munich restaurant of Adolf Hitler, near to his apartment, when it was known as the Osteria Bavaria. Karl had booked a table, positioned in a secluded corner, set apart, and surrounded by white columns supporting a mock semi-circular roof above the seating in a representation of a piazza. There seemed to be a fatalistic reason for his choice, as though they were closing a chapter on history. Explaining to the Patron the need for discreet privacy, Karl had paid to have the tables in the immediate vicinity kept free. Although they had eaten there previously, this occasion took on a more pressing resonance. They had ordered a bottle of Chianti, when Friedrich arrived, clad in his signature flat cap, in a long coat. He bowed to Inge, then wiped his glasses awkwardly before lifting her right hand to kiss it.

"Fräulein Rauff, your future husband has placed me in impossible situations, and danger, but you know what, I have already missed him since we returned. I will, however, not be going on vacation with him again any time soon." He removed his coat, handing it to a waiter, revealing a dark grey suit and tie worn beneath. A moment later, Karl's sister, Gretchen, arrived, her greying hair tied back, wearing a black polo-neck sweater over matching trousers under a cream coat. Fifteen minutes went by as they attempted light conversation, then, moved on to discuss the rising civilian casualty figures in Gaza, and their shared concern over the overwhelming nature of the Israeli military assault. Karl pointed out that their overdue guest, whilst being Jewish, shared these concerns. It all seemed a little surreal as all knew the gravity behind the reason for their meeting.

Just as Karl began to feel a sense of unease, Benjamin arrived dressed in an immaculate black coat, with a velvet edged collar and a cream scarf. "Sorry to be late; a little unforgiveable, I know, but just swung around a few blocks with my driver to make sure we had no unwelcome guests." He slipped out of his coat to reveal a well-cut mid-blue three-piece suit, worn over an open neck white shirt. He kissed the hands of Inge and Gretchen; then, looking furtively round, "I trust, bearing in mind where we are, we will not be joined by anyone in uniform sporting a small moustache!" They laughed and the moment lightened as he sat down, extending his glass for Karl to fill.

Karl began, "I have fully briefed my sister, upon our…inheritance, shall we call it, and she shares my discomfort with the impossible situation this places us in. Gretchen, perhaps, you may wish to speak."

Gretchen's words were spoken clearly and concisely, in a precise manner, reflecting a lifetime of intolerance of those who failed to live up to expectations. "First, let me say I have no argument with the past; mistakes were made, and continue to be made by those in power. The horrific current events in the middle-east witness this, demonstrating the hypocrisy of our leaders in failing to unite in demanding a cease-fire. But, looking back to the dark days of the war, I am aware that much of the *Raubgold* was looted from the countries which we occupied, and also, that it was driven by a mis-guided policy whereby we plundered from elements of society which included your race, *Herr* Weiss. However, I do not condemn the brilliant actions of my father and grandfather which helped us rebuild Germany after the war. In my view, the world would have been a better place if we had joined forces with the Western Allies against the Russians. So, I do not share my brother's views and I applaud *das Geheime Vierte Reich*, which, yes, I know about, for the work which they have undertaken to invest in our industry. I am, however, lucky enough to have inherited much, and worked, like you, *Herr Völker*, in an accounting role from which I have prospered. This has been within an organisation supported by *VVF AG* which, as I think we all know, is an investment group set up by the Nazis at the end of the War."

She stopped as a waiter took their orders, resuming by holding her hands up, "So, I have no need of the assets my father has pledged. I am willing to only accept a small part, which will be re-invested in German economic development. Of the three 12.5 kilo bars of gold my father left for me, I will take only one which will be used for this purpose. I do not feel we should condemn all of the past, but learn from the mistakes and, yes, the barbaric abuses of power exercised by some. However, I have listened to my brother at length, seen what our father left for us, and been deeply moved by what I have learned, not least about the horrors inflicted on others." She turned to look at Benjamin, "Therefore, the rest of what my father left, *Herr* Weiss, I will surrender to your *World Jewish Restoration Organisation*."

Benjamin looked shocked, then held his hands up in a gesture of thanks, saying, "I am speechless, *mein herzlicher Dank,"* (my heartfelt thanks) as Karl spoke.

"I am so grateful to my dear sister for this gesture but, unlike Gretchen, I condemn all that National Socialism stood for and feel the shame of the past hanging over me like a dark shadow; this has been so all my adult life. I too, have no need of my so-called inheritance, and so, I will pledge all of mine to the *World Jewish Restoration Organisation*."

Benjamin stood, walked to Karl, and, with tears in his eyes, hugged him. Karl's voice was shaking with emotion as he continued, "I have seen and learned so much these last weeks that has horrified me, particularly discovering the complicity of so many." He stopped, the moment adding emphasis to his words, then placed his hand on Inge's shoulder,

"Inge, I know you have something you wish to reveal, but first, I think we need Champagne." He raised his hand to a waiter, ordering two bottles of *Dom Perignon*, nodding to the surprised waiter with a smile, to confirm he meant it.

Inge now spoke, her voice wavering: "I have been invested in this from the outset, and not just because I love and respect Karl, or that he is to be my husband, but there is much more. You all know me as Inge Rauff, yet, once, I despised that name, and, like Karl with his name of Spacil, I wished to disassociate myself from it. You know why? My grandfather was a man by the name of Walther Rauff. He was an upper ranking SS officer, as a *Standartenführer,* and worked directly under one of the architects of the 'Final Solution', Reinhard Heydrich. He was considered highly efficient in assisting with the *Judenfrage.* (Jewish problem) Not only this, but my grandfather helped invent the gas vans that they used to exterminate Jews, disabled people, communists, and any they did not like. You know what they did?" Her voice was shaking with her feelings. "They connected hoses from the exhaust of the vans, through the floor, and then they crammed people inside them, and left the engine running, creating mobile gas chambers, suffocating those inside. I have lived with this guilt inside me…" She broke off, trying to hold her feelings in check, and Karl put out a reassuring hand, but she waved him away. "No, I must continue… my grandfather was responsible for the deaths of around 100,000 people, some say many more, but this is not my point; it is what came after…

"You see, in 1945, he was wanted by the Allies as a war criminal. You will not believe what happened; the Catholic Church saved him, but not in the way you might think; he escaped capture with the help of the Church, under the authority of a senior bishop, closely associated with the Vatican, Bishop Alois Hudal."

She stopped, as their meals were served, taking a long sip of her wine. The first bottle of Champagne arrived, and, as Karl nodded to the waiter, his face betrayed the pain of hearing more of what she had confessed to him. They began their meals in silence. Somehow, it did not seem appropriate to talk. Then Friedrich spoke softly, looking at Inge, "I have often questioned myself in life, but never more so than, perhaps, in recent days. Please do continue, *Fraulein.*"

"*Danke,* Friedrich, Karl speaks highly of you." Inge smiled at him, breaking the tension before continuing. "You see, the values they talk of, trust, justice, and morality were nothing. You know what? After the war, my grandfather worked for Syria, then he was recruited by the CIA, West German Intelligence, and even the Israelis. He was deeply involved with Operation Condor, the US sponsored covert actions to eliminate or murder left-wing groups in Central and South America in the 1970's and 1980's. He moved to Chile, assisting the regime of President Pinochet who refused extradition requests for him to stand trial for war crimes. Now, our Intelligence service, after all this was discovered recently by the press, say it was a mistake to recruit him, as though this was an isolated error. You know what, our BND was riddled with former Nazis and even the head was a former SS officer. My grandfather was recruited by Rudolf Oebsger-Röder, another former member of the SS who was also guilty of war crimes; he was working for West-German intelligence. Shall I tell you who paid Walther Rauff's legal fees when he resisted extradition? Our German Intelligence service. They even gave him money to set up a business in Chile. The hypocrisy is staggering.

"When Karl first began looking into this after his father became ill, I contacted my police colleagues who had access to the *Bundesarchiv*. I discovered so much; it is just beyond belief. The list of those guilty of horrific crimes who escaped justice is unbelievable, and those who helped or contrived with them. Now, we have more incontrovertible evidence with the recovery of information which reveals the identity of those who accepted Nazi assets in the document recovered from London, *die Ehrenarier Treuhänder Deutschlands,* and the *Transaktions Aufzeichnung* which Karl's father left for him. What do we do with what we have? The revelations would change our perspective of history, cause civil unrest, and potentially destroy many global institutions. We now know the depths of depravity to which these so-called respectable institutions sank, with the involvement of powerful people, and corporations in a scandal that exceeds anything we have ever seen. How could they? The victims cried out but no one listened; even after the war. *Gott,* this needs to be exposed, written about, but then, if it is, what difference will it make? They got away with it; they always do. I'm sorry," she sobbed, holding her head in her hands, as Karl placed his hand around her shoulder.

He turned to Friedrich, "That just leaves you, my friend. You work for the GVR."

Friedrich was shaking his head, "Not any more, *mein Soldat-Kämpfer*. I am finished with all of this; I have seen and heard too much and I'd like to announce my official retirement. I wanted excitement, and I got it; but I have learned that history is always written by the victors. I recall the very apt words of Hermann Göring at his trial for war crimes at Nuremberg, *"Der Sieger wird immer der Richter und der Besiegte stets der Angeklagte sein."* (The victor will always be the judge, and the vanquished the accused) Perhaps, I will return to your saying from the bible, Benjamin, that tells us to only follow justice. Let us drink to justice."

They all touched their glasses together.

"*L'chaim!*" (to life) Benjamin added, "…because that is what this all cost, the life of so many precious individuals. But, let us lighten a little now; we have some things to celebrate. Remember, I warned you that we Jews are pragmatic. First, the fanatics in the *Reichslegion* have not been successful in obtaining the gold, and, equally, the GVR have gained nothing. They know nothing of the six 12.5 kilos of gold representing your inheritance, and we, my friends, have the rest. The British police are also unaware of how much gold was taken from the scene of the crime at Hatton Garden. No one knows what we know. The GVR will have to formally claim what is left from the British Government. Our two former police officers will say nothing. You might say that ours is the perfect crime, because there is no record of what we have taken."

Karl raised his hand, looking puzzled, "But what will happen when they discover that two 12.5 kilo bars of gold were removed from police secure storage worth two million dollars? They will surely come after us."

"Ah remember," Benjamin replied, waving his finger, "I told you; subtlety is sometimes needed. You may recall our friend, Mr Seed, residing in Belmarsh Prison. I visited him again and said that we might have a slight problem with his release. I explained that two gold bars were missing and that this was blocking progress on his case. I also told him that there were some very nasty and violent Nazi people who would love to know who stole them. Naturally, I said I was concerned for his wellbeing, but if he could assist with locating these bars, then, any danger to his life would be removed, and that he would have earned the £2,000 I would give him. I even took a 1 kilo bar of gold to show him, which I offered to leave with a trusted third party if he could assist. He was most grateful for my intervention and very helpful. He volunteered that he and his accomplice, Perkins, who passed away in 2018, had hidden them in a grave at Tower Hamlets Cemetery."

"How does that help with the missing gold we took from evidence storage?" Friedrich looked puzzled.

Benjamin had a wry smile on his face, "Ah, well now, you may remember how you were tutting when we met the charming Lydia Thorson at the police evidence storage centre. We had a lovely dinner together on Saturday, after she had assisted in my returning what rightfully belongs to His Majesty's Forensic Archive service. So, you see, no gold is missing."

Tuesday 16th January 2024 9:00am
Office of the Prime Minister, 10, Downing Street, London

The large blue double doors, with their gold trim, opened, and the PM's private secretary, Elizabeth Perelman, entered, holding some files in her hand. "The home secretary is now here, Prime Minister. Do you want me to take notes for a briefing."

The prime minister was sat at his red leather-topped desk, in a white shirt and striped tie, his dark blue jacket hung off the back of his chair. "I think not, Elizabeth; not at this stage. This is all bordering on some very sensitive areas and I am hopeful that we can keep any formal records to a minimum. If you ask Sir Richard Moore and the home secretary to join me, and inform the press office that no record of this meeting is to be released. I will not activate an electronic recording of our discussions. Oh, and can you get someone to organise coffee?"

Moments later, the doors were opened again, and both men entered, holding document folders. They pulled out cream upholstered seats from the table near the PM's desk to face him.

"Coffee is on its way, gentlemen, but hopefully, we can knock this awful business on the head before it gets further out of hand. What's the security situation, Sir Richard?"

The head of MI6 glanced at his notes. "Pretty much resolved, Prime Minister. I'm glad and relieved to report that the German Intelligence agents departed last Thursday. So far, their identities do not appear to have emerged, despite the press being on the case. The extremist paramilitary wing of the German far-right *Reichslegion,* known as the DA, have all been neutralised. We have three DA fatalities, plus three injured who have already been transferred to hospitals in Germany under guard; we took five prisoners who have been taken by the BND for interrogation. We do not believe we have any further suspects at large nor any DA cells remaining on UK soil. I am waiting for an update from one of our agents assigned to the operation. You may recall he was given special clearance to supervise access by the BND agents to the Hatton Garden evidence we still hold, including the gold. However, he has taken unauthorised leave for a trip to Israel; I'm afraid that whilst he is effective, he is a bit of a maverick."

"Most inconvenient; I trust he hasn't stolen it," the prime minister said, attempting a brief chuckle, turning to the home secretary, "So James, how are things your end; and have we checked the evidence is still safely stored with the police?"

The home secretary looked a little uncomfortable, speaking hesitantly, "Well, Prime Minister, it certainly seems that we are back where this all started, except, of course, with an awkward press story over the shootings; but I'm afraid we do have a rather strange anomaly."

Rishi Sunak leaned forwards, "I hope this will not add to our difficulties, Home Secretary."

The home secretary's brow was furrowed, "Well, we can account for all the gold the police originally recovered, but the extraordinary thing is that the serial numbers of two of the bars do not match our records."

Just over two weeks later, on 2nd February, a secure package arrived at Karl's apartment for which he had to sign. The postmark identified the source as being Israel. Inside was a hand-written note,

'Dear and valued friend,

We have shared much together.

I wanted to express both my admiration for your humanity, and my thanks for all you have done in helping to return a little of what was taken from those families whose forebears suffered so much in The Shoa.

Please forgive me, but I used my security clearance to obtain your bank account details and, in there, you will find an appreciation has been deposited. This will not show an identifiable source, and how you use this is, of course, for you to decide.

Perhaps, you might purchase a villa here in Eilat.

I have sent a similar message and gift to Friedrich. I know he will be quick to calculate the value of what I have enclosed!

Take care, my friend, and let us share a drink in happier times, perhaps on the veranda of your villa.

'The LORD makes some poor and others rich; he brings some down and lifts others up.' 1 Samuel 2:7

L'chaim,

Benjamin'

Karl opened the package, inside which was an ornate wooden box, inlaid with a brass pattern, and a metal clasp on the front. He opened it to reveal three gold coins, set in blue velvet, labelled 200, 100, and 50 Lirot. Each had an image of an ancient oil lamp stand, surrounded by olive sprigs. In the lid of the box, within a gold plaque, were the words, *'Shalom alekem'* (Peace be with you)

Postscript

What happened to them?

Hermann Abs: 15 October 1901 – 5 February 1994 The most powerful banker of the Third Reich. After the war, he became chairman of Deutsche Bank, and contributed to the reconstruction of the West German economy, working closely with Chancellor Konrad Adenauer. Helped finance the rebuilding of heavy industry, and became a highly respected figure in post-war international banking and finance, ironically playing a part in negotiations over Jewish reparations. Appointed by the Vatican to examine banking irregularities following the collapse of the Banco Ambrosiano of which the Vatican Bank a was major shareholder in December 1982.

Martin Bormann: 17 June 1900 – 2 May 1945 The powerful head of the Nazi Party Chancellery attempted to flee Berlin on 2 May 1945 to avoid capture by the Soviets. Various stories emerged of his demise in Berlin with his body purportedly recovered in 1973 in an excavation. DNA tests in 1998, later challenged, confirmed his identity. His ashes were scattered over the Baltic Sea in 1999. However, consistent reports place him in both Chile and Argentina right through to the 1970's. Sources say he was running a Nazi movement infiltrating Germany until his death. Bormann was found guilty in the Nuremberg trials of war crimes in absentia.

Brendan Rendell Bracken: 15 February 1901 – 8 August 1958. In 1945, after the end of the wartime coalition, Churchill's former Parliamentary Secretary, Bracken, was briefly First Lord of the Admiralty in the Churchill caretaker ministry, but lost the post in the general election won by Clement Attlee's Labour Party. Bracken lost his North Paddington seat but soon returned to the Commons, as Member of Parliament for Bournemouth in a November 1945 by-election. He was a relentless critic of the Labour government's policy of nationalisation and retreat from empire. In early 1952, he was elevated to the peerage as Viscount Bracken, of Christchurch, but never used the title or sat in the House of Lords. His best-known business accomplishment was merging the *Financial News* into the *Financial Times* in 1945. At that stage, he was also publishing *The Economist*. In 1951, with his love of history, he helped found *History Today* magazine.

Cardinal Antonio Caggiano: 30 January 1889 – 23 October 1979 Played a part in helping Nazi sympathisers and war criminals escape prosecution in Europe by easing their passage to South America. Elevated to Cardinal on 18th February 1946 by Pope Pius XII. Liaised with President Juan Peron on assisting war criminals to flee to Argentina. Appointed Archbishop of Buenos Aires in 1959 and became head of administering to Catholics in the Argentine armed forces. Lived until the age of 90 and Buried in the Metropolitan Cathedral of Buenos Aires.

Sir Winston Churchill: 30 November 1874 – 24 January 1965 Churchill lost the post-war General Election in July 1945 to Labour under Clement Atlee. Labour were elected again in 1950, but lost to the Conservatives in 1951 when Churchill returned as Prime Minister. However, he was 77 and suffering from ill-health. He had a number of strokes in office but remained dedicated to his role, only resigning in April 1955. He had been knighted by Elizabeth II on 24th April 1953. Churchill remained active and was privately critical of his successor, Antony Eden, whilst continuing to play a role in advancing British causes overseas after his 'retirement' In his last years, he spent much time at his home of Chartwell and on the French Riviera. He suffered a final stroke in January 1965, passing away two weeks later. He was given a state funeral and lay in state at Westminster Hall for three days.

General Lucius D. Clay: 23 April 1898 – 16 April 1978 The deputy to General Dwight Eisenhower became deputy military governor of Germany in 1946, and military governor in 1947. He organised the Berlin air-lift when the Russians blockaded West Berlin. Controversially, he commuted many death sentences for Nazi war criminals. In 1950, he was appointed chairman of Continental Can Company, then from 1962 to 1973, he became a partner in the global financial investment group, Lehman Brothers. He was a close advisor to both President Eisenhower and President Kennedy whom he accompanied on the famous Berlin visit where he gave the speech, "Ich bin ein berliner…" Berliners placed an inscription at his grave thanking him for their freedom.

Allen Dulles: 7 April 1893 – 29 January 1969 The lawyer and wartime director of US Intelligence or the OSS in Switzerland became the first director of the CIA in 1952. He served in this post throughout the Cold War, resigning in 1961 (at the behest of President Kennedy) after a series of intelligence issues including the failed Bay of Pigs invasion against Fidel Castro in Cuba. He was presented with the National Security Medal by JFK the day before his 'resignation'. After Kennedy's assassination, he was appointed to the Warren Commission by President Johnson which many believe covered up the truth behind Kennedy's assassination. There were serious allegations that he 'coached' witnesses to ensure that evidence given fitted the narrative.

John Foster Dulles: 25 February 1888 – 24 May 1959 The influential lawyer who worked during the war to structure a post-war Europe envisaging a pan-European Federal system. He was actively involved in the planning for the creation of the United Nations believing that there needed to be a strong body to enforce peace and international law. He became an advisor to President Truman and served as a US delegate to the UN. Dulles was strongly opposed to the use of nuclear weapons against Japan and helped to create the post-war treaties with Japan. Dwight Eisenhower appointed him as Secretary of State where he promoted robust anti-communist policies. He remained on post until one month before his death from cancer.

Walther Funk: 18 August 1890 – 31 May 1960. Named by Adolf Hitler to remain as Reich Minister for the economy in his last political testament, Funk was arrested by the Allies on 11th May 1945, and sent to a prison camp. He was tried at Nuremberg, accused of complicity in the stealing of property from the Jews, war crimes, and crimes against humanity. Funk was visibly upset and emotional during his trial on hearing the evidence of concentration camp atrocities. He stated he had little power in the regime but accepted moral guilt for signing off on orders that others required carrying out. He was given life imprisonment and incarcerated in Spandau, being released in 1957 due to ill-health, dying three years later from diabetes.

Friedrich Flick: 10 July 1883 – 20 July 1972 Having been deeply involved and hugely benefitting in his iron and coal business empire from slave labour, and appropriation of assets seized by the Nazis, Flick was arrested on 13th June 1945, and tried at Nuremberg in 1947. Flick employed 48,000 forced labourers in his munitions, steel, and coal mines, 80% of whom perished. Despite this, he steadfastly refused to acknowledge any guilt whatsoever, stating: "nothing will convince us that we are war criminals." He was released on 25th August 1950, and rapidly took back the reins of his business empire, becoming the largest shareholder of Daimler-Benz and other leading businesses. He became one of West Germany's richest people and was feted with awards and honours. At the time of his death, he had amassed 330 companies employing over 300,000 people.

Reinhard Gehlen: 3 April 3 1902 – 8 June 1979 Surrendered to US Intelligence in Bavaria on 22nd May 1945. Gehlen offered the US invaluable intel on the Russians he had gathered as a senior German intelligence officer. Much of the hidden information he used as a bargaining chip for his own advancement, becoming a spymaster, with many other former Nazi officers for the United States in the Cold War. He set up the 'Gehlen Organisation' recruiting many former SS, and others from the Gestapo to work with him against the Soviets and the East German regime. In 1956, he transferred his operation into the Bundesnachrichtendienst (BND, Federal Intelligence Service) and became president of the BND until 1968. He was awarded the Grand Cross of the Order of Merit of West Germany in 1968.

Hermann Göring: Surrendered to US forces on 6th May 1945. Tried at Nuremberg, he admitted loyalty to Hitler but claimed he had no knowledge of the atrocities being committed in the death camps. His trial lasted 218 days during which he put up a vigorous defence and had to be separated from other Nazis whose testimonies he tried to influence. He was convicted of conspiracy, crimes against peace, war crimes, and crimes against humanity in 1946 and sentenced to death by hanging. He requested that he be shot as a soldier rather than hanged but the court refused. Göring made a number of acquaintances with his captors who found him engaging, and to whom he gifted some of his personal possessions. He allegedly committed suicide by ingesting cyanide the night before his scheduled execution.

Paul Hechler: Unable to trace reliable records. However, he continued to serve in post at the Bank for International Settlements until December 1945, seven months after the end of WWII.

Reinhard Heydrich: 7 March 1904 – 4 June 1942 On 27th May 1942, Heydrich was travelling in a Mercedes convertible in Prague, and was ambushed by a team of Czech and Slovak soldiers who had been sent by the Czechoslovak government-in-exile to kill him in an operation called Anthropoid; the team was trained by the British Special Operations Executive. An anti-tank explosive was thrown against the car, which resulted in serious injuries to Heydrich. He was visited by Himmler in hospital but suffered from an infection and died from his injuries on 4 June.

Heinrich Himmler: 7 October 1900 – 23 May 1945. Himmler last met with Hitler on 20 April 1945, Hitler's birthday, in Berlin, and Himmler and swore unswerving loyalty to Hitler. At a military briefing on that day, Hitler stated that he would not leave Berlin, in spite of Soviet advances. Along with Göring, Himmler quickly left the city after the briefing Realising the war was lost, Himmler attempted to open peace talks with the western Allies, offering that German forces would join the Allies in an offence against the Soviet Union. This he did without Hitler's knowledge. Hitler learned of this on 28th April 1945, dismissing him from all his posts, and ordered his arrest. Himmler was detained and arrested by British forces and purportedly killed himself in British custody.

Adolf Hitler: 20 April 1889 – 30 April 1945? (1962) After midnight on the night of 28–29 April 1945, Hitler married Eva Braun in the *Führerbunker*. On 30 April, Soviet troops were within five hundred metres of the Reich Chancellery when it was reported that Hitler shot himself in the head and Braun bit into a cyanide capsule. In accordance with Hitler's wishes, their staff stated their corpses were carried outside to the Reich Chancellery garden, where they were placed in a bomb crater, doused with petrol, and set on fire. Berlin surrendered on 2 May. The remains of the Goebbels family, General Hans Krebs (who had committed suicide that day), and Hitler's dog Blondi were discovered by the Soviets. There is no evidence that any identifiable remains of Hitler or Braun (with the exception of dental bridges which could have been removed years later) were ever found by them. Credible reports emerged that Hitler and his wife were flown out of Berlin, and rendezvoused with a U-Boat taking them to Argentina. Witness reports from Argentina claim Hitler died there in 1962, having vowed never to participate in public life again after the betrayal he claimed to have suffered.

Wilhelm Höttl: 19 March 1915 – 27 June 1999. The former Nazi acting head of Intelligence in Central and South-East Europe had access to many secrets which he used to advance himself after WWII. In May 1945, he surrendered himself to American authorities in Bad Aussee after which he testified against former Nazis at Nuremberg. After a brief period of imprisonment, he worked for the US Counter Intelligence Corps in espionage against Russia in Austria. He opened a school in Bad Aussee and wrote a number of books. He later received the Cross of Merit for his work as a school director and historian. Many believed he had amassed a fortune as a result of receiving stolen Nazi gold in exchange for helping Nazis to escape capture.

Bishop Alois Hudal: 31 May 1885 – 13 May 1963 Formerly close to Pope Pius XI, he became more distanced from the Vatican following WWII. After 1945, Hudal worked on the ratlines, helping former Nazis to find safe haven and escape trial. He viewed it as "a charity to people in dire need, for persons without any guilt who are to be made scapegoats for the failures of an evil system." Hudal actively assisted many senior and notorious Nazis, not only in escaping, but also in gaining employment or setting up business. He was unrepentant, condemning the "show trials and lynchings" of the Allies. He believed that the greater evil was that of the communist threat. Up to his death, he worked to obtain amnesty for former Nazis.

Ernst Kaltenbrunner: 4 October 1903 – 16 October 1946 The former Chief of the Reich Security Main Office, and major perpetrator of the Holocaust, was apprehended by US forces on 12th May 1945 in a mountain region of Altaussee, Austria. He tried to hide his identity but when he was embraced by his mistress and the wife of his adjutant whilst walking with US troops, he was discovered. Following a trial at Nuremberg, he was convicted for war crimes and crimes against humanity, despite protesting his innocence against overwhelming documentary evidence. He received the sentence of death and was hanged on 16th October 1946.

John Maynard Keynes, 1st Baron Keynes: 5 June 1883 – 21 April 1946. As the War neared its end, Keynes was chairman of the World Bank Commission where he advocated The Keynes plan, which argued for an international currency and global management of currencies backed by an international trade and payments system. However, on almost every point where he was overruled by the Americans. Many argue Keynes was later proven correct in his theories by events. Two new institutions, later known as the World Bank and the International Monetary Fund (IMF), were founded as a result of Keynes advocacy which supported those countries most exposed to trade deficit issues. After the war, Keynes continued to represent the United Kingdom in international negotiations despite deteriorating health. He succeeded in obtaining preferential terms from the United States for British debt. His economic theories had a profound influence both during and after his lifetime continuing to the present day. Keynes suffered a heart attack, immediately after returning from negotiating improved debt terms with the USA and passed away at Tilton, his farmhouse home near Firle, East Sussex, at the age of 62.

Bernhard Krüger: 26 November 1904 – 3 January 1989 Having run the massive bank note forgery operation from Sachsenhausen concentration camp, in May 1945, Krüger and his team of prisoners were transferred to Ebensee concentration camp in Austria where they were liberated. After the war, he was detained by the British for two years, then turned over to the French for a year forging documents for them. He was released in 1948 without any charges being pressed, and returned to Germany. In the 1950s, he went before a denazification court, where inmates under his charge at Sachsenhausen provided statements that resulted in his acquittal. He eventually worked for the company that had produced the special paper for the Operation Bernhard forgeries.

Meyer Lansky: July 4 1902 – January 15 1983. Lansky was very active in organised crime after the War, developing interests in hotels and casinos, whilst also involved in blackmail. It was rumoured he extorted favours from J Edgar Hoover with compromising photos of the FBI boss. He developed a business empire centred on Cuba (before the revolution), and Las Vegas. Lansky was never found guilty of anything more serious than illegal gambling. He was one of the most financially successful gangsters in American history. Before he fled Cuba, Lansky was said to be worth an estimated US$20 million (equivalent to $184 million today. When he died in

1983, his family learned that his estate was worth only around $57,000 (equivalent to $174,371 today)

John J. McCloy: March 31 1895 – March 11 1989. After the war, he served as the president of the World Bank, U.S. High Commissioner for Germany, chairman of Chase Manhattan Bank, chairman of the Council on Foreign Relations, and was a member of the Warren Commission investigating the death of President Kennedy. He was a prominent adviser to all presidents from Franklin D. Roosevelt to Ronald Reagan. In his work on the Warren Commission, he did not initially believe in the lone gunman theory but later changed his mind adding to the conjecture about the JFK assassination

Thomas McKittrick: 14 April 1889 – January 21 1970. From 1946 to 1954 McKittrick worked for the Chase National Bank, becoming a senior vice president and director. He headed a survey mission for the International Bank for Reconstruction and Development to India in the 1950's. He was even lauded by those whose stolen goods in the form of looted Nazi gold he had traded: McKittrick was invited to Brussels and decorated with the Royal Order of the Crown of Belgium. The honour was "in recognition of his friendly attitude to Belgium and his services as President of the Bank for International Settlements during World War II."

Henry Morgenthau Jr: May 11, 1891 – February 6, 1967. The author of the Morgenthau Plan advocating the break-up of the German post-war economy was responsible for a policy enacted by US Treasury officials in the immediate post-war period where they were seconded to the Army of occupation, acting to restrict German recovery for almost two years following the resignations of Morgenthau. However, they resigned when, in July 1947, when a new policy under President Truman, mandated a productive Germany. In 1945, when Harry S. Truman became President, Morgenthau insisted on accompanying him to Potsdam by threatening to quit if he was not allowed to; Truman accepted his resignation immediately. Years later Truman also referred to him as a "block head, nut". Morgenthau devoted the remainder of his life to working with Jewish philanthropies, and became a financial advisor to Israel.

Sir Otto Niemeyer: 23 November 1883 – 6 February 1971. He served as a director of the Bank of England from 1938 to 1952 and a director of the Bank for International Settlements from 1931 to 1965, including a period as Vice-Chairman from 1940 to 1946. Niemeyer was briefly mooted as successor to Sir Montagu Norman in 1944, as Governor of the Bank of England; his candidacy was vetoed by Winston Churchill. He was a governor of St Paul's School, Marlborough College, and the London School of Economics, serving as chairman of LSE from 1941 to 1957.

Sir Montagu Norman: 6 September 1871 – 4 February 1950. Retired from the Bank of England, where he had spent most of his working life, in 1944. Following his retirement, he was raised to the peerage as Baron Norman, of St Clere in the County of Kent, on 13 October 1944. He had a fall at his estate at Thorpe Lodge, Airlie Gardens in Kensington in 1944, sustaining an injury from which he never recovered. He died on his home from a stroke in 1950.

Oswald Pohl: 30 June 1892 – 7 June 1951. After the war, the former head of the SS Main Administrative Office and the head administrator of concentration camps, Pohl, went into hiding, and worked as a farm hand. He was apprehended in 1946, stood trial in 1947, was convicted of crimes against humanity, and sentenced to death. During his trial, he did not deny his knowledge of the mass killings of Jews, Pohl presented himself as a mere executive, accusing the prosecution of being guided by feelings of hatred and revenge.[1]After repeatedly appealing his case, he was executed by hanging in 1951.

Emil Puhl: 28 August 1889 - 30 March 1962 Despite being instrumental in moving Nazi gold during the war, and for ensuring gold (including teeth and jewellery) removed from those murdered in the death camps reached the Reichsbank, the former president of the Reichsbank only received a prison sentence of five years at Nuremberg. He was released in 1949 for good conduct.

Paul Josef Goebbels: 29 October 1897–1 May 1945. On 30th April 1945, the infamous Reich Propaganda Minister was appointed Chancellor of the Reich under the terms of Hitler's will, but on 1st May 1945 Goebbels and his wife, Magda. Committed suicide after poisoning their six children with cyanide in the Führerbunker shortly before it was over-run by Russian forces. He confessed to having only disobeyed Hitler once, when he refused to leave Hitler's bunker.

Walther Rauff: 19 June 1906 – 14 May 1984. The SS officer man who masterminded mobile gas extermination vans escaped justice via the Ratlines, which he had helped organise. assisted by members of the Roman Catholic Clergy. Escaping from an Allied internment camp, he was sheltered in monasteries. Rauff worked for Syrian Intelligence, then was recruited by Israeli Intelligence. He also carried out work for the West German Intelligence (BND) As he was hunted for war crimes, he went to Chile and assisted their military, remaining there until his death despite there being many requests for his extradition. It is thought he was directly responsible for over 100,000 deaths of Jewish, Roma, and those with disabilities.

Hjalmar Schacht 22 January 1877 – 3 June 1970. Despite serving as Reichsminister for Economics until 1937, Schacht was not a supporter of the Nazi regime. After the failed plot to kill Hitler, he was arrested and spent time in concentration camps although he was not involved in the plot. In late April 1945 he and about 140 other prominent inmates of Dachau were liberated on 5th May 1945 after being abandoned by SS guards taking them to Tyrol. He was put on trial at Nuremberg for "conspiracy" and "crimes against peace" Schacht pleaded not guilty citing in his defense that he had been in contact with Resistance leaders and that he had been imprisoned in concentration camps. Despite Russian objections, he was sentenced to only eight years imprisonment which was overturned on appeal. He served as a hired consultant for Greek tycoon, Aristotle Onassis, during the 1950s and also advised the Indonesian government. He founded a bank in 1953 and gave advice to developing countries. He was respected internationally as an economist.

Hermann Schmitz: 1 January 1881 – 8 October 1960 The Chief Executive of the major German manufacturer IG Farben, had been a leading business supporter of Hitler's regime. His factories, including BASF employed slave labour and had execution centres in some locations. He was arrested and charged at the IG Farben Trial in 1947, during which he was sentenced to four years imprisonment (including time already served) for war crimes and crimes against humanity through the plundering and spoliation of occupied territories. He was released in 1950 and went on to become member of the administrators' council of Deutsche Bank in Berlin, as well as the honorary president of "Rheinische Stahlwerke AG.

Friedrich Schwend: November 6, 1906 — March 28, 1980. Schwend surrendered to American troops in Tyrol on May 12, 1945. He revealed his hiding places in Austria and South Tyrol. He revealed some gold to the Americans on his capture. From 1945 to 1946, Schwend worked as an informant for the Counterintelligence (CIC) helping to "flush out" other former SS members in Europe. In 1945, he joined the Gehlen Org, and in 1946 he escaped to Peru via the ratlines, where he opened a restaurant. Despite the restaurant being successful, he became involved in money counterfeiting, drug trafficking and arms dealing. In 1972, Schwend was detained in connection to the murder of businessman and it was discovered that Schwend had given refuge to the notorious Nazi, Klaus Barbie. Schwend was deported to West Germany in 1976, where he was given a two-year suspended sentence for the murder of one of his agents in Italy during the war, for which he had received a 21-year suspended sentence from Italy. In 1979 he returned to Peru, living there until his death.

Otto Skorzeny: 12 June 1908 – 5 July 1975. Involved in secreting the gold taken from the Reichsbank in 1945 by the SS. Skorzeny assisted with the establishment of *Der Spinne* helping former Nazis escape after the war. He was imprisoned after the war but escaped in 1948 wearing a US army uniform. Worked for various countries in military intelligence and training until the end of his life. He was recruited to work covertly by Israeli Intelligence in the early 1960's and implicated in a number of controversial kidnappings and shootings. He spent some time in Argentina helping train the military and was rumoured to have had an affair with Eva Peron. There were some claims he had involvement in the assassination of President John F. Kennedy in November 1963 but there were no proven links. Skorzeny accumulated enormous wealth investing in major industrial projects, and owned property in Ireland and Spain where he died of lung cancer.

Josef Spacil: 3 January 1907 - 13 February 1967. On 8 May 1945 Spacil changed into an ordinary *Wehrmacht* uniform and joined a group of retreating soldiers surrendering to US troops. Spacil gave his name and rank as "Sergeant Aue". However, his real identity was soon revealed and after interrogation he revealed the location of some hidden, buried gold to US Intelligence. Following interrogation, he was described as "a fanatical Nazi". US Intelligence suspected Spacil of having secreted some treasure which he was not revealing, but were unable to prove anything. Spacil formally testified against his former boss *Obergruppenführer und General der Polizei und Waffen-SS* Ernst Kaltenbrunner at the Nuremberg trials. After the war Spacil was employed as a clerk in Munich. There are claimes that Josef Spacil secretly financed and owned a chain of supermarkets.

Árpád Toldi: (No dates of birth and death traced) The Hungarian SS officer, who had commanded the gold train which left Hungary in 1944, mysteriously disappeared. Toldi and his family left the train with a large amount of gold on 30 March 1945, as the train crossed into Austria - the Russian Army was only 16 km behind. Toldi's convoy tried to enter neutral Switzerland 10 days later, but were refused entry. Toldi then turned to SS officer Wilhelm Höttl, to whom he handed over 10% of his convoy's goods in return for both German passports and Swiss visas for all of his family. Toldi and his family then successfully entered Switzerland, but he was detained in Austria later that year, interrogated by Allied authorities, but released and was traced again.

Jacob Wallenberg: 27 September 1892 – 1 August 1980. From the mid-1940s, Wallenberg was on the board of numerous major businesses, and became vice chairman of the board of the Swedish Bankers' Association. In

1952, he became a board member of the Nobel Foundation. Wallenberg was appointed by the Stockholm School of Economics Association as a member of the Stockholm School of Economics Board of Directors which is the school's highest executive body, Jacob Wallenberg's biggest hobby dominating the sport in the Nordic waters, He was chairman of the Royal Swedish Yacht Club (KSSS) for many years

Marcus Wallenberg: 5 October 1899 – 13 September 1982. Led and reconstructed many of Sweden's largest companies after the War. In 1946, Wallenberg became CEO of Stockholms Enskilda Bank until 1958 when he became vice chairman of the board. In the 1950s, he was chairman of the board of AB Atlas Diesel, LM Ericsson, Scandinavian Airlines and the Swedish Bankers' Association. Wallenberg was a board member of ASEA (chairman from 1956), Stora Kopparbergs Bergslags AB, Federation of Swedish Industries (vice chairman from 1959, chairman 1962-1964 and the International Chamber of Commerce as well as chairman of its Swedish National Committee from 1951 to 1964 and was CEO of the English-Swedish Chamber of Commerce. Wallenberg was also chairman of the Royal Lawn Tennis Club (*Kungliga Lawn Tennis Klubben*) and he became honorary chairman of the Swedish Tennis Association in 1953. He became a member of the Steering Committee of the secretive Bilderberg Group from 1954 to his death in 1982 and held many other board positions including the Nobel Foundation.

Harry Dexter White: October 29, 1892 – August 16, 1948 After being a senior US Treasury Department official promoting controversial policies for post-war Europe, he was accused in 1948 of spying for the Soviet Union, which he adamantly denied. He was never a Communist party member, but he had frequent contacts with Soviet officials as part of his duties at the Treasury. That he passed sensitive and classified documents on to people he knew were agents of the Soviet Union has been confirmed, although hard evidence only came over time in a US counterintelligence operation known as the Venona Project, plus the opening of the Soviet archives in the 1990s. After giving evidence at the House Unamerican Activities Committee in 1948, White suffered a heart attack, and died after a further attack days later, aged 55.

Hatton Garden Heist Timeline

The full details of how crooks pulled off the most daring robbery ever

A mixture of careful planning, sheer boldness and ingenuity gave this gang of aged robbers their crack at a massive fortune. Most of the gang were over 60, whilst Brian Reader, the mastermind, was 76. All were considered to be 'professional' crooks involved in a number of previous large robberies.
It was seemingly designed to be one last job as a gang of ageing crooks pulled off possibly the most daring raid in history.
Al least £14 million in gems, bullion and precious stones were robbed from safes after they broke into the vault of Hatton Garden Safety Deposits Ltd.

Three years of planning

Prosecutors suggested the Hatton Garden heist was at least three years in the making.
As early as April 2012, the thieves were searching online about how to use different types of drill.
By May 2014, the planning became more specific, with evidence of research into the Hilti DD350 drill used to hollow out three large holes in the thick, concrete wall.
It is believed the gang started scouting out 88-90 Hatton Garden around January 2015.
Certainly, it was around this time Lionel Wiffen, a jeweller in the building, spoke of feeling "uneasy" and that the place was being watched.
The planning proper appears to have begun at The Castle pub in Islington mid-January.
Using mobile phone and vehicle-tracking data, police were able to establish that ringleaders Jones, Collins and Perkins began meeting at the trendy gastropub, usually on busy Friday nights.
Jones would usually call Wood the next day to keep him updated on their plans.
John Collins, 74, admitted his role in plotting the Hatton Garden Easter raid which saw valuables worth more than £14 million stolen

Thursday April 2nd 2015 - The Heist begins

8:20pm
Just a few hours after the security guards at the Hatton Garden Safe Deposit Ltd left, the gang assembled.
Brian Reader, 76, the eldest of the gang took two buses, even using someone else's Freedom Pass - which provides free travel for the over 60s - to get to the scene.
The others arrive in a white van. John Collins, 75, drove and initially parked up on Leather Lane around the corner from 88-90 Hatton Garden.
First Danny Jones, 60, and Carl Wood, 58, got out and walked up and down Greville Street where there is an entrance into Hatton Garden courtyard, checking out the building.

9.22pm
Neighbouring jeweller Lionel Wiffen, locked up and finally left the building.
The gang were watching and now their slick plan went into action.
Although a number of CCTV systems covering the area were stolen, the thieves missed one placed above a fire exit which caught much of the action. Street CCTV also captured some of the key moments.
First, a red-haired thief, who has not been identified and has become known only as 'Basil', walked from Greville St and gained entrance to main doors of 88-90 Hatton Garden.
Wood and Jones got out the van and Jones came to stand opposite the fire exit door by a telephone box.
He appeared to have something to his ear, possibly a walkie-talkie which would explain the lack of mobile phone activity by the gang during the raid. They then appeared to return to the van.

How did 'Basil' gain entry?

The main wooden doors were secured with a mortise latch which locked automatically when the doors were slammed shut.
Immediately behind, there was a magnetic glass door, opened with a four-digit pin-code outside business hours (i.e. 9am-6pm).
All tenants of the building had a key for the main doors and knew the four-digit pin.
As there was no sign of forced entry, police suggested during the trial, Basil must have had keys and known the pincode.
The main building key was one which could be easily copied by a locksmith, the court heard.

Experts also suggested it might have been possible to open the magnetic glass door by either covering the magnetic contacts or by 'rippling' (violently pushing and pulling them).

What happened next?

No one knows for certain - but what police found later left some clues. Once inside, the lift car was moved to the second floor and was disabled: the door sensor was left hanging off so that the doors would remain open.
This opened a short drop down the shaft from the ground floor to the basement; at the bottom, the shutters were then pulled open on the inside.
On the ground floor, a handwritten note had been stuck next to the lift, which had not been there before: it said, 'Out of order'.
Metropolitan Police picture released showing first picture showing inside of Hatton Garden vaults after multi million pound raid.
One or more of the four men crawled out of the lift shaft and into the airlock to the cupboard beneath the stairs, and cut the grey, telephone line cable, coming out of the alarm box.
The GPS aerial was broken off, significantly reducing the signal range. After attacking the alarm, the cover on the electrical box underneath the desk (which powers the outer sliding iron gate) was removed and the wires were cut.
This stopped the power to the iron gate, allowing it to be pulled open; the manual key-operated door release does not appear to have been touched.
The lock was broken off the wooden door to HGSD, leaving a hole in it.
This allowed access for larger machinery and easier passage to and from the vault.

The gang move in

Once Basil entered through the main doors, he waited until Mr Wiffen had left the premises, before he then opened the fire exit door to allow others in.
To gain access to the Hatton Garden courtyard, all that was required was to pull back the two bolts on the basement door; the door to the staircase from the ground-floor lobby was never locked.
The white transit van then arrived from the direction of Leather Lane and stopped outside the fire escape.

Brian Reader, Terry Perkins, Danny Jones and Carl Wood got out and started to unload bags, tools and two wheelie bins, which they carried (or wheeled) in through the fire escape and down the stairs.

Large metal joists were also ferried down the stairs: they would become important.

A CCTV camera above the fire escape captured much of this to-ing and fro-ing.

Reader, distinguishable also because of his stripy socks and brown shoes, was wearing a scarf that would eventually be seized from his home address at Pentire.

He also wore a yellow hard hat and a hi-visibility jacket with "GAS" written on the back.

Perkins was dressed in dark clothing, with a hi-visibility waistcoat, a yellow hard hat and a white surgeon-style mask.

Collins sets up as lookout in office across street

Back out on the street, the white van moved off, continued round the block, and parked in Cross Street.

John Collins got out and walked to the back of the vehicle.

It appears that the burglars had forgotten something in the van as he was joined by Daniel Jones who had run to where it parked from 88-90.

Jones collected a green crate and returned to the fire escape; he carried it, then the wheelie bins down the stairs, assisted by Carl Wood.

Collins can then be seen walking along Hatton Garden to the crossroads with Greville Street, wearing a green quilted jacket, a flat cap and carrying a brown briefcase; he then went into 25 Hatton Garden.

How he got in remains unclear, but he spent some time at the door of the property as if he is trying to open it.

The court heard there was "an abundance" of keys to the main door of these premises in circulation at the time.

From 25 Hatton Garden, Collins had a clear view of both doors to 88-90 Hatton Garden, which now had Perkins, Reader, Jones and Wood inside. Collins positioned himself there as a lookout.

There was no sign of a break-in at 25 Hatton Garden when tenants returned after the bank holiday weekend.

The court was told Collins "may have secured a key through one of the many contractors who appear to have had one".

10.23pm
After about an hour it appears there was a need to communicate with Collins as Danny Jones again exited the fire escape door and came out onto Greville street and towards 25 Hatton Garden.

Midnight - 00:18 Friday, April 3
Police believe the gang managed to open the outer iron gate into the vault soon after midnight. At 00:18, the alarm finally managed to send an SMS message to the monitoring company: opening the outer door is likely to have improved the signal to the panel.
The monitoring company called Alok Bavishi.
His family, of Sudanese origin, owned HGSD Ltd. Alok was told that the alarm was signalling.
He was also falsely told police were on scene. Alok rang security guard Kelvin Stockwell who agreed to go back to Hatton Garden.
Alok himself was not originally intending to accompany him, but then decided he would as Stockwell was by himself and the police had been called, or at least he thought they had.

01:15 Friday, April 3
Security guard Mr Stockwell arrived at Hatton Garden at about 01:15. At this point, lookout Collins had fallen asleep and failed to alert the gang.
Stockwell had a look through the main door and did not see anything amiss.
As a result, he called Alok Bavishi, who was by then five minutes away, to say that the main door and the fire exit appeared secure.
He informed him, wrongly, that it was a false alarm. Both men returned home, as the attempts to access the vault continued inside.

01:15 - 7.50am Friday, April 3
The men spent the rest of the night into the morning cutting through the second sliding iron gate.
The gang were left with just one more obstacle, but it was to prove the most difficult.
How to break into the main vault containing the safe deposit boxes crammed full of hugely valuable loot?
Rather than attempt to crack open the vault door, the gang had an alternative, and much more audacious, plan which had been three years in the making.
It was to a two-stage operation; first drill through the two-metre thick concrete wall of the vault, then use an hydraulic ram powered by a pump and hose to push over the metal cabinet containing the safe deposit.

The burglars would then be able to climb through the hole and into the vault.

The gang put to use the specialist drill, the Hilti DD350, to create three adjoining and circular holes in the thick, concrete wall immediately to the left of the vault door.

This left the 25cm by 45cm breaches which astonished the world when pictures from the raid later emerged.

The Hilti DD 350 is known as a 'diamond core drill' designed to bore through solid materials like concrete and stone.

These power tools feature hollow cylindrical drill bits fitted with teeth – known as cores – which grind away the surface to create a hole.

The DD 350 costs £3,475 when bought directly from manufacturer Hilti, a major producer of construction and engineering equipment which is headquartered in Liechtenstein.

Phase one of the plan went off without a hitch. But the gang ran into a problem during phase two.

On the first night, the hydraulic ram did not manage to knock over the cabinet which was bolted to the floor and the ceiling.

It is not clear why this wasn't successful, but investigators believe it may be that the gang didn't use the equipment properly and the base broke.

Either way, at 7.50am on Friday morning, Wood, Jones, Reader and Perkins left Hatton Garden empty-handed. Reader was not to return.

It has been speculated he walked away from the raid believing it could not be completed. His fellow criminals however, had more determination.

4.30pm Saturday, April 4

As the others returned home, Danny Jones made a visit to Machine Mart and D&M Tools - two specialist tool shops in Twickenham. Jones went into D&M Tools first but left without making a purchase.

In Machine Mart he bought a new pump and hose manufactured by Clarke. A receipt showed he gave his details as 'V. Jones' of 'Park Avenue, Enfield, Middlesex EN1 2BE'.

8pm Saturday, April 4

Jeweller Lionel Wiffen returned to his office adjoining Hatton Garden Safe Deposit Ltd with his wife to make arrangement for an electrician who was due to visit the next day.

When he arrived at the fire exit on Greville Street, he found it unlocked and ajar, which worried him.

He checked the door from the courtyard into the basement: it was bolted from the inside which must have been done by Basil as he left.

They cleaned and rearranged the office for about an hour, locking the Greville Street fire exit when they left at about 9pm.

10.04pm Saturday, April 4
The gang returned to have another go on Saturday evening.
Again, the mystery thief 'Basil' was able to enter 88-90 Hatton Garden through the communal street-level door while Jones, Wood and Collins waited near the fire escape.
During this time the three appeared to enter into a discussion and Wood decided he now also wanted 'out'.
CCTV showed him leaving via Leather Lan and he did not return.
A bugged conversation between Jones, Perkins and Collins later appeared to confirm this when Perkins said "he thought we would never get in".
Basil again let the gang in through the fire escape and Jones was seen on CCTV bringing in the new hose and pump.
This time the burglars made the crucial breakthrough. Using metal joists to give it more purchase, the hydraulic ram finally managed to push the cabinet over and into the vault.
Once inside, the gang grabbed as many riches as possible.
They jimmied open 73 of the 999 safe deposit boxes containing jewellery, precious stones and gems.

05.44 - 06.44am Sunday, April 5
As dawn broke, the gang emerged from Hatton Garden, their arms filled with loot.
Jones was first, carrying the pump and hose back to the van.
Perkins soon joined him and together they brought the two wheelie bins and several bags, all full of jewels and other valuable items, up the stairs to the fire escape.
Due to the weight of the bins, this proved to be a difficult task. Collins, meanwhile, left his lookout post and walked along Greville Street into Leather Lane to where the white van was parked.
He drove the white van round to the fire escape.
Collins remained in the van whilst Jones and Perkins loaded the obviously very heavy wheelie bins and bags into the van; 'Basil' joined again carrying the bin bag on his shoulder having exited the ground floor doors at 88-90 Hatton Garden. 97.
At 06.44am, all four left the scene in the white van and drove east having stolen an estimated £14million in loot.
It was the biggest burglary in English legal history.
Source: Daily Record – January 2016

My Thanks

I would like to thank those who have assisted and supported me in the writing of this book. The input and encouragement of those around me have been enormously helpful factors.
You know who you are.

I am also grateful for the fantastic feedback from readers of my previous books, especially the enormously positive response I received following the publication of 'The Barbarossa Secret', and my last novel, 'Fission',
which, in no small way, motivated me to continue.

Finally, I specifically wish to thank my team of incredibly dedicated proof readers:

Ashley Best
Mair Herbert
Wendy Munro

I am so indebted to them for their incredibly valuable input in rooting out errors, making suggestions, and their positive feedback.

Social Media

https://facebook.com/christopherkerrauthor

https://christopher-kerr.co.uk

https://x.com/chriskerrauthor

https://instagram.com/christopherkerrauthor

About the Author

Christopher Kerr has enjoyed a varied career as a civil servant, marketing executive, and entrepreneur. He now concentrates on writing, which has become a passion, based upon a keen interest in history, politics, and current affairs.

Christopher's genre is historical/contemporary fiction, set against actual events and real people, to give added authenticity, and perspective to human drama.

His debut novel, 'the Covenant', was published in 2021, followed by 'The Barbarossa Secret' in 2022, 'Fission' in 2023, and 'Bullion' in 2024.

Christopher lives in a quiet village in North Wales where he is currently planning his next novel, 'Flight of the Eagle', which explores the hidden truth behind the fall of the Third Reich, and how secret organisations were formed in the post-war era affecting present-day global governance.

Other Books by Christopher Kerr

'The Covenant' – Published 2021

'The Barbarossa Secret' – Published 2022

'Fission' – Published 2023

Printed in Great Britain
by Amazon